Haunted HEARTS

Little Hope Series, Book 1

ARIANA CANE

All roads lead to
Maine.
But do they end
there?

Author's note

This book touches on a few heavy topics. If you have triggers (DV, IPV, PTSD), please be careful reading.

If you find yourself in the same situation as Freya did, please talk to someone. What you are going through can be fixed, no matter how desperate your situation might seem. Please don't be ashamed. Talk to someone. And you will never end up alone. Never. There is an Alex out there for you.

If you find yourself in a situation as Alex did, please talk to someone. I'm not a professional, but I've seen it happen to people close to me, and I can surely tell you that PTSD is a bitch that can be caused by many things, but it's *manageable*. People can help you to manage and fix it. Please reach out to them.

You are not alone.

P.S. And remember, abuse and PTSD don't have genders.

Chapter One

F REYA

It's pouring rain outside. Like *pouring* pouring, as if somebody from up above flipped a switch and decided to flush me off the road—a very dangerous road—in a torrential downpour. These Maine mountains are beautiful but deadly if you're an idiot—which, apparently, I am—because who decides to drive on it in a rear-wheel drive in mid-April when the snow is still looming in the air like a threat. Especially since the snow is looming a little bit longer and infinitely heavier than normal, creating a lethal mixture for the perfect roadkill. You guessed it, that's me, unfortunately.

But I didn't have a choice in my journey. God, I wish I had. I probably would've prepared a little better, which would've included making sure my car was more equipped to handle such weather. Like, for example, getting *appro-*

priate tires for driving on an icy road downhill. I had to escape that piece of shit I used to call my husband and the situation I found myself in, so I've been on the road ever since. And while I don't regret for a second leaving the man who proved himself to be the worst mistake of my life thus far, I'm not feeling so great about ending up on this particular route. You win some, you lose some.

The only good thing that came out of that monstrosity called our marriage was the car. Well, along with a very significant sum of green that I don't have any use for. The moment I got the money, though, I bought this car as minor compensation for the abuse I suffered. *The* car. A 1967 black Chevy Impala. There are some things from your teen years that just don't leave you, and hey, if the Impala can survive all the hell it went through on *Supernatural,* it's bound to be safe enough for me. I'd wanted it since I was a teenager when the idea of a car like this represented *freedom.* There was no greater feeling than that moment when I first sat in it and started the engine.

No one told me that it's not an easy car to drive though. This is the first time I've ever really driven it for so long, but after the first hundred miles or so (a *very* long hundred miles), I'm now a pro, and I *finally* had that feeling that I imagined all those years ago.

I'm free!

Until I hit this damn mountain road on naked wheels in one of the worst snow-rain-whatever-you-call-it-storms I've ever seen.

I reach for the coffee cup that I got two states ago at a gas station and take an insufferable sip. The now-cold dark roast with a ton of heavy cream and sugar (yeah, just because I like it sweet) tastes like old garbage, and I screw up my nose as I force it down, gulping with a grimace. I need to stay awake and alert if I have any hope of making it out of this alive, and drinking shitty coffee just about does the job, even if the taste of it makes me wonder if I really do want to get out of this alive. I knew I should've stopped the last time I saw somewhere that might have had decent coffee and a warm meal, but I stupidly thought I could push through until I found a place to sleep so I *wouldn't need* this garbage masquerading as a beverage right now. Little did I know...

It's rain-snowing even more now, and I can barely see the asphalt under even the highest strength my lights will go.

I turn a tight corner and hear a popping sound at the back of the car as the car swerves drastically toward the left. I grip the steering wheel until my knuckles whiten with effort and try to keep myself steady. It's not working, and I let out a violent string of curses in the hopes that something or someone will listen to me out there and save me from a messy death off the edge of a mountain. In this storm and this particular section of Middle-of-Nowhere-Maine, the likelihood that someone is going to find me in time feels pretty slim.

Of course I'm going to die just as I get a taste of newfound freedom. What have I ever done to the universe to deserve such a terrible end?

The car comes to a stop, and I hold my breath, refusing to let go of the wheel, just in case I'm about to face an even more precarious situation than before. I slowly peer out the window and manage to make out that I'm still on the road. I was seconds away from smashing into the cliff face that juts out on the other side of it, but I'm alive. I'm alive!

I relax my grip and laugh out loud. I'd never been so convinced I was going to die. The last thing I would've ever consumed on this earth was shitty coffee that tasted like mud.

I'm leaning back in my seat and trying to calm my nerves when a knock on my window makes me scream. When I slowly bring my gaze to the glass, there's a man standing there. I can't see his face, but I can see that he's wearing a dark baseball cap pulled low over his eyes.

He gestures for me to roll down the window. I'm alone on the road and haven't seen another vehicle for at least forty minutes. It's almost midnight. I swallow nervously, mostly at the bulk of him that takes up almost the entirety of my window. He taps on the glass again, and I reluctantly roll it down the tiniest bit I can.

Where the hell did he come from? How could a human being even walk through this storm? Maybe driving the car from *Supernatural* inevitably comes with bumping into ghosts here and there.

"Can I help you?" I ask carefully.

"You all right?" His voice is raspy, like he hasn't used it in a long time. I try to get a good look at his facial features, but they're still hidden under the cap. Damn. I have no hope of identifying him now. He must be drenched, standing out in this rain; however, he appears not to notice it at all, let alone mind it. He's standing with his hands in his pockets, letting the rain sluice down his frame. And *me*, actually. Some of the rain is trickling through the crack in my window, and I'm terrified of getting the interior of my baby wet.

"Yeah." I clear my throat and remember I should probably keep him calm. I've watched a few true-crime shows in my time—maybe more than is healthy—and one of the rules always seems to be never to agitate the killer. Be friendly and get the hell out of there as soon as possible. Also, pay attention to the details of what he looks like, but I can't get a good picture of that at all. And yet, I put him into a category of people whose place is on a true-crime TV show just because I met him on a lonely road, wearing a cap in the night—*you're a hypocrite, Freya.* "I didn't see you behind me."

I sneak a peek in my side mirror and spot a truck several feet behind me with dimmed lights. How the hell didn't I notice him earlier?

"Didn't want to blind you. The rain's doin' a good enough job of that." He just read my mind and voiced the concern that's probably written across my forehead in neon letters. Strangely, his voice sends a shiver down my rigid spine.

Because I'm scared, of course. *That's the only reason why.*

The last motel I slept in had weird people creeping around the hall, and I hadn't felt safe enough to sleep. My lack of shut-eye must be the reason why I failed to notice a giant truck behind me. Even in this rain, I should have been more aware of the situation if I was planning on getting out of this shitstorm—quite literally—alive.

"Your tire's blown. Need help changing it?" he rasps.

This feels all too suspicious for my liking. A good Samaritan with a sexy voice on a lonely, treacherous road in Maine at night in a rainstorm, and I haven't seen another soul for miles? It all feels a little too much like a Stephen King novel.

"No, I'm good. Thanks, though. I can change a tire myself." I've never changed a tire in my life, but my skin prickles at the thought of a man assuming that I'm weak and incapable just because I'm a woman. I'm five seven and somewhat fit—meaning I can run, especially when my life depends on it, which I seem to do more often than not. Right now, though, I'm looking more and more like the average woman I am, and the guy standing in front of me is definitely not an average man—he's a giant. I wish I could see his whole face, but only the lower part of it is visible. And that part is very intriguing.

His jaw sets at my words, but he looks almost amused at the idea. From what I can see, anyway, since I can still only make him out from the nose down. He sighs and tugs his cap even lower. How can he even see at all?

"Need a ride to town?" His voice *feels* a little softer now as if an ancient, unused mechanism finally got some good ol' oiling.

"No. I'm perfectly fine," I squeak. "But thanks."

He clenches his jaw, strolls back to his truck, and takes off. Just like that. If he's a serial killer, he must figure I'm not worth it. Maybe it's his night off from brutally murdering stranded travelers in the middle of the night. But if he's *not* a serial killer, I probably just sent away my only hope of getting off this mountain some way other than in a body bag. I truly am an idiot. I bang my head on the wheel and groan. Looks like I need to learn how to change a tire, I guess, and fast. Nothing like being thrown into the deep end of a new skill in the middle of a storm, high up on a mountain. Just what I needed.

I get out of the car and am instantly drenched to the bone. I try to cover my head with my hands, but the attempt is useless, and I shiver uncontrollably. God, I hate the rain. Especially this brutal April rain-snow-icicles-from-the-sky thingy that I'm not used to and *never* want to experience again.

I look at the wheel and see that the stranger is right—my rear left tire is completely blown out. I stand up and let out an agitated scream, and after, I feel a little better. I scream again because it feels good, and it's not like anyone can hear me out here.

"God*dammit*," I hiss at myself.

I whimper and lean on the car. After taking a few steadying breaths and feeling sorry for myself for a long, pathetic minute, I get my phone out of the car's console.

"Right," I tell myself sternly. "You've got this. You're a strong woman. You don't need a big, burly man to help you with this easy-peasy task."

Silently thanking my cell phone provider for the one single bar I have up here, I Google *what to do when you blow out a tire*, then wait for an eon as the page loads. Just as it does, I notice the phone is getting too wet and is about to complain about water exposure.

I drop my head back and think about screaming again. It doesn't change the situation but sure does relieve some of the pressure in my brain.

I sit my soggy ass back in the car, giving up on keeping anything dry in this rain, and study YouTube to learn how to change a tire.

They tell me that it will take me ten minutes to change a tire on a regular sedan. Liars. It takes me an hour and a half—two hours, if you include trying to find the tire-changing kit I didn't even know I had in the trunk.

As a result, I'm driving on a donut and cursing my suspicious nature for not accepting a stranger's help. With the memory of his coarse voice, I shiver again. It's got to be illegal to have a voice like that. It's straight from any woman's hot fantasy, mine included. And at such an inappropriate time, no less.

After changing the tire, I check Maps and find a small town at the bottom of the mountain called Little Hope.

Does it mean that there is still a little hope left? Or is it that we're relying on simply a little hope? Either way, I'm heading toward Little Hope and praying like hell it's something positive. I wonder briefly if it's the town that the stranger mentioned but eventually decide I don't have much choice in the matter regardless.

I finally make it to Little Hope within the hour. I had to drive slowly on the wet roads that turned into some sort of icy mush and on the donut. The whole trip left me terrified every time I felt the slightest tug on the wheel.

By the time I reach the town, I have *very* little hope left. My back hurts from the constant strain of holding onto the wheel for dear life.

It's almost three in the morning when I turn onto the poorly named Main Street. There are no motels in sight, everything is shut down and closed, and I can't find so much as a gas station around. I groan and park next to a Dunkin' Donuts, crack the window open—I don't want to end up on a show titled *Ten Stupidest Deaths in the U.S.*—and fall into a damp, restless, uncomfortable sleep.

I'm awoken with a start by a sharp knock on my window, right by where my head has been awkwardly resting all night. Why do people around here keep doing that? I slowly blink my eyes open and turn my stiff neck to face the owner of the knock. A young, attractive cop with short blond hair is staring at me through the glass. I smile halfheartedly at him, trying to mitigate what has to be an otherwise atrociously early-morning, tired appearance. He doesn't return my smile, and his attractiveness goes down a notch. Shame.

"Is anything wrong, officer?" I roll the window down

completely, enjoying the smell of rain-soaked earth and fresh air. It's sunny, and the sky above is a glorious shade of marine blue. The air is chilly, but that's just what I need to be totally awake. I keep a plastic smile pasted on my face as the officer notices me gazing at the scenery.

"License and registration, please." His request is curt and professional.

"Have I done something wrong?" I inquire evenly. At this point, I'm fed up with my situation, lack of security, and aching back from sleeping in a fetal position, so my grouchiness is justified. If he has a valid reason other than catching me doing the unthinkable—sleeping in my own car outdoors—I'll comply, but I refuse to be bullied by him. I spent all of last night being bullied by the elements. I've done my time.

"Did you sleep out here, ma'am?" His tone doesn't waver.

"I did. Yes. I believe you woke me, so you know I did." I can feel my temper beginning to rise in my gut. And after the week I've had, he is the last drop in the overfilled basket.

"Why?"

"Because I couldn't find any motels."

The officer looks around us. "Yeah," he draws out in a flat tone, "we don't have many around here."

"Well, then that would be *why* I slept in my car." I'm not trying to irritate him any more than he's trying to irritate me, but now we are both staring at one another—irritated. God knows I don't need problems with the law now. So I sigh and lean back, trying to gain my composure.

"Well, there's your answer." I wave my hand at him. It's more a spontaneous gesture and not aimed to irritate him, even though he's irritated me enough already. He follows my hand and squints his brilliant-blue eyes at me. Awesome, I did it anyway. I sigh and lean back in my seat.

"What is your business here in Little Hope, ma'am?"

"Just passing through."

"Is that so?"

"It is so." I rub my eyes and try not to give him a sardonic look. I'm tired, I reek, I'm still a little damp and a lot cold, and I desperately need to pee. "Look, it was pouring rain, and my tire blew out on the road in the middle of nowhere at midnight. This Cinderella"—I point to my probably hideous face—"needed a safe place to park her pumpkin carriage, so she didn't die in the damn mountains. Because lo and behold, there is no motel and *no* fucking hope in this little damn town you call Hope!" I shut my eyes and try to breathe out slowly, mentally cursing myself for the outburst. When I open them again, the cop's face has softened.

He leans on my window and gives me a small smile. "I'm sorry, ma'am. Looks like you had a rough night. Little Hope isn't so bad, and the people here are friendly."

"Yeah, I can see that," I answer sarcastically. Between this guy and the jerk with the truck from last night, I don't believe him—though, to be fair, the guy from last night tried to help me, and I sent him away, but I'm allowed to complain internally. The cop laughs, and his face changes in an instant. He is *gorgeous*. Like, *GQ*, drop-dead gorgeous. My mouth is suddenly drier than it was before. I probably look like I just crawled out of a grave. Smell like it, too, I'm sure.

"Name's Jake," the officer says, standing up with a small huff of effort. "I can't give you a place to stay, but I *can* give you a cup of the best coffee around these parts."

I doubtfully look at the nearby Dunkin', and he laughs. "Donna is dealing her own supreme roast under the table. Let's go."

He waits for me to open the car door and keeps smiling, his whole face lighting up. It's a nice view to wake up to, and I almost forgive him for waking me up. Almost.

As we walk to the building, I try to furiously comb through my hair with my fingers and keep a healthy distance. Damn, do I need a shower?

Jake opens the door and grins as I walk past him. A lady in her fifties with big seventies-style peroxide hair and blinding blue eyeshadow welcomes us with a bright smile. Well, Officer Hottie I'm standing next to. I doubt she even sees me here.

"Isn't it one fine morning today, Officer Jake?" she says, tilting her head, a blush warm on her cheeks. "All that rain last night, and I thought we'd be a frozen lake this morning!" Her good humor is directed at him and him alone. Clearly, somebody has a crush on him.

"Mornin' Donna. How're you doing?" Jake is drawling his words like he's from the South. Not two minutes ago, he was *very* New England.

"Better now, sugar." Donna finally notices me, looking like someone Jake hauled up from the bottom of a lake, and one thick eyebrow rises into a curious crescent on her forehead. "Now, who do we have here?"

Jake gives me a troubled look, likely remembering he never got my license or even my name.

"Freya. My name's Freya." I try to smile but fail. I'm too frustrated to smile. I notice a bathroom and want to head toward it, only to be stopped by Donna's next question.

"Ah, so it was you in the parking lot. I don't normally take too kindly to people parking in my lot, but any excuse to call Jake here is fine by me. All right, honey, I'll get you a cup of coffee. Jake, sit down and chat with me. Your house still standing?"

I leave them to talk and hurry toward the bathroom. After I pee, I brush my teeth and wash my face using the travel-size pouch of toiletries in my bag. Good thing I keep it there. In fact, I have pretty much everything inside my bag. If the apocalypse strikes, I'm the best bet for survival, so come and befriend me. Bring minty cookies, too. I love those.

When I walk back to the counter, Jake is leaning against it, his body looking mighty fine in his uniform. Men in uniform shouldn't be allowed on the streets. He's taller than me by at least half a foot and obviously well built. The shirt of his uniform is straining against tight muscles, and his pants drop neatly over a perfect ass. What a fucking tease.

He has two takeout cups in front of him and hands one over to me once I'm in front of him. I accept it with a smile and take a sip.

"Oh, my goodness." That is *so* not Dunkin' Donuts coffee. "What *is* that?"

They both laugh, and Jake turns to smile at Donna. "Donna used to have the best coffee shop in the county, but she was forced to close it due to—"

"Jake." Donna interrupts sharply, cutting him off with a slightly chastising frown.

Jake grimaces at Donna but continues anyway. "The building was sold, which meant that..."

While he continues the story that I am absolutely not paying attention to, my gaze wanders outside, and I notice a truck parked in the lot that seems eerily familiar. How I could know someone from here is a mystery to me until a tall man steps out from the driver's side. I recognize the well-worn baseball cap and leather jacket that has seen better days. I know I told him to leave me alone, but the nerve he has to leave someone alone in the middle of a mountain! And in the rain? With a flat tire? In the dark of night? He pisses me off, and I don't know why.

The friendly chatter around me has stopped, and I turn toward Jake. His face is sharp, his brows furrowed.

"He's bad news," he informs me without preamble, a scowl just barely evident through the tautness of his lips.

"Who is he?" I ask, trying not to let my instinctive skepticism of Jake's unasked pronouncement show on my face, though my eyebrow wants to shoot up at his sudden vehemence.

"Trouble," Jake snaps.

"Oh, yeah? How so?" I feel a little defensive of him and a lot hypocritical, seeing as I was just mentally calling the guy a jerk for trying to help me.

"Was in the navy. Didn't come back the same."

I look out the window at the guy. "Did he get hurt?"

Donna sticks her nose up in the air. "Yes. Poor guy defended our country, got hurt, and now people treat him like he has leprosy. Alex is just as necessary to this place as you are, *officer*." Donna glares at Jake, and all those lovey-dovey looks are gone. Jake throws his hands up in defense.

So his name is Alex...

"Didn't mean anything bad, Donna. Just warning a new citizen, that's all."

I put a finger up. "Thanks, but I'm just passing through. I need someone to look at my car and find a new tire, then I'll be on my way. I really won't be here long."

Jake is still too busy glaring at Alex through the window to pay me any attention. "You'd do yourself a favor by staying away from him," he advises without a glance in my direction. It's like he's trying to win a staring contest with Alex, who doesn't know it's happening.

"Why?"

"He... has issues." Jake shakes his head.

"Don't we all?" I mutter under my breath.

Jake finally moves his eyes to me. "Not to his level, no."

Donna smacks her cup on the counter, gives Jake the stink-eye, and leaves us be. I raise an eyebrow at Jake.

"Donna is a friend of Alex's mother," Jake explains. "She's as good as the rest of us at gossip, unless it's about him."

That situation makes a lot more sense. I turn to look for Alex through the window again, but he's gone.

"Just in case, Freya, stay away from the guy while you're here. He isn't stable." He looks very serious and very... paternal.

"I'm just passing through," I remind him for the second time. "Don't think I'll meet him again."

"Again?" Of course that's what he picks up on.

Damn. "Yeah," I sigh. "When my tire blew out yesterday, he was driving behind me and stopped to help."

"Alex? Stopped to help?" He chuckles, and for some reason, his tone irritates me. "He doesn't usually interact with people. And for a good reason." He sips his coffee with so much gusto that I suddenly lose my appetite. This guy gossips harder than a sorority girl. "You know, we went to school together."

"Ah." Things are starting to click into place now.

"He was this super popular jock. Every guy wanted to be him. Every chick wanted to be with him. Then he finished school and enrolled in college but never finished once he enlisted. Dragged my brother along for the ride, too. Then five years ago, he came back like that." He points to the left side of his face.

"Like what?"

"Burnt." He waves his hand to indicate his face in

general now. "He was dishonorably discharged. Knowing him, for a good reason, I'm sure." He takes another sip, looking so smug with being on this side of the story. I can imagine Jake being one of those wishing badly to be him. He would have looked like a nerdy kid that had to grow into his looks.

Deciding I'm done with this gossip session, I place my coffee back on the counter.

"I think I'm out of here. I'm going to find the nearest mechanic and get the hell outta here." I try not to show how much this interaction rubbed me the wrong way.

Jake smiles. "It was a pleasure. Hope to see you around."

I hope not.

Chapter Two

F **REYA**

I walk to my car and wait for Officer McGossip to depart. I don't want his help anymore, but I do need *some* help. At the very least, my coffee is still sitting on the counter, and I need that baby like a lifeline right now if I've got any shot at getting out of here.

When Jake finally leaves, I jog back inside. Donna greets me with a tight-lipped smile and a wary expression.

"Is there any chance I can have a cup of coffee and a donut to go?" I ask carefully. She leans on the counter and rolls her lips between her teeth as she studies me. I feel like prey.

"Did it work?"

I stare at her impassively. "Did *what* work?" I respond, though I suspect what she means.

She jerks her chin in the direction of Jake's last appearance. "Do you believe all the shit he spilled?" Nice Donna is gone. Dubious Donna is out in full force.

"About Alex? I don't know either of them enough to believe anything. He stopped by my car on the mountain yesterday to help me with the tire and... Well, you saw almost all of the interaction I had with Jake."

"Alex stopped to help you?" Donna's face lights up. "Good for him! And for you."

"I actually didn't accept his help." I feel awful about that now. I don't know why, but it feels like I did something wrong.

Donna's eyes narrow to slits almost instantly. "It was after you saw his face, wasn't it?"

"I haven't even seen his face!" I defend myself with a huff. "Judgy much? He wore a cap! It was also raining, the middle of the night, and I was alone and scared shit-less to leave the car when a huge stranger was hulking outside."

She gives me another distrustful gaze before slowly relaxing. "He was always a big boy." She smiles fondly, hopefully realizing that she would have done the same if she hadn't known the "big boy" personally the way I hadn't. "He always wears that silly hat."

"Why?"

"Because of the burns on his face." Donna turns to get my coffee and keeps chatting as she does. "Those burns... they're nasty, but that's not why people step aside when they see him. People here try to avoid him. It's difficult to look at the face of a person you knew and see someone you don't." She clucks her tongue against the back of her teeth and sighs sadly. "I remember how he looked then, and my heart bleeds every time I look at him now. It's easy to be empathetic toward what he must go through, bearing that on his body so plainly... I don't know. I think he wears the cap to help other people, not himself."

"Oh," I whisper.

"He has a temper too. Before the army, he was always an unpredictable child, but after... he changed, that boy. His mama is worried. All of them are worried. And those damn rumors." She shakes her head. "Honor is all we have sometimes, and him being... like he is... doesn't help."

I watch her carefully. "You don't believe it, do you? The rumors? Jake mentioned something about being dishonorably discharged."

"I've known that boy since he was two. I can't imagine him doing anything dishonorable." She purses her lips and looks sadly at the cup as she hands me a coffee and mindlessly starts cleaning the machine she'd been using, almost like she's moving on autopilot. "His family is worried about him. He hasn't talked to anyone since he got back. Well..." She pauses to scratch at her chin. "Not *talked* talked. Shared with anybody, if you know what I mean."

"I do." I nod, although I'm not entirely sure I do know. From a professional point of view, I can assume that she means a therapist because that's where we would send anybody with PTSD when I worked at the hospital, which he must have. From another standpoint, I've never had a real family that would ever want to hear about me and my life. I imagine that no one is particularly worried about my whereabouts either—my ex-husband excluded unless it's my dead body located in a ditch. So, what do I know? "He has a big family?" I ask to distract myself from looking over my shoulder like I always do when I think about who might be watching from the bushes.

"Big and good as they come," she confirms with a small smile as if picturing them. "But he doesn't see them much.

Prefers to keep to himself and hide from the rest of the world." She shoves a donut into a bag and passes it to me. "Anyway, I'm no better than Jake. Where are you headed next?"

I debate on telling her the truth or a simplified version of it. "I'm looking for a place to stay for a few months. But *right now*, I'm looking for a place to get my tire replaced. Can you point me in the general direction of an auto shop?"

Donna nods her head in the direction behind me. "Closest auto shop is about a mile down that road." She raises her eyebrows, and I almost feel like she's smirking at me. "Jake's brother owns it, a matter of fact. You'll have to hurry if you wanna catch them—one of the guys is having a birthday barbeque today, so they're closing early."

Oh, man.

"*Or*," Donna says with a sly grin, "Alex does some restoration work. He might be able to find something for your beauty out there. I'm pretty sure he's the better bet anyway, since he works with older cars."

I can't quite figure Donna out. First, she was ripping into me about judging Alex's burn scars, and now she's trying to send me to him? Not to mention calling a very nosey cop on me.

"Well, I'm not taking my chances on that road in the middle of a rainstorm on the off-chance he deigns to stop and help me again, so the auto shop will do just fine." I jump off the stool and look back at her. "One last thing: is there anywhere I can stay while I'm here? A hotel? A barn? A prison cell since you've got friends on the force?" I joke, smirking. Then I sigh. "I really just need a bed."

Donna chuckles at my teasing. "We have a bed and breakfast, but it only has six rooms. As far as I know, they're pretty booked up on holidays. And with Easter coming up..." She trails off, but I can predict the end of her sentence.

"How do I find them?"

"The Dancing Pony is just down the street." She waves at the door.

Everything here is *just down the street*. I have a feeling it's no exaggeration.

"Dancing Pony?" It sounds more like a strip club than a cute bed and breakfast. I can imagine the song "Pony" by Ginuwine being played by the staff every time somebody enters the building. I'd be down to staying at a place like that for a night or two.

"Yeah, they have theme nights and all that." She blushes a little, and I wonder what type of theme nights they might host at that place.

"I'll try them. Thank you, Donna."

Donna watches me walk to the doorway before calling out again. "If the Dancing Pony can't take you, come back here. I'll find you something." She points to the main road in front of us. "If you turn left at the intersection down there and head up the mountain, you'll see a wide turn about two miles in. Turn there and keep on driving. You'll find Alex's house. The boy likes his privacy." She grins impishly.

"Can't blame him," I murmur and glare at her, but she just shrugs.

"Just in case that might be useful information."

"Thank you..." I reply slowly, my brow puckered.

"Good luck, honey. He is a good boy." She leans her body on the counter and taps her finger against the plastic surface, looking a little tired.

I shrug right back at her. "I have no idea what you're talking about."

She exhales a laugh and disappears from view as I stand there, confused as to what just happened.

Yesterday I was too exhausted and panicked to really take in the surroundings, but on my way to the Dancing Pony, Little Hope's only bed and breakfast, I see that the town is actually very quaint. A homey, small-town, waving-to-everyone sort of place. The stores all have family names—Morrison's General Store, David & Son's, Dr. Thompson Dentistry—and it all gives off a merry, Hallmark-esque ambiance. I feel like I'm about to step into fluffy snow with a sprig of mistletoe hanging over my head, and a cute guy with dimples will pass me by at midnight.

Today the town looks much more cheerful, and the Main Street name doesn't seem so dumb anymore. The people on the street look *normal* and happy, greeting each other on the street and no doubt asking after the family. Or if they're Donna or Jake—gossiping. These streets must be a nightmare if you're unlucky enough to happen to become the center of gossip. The sun gives everything a bright, vivid shine after the downpour last night, and even through my windows, it smells clean and fresh. Almost, surprisingly, like... *hope*.

A few people curiously look at me driving down their streets—my car new and foreign to their small-town life—but no one pays me more than a couple of seconds of their attention. Good. I'm not here to be a spectacle. I'm here to keep my head down and get the hell out. Which this car is *not* suitable for. So, kudos to my very "smart" decision of choosing the very rare Chevy Impala that every single nerd wants.

I pull up in front of the Dancing Pony and sigh—it's so *not* a *Magic Mike* set-up. It looks like a set piece from *Lord of the Rings*, complete with ivy trailing up the stone exterior. How ivy is alive and well during such weather is a mystery to me. Must be the Hallmark magic in the air.

The main door is unlocked, and I walk into the foyer to the sound of a tinkling bell announcing my arrival. The inside is just as quaintly decorated as the outside. It's dimly lit, but there's a roaring fire in a living room area, a lot of exposed brick, and dark-wood accents. The wooden desk itself has an eclectic mix of little potion bottles, worn books, old maps, and unlit candles.

"I'm sorry!" A soft, musical voice comes from behind me, and I turn to see a woman hurrying around to the other side of the desk. "I heard the bell, but I got tangled up cleaning a mess in the kitchen!" She comes to a stop behind the desk, and I gape at her for a moment, realizing I'm staring harder than I did at Alex. She has long, ash-blonde hair parted around fake elf ears, and she's wearing a long, beige dress that looks difficult to move in. Her bright-blue eyes twinkle in amusement at my openmouthed perusal of her attire. "Sorry. Theme night. My husband and I are huge *Lord of the Rings* fans, if you can't tell." She giggles. "We like to host gatherings here with a specific theme. Dinners, games, *Dungeons & Dragons*... all the fun stuff for a place like this."

I look around the room again and smile. "I bet it's awesome." No sarcasm there. I'd played *Dungeons & Dragons* in high school and loved it. That was one of my very few pleasures in life because it didn't require money or friends, just a few socially awkward kids when one of them had a worn-out playing set. I stand up straighter and remind myself of what I'm here for. "Any chance there's a room available? I've heard you get busy around Easter."

Her smile drops. "I'm sorry, we don't have any vacancies right now. We have a game week, so we're all booked up."

Perfect.

I purse my lips and try to ignore the surge of disappointment that lances through me. "Okay... er, how close is the next place that *does* have rooms?"

She winces. "Not for fifteen miles or so." She points in the direction I'd just come from, which was *not* on the agenda.

"Thanks for your help," I say with a disheartened smile. It's not her fault she's fully booked up, but it doesn't change the fact that I'm screwed.

She looks crestfallen to me. "Look, if you give me your number, I can call you if a room becomes available, if you'd like that? How much longer do you plan on staying in Little Hope?"

"Not long, hopefully. No pun toward the town," I tack on apologetically. "I just need to be... somewhere. I need to get my tire replaced, and then I'll be back on the road." I scribble my number down for her on the back of a business card she handed me from a small pile on the desk along with a pen and smile weakly at her. "*But*, if something comes up in the next day or so, please, give me a call."

"Good luck!" the elf says, and I wave at her as I leave.

Well, that was a big ol' waste of time, I think to myself as I grumble my way back to the car.

I pass a small grocery store, and my stomach growls, reminding me that we're surviving on a donut —a real one, this time—and two cups of coffee.

By the time I return from grocery shopping, where I grabbed all the snackables in sight, peering through a few store windows lazily and sitting on a park bench to get a sense of my surroundings. As I'm scrolling through social media—for a glimpse of my old life—I realize with a sinking heart that I've missed the window for getting to the mechanic to have my car looked at.

I groan and get in the needy hunk of metal and chrome, having no choice but to head up the mountain path, following Donna's directions.

The trip is short and uneventful, which is a nice change while driving on a donut.

The area is full of lush, green vegetation, still wet from the downpour, and what must be Alex's cabin emerges through the trees as if it belongs there; the dark, rain-soaked wood and black trim make it look cozy and inviting. *Nothing like the man inside it,* I think. I expected a cabin but didn't expect anything like *this*. It looks like something a cute, artsy type would buy when they needed a respite from the rest of humanity.

I park the Impala next to his now-familiar truck and climb out into the fresh air. I inhale deeply and take a second to enjoy the solitude. It puts me on edge after a minute, but those few breaths of mountain air help some of the tension leave my shoulders. I walk to the door and knock.

Nothing.

My car isn't exactly silent, so he must know somebody is here. I knock again, and still nothing. I frown and contemplate my options while I continue to knock.

"All right... *What?*" A growl comes as the door swings

open, and I face a chest covered in red plaid. A very wide chest.

I gulp. The shirt he's wearing covers his arms from shoulders to hands, buttoned all the way up his neck. God, that neck. I involuntarily swallow the sudden need for a drink and look up. He is wearing the same cap low on his eyes, but no matter how low he tries to pull it, I can still see the webbed mapping of scars that I now know were burns left behind. They *are* nasty, but not in a repulsive way. They look extremely painful; the corner of his eye pulls down, and half of his cheek is jagged with red scar tissue. I follow them down his throat.

How did I miss this on my first assessment? Judging by the way they snake into and below the collar of his shirt, the scarring must go all the way down.

"Are you done?" he rasps, and I have to check if I'm still standing. That voice... At least I know now that it *was* from his voice and not just an adrenaline surge when we first met.

"It looks painful," I blurt and instantly smack myself on the head. Mentally. Although he would probably enjoy it physically.

The nerve on his jaw ticks, along with his good eye. I clear my throat. "I need help with my car, and the mechanic is closed. The lady from the coffee shop said you might be able to help me."

He crosses his arms over his wide chest, and, dammit, just like that, I'm distracted again. I sigh dramatically.

"Look, thank you for stopping to help me yesterday, but I was alone on a dark, lonely road, and you're a big guy. And a stranger." I stick my jaw out a little. He looks me up and down and relaxes a little. I take it as a good sign and continue. "I changed the tire to a donut, but I can't drive far on that thing. Can you please help me?"

"Did you get wet yesterday?" he drawls unexpectedly, and it takes me a second to figure out that he means from the rain.

"Yeah," I answer. *Obviously.* "It was a *rainstorm*. I don't really know how one was supposed to stay dry."

"Good." And he closes the door in my face.

What the actual fuck? I just explained to him why I'd refused his help last night with a perfectly reasonable explanation. What the hell does he want then?

"Asshole!" I yell at the door and storm back to my car.

About a mile down the dirt road, the donut gives out on me, and I get stuck in the middle of nowhere. Again.

This time I have no cell reception, no more donuts in the truck, and no more mental capacity.

I break down and cry. For how long, I don't know, but when I'm back in the land of the living, it's dark outside, and the surrounding forest is making weird noises.

I don't know what type of animals—or people—are lurking in the dark. I check all the doors, crack a window open and try to fall asleep. I hadn't taken a shower in two days, and I ate a Kit-Kat and a bag of salty chips for dinner. Life is bad, but I've had it worse.

Though when I fall asleep, I can't stop thinking that maybe I made a mistake going on this crazy trip and should have stayed.

Running away never helps.

Chapter Three

F**REYA**

I wake to the sound of a tap on my window. *Again*. It's becoming a habit already.

"The fuck you doing here?" A coarse voice filters through my half-consciousness. A tall figure in an already-familiar cap is hunched to look inside the window.

"I'd gladly move, but I can't." My own voice is foreign to me. I bet I was in a deep sleep cycle when this jerk woke me up.

"Why?"

"The donut shit the bed, so I'm stuck here." I accidentally hit my knee on the wheel and groan in pain.

He grunts something under his breath before adding more coherently, "Can't you call someone to pick you up?"

"I'm sure you're well aware that I'm not *from* around

here." That should explain everything. I roll over and settle back to sleep.

"The fuck are you doing *now*?" He's definitely growling.

"Trying to sleep. Do you mind?" I give him a look over my shoulder.

"I do, actually. You're on my property."

"This car is *my* property," I counter smugly.

"Well, your *property* is on *my* property, and I'd like it to be *off* it. *Now*." His nostrils flare.

I sigh. "I don't know if you can tell, but there is literally nothing I can do right at this moment." I spread my arms as far as I can in the cramped space. "In the morning, I'll go to the road and hitchhike a ride."

"Open the door," he growls.

"No. Go away." I'm a little scared now. *Fine*, a lot scared. This huge grizzly of a man is growling at me through my window—which feels all too breakable right now—and he doesn't look very pleased to see me again.

"Open. The. Door." He accentuates every word, which makes me almost pee my pants.

"Why? So you can prove me wrong and murder me?" I yell.

He squints at me. "No. I'll give you a ride to town."

"I don't need a ride to town." A lock of hair falls over my eyes, and I try to sweep it aside with a huff.

"You just said you'll catch a ride there in the morning."

"Yeah, *in the morning*. What will I do there now?" I'm fully awake now. *Thank you very much for such a restful sleep, you ill-mannered behemoth*, I think grouchily to myself. All I need is some damn sleep. Life on the run tends to drain your energy like nobody's business. I feel like I could sleep for fifty hours straight.

"I don't know," he spits sarcastically. "How about staying at the Dancing Pony so you can keep the fuck off my land?"

"Aren't you a smart one?" I fake-smile at him. "They're fully booked. I need a ride—*in the morning*—so I can go to another auto shop to fix my damn car because I made a mistake by putting all my eggs into this"—I point at him—"basket."

His growl is even louder. "Get out of the car."

"No, dude." I shake my head again, wide-eyed. "You are seriously scaring me right now."

He steps back and takes a deep breath. "Just get out of the car, so I can give you a ride."

"Where to?" I ask suspiciously. Didn't I just say I have nowhere to go? Will he give me a ride to the nearest slaughterhouse?

He pinches the bridge of his nose and takes a deep breath. "Christ, woman, you can stay on my couch for the night. I'll drive you to town in the morning." All the fight has left his eyes. I give him a once-over and try to listen to my spidey senses. They're quiet. I don't feel any dangerous vibes coming off of him, but then I remember Jake's warning. I chew on my lip. He sees my hesitation and rolls his eyes, then tells me in a borderline-exasperated voice, "This driveway leads to the main road. Some people take wrong turns. You don't want to end up here when some trucker decides to look for a place to nap. Or a bear decides you smell too good to pass up."

He's not wrong. Choosing between two evils—this enormous bear of a man or an unknown truck driver—yeah, the choice is obvious. But he's so wrong about the smell. Any bear would run away screaming if it got in close proximity to me.

His words make sense, and at this point, I'm too tired to even care if he ax-murders me. I open the door and grab my keys and bag before following him to his truck and climbing inside. Immediately, I'm hit with the most delicious smell. It's dark and spicy. It's not a chemical smell, so it doesn't seem to be cologne or air freshener, but it's all... *man*. And old leather and heavy masculine sweat. I didn't know that combination could be so lethal.

The ride to his house is short and quiet. I see on his dashboard that it's one-thirty in the morning.

"What were you doing out there this late?" I question, getting out of the car as he pulls up to the cozy cottage he calls home. He grunts something under his breath as he unlocks the door that I can't make out, but I don't ask him to repeat it. He was probably out burying a nosey busybody in his backyard. I shiver again—not a good thought to have while walking into a stranger's house. Well, not a stranger anymore. I know his name. Sort of. The last name is irrelevant. Plus, Donna knows I might've headed this way. If I go missing, I bet Officer Jake would be eager to nail the town weirdo to the wall.

Oops. That didn't come out the way I intended, but I'll put the image in my spank bank anyway.

To be fair, he doesn't know me either, yet he's taking a chance on me. Not many people ever have.

He walks inside without inviting me to follow him in, but I walk behind him regardless and gently shut the door while I study my surroundings. I'm surprised by the homey feel. It's open concept, just one large room with two doors on the far side—a bedroom and a bathroom, I presume—a small, open, dark-cherry kitchen, a cozy fireplace with real fire—a treat—and a brown sofa that looks so divine that I want to lie on it immediately. That could also be from the heavenly idea of stretching my legs fully for the first time in days. The dark colors prevail in the interior, with just a few colorful strikes here and there in the form of a couple of pastel pillows, a red throw, and orangey bear figures on the shelves and over the fireplace. Bears... hmm... nothing suspicious at all.

"You can take the bed," Alex grunts, nodding toward the bedroom's open door. "It's through there."

"Where will you sleep?"

"The couch."

I eye the sofa. It's a standard couch with three seats. Looks comfortable enough, but I then eye *him*. He is insanely tall. In fact, I've never been this close to a person of his size. He's easily seven, maybe eight inches taller than me, and the span of his shoulders is twice that of mine. And I'm not a petite belle, but standing next to this man, I feel intimidated. An awful lot.

He lets me look him up and down, his gaze hidden in the shadows of that horrible cap. God, I hate that cap. I wish I could see his eyes.

"You're way too big for this couch. I'll sleep there." I walk toward my self-appointed sleeping arrangement and sit on the soft cushions. It's heaven.

"I've slept in a lot worse places," he grumbles.

"So have I." I curl up on the sofa and yawn loudly. "I'll wake up in a couple of hours, and then I'll be out of your hair."

I don't hear if he answers or not before I succumb to the heaviness of my eyelids and fall asleep.

I wake to the smell of freshly brewed coffee and the sound of birds twittering in nearby trees. Before I open my eyes, I take a second to relax in the fluffy comforter that lies around my shoulders. I don't remember placing that over me last night, so Alex must have done it while I was asleep. The same smell from the car washes over me, and I want to bury myself in it.

I hear Alex making something on the stove and blink my eyes open to find him. I can't help the large stretch as my body remembers we're no longer stuck in a car, and as hard as I try to do it quietly, Alex hears me and turns to look at me. He's wearing a long-sleeve black Henley, dark, worn jeans, and, of course, his faded navy cap. I didn't have a chance to look at him properly when I first met him because I was scared, pissed off the second time at his door, and exhausted the third. Now, I can appreciate all of *that*.

His dark hair is a little on the longer side, curling along the edges of that awful cap. The scarring on his face in the morning light is still the same to look at. No better, no worse. It's just... there. It isn't pleasant to look at by any means, but not nearly bad enough to send me running for the hills. Quite the opposite, actually. That scar has a story. Although an unpleasant one, it was what shaped him into the man he is now.

A little sparkle of interest pangs in my chest, restarting my frozen heart.

He is watching me watch him as he leans against the granite kitchen counter with a coffee in his hand, returning my stare. His eyes travel down before there's a subtle quirk to the edge of his lips that he tries to hide with a tilt of his mug.

Looking down, I notice my nipples peeking through my T-shirt. When I'd gone to sleep in my car, I hadn't expected company, so I took off my bra. When he picked me up, I forgot to put it back on. I cross my arms over my chest and rally a smile. "You should have woken me earlier."

He shrugs and says nothing before pointing to the door next to his bedroom. Through the open door, I can see the beige sheets rumpled from where he slept in it. *Fuck*, that's an image. "Bathroom is in there."

My smile drops. "Right. Thanks."

I grab my bag and scurry to the bathroom—not even letting myself take another peek inside his bedroom—then close the door and make sure it's locked. I still feel like his eyes are on me, and I quickly scan the small washroom, a weird sensation settling into my gut.

The bathroom is clean and simple. A shower, a toilet, and a small white vanity are really all it is. I relax.

I peep inside the medicine cabinet, but there are only a few shaving items, a toothbrush—only one, which feels way more important to me than it should be—and two prescription pill bottles. Both are full. I debate with myself if I want to look at the names on the bottles and see if I recognize what they're used for. I do. I *so* do. But the guy offered me a bed so I wouldn't get mauled by bears, so the least I can do is respect his privacy. I close the cabinet and take care of my needs.

After the hottest shower in the universe, a relief from the pitiful showers that the motels have offered me thus far on my journey, I'm starting to feel human again.

I wrap myself up in a towel, then groan, tipping my head back as I realize I forgot a change of clothes in the car since I only grabbed my handbag.

I open the door and peek into Alex's bedroom, trying not to look around too much since I wasn't invited in here. I spot a pile of neatly folded shirts on the dresser right near the door. *Perfect*. He might kill me for it, but at least I'll die with my modesty intact and not buck-naked. The dark-gray shirt I plucked from the top of the pile reaches me mid-thigh, which is perfect for my lack of underwear... which brings me to conclude that I might have spoken too soon. There is no way I'll put my old panties on. Everyday liners can only get you so far.

I walk out into the kitchen, and Alex's coffee mug pauses at his lips. He's now sitting at the square dining table, wearing the same cap, of course, but his gaze is locked on my outfit.

"The fuck are you wearing?" he growls, smacking his mug onto the table, the remaining liquid splashing everywhere.

"All my clothes are in the car, and I haven't taken a shower for a while," I try to explain, already knowing it will fall on deaf ears.

"Not my problem," he growls through gritted teeth.

"I can't put the same stuff on," I weakly try to reason. I knew I was taking liberties borrowing his shirt, but I wasn't expecting... well, *that*.

"Not my problem," he repeats and slowly stands up. I gulp down a sudden rise of fear. Maybe Officer McJudgy had been right after all.

"I'll get it to a dry cleaner and return it to you, I promise," I assure him quickly, trying to appease him. "Or buy a new one. I really don't have anything to wear now." My voice is getting smaller while his—getting louder, and I hate myself for that. I hate this familiar reaction of my body to an alpha male presence. I thought I'd cured myself of that sickness. Guess I was wrong.

His jaw ticks again, and I can see the edges of his eyes narrow under that goddamn cap.

"Fine," I snap. "Do you want me to take it off?"

"Yes," he growls, and I act before I think—I turn around and pull the T-shirt off, throw it onto the chair, and stride toward the couch, where I wrap myself in the comforter I left there earlier.

The silence in the room is suffocating, but I turn to look at him as I make my way to the door. His mouth is open, completely gobsmacked by what I just did. His gaze trails down my body as if he still sees it as exposed, and I watch his thick, scarred neck move with a swallow.

"Happy now?" My chin is raised in defiance.

His gaze moves up to my face. "What the *fuck* did you do that for?" His voice is quieter now. And lower. So much lower.

"You told me to take it off," I respond, shrugging under my massive covering.

"I didn't know you didn't have anything on under it!" His voice rises an octave.

"And I told you I don't have any spare clothes with me!" My voice is higher as well. We're moving toward full-blown yelling.

"Put the shirt back on," he growls.

"Why?" I challenge, my jaw tight and body rigid.

"Just put the damn shirt back." He stands and walks to the chair, where he grabs the shirt, tosses it at me, then turns around, giving me privacy.

I slide the shirt back over my shoulders and down my sides, then take a seat.

"Can you please give me a ride to the auto shop?" I ask quietly. Two minutes ago, everything seemed surreal, and I was that different, brave, bold person. And now, my showing off just feels stupid and immature, and I'm back to being... well, *me.*

He scowls and walks to the stove, piling up a plate with eggs, bacon, and toast before placing it on the table. Who he is scowling at is a big, fat mystery to me. Then he points at it and turns back to pile up a second plate. "After you eat your breakfast."

"I'm not hungry. Can you just please give me a ride?" My nose is tingly, my eyes are burning, and my voice is almost inaudible.

He takes a deep breath and wipes his face with his huge paw. "Look, I'm not really the social type. I don't do good with people." Then he takes another deep, cleansing breath. "Eat." Then he adds in a gentler voice, "Please."

"Thank you," I answer softly, refusing to make eye contact. I feel like it was important to agree, and not because agitating a person with a bad temper isn't a good idea, because it's not. But here, he *needed* me to agree and accept this small social step.

The room is silent, apart from the both of us eating breakfast, but it's not uncomfortable anymore. I can't help but sneak looks at his half-hidden face while he's lost in his own thoughts, staring into the depths of his coffee cup. *Great, while he is busy, I can ogle him a little*, I think to myself. His shoulders are so wide, and that chest is mouth-watering. I wonder if he has that tickly chest hair... He's like a mystery box you desperately want to unwrap. Very slowly and rife with anticipation, knowing the goodies will be rewarding.

He hugs the mug with both hands, and his fingers are long and thick. *I'd like to feel those fingers trace... Stop, just stop, Freya! What are you thinking?* I shake my head a little to get myself off of the cloud nine I'm currently sitting on.

I wish for a second that I'd met him before now. When I

had the chance to have a normal life and normal relation-ships. Before I was so messed up.

He must notice my stare because he looks up and stares back.

I glance at his cap. "Do you wear that at home because of me? Trust me, I've seen worse." He doesn't respond. He just stares at me under the frayed edge of the faded navy material as if it were a bulletproof shield. "I mean, it's only fair. You've seen... a lot of me. The least you could do is show me your face."

He hesitates, and I watch his jaw set in indecision before slowly removing the cap and placing it next to him. Deliberately keeping it close for my sake, I presume, in case I cry and run away, scared of his appearance.

The left side of his face is badly damaged. The hairline is uneven, but the ropey web of scars doesn't go all the way to his hair. I can see why he wears his hair long: anything to cover the damage. Half his cheek and jaw are damaged too, which explains why he keeps himself clean-shaven. It would be even more obvious if only half his face had hair.

After a lazy trail of my eyes over the affected area of his face, I reach his eyes. They are striking moss green, sharp, and fiercely observant, probably due to years of being able to hide them behind cap brims. He could watch without being watched. I stare into his eyes, trying to get a feel for the type of man that sits before me.

He drops his gaze first, clearing his throat and looking into his coffee mug. I'm probably the first person he's let look him in the eye in a long time, and it shows in the uncer-tainty radiating from his body.

"You have beautiful eyes," I comment, then return to eating. He looks at me like I just spouted a horn between my eyes and started shitting rainbows in his kitchen simultaneously. "What?" I ask. "Do I have food on my face?" I start wiping at my mouth and cheeks. He shakes his head and grabs his coffee again to take a sip, but the move feels more like he's trying to hide behind it. I doubt there's any coffee left in it at this point.

We finish eating—and drinking—in silence. I take my plate to the sink and wash it. He comes over with his mug, so I grab it and wash that too. He doesn't move from my space. Standing two feet from me, he towers over my not-so-small frame. I usually don't like large men who represent obvious domination in my book, which is funny, considering how his looming presence doesn't even intimidate me anymore. In fact, his presence is inexplicably calming, somehow.

"Give me your keys." He's right behind me, which should send me running for the hills, but his breath causes shivers and not those born out of fear.

"What?" I whip around and almost smack my face into his chest. That sounds way too familiar for my liking—making me stay, taking my keys...

"Give me the keys so I can bring your bag. You can't go into town with a bare ass."

"Right." I feel my cheeks heating. The cheeks on my face, those cheeks. Again, what on earth came over me at that moment when I took his shirt off? "I only have one big suitcase in the trunk. If you could get it, that'd be great."

I retrieve the keys from my bag and hand them over. He takes them carefully, avoiding skin-to-skin contact. I feel a little offended because, *hell,* I'm not that bad to look at, and I don't smell bad. Anymore.

Before exiting, he quietly adds, "Good girl," and walks out the door.

When he disappears outside, I take residency under the

comfy comforter and pull my phone out of my bag. When I press the power button, it all comes rushing back, crashing into me at full speed.

"You think you can hide?"

"You think you can run away from me?"

"You think you can take what's mine?"

"You're nobody, and you'll always be nobody. Just dirt I found on the side of the road. You. Are. Nobody."

"I will find you, and you know what will happen then. Because you know I don't like to waste my time."

"You spend a cent of it, you'll regret it."

All the messages are from an unknown number. Dang it, he figured out this number too. It doesn't even have a name attached to it—it's the freaking prepaid cheap stuff.

Erik always had ways of getting any information he needed, making him a mighty person among his... *associates.* But now, him having too much information might give me leverage. If I only knew the right way to utilize it.

I'm staring at my phone with something that has to look like murderous intent when Alex comes back. He stops at the door.

"Are you okay?" I can almost detect a note of concern in his voice. Almost. Then it's gone.

"I'm good." I stand up. "Did you bring it?"

He extends my suitcase toward me, which I know for a fact is not light, yet he's holding it with an outstretched arm like it's nothing. "Thanks." I grab the suitcase, and it lands on the floor with a loud thud. I jump at the unexpected noise, then quickly collect myself and roll the suitcase to the bathroom.

Before entering the bathroom, I turn around to say, "Alex, it might not seem like it, but I really appreciate what you did for me."

Color rises on his good cheek, and it looks awfully cute. The grumpy giant is turning out to be a shy guy.

I change into a fresh pair of skinny black jeans and a loose baby-pink sweater. I have a jacket in the car in case I need it. It is April in Maine, after all. I pack everything back in it and roll my suitcase to the door. "I'm ready."

"Your car is a beaut."

"Thanks," I answer proudly. "When I was a kid, I watched this show and wanted to have a car just like that because, for the characters, the car was their home, and I wanted the same. Nobody told me it's a stick, though." I chuckle.

"*Supernatural.*" There is a smile in his voice.

"Yes! You've watched it too?"

"Before the navy." He looks sheepish, sharing this information about himself with me.

"How long were you in the navy?"

"Seven years," he grunts.

"Wow, that's a long time in the service. Did you leave because you were injured?"

"No." He cuts me off, and the mood shifts to Antarctic-degree chilliness.

I shouldn't have pried—I remember what Donna said—and this line of questioning would never bring any good. But silly me was hoping he would open up like a flower to my sun. Yeah, right. For a man like him to be dishonorably discharged might have hit hard. But for the love of me, I cannot imagine this man doing anything dishonorable.

Donna was right. Yes, he is an asshole to me sometimes. But he stops in the pouring rain at night to help a stranger change a tire. Yesterday, he didn't have to give me a place to stay, but he did. Even after the army—excuse me, *the Navy* —he still serves. I think it's in his blood. I don't believe people who serve this country and enlist to help others can switch it off once they come home. I think it's a default setting of sorts. A protector mode.

"I'm sorry if I asked something I'm not supposed to."

"Did you pack all your shit?"

And just like that, I'm back to the land of hating his guts. "Yes." I grab my suitcase and tread to his truck. "I found their phone number. I'll call them to pick me up with my car, so you can drop me off at my Impala."

"I'll drive you to the shop." And he's back to growling as well. Great. He walks up to me, pries the suitcase from my fingers, and drops it in the trunk of his truck. I sit inside, boiling. Even the sexy smell can't calm me down anymore. For a second there, I thought he might be an actual human being, but he is a darn animal with a stick so high up his ass that it prevents him from speaking normally. Only grunts, growls, and snarls.

Chapter Four

FREYA

Alex is completely silent on the way to the auto shop. The whole fifteen minutes, not a peep. Doesn't spare me a glance, doesn't so much as hint at opening his mouth. By the time we make it to the auto shop, I am eager to get out of his presence.

"I'll leave your suitcase in your car" is the first thing he says to break the heavy silence.

"I'll take it now," I argue.

"No, you don't know where you'll stay. I'll leave it in your car, so you don't have to drag it around the town." He sounds surprisingly logical, considering our very irrational morning.

"How will you open the door?"

"It's an old Chevy, for fuck's sake."

Right, like that should explain everything.

"Okay. Thanks, Alex," I mutter. "I mean it."

I'm about to get out of the car when he grabs my hand. His palm is dry and warm. I glance at the place where our skin is connected—his hand completely swallows mine.

"Look, it's better if he helps you." His eyes are troubled, and only then did I notice that he's not wearing that default cap of his.

"Whatever." I pull my hand back and climb out. "Take care, Alex," I say quietly.

He turns his head to the road, and the engine roars to life. He jerks his chin in the direction of the auto shop. "His name's Justin. He'll help you."

I barely have time to shut the door before he speeds away. I scowl—screw him and his mysterious ways.

I take a deep breath and turn toward the building before me. It's the typical toxically masculine, greasy, sexist nightmare I've learned to expect from places like these. There are wheels stacked up along the wall outside, a weather-beaten sign that says Sal's Auto Shop, except that it's missing all the O's and the bottom half of the P. Dirty rags are lying next to pools of jet-black grease, and I can see at least two burly men wearing coveralls. My jaw tenses, and I go to take a step toward what I assume is the main door, but it's blocked by a beat-up fender, presumably from the totaled car currently being pushed into place on the other side of the lot. Before I get a step farther, a tall blond guy steps out into the sunshine from the main garage and squints at me.

He looks too much like an older version of Jake to be anyone other than his brother. He wipes his hands on a rag equally as dirty as the whole shop and tucks it into his belt loop. "Hey."

I smile as professionally as I know how. "Hi, there. You're Justin, right?"

"I am."

The men in this town seem to lean toward quiet and brooding, as he doesn't say anything else. I clear my throat and force that smile to stay on my face. "Well, uh, Donna at Dunkin' Donuts said you can help me with my car?"

He nods slowly before looking around us, and I chuckle awkwardly.

"It... it broke down on Alex's..." I wince. "I don't know his last name. Tall guy. Wears a cap. Lives up—" I stop as Justin raises his eyebrows, a look of amusement on his face. "You know who I'm talking about," I guess sheepishly. "Well, my car broke down on his property."

Justin rubs his chin. "Crowley."

"Excuse me?"

"It's Alex Crowley." He nods his head toward the garage office over the stranded fender, and I follow him as he starts moving in that direction. "And he's better equipped to work with your car."

"How do you know what kind of car I have?" I question slowly, a little apprehensive now.

He laughs. "My brother has a mouth on him, and I believe you've already met him. Plus, it's a small town."

"Officer Jake, right?" I distractedly amble around the room, feeling out of place.

"Mmm-hmm... Don't hold it against me," he jokes with a crooked grin. He rounds the desk and types something into an old computer, his dirty fingers clacking on the already-dirty keyboard. "A week."

"A week of... ?"

"*Wait.* For your wheel."

My jaw drops. "I just need a tire, and I can be on my way," I protest. "You've got stacks of them right out there!" I jerk a thumb over my shoulder to where I can see some through the window.

"You need a whole wheel."

"And how do *you* know?" I growl. "You haven't even seen my car."

Justin looks over at me and smirks yet again before holding up his phone, where there's a photo of my car wheel. My mouth drops open again. "Alex sent it," he informs me.

"Wants it off his property, more like," I grouse. I cross my arms and scowl, then, trying to regain control of a situation that feels distinctly like it's spiraling out of my control, take a reassuring breath and straighten my shoulders. "Not a problem. Give me a new *tire,* and I'll be out of your hair. Name your price, and I'll double it. I don't mind."

Justin leans on the desk and folds his arms, regarding me closely. "You won't get far without a new rim. It's bent to hell and back." He laughs at his own joke, which I don't find amusing. "You'll just get stuck next town over if you don't. Or in the middle of nowhere." He looks past me out to the street beyond. "I wouldn't be alone out there by myself if I were you."

I snort at that. "I can handle myself against wayward men. I've been doing it for years."

Justin laughs. "I was thinking *bears*, sweetheart. You're in the middle of Maine. We've got more bears here than men."

I'm about to start fuming. "Can Alex get it done faster?"

"Doubt he'll help at all. Considering..." He doesn't finish the sentence, letting me assume the worse. Oh, right. He tried to get rid of me by dropping me off here at the crack of dawn.

"Oh my gosh, I don't have cooties." My eyes roll so far back in my head, they're on the verge of being stuck there.

"The jury's still out on that." He sniggers. I want to smack him across his handsome face but refrain from doing so because he's my last hope of getting out of Little Hope. He must have read something on my face because he laughs, and the atmosphere eases a little. "How do you know Alex, by the way?"

I shrug. "He helped me."

"Did he?" He squints his eyes. "Interesting." He steps closer and intently watches my face. "And how did he do that?"

"That will be none of your business, Mr. McNosey." I squint right back at him. He lets out a full belly laugh.

"Fair enough. But seriously, I don't have any wheels like what you need. It's a rare car, and I don't specialize in that. It'll take a week for it to arrive." He waves at his computer.

"Can't you just put on a tire? Any tire? Anything? Please." I'm not above the begging at this point.

"You need a wheel. Trust me." He does a double nod.

"*Trust you*, huh?" I challenge him, irked.

"Or don't." He laughs again. "But it'll still be a week."

I sigh in exasperation and drop my head back. "*Fine*. I'll wait a week." I purse my lips as Justin gives a smugly satisfied nod. "But is there somewhere I can stay for a week? An Airbnb? An abandoned trailer? Somebody's sofa? *Anything?*"

Justin frowns dismissively. "Call The Dancing Pony. There will be—"

"Already have. They have a game week all week, and they're all booked up."

Justin sighed. "Of course they do." He picks his phone

up again. "Give me your number, and I'll try and find something for you."

"Really?" I whisper. "You'd do that? I mean, literally anywhere other than a bench on Main Street would be perfect."

He gives me a faint smile as his fingers pose over his phone, ready to type in my number.

"Oh... I don't know it by heart. Let me..." I get distracted turning the cheap supermarket cell on and finding the number that I'd saved as a contact, but I can sense Justin's eyes on me. He clears his throat as I rattle off the number.

"How long have you had that phone for?" he inquires, his tone awfully suspicious.

My eyes dart up to his, and I see he's studying me closely. "Uh, not long. It's a new phone. My other phone was accidentally run over by a truck on a highway in Ohio. You know how it is." I smile wide.

"I don't." His smile is gone.

"And how is that any of your concern again?" I didn't come here to be questioned by Mr. McNosey, who turns into Mr. FBI at midnight.

"Just looking out for my best friend." His voice saddens.

"And who might that be?" I ask conversationally.

He points in the general direction of the road where I just came from. "He just dropped you off."

"Oh. Him." Makes more sense now, but not really. If they're best friends, surely Alex would have mentioned something before dumping me here. So, just to be a little bitchy, I add with a sweet smile, "You don't exactly seem like best buddies anymore. Got into trouble over a girl?"

"No woman could have come between us." His face changes, and he doesn't look anything like the smiley scamp he was two minutes ago.

"I'm sorry, Justin. I didn't mean anything by that." And just like that, I've hit the wrong nerve. Me and my big mouth.

"We enlisted together, you know. We'd been in the navy for three years. Then..." He stops himself, looking for the right words, then swallows audibly and averts his eyes. "Something happened with me... and I had to be away for a while, so I wasn't there for him. I can be there now." He gives me a pointed look, daring me to hurt his friend. And I sense there is a lot more to that, but I'm not dipping even my pinky toes into their story. However, I'm not above dipping them into his own shit since he's being mean to me, and I'm getting a free pass to be mean back.

"Went to jail?" I venture casually.

His eyebrows shoot up to the sky. "How did you know?"

"Wild guess," I lie.

"Right." He watches me carefully now, suspicion clear on his face. "What did you say you do for a living?"

"I never did," I say almost singsong, smiling serenely.

"Right." He scrubs at his eyes again, and only now do I notice that the poor dude looks exhausted. He has dark-purple bags under his eyes, and his skin looks dry and cracked.

"When was the last time you slept?" I ask, tilting my head as I peer at him.

"Seriously, man. How do you know the right questions to ask?" He takes a step back, looking a little scared of a little ol' me, which is comical coming from such a huge guy. I fight a snicker.

"When?" I demand, pulling out the authoritative voice I used with my worst-behaved patients.

"About three days." Then he adds with a cheeky smile, "Ma'am."

"You're about to crash," I inform him. "Probably should go home."

"I live above the garage." He points a finger upwards.

"Smart," I nod.

"Tell me about it," he sighs tiredly. "I can offer you to stay at my place…" He probably notices the change in my face because he adds quickly, "Just to wait out for the wheel. But my sleep problems and all that." He spreads his arms like it's supposed to explain *all that*. It doesn't.

"Again, I don't need a wheel. Just a tire. A donut will do. I just need to get the hell out of here." And we're back to square one.

He chuckles. "I see Little Hope is growing on you."

"Like a fungus." I rub my eyes. I'm tired. Tired of this conversation, tired of this town, just plain *tired*.

"Look, why are you here?" He places his hands on his hips.

"Because I need to fix my damn wheel—*tire*, I mean!" He's exhausting me with this banter.

"No, I mean, why are you in this town?" He widens his eyes like I was supposed to catch his meaning.

"Because it's on the way?"

"On the way to where?" And Justin is back to being Mr. FBI.

"Where I'm going to." I squint at him again.

"And where is that?" He crosses his arms over his chest, his tone mocking.

I'm defeated. "I seriously don't know how we arrived at this Dr. Phil shitshow."

"Yeah, I missed that moment too," he admits, his hard stance deflating. His weak smile is tired.

"I'm just looking for a place to stay for a few months." A partial truth.

"Then why not stay here?"

I give him a dry look. "How about *you don't even have a motel for me to stay in* as a reason why?"

"It's this week only. Then the place will be empty." He shrugs his wide shoulders. "And as I said, I'll ask around for you."

"And what about my car?"

"I'll fix it." He cuts me off, then adds more softly, "But it will still be a week of wait. You probably could use this week for your own business. You aren't on vacation either." Not a direct question but a very correct assumption.

One sleazy town, I complain mentally with a defeated sigh. "You won with your week. When will you get my Chevy here?"

His smile is devilish.

ALEX

As I'd promised Freya, I placed her suitcase in her trunk. The locks on her car are flimsy, and I'm surprised she made it this far without being robbed or worse.

I lean against the side of the old Chevy and fold my arms as I hear the crunch of tires on gravel. It had better be Justin's tow truck and not yet another trespasser who thinks they can stay the night and wear my shirts on their tight, naked bodies. If it's one of the more silent employees of the garage, even better.

It's not. Of course it's not.

Justin gets out of the truck and aims a steely gaze at my face. "She's shady as fuck."

"Didn't ask your opinion," I grunt. I'm in no mood for friendly chatter.

"You still got it. She has a cheap phone on her that she doesn't even know the number for. Real keen to get out of here." Justin nods at the car I'm leaning against. "Anything looks suspicious there?"

"Not that I was looking or was interested in your input." Does he just assume we're best buddies again, and because of that chick, we're back on track, solving yet another mystery? I don't have friends anymore, and I don't *need* them. Just how I like it.

Justin snorts and peers in the window of the Chevy. "Anything interesting, though?" He purses his lips, and I shake my head, seeing the wheels turning in his and knowing exactly what he's about to say.

"She ain't staying with me."

Justin splays his hands like a plea. "I don't trust her staying with anyone else. Something's odd, Alex. You know it as well as I do. Besides that, where the hell else will she stay?"

"Not my problem." I stand up and start prepping the Chevy to be transported back to the garage.

Humming my approval of Justin's choice of a flatbed tow truck so the beauty won't get damaged during the transportation, I climb inside Freya's car, so I can start it and turn the wheels straight.

"Oh, but it is. You let her stay at your place once already. Don't sentence this town to host some weird schmoozer on the streets."

I roll my eyes—schmoozer, my ass. That girl couldn't sweet-talk anybody even if she tried. "Get Jake on it, then. Ask Ken to do a background check, find a parking ticket, and lock her up. I don't know. Order the fucking wheel and get her out of here." Then I turn to him. "And so you know, this conversation was a one-time deal. Bye, Justin."

A dark cloud crosses Justin's face. "You used to be different. You cared about people."

"Why the fuck should I care about her or the people in this town when they don't give a fuck about me?"

He shakes his head and scowls, bending to finish attaching the fender of the Impala onto the back of the tow truck. "You're a real ray of fucking sunshine, Alex."

I don't respond. I watch silently as Justin secures the Chevy and climbs into the truck cabin. He flips me off and reverses out the drive.

I wait until the sound of the engine fades away before trudging back toward the house, keeping an eye on my surroundings the whole time. I reach into my pocket, pull out the hairband Freya left in my bathroom, and scowl at it.

Yep. She's trouble, all right.

FREYA

I roam through Little Hope, trying to find something to occupy myself with while I wait for Justin to call me. I doubt he's even trying to find a place for me to stay. And here comes the million-dollar question: *Where will I sleep tonight?*

I wander into a diner conveniently located on the same Main Street and flop into a seat facing the window. It's small, quiet, and cozy, but a few people are standing around talking to each other as they wait for to-go orders and a group of elderly women gossips over coffee in the corner. One of them has her eye on me, and I gather that's where the hub of gossip comes from. Officer Jake walks in and grins at the group of women, then perches on the edge of the neighboring table and leans in to talk to them. Ah. Makes sense.

Everything on the menu looks fatty and delicious and has funny names of famous people. I can't decide what I'd like to eat. It wasn't that long ago that I ate breakfast at Alex's, so hunger doesn't force me to go into a rage of ordering everything. Yet.

The waitress, a quirky, twenty-something girl, stops to take my order. Despite the chilly weather, she's wearing a short-sleeve shirt that displays colorful tattoos. She has her ash-blonde hair tied up into a long, sensible ponytail and a piercing strung through the bottom half of her red-painted lips. She looks out of place here, in this small, conservative-looking town, and I think of her as a kindred spirit.

"Morning. What can I get you?" she chirps.

"A coffee with cream and..." I trail off, flipping through the menu again. "I'm sorry... I can't decide."

The waitress grins. "Let me help. How was your morning?" She rests her hand on her hip and smiles.

I look at her and see a genuine question, not a jab. I close my eyes and sigh as I think about the headache that has been the last forty-eight hours. Or ten years.

"That bad, huh?" the waitress says with a chuckle and points at the menu. "Try a Lonely Kurt. It has enough calories, fat, and sugar to keep an army going, and after a bad morning, it tends to help people."

I laugh. "Sounds like a plan. Thank you."

She takes my menu. "I'm Kayla, by the way. I don't recognize you from around here."

"I'm not. Just... an unexpected visit." I wave my hand

wearily. "My car broke down, and now I have to wait a thousand years for it to get fixed," I groan. "Ugh, I'm sorry. Bad morning. I'm Freya."

Kayla smiles and holds up her notepad. "I think you might need two Lonely Kurts." I laugh as she starts to walk away before calling back over her shoulder, "Welcome to Little Hope, where there is *no* hope left."

Her call got Jake's attention again, and he scowls at Kayla menacingly, almost like he wants to... hurt her? That definitely gets *my* attention. I didn't like Jake much from the outset due to his non-stop gossipmongering, and now, I don't like him even more. He walks toward me and grins a little obnoxiously as he settles into the chair opposite from mine. "Hello, again. You're still here."

"I'm sure you know as well as anyone that I'm still here," I say slowly, not wanting to be too friendly with a guy who just sent such a malicious glare to a very nice girl—one who's my possible kindred spirit, no less.

He chuckles. "How's that car going?"

"If you'd tell your brother to hurry up, much better," I reply flatly.

"I'm afraid I can't tell my brother how to do his job." He shrugs good-naturedly.

"Why not? I'm sure he tells you how to do yours." I eye him over the coffee that Kayla has just walked up to set down in front of me.

"That's what older brothers are for." He smirks, not sparing Kayla a glance.

"I wouldn't know." I smile at Kayla as she follows up the coffee with the Lonely Kurt, placing it down gently. It's an excessive amount of food consisting of sausage, bacon, eggs, and French toast with strawberry syrup.

"Hi, Jake," she enunciates evenly, while he completely ignores her.

"Thank you, Kayla," I respond, purposefully loud enough for him to hear it and experience the appropriate feeling of shame that he should have for his rudeness, but he doesn't react. Kayla just smiles sadly and leaves.

"You were very rude to her," I state icily.

"It's what she deserves." His nostrils flare as he glances at Kayla standing at the counter, looking down at her notepad. My mind goes into overdrive at his callous response.

"Well, that's a fucked-up thing to say," I snap at him, scowling.

"Trust me, she does." His features cloud with hatred, and I feel like I want to run away as far from him as possible. He might look like a chill surfer dude, but he's got one hell of a mean streak. "Let's change the subject. You an only child or the eldest?"

I smile blandly at Jake. "None of your business." I have no interest in being friends with him—hoes before bros because Kayla and I are now friends, and us ladies have to stand together—nor do I want to share the details of my personal life with a meddlesome cop.

Jake hums under his breath before chuckling in a tone that sounds distinctly condescending. "Where are you headed after this?" He prods further. "I imagine someone must be waiting for you."

"Nope. Just me." I stab my knife into the middle of my French toast and hold it up in the air, taking a bite out of the side of it like a savage. He wants a show? He'll get a show. "Sorry, a girl's gotta eat," I cheerfully and sarcastically apologize through a mouthful of food. "The smell of blood always gets me so hungry." And then I ravage another piece of syrupy toast, imagining his bloodied neck under my teeth.

Jake frowns, looking aptly disturbed, before slowly standing and making his way back over to the gossip hub. I watch him as closely as he's watching me before Kayla comes back and takes his place across from me. I put the toast down and wipe my mouth, slowly assessing the mess I created with my open-mouthed chewing, then I take a sip of my coffee and try to act normal again. "Sorry," I whisper to Kayla.

She bursts into laughter. "Your breakfast is on me. His face was totally worth it."

"Well, thank you!" I grin and dig into the rest of my Lonely Kurt.

Just as I'm about to swallow a chunk of delicious goodness, Donna bursts into the diner and plops onto the seat next to mine.

"Thought I saw you," she chirps and pulls a strip of bacon from my plate. I glare at her. You don't come between a person and the bacon. "I got bad news for you, hon."

I stop chewing. "What?"

"I can't find anywhere for you to stay. We're a small town, and nobody's renting out. I'd take you for a couple of days, but I got no room, hon. Sorry." She offers me an apologetic smile, which then abruptly turns almost manically angelic when she continues, "Guess you'll have to stay with Alex!"

Yep, I see now how all that works here.

"He's not renting out either," I reply neutrally.

"Did you ask?" She perks up, trying to steal another strip, but I pull my plate away and glare at her.

"Sort of," I hedge.

"Oh." Her smile deflates. "I really didn't find you a

place, then. I'm sorry, hon." She looks sincere, and I don't have the heart to be rude to her, even though Jake activated my bitch mode mere minutes ago.

"It's fine, Donna. Don't worry about me." I try to convince her, while wondering how I could convince *myself* that everything will turn out fine in the end, too.

Chapter Five

F**REYA**

Justin texts me just as I get Kayla to wrap up my leftovers. He's going to meet me outside the diner with his tow truck, and we're going to get my car. I have no idea where he's organized for me to stay, but at least *something* is moving along.

I wait for Justin at the diner counter while Kayla flits around the floor, taking orders and delivering dishes.

I watch Jake leave the diner, throwing one last questioning look at me and a hateful one at Kayla, but I turn away from him.

"Don't mind him," Kayla says as she watches the exchange, coming to stand by my shoulder. "He thinks he's better than all of us. He isn't." She turns away to wipe down the counter, and I smile at her. "He and his brother," she sighs. "He works at the mechanic—"

I check my watch and breathe a measured exhale, trying to mitigate my exasperation. "I've met him. He's supposed to pick me up, but he's late."

She quickly turns to look at me, her eyes narrowing. "What? Why?"

"Because we're supposed to collect my car from Angry Alex's house? Why?" I look out through the window again. "Are you a couple?"

Kayla's eyes go wide before she bursts into laughter. "Hell no!"

And just like that, I like her a little more. Not that I don't like Justin, because I do, he seems pretty nice and genuine and even offered to help, but he's guilty by association because I *so* don't vibe with Jake.

At that moment, Justin pushes open the door. He sets his jaw and walks toward me, walking past Kayla as if she doesn't exist. She could be standing there naked, and he wouldn't give her the slightest ounce of attention. He leans on the counter, facing me, and grins a cheeky smile. "I found a place you can stay."

"Oh, good. Where?"

"With me." He shoots a quick glance at Kayla, lasting just half a second; I barely registered it, but it was there.

I can almost feel Kayla's soul leave her body, and I roll my eyes. So they're not a couple, but she wouldn't mind being one, and for somebody who's supposedly indifferent toward her, he's a little too preoccupied with her knowing that he's offered his place for me. *Interesting*.

"No, thank you," I tell Justin crisply. "I'll take the bears."

He purses his lips and runs his gaze down my face before grinning again. "Okay, fine. Let's get your car and see where we go from there." His disappointment was short-lived, and I sigh in relief.

"Fine." I lean over the counter to Kayla and whisper in her ear. "He's an asshole, but I need him right now. I'm sorry."

She smiles shyly. "I would offer you to stay with me, but I don't have—"

"I don't think she wants to stay in your dumpy little trailer," Justin says, speaking to her directly for the first time. There's such malice in his voice that my heart starts racing. I narrow my eyes at him.

"She wasn't talking to *you*," I snap before turning to Kayla. "Thanks for the offer. I'll find somewhere to stay. See you soon?"

She gives me a weak smile, and I push past Justin out to his truck.

ALEX

I stand next to the wine at the supermarket and add two bottles to my cart. I need more than that to forget the fiasco in my kitchen this morning. When I spot Officer Attleborough hurrying down the aisle toward me, I add another two.

"Alexander," he starts, bowing low with a sarcastic sneer. I scowl at him and make a move to dig the metal cart into his shins, but he hops out of the way and pouts theatrically. "*Hey.* I'm an officer of the *law* now. You'd better watch yourself."

"You're a pain in my ass. Unless you're here to tell me off for eating meat again? That's not a problem with the law." Since Jake got his badge, he's become even more insufferable.

"Um, *yes*." He peers into my cart and screws his nose up. "Some poor pig was born and raised to *die*, Alex, so that you can get your fill." Then he shoots me a nasty smirk, adding, "Just like your friends."

That was a low blow, and a swell of knotted fury in my gut tints the edges of my vision red.

"That'll be you if you don't shut up and leave me alone," I growl, opting to push my cart past him rather than stuff him into it and send it rolling down the mountainside and straight off a cliff. He just *had* to dig his heel into that gaping wound.

He catches up to me and stymies my forward progress. "*So*," he starts, grinning widely and sticking his thumbs behind his belt buckle, "I need some information about your new girlfriend. Not going to lie, Alexander, she's a bit of an odd one, even for you. But I guess you don't have many other options these days."

I stare at him with a deadpan expression, but he doesn't stop talking long enough to notice. He studies the rows of oil in front of him and eventually pulls one off the shelf.

"She eats food *very* strangely. She looked like a serial killer. Is she one? Have you asked her? Is that in your criteria for who you're going to sleep with?" He laughs sardonically and looks at me. "Who am I kidding? You don't have criteria."

"Are you done, Jake? Because you're about to be *very* done."

"I'm an officer of the—"

"Yes. Law, I know. Yet *I* am the one that knows how to actually use that gun of yours."

He sticks a foot out to rest on the bottom rung of my cart

to thwart my getting the hell away from him, then turns serious. "Freya is hiding something. What is it?"

I lean slowly down to his face and enjoy the strain on Jake's face as he resists looking away. "I'm not her keeper," I whisper. "And she's not my girlfriend. Go bug *her* if you're so upset about it." I hold my hands up before pushing the cart past him as I give him a mocking salute. "Glad to be of service, Officer of the Law."

I leave him standing in the aisle alone with a scowl on his face.

FREYA

Justin and I pull into Alex's driveway, and I sit up straight in alarm. "My car's not where I left it, and it's not here."

Justin lazily looks over. "Oh. So it's not. Maybe Alex moved it."

"With *what?*" Justin isn't stopping, and I turn to him with a scowl. "*Justin*. My *car* is *gone*! I need that car!" I sink back in my seat and whimper. That car is all I have of *mine*. "I knew I shouldn't have left it. That's my baby! We need to... I guess... call your brother?" I wince. "Oh, that's not going to go well."

Justin frowns over at me as we pull up in front of Alex's cozy house. "Had a run-in with Jake?"

"Sort of," I growl and get out of the car in a huff, storming toward the place where I last saw my baby. Maybe there will be... clues. Or something. Fuck. I don't know how to find my missing car. It's an old Chevy that can't drive on three wheels. It shouldn't be too hard to find.

"Freya!" Justin hollers. "Bears."

I flip him off and continue walking until I hear him laughing behind me.

"I picked it up already!" he calls out, sounding positively delighted with himself. "It's already at the shop."

I halt and turn to face him. He's got one foot still in the truck cabin and is leaning casually on the roof of it. "Then why the fuck are we here?" I snarl.

He gives me an evil grin, climbs back into the cab, and starts the engine.

"Hey!" I run back to try to get him to let me in, but he locks the door. "Alex isn't even home!"

"Oh, I know. I saw his truck at the grocery store. He's doing all his errands today. He'll be back later." He chuckles wickedly.

"So, why...?" I can't finish the sentence because the bastard takes off. "*Justin!*" I screech.

"The spare key is on the top of the entrance beam on the left!" he yells back through the open window. "And look out for bears!"

This sucks. This asshole really just left me on the doorstep of another asshole.

Freaking Little Hope and its inhabitants. Fuck them all. Well, not *all*, I suppose. Kayla was okay.

"Fuck, fuck, *fuck*," I hiss, kicking at a random plant that was growing over the drive. There's a fluttering of movement once I've kicked it, and I squeal, skittering onto the porch and pressing myself against the wooden door, eyes wide.

A bird flies out of it, audibly annoyed at my interruption, and I let out a sigh of relief. I plop down on the step leading up to the porch and wait for Alex to appear.

I have several hours to cool off before Alex's truck appears between two trees. I haven't used the spare key because it seems too invasive, especially with a private guy like Alex. I need to pee, and even though I'm in the woods and there's a bathroom behind every bush in sight, Justin's words about bears roaming the area keep me glued to the porch. I don't want to be eaten while squatting behind a raspberry bush. I slowly chew the leftovers of the Lonely Kurt, a granola bar I found in my purse, and take sips from the bottle of water I'd tucked in the side pocket.

I dread turning either of my phones on because I'm scared of what I'll find or what someone will find out about *me*, but I need to know if that elf from The Dancing Pony has come through with a room. I know she hasn't, so I decide not to even bother. I can't sleep in the car because the car was towed—hopefully—and I can't stay here because... well, nobody has invited me to. Simple as that.

I'm lost in self-pity when Alex strides toward the house, a storm cloud thundering over his features. "What are you doing here?"

"Funny story, your best friend Justin dropped me off here and then left. Now, I am *stuck here*." I spread my arms with a thoroughly *done* expression.

"Why the fuck would he do that?" He's taken aback.

"Exactly my question." I roll my eyes before exhaling a long, low breath. "Can you give me a ride to town? The only taxi service refused to drive to your house, and the only other person who has my number is the man who dropped me off here." No Lyft or Uber here. Just two local cab drivers who said they "aren't climbing up that mountain to be shot in the ass," which left more questions than answers about my morning host, if I'm honest.

"Where will you stay?" he asks eventually, stepping around me and unlocking his door.

"I'll figure something out." I sigh resignedly, scrubbing a hand over my tired face.

"You won't. At least not right now." He pulls the cap off his head and rubs his eyes. "C'mon, you'll sleep here." He walks past me and grabs my bag.

I'm prideful but not stupid. I don't want to sleep outdoors where bears could feast on my muscular thighs, so I follow him inside.

He strides toward the other mysterious door that's been calling to me like a siren, right next to the bathroom. "You're sleeping on the bed."

"I'm not." He keeps walking. It's kind of a short distance for such a long walk, so I assume he's dragging out the time it should take. "Alex, wait. I'm not sleeping on your bed. I like your couch."

"You are." He cuts me off and disappears into the smaller room. I curiously follow him.

So this is the bedroom. In the morning, when I took a quick peek and grabbed the shirt, I didn't even glance around—yep, not even once—but now, when I've been officially invited, it's a whole other story. I shamelessly look around, noting that the room follows the same design pattern and accents as the rest of the house—the same dark colors, the same simple and cozy style. A huge, soft-looking rug under the king-size bed with a brown, solid wood headboard. Two matching night-stands with pretty, pastel lamps on the top. A three-drawer dresser by the door that I'm already familiar with.

"Here," he says, pointing at the bed.

"Look, I'm not trying to be stubborn." He raises a brow

at my words. "I'm really not. You are a huge guy, and there is no way you can fit on that couch where I've already spent a perfectly relaxing night."

"I can fit in tight spaces."

When the realization of what he'd just said settles in, his cheeks pinken. Well, his good cheek does.

"I bet you can." I can't help but joke at his expense. He gives me a half smile that completely transforms his face before dropping my bag on the floor. Being a smart girl for a change, I stashed a couple of clothes in my bag that morning because Alex was right—I don't want to drag my suitcase around town all day long.

"You sleep here," he says like a caveman. And then he leaves. He comes back a minute later with a pile of light-gray fabric in his hands. "I brought clean sheets."

"No!" I yelp, and my cheeks instantly heat. How can I explain to him that I'd love to sleep bathed in his smell? That the air in his car pulled out of me a Pavlovian response, and my mouth was watering the whole drive into town this morning? And even while he was being a jerk, too. My body and mind can't seem to agree on what's common sensical in terms of body chemistry we should obey. "I mean, you don't have to. I'll change it tomorrow morning for you." I try to smile off my embarrassment but fail miserably.

"Whatever floats your boat."

"Yep," I reply because I don't know what to say that will erase my stupidity.

Before he walks away, he says quietly, "Whatever you're running from, I can help."

Not wanting to show the stark vulnerability I feel wash over my face, I turn away to root through my bag, searching to make sure that nothing is missing. "You don't know what I'm running from," I mumble.

"*You* don't know what I can do."

I stop looking through my bag and turn to stare at him. "Okay," I whisper.

He gives me only a faint smile, but it's enough to start my heart racing.

Chapter Six

A^{LEX}

I'm a fucking idiot, I think to myself as Freya continues to gaze at me, her hands shoved into her bag and her eyes wide. Why is she in my house again? Oh, right, I let myself be led around by my dick for a moment of weakness.

And that asshole, Justin. I know what that sleazy fuck did there.

She stops ravaging her bag and stands up from the floor. "Are you hungry?"

"No."

"Liar." She walks past me and opens my fridge. "I'm making lasagna."

"Please," I say dryly. "Make yourself at home."

A flush of red stains her cheeks, but she continues to grab things out of the fridge, ignoring my comment.

I don't really know what to do while she's cooking, so I

sit at the dining table and watch her. She starts stirring something on the stove, filling the room with a sizzling beef aroma. She scowls when she notices me watching. "Please don't sit there."

"Just making sure my house still stands by the time you're done."

She turns around and points a knife at me, puckering her lips as if it should scare me. I bark something that might resemble laughter and smirk. "Tell me about why you're here."

She turns to me and smiles a fake-ass smile. "How about *instead* of having this fantastic conversation, *you* go have a shower, or... I don't know... go chop a tree down or whatever manly thing you feel you need to do."

I fold my arms. "I need to know who's taking refuge in my home."

The goddamned tease dips her finger into the meat mixture on the stove and makes eye contact as she slides it in her mouth past her lips. Her eyes are bright with some unfamiliar feeling I haven't been a recipient of for a long time, and my mouth falls uncharacteristically dry.

"Okay, shower it is," I mutter, getting up from the table and walking painfully to the bathroom. I close my eyes and lean my palm against the door, resisting a groan.

I'm a fucking idiot.

FREYA

While the lasagna is in the oven, I take a shower once Alex is done with the bathroom. I walk out to the delicious smell of it wafting throughout the small house.

Alex's busied himself with watching some explosion-filled action flick on a flatscreen TV mounted above the fireplace that looks to be a top model, but I see he's already changed the sheets on the bed and has it made up for me. Bummer.

I change into my favorite green yoga pants and an over-sized white T-shirt, my favorite comfy outfit to lounge around in, patting myself on the back for shoving these particular articles of clothing into the bag in the morning. My pants just happen to be the same color as Alex's eyes. A pure coincidence, that's all.

When I emerge from the bathroom, the timer on the oven has long since run out. Alex stands stoically by the window with his hand wrapped around a glass bottle. The cap is nowhere in sight, and his sleeves are rolled up casually at his elbows. It's the first time I've ever seen him look so relaxed.

"Have you eaten already?" I venture, hoping not to startle him.

He doesn't look at me as he answers, "No, not hungry."

"Okay." No man in history has ever been *not hungry*.

I retreat to the kitchen to fix a salad. When I pull open the oven, a mouthwatering smell hurricanes into the space, and I watch Alex from the corner of my eye. While the delicious aroma suffocates the living crap out of me and makes my stomach growl with a hankering for real food, I hear a rustling behind me. Alex slowly trudges into the kitchen, clearly haven given up on resisting the smell.

"What are you making?" He tries to sound grouchy, but I only smile to myself because it's just what I expected from him.

"Lasagna and salad. Do you want some?" I ask.

He shrugs. "I could eat."

"Good. Sit down then." I point at a stool with my spatula.

"Yes, ma'am," he shoots back, settling onto the seat.

I grin wider. It's the first note of natural, unconditional lightness I've sensed in Alex since we met. I heap a generous portion onto his plate and set it in front of him. He digs in without waiting for me, shoveling my cooking into his mouth with gusto. I can't help but be hit with a ray of satisfaction in some strange, seemingly primitive way that I just fed a male. This male, not just any male. Like he is *my* male. I feel like thumping a fist on my chest with a warrior shout. It feels like a personal success to see him chewing my food as if his life depends on it.

His plate is empty in minutes, and he's eyeing the stove.

"Want some more?" I offer, and he nods. He makes a move to stand, but I'm faster. I press his shoulder down, urging him to stay seated, and take his plate.

Between the groans coming out of his throat and the way he's savoring each bite, I can tell he is definitely enjoying this meal.

"That's good," he admits between bites. "You know how to cook?"

"Just a few things. Nothing crazy."

"I'd say this is crazy." He points at his plate, and my cheeks heat at his praise. What is wrong with me? "I haven't eaten a home-cooked meal for... ten years, I think."

"What?" I blurt, surprised. "But what about your family? I heard it's big. Doesn't your mom cook for you sometimes?"

He stops chewing and gives me a cold look. "Somebody's been busy gathering gossip, I see." He's peeved by my inquiry, that much I can tell. "My mom is dead, so no, she doesn't *cook for me sometimes*."

My brow knits even as I internally wince from my misstep. "I thought your mom..." I remember Donna mentioning that his mom is concerned about him.

"If you mean Stella, she isn't my mother." His lips form a flat line before he gets to his feet and carries his dishes to the sink. I don't know who Stella is, but I'm scared to ask.

"I'm sorry, Alex," I attempt to apologize, but he just waves his hand dismissively, washes his plate and silverware, and retires to the couch. My only intention was to make his day better and to show him how thankful I was, but in the end, everything turned out to be a downer. It feels as if it always does, and now I feel like crap.

I clean up the kitchen after my mess and position myself to covertly creep on him for a moment. He's seated on the couch with his glass back in his hand and gazing into the fire he started before dinner. The air is chillier in the evening, and the fire adds just enough coziness and warmth for me to feel a little better. I straighten my shoulders and walk to the battlefield. I take a seat on the couch two feet away from him and look over.

"Alex."

He doesn't acknowledge me, so I lightly touch his hand, and he tenses. His forearm bulges at the contact, and a pronounced pulse on his neck is visibly increasing speed. His gaze moves down to where our hands are connected and then to my eyes. He doesn't look pleased. Gone is the dry humor and sarcasm, and in its place is a deep-set anger that seems forever just below its boiling point.

"I don't like to be touched," he growls, tugging his hand from under mine. His voice is rough, and I sense not just a desire to be left alone but that not only he doesn't like it but *can't stand it.* I've seen it before, people with different sorts of PTSD retracting inside themselves like turtles, recoiling as if physical contact makes them ill. It could be because of the obvious reason—his burns and what caused them—or maybe something else.

I quickly withdraw my hand and place it on my lap. "I'm sorry," I apologize again. "About that and about mentioning your mother. I haven't been gossiping about you, I swear."

"I don't care." His voice is gravelly.

"I do. I don't gossip. Trust me, I know firsthand how badly it can hurt." I swallow down a painful lump in my throat. Yeah, I know it, all right. Some busybodies make it a hobby to spread rumors around, and I paid for those lies every time coming back home when I had to stay late at work because we had some sort of emergency, but by the time I got home, my ex already had heard a different story on where I might've been and who I had been doing it with. I don't know who made up those lies till this day—or maybe it was just him, fabricating reasons to justify beating me bloody. "And I want to thank you for letting me stay here."

"I didn't have a fucking choice." From his sullen expression and the rigidness of his posture, he doesn't look thrilled to feel cornered like this.

"I know. And again, I'm sorry." I sigh. "I'll pay you for these two nights."

"I don't need your money," he grunts back.

"Okay, but maybe there's some way I can repay you," I say persistently, then cringe internally. Even to my ears, it sounds corny, like a cheap porno where the plumber takes his "payment" as some action between the sheets.

If he hears it in the same mortifying way, he doesn't show it, his expression flintier and more detached than ever. "Yeah, you can. Be fucking gone in the morning."

I fend off a flinch at his harsh reply. I'm seriously

considering leaving now and walking back to town, taking my chance with bears—real ones, not the rude grizzly of a man sitting stonily beside me—and wayward truck drivers. I lift my gaze to the ceiling, blinking back sudden tears, which I resent for appearing in front of him. Then I pop up from the couch, walk over and into the bedroom, grab my bag, and start shoving inside everything I took out before. It's not much, so the whole process takes about a minute, but it feels like an age as I move with the overheated, itchy feeling of rejection. I zip it up and stride to the door, dragging it behind me.

When I start to yank the entrance door open, a big hand smacks against it right in front of my face, pushing it shut again. I keep looking ahead, refusing to give him even the slightest glance. I tug at the knob again, but the door doesn't budge. Obviously, it's like trying to move an island with a spoon because the grizzly has decided to hold it hostage.

"Freya." His voice is rough. *I don't get tingles anymore from that, you motherfucker. I get darn hives from your proximity.* "Look at me."

I refuse. I'm done looking. I'm done *trying*.

"Freya." There is so much in that word—my name—that, despite cursing myself with all that is mighty, I still can't help but turn to look at his face, rotating in place. He's so close, the closest he's ever been to me. From here, I can see little brown dots breaking up the forest green of his irises. Half of his left eyebrow is gone, and the corner of his mouth on the same side pulls down. But his lips are so full, too pillowy for a guy. They look so soft that I involuntarily lick my own. His eyes dip to the movement, and his throat works with a swallow. I suddenly forgot what I was mad about.

"When are you leaving Little Hope?" The movement of his lips takes me out of my mouth-induced trance.

"I don't know," I answer honestly, my voice nearly a whisper.

"Look." He drags his hand over his face. "I'm not a good person to be around." I wait for him to continue, but he seems to be waiting for me to pick up the thread and ask the questions.

I let go of the suitcase handle and cross my arms. *Not falling for this one, buddy. You got something to say, say it.*

After a few long seconds—minutes? —he finally sighs in defeat and concedes, "I have a pretty fucked up case of PTSD, and I'm not... *safe* to be around."

Pulling on my years as a nurse, I strive to keep a steady gaze and a neutral expression. "Are you violent?"

"Yes." A very sure and very curt affirmation.

I can't stop my brow from creasing at this. "Do you think you might hurt me?"

"I don't just think. I know I will." He sounds awfully positive.

I chew the inside of my lip as I mull this new, admittedly concerning confession over. Now Jake's warning makes more sense. "Have you hurt anybody before?" I press.

A weighted pause, then a quiet "Yes."

I mull over that, weighing my options here. "In the military? You hurt somebody in the military?"

"The navy," he says, correcting me. "And yes, I hurt people then, too."

"Too?" My brows shoot up. "Where else?"

He is silent for a moment. "Here. When I came back."

My shoulders drop. If he's talking about his PTSD and violent outbursts voluntarily, it must be pretty bad. Who did he hurt? And how? Was it his girlfriend? Or Justin? Maybe that's why they aren't really friends anymore. I want to ask all those questions, but instead, I ask, "That's why you live here like a hermit?"

A short nod. "Among many other reasons."

"And that's why you don't want me around?"

"Among other reasons." A small smile shines faintly through his melancholic mask.

"Are you in therapy?" I ask, hoping like hell it's a yes.

"No." He sighs, and I stifle one of my own. "I tried for a few months when I came back, but it didn't do shit."

I'd seen it often enough. Severe PTSD can't be cured with a magic wand in the blink of an eye. It takes time, determination, and a *desire* to get it under control. And even after all the correct steps have been taken, it lingers for years.

Alex doesn't seem like a person who even *wants* to be cured. Quite the opposite. He looks like someone content to wallow in his misery, to let the pain cover up the fear he still feels. I *so* don't need this in my life. I have enough of my own shit to deal with. *Don't add more. Just don't, Freya.*

All I need to do is fix my problems without gathering others' along the way, and my main problem as of right now is my homeless situation.

"I really don't have anywhere to go," I whisper, feeling suddenly as weary as he'd suggested I would be earlier. "Justin said it'll be about a week for the new wheel to arrive." I press my forehead against the door. "I don't have anywhere to go." I feel like I'm speaking more to myself than to him, voicing the bleak thought I haven't been able to stop from cycling through my mind for what feels like my entire life. "Nowhere." And I drown in self-pity.

This is the first time I've allowed myself to do so since I

left my husband—or escaped, to be precise—and in front of a stranger, no less. Yes, I've cried, but it was because I was dead tired, and tears were a natural way for my body to release pent-up stress. And now I just feel sorry for myself because I know nobody else out there will feel sorry for me instead. There's only one person on earth who cares that I'm alive, and that one person wants me dead.

Everything suddenly overwhelms me, and I cover my mouth with my hand to stifle a sob. This constant moving from place to place? I've lived all my life like a nomad. I just want a place I can call home.

"Freya." His voice is barely audible. He groans like he's in pain, then grabs me by my shoulders and smothers my face against his chest. His heavy arms hold me tight. The top of my head nestles right under his chin. I hesitate for a moment but then wrap my arms around his middle. I try not to focus on how good he feels under my touch, or how my face smushes between his well-developed pecs—so well-developed that I can barely breathe—or how his back muscles bunch under my fingers every time they skim over his plaid-cloaked skin. "You can stay here until your car's ready."

I jump at his voice. He'd *just* told me that he didn't like to be touched, and here I am, doing exactly that. "I don't need your pity."

"Good, because you're not getting any. Just be quiet and don't overthink it." His voice is steady, so different from moments ago.

I start nodding vigorously, which knocks his teeth together and probably almost out of his mouth, which causes him to chuckle. "Okay, then," he says, bringing me closer for a second before releasing me.

I take a step back and look up at him. He seems tired, very-very tired. And I'm not sure it's just physical.

"But we have to go over some ground rules."

"I'll pay you, I have money," I assure him eagerly, nodding like a dashboard bobblehead. I'm so happy, and it's not because I found a place to sleep; I'm not scared to spend a night in a motel or a car. For some reason, unbeknownst to me, I sense a kindred spirit in him and even feel oddly comfortable in his crabby presence. Even though I want to throttle him fifty percent of the time. Or seventy-five. Give or take.

He shakes his head. "No, it's not about money. I need you to stay away from me as much as you can. Our contact has to be minimal."

I'm about to go into fight mode when I realize that he's trying to protect me from himself, not insult me. The snarling and snapping are his defensive mechanisms, and I'm adult enough to acknowledge that. So, instead of being an immature ass, I find myself nodding.

"Good," he says. "You'll take my bedroom."

"Wait." I hold my hand in front of his face. "That's where this compromise has gotta bend. I'm not taking your bed. You're a huge guy, for heaven's sake. I'll be fine on the couch."

"Stop fighting me on this. We've already been here, and I told you, I've slept in worse places."

"And *I* told *you*, so have I."

That causes him to squint his eyes at me. "Fine," he grumbles, ceding to me. "Take the couch." He leaves me standing there and treads to his bedroom. I hear some shuffling, and then he emerges with my comforter—yes, it's already *my* comforter—and two pillows. He drops them on the couch and strides to the kitchen. "Take anything you need."

"Thank you," I say quietly. "I mean it. Thank you."

He shrugs one shoulder, like it's no big deal that he went against his own word and let me stay here. I make my bed and fluff both pillows, glancing at Alex to see if he's watching. When I see that he is not, I sniff a pillow. Thank God, he gave me one of his own. And it smells like safety. Such an absurd thought and such a ridiculous statement, but a true one regardless. My brain chemistry finally decided that Alex is "good," and we go toward him like a stray dog toward the first human who shows it compassion.

A low grunt comes from the kitchen, and I find Alex slowly rotating a shoulder on his bad side like he's trying to ease the pressure. He winces a little and tries to massage it, but he can't get a good hold on the angle he'd need.

"Let me help you." I start walking to him, but he jumps back and growls like a wounded animal.

"No."

"You're in pain," I insist, fighting an eye roll. "Let me see." I stop in front of him. As a typical guy, he immediately starts playing the macho man, but he clearly doesn't know what he needs, which is help.

"I said no. I don't need your help." He tries to walk past me, but I grab his forearm. I didn't expect it to be this thick, so my initial gesture of trying to make a power move turns out to be a pitiful attempt of stopping a bulldozer with a nail. He easily removes himself from my grip, but I don't give up and grab his hand instead. Tingles shoot from the place where our skin touches. His palm is rough and dry. We both look down at our locked hands, and he tries to pull his from mine. But he isn't trying all that hard, just a lazy tug. And another. I squeeze his hand.

"I'm a nurse. Spent a lot of time in the emergency department." I'm trying to get ahold of his eyes, and when I do, I lock onto them for dear life, hoping he will see in them what I'm really trying to say—that I will not get scared, no matter what I'll see. "I've treated bad burns. I've treated *really* bad burns. I've treated burns still smoldering."

He might be self-conscious about the scarring like most people are. As a very attractive man, he probably had a lot of female attention before the accident; even though I don't know what happened, I can bet my Chevy that it's changed him, and he isn't such a lady magnet anymore. Not because of his scars—let's be honest, we love a good broody, damaged hero—but because of his "fuck off" attitude. His broodiness seems to have eventually outgrown his sexiness, and now, only *assholishness* remains.

His gaze is trained on mine. The silence is heavy. Then he sighs. "It's tight."

"Have you put any oil on it?" I question casually.

"No," he grumbles.

"Okay. Do you have any?"

"No." Then he thinks for a moment, then hazards, "Olive oil?"

"That'll do it. Let me check something, though." I run to my bag, and of course, it's there—a travel-size baby oil. Perfect. I race back with my discovery and too much enthusiasm than is appropriate for the situation, and Alex is standing in the same exact spot I left him. "Take off your shirt."

He gives me a sideways look and pulls his plaid shirt off. He has a T-shirt underneath, and I see that his left arm is scarred down to the elbow. The burns affected the deeper layers of his skin, and the damage is considerable. In some places, he looks to have gotten skin grafting and full-thickness grafts at that. The damage on those spots might have run very deep if his doctors had decided to go with a risky procedure like that. They did a good job, though, as right now, those spots look almost normal. In some places where the skin looks leathery, the ridges are thick and shiny, and the grafting was clearly done on the top layers only.

I lightly tug on his T-shirt. "This too."

He regards me silently before he yanks it off over his back. I always find it fascinating how such a simple gesture can look so manly.

And oh, boy, does he look manly.

He's half-naked and gazing at me with a tense gaze, looking like he doesn't know whether to run or stay put. There's a smattering of chest hair across his broad upper body, and his pecs are pronounced and mouth-wateringly large. His abdomen is cut. Washboard cut.

My gaze dips lower, and it's there. *It* is there. That delicious V thing. I've seen those before but never touched one. And now it is here, right in front of my face. My throat is suddenly dry, and I try to swallow. It happens only on the second try. My hand is itching to touch this mysterious V when he clears his throat, and I realize I've been caught staring. I feel my cheeks heat, and I look up. His eyes have a funny spark I've never seen in them before.

Right. Back to business. I stop looking at the entire image of the gorgeous man in front of me and switch to nurse mode, solely assessing the damage to his shoulder. It's definitely not as bad as I expected.

Judging by his behavior and his constant desire to wrap himself up to his nose in clothing, I thought it would be unbearable to look at, and he wouldn't have a clear patch of skin. In reality, the majority of the scarring stops on the left side of his chest, right along his nipple. It's to the same degree as his face: pretty deep in the skin tissue and poorly treated after the surgery, but not excessive. The scars are raised and angry—too much nerve damage and not enough physical therapy. I walk around him slowly, and he tracks me with a gentle turn of his head.

Left part of the chest, half the neck, arm down to an inch above the elbow, and about the same amount on the back, as is on the front, I log in my head.

I gesture for him to sit on a stool in the kitchen, then I open the bottle of oil, pouring a small amount into my hands, and rubbing them together to warm it up. Alex's eyes follow my every move, but neither of us says a word.

I start with his arm first, noting how huge and solid the muscles under my hands are. I wonder if he had them before the accident or gained all that beef later. If it's the latter, that would've hurt like a bitch while the skin was stretching. I don't ask. I massage his sore, angry skin while he watches me, alternating between looking at my hands and my mouth. His features are pinched tight, but somewhere along the way, they relax, and he shuts his eyes.

I move to his back and follow every single ridge there, using small, gentle circles to soften up the skin, hopefully.

When my fingers brush up his neck and touch a spot behind his ear, he shudders, and I hear a rough swallow slink down his throat. I keep massaging, trying to ignore the heat pouring into my belly. Such *appropriate* timing. How am *I* getting turned on by this? He's in pain, and I'm getting aroused. Maybe *I* need a good shrink, too.

I also pour more oil into my hands and warm it up before rubbing the non-injured side of his neck. His muscles are so tightly coiled and tense there. I'm still behind him and can't see his face, but suddenly he seems to melt under my touch, his neck lolling forward and his breath coming out in a slow, even rhythm. I think he's fallen asleep until he shifts his shoulders under my touch, feeling their new sensitivity.

I move to his front and glide my fingers across the burn on his chest, testing his pain level. I don't like that I can see his face. It makes this so much more intimate. His eyes flutter closed again when I apply the right pressure and travel up toward his neck.

I glance at my hands, which are in the same line of view as his legs. I glance back at his scar.

And then I glance back because it surely wasn't... my eyes widen. He *is* hard. Like, *hard* hard. I can see the outline along his left leg. And his timeworn jeans are so conveniently washed out that I can see an *actual outline.* I swallow nervously and look at Alex's face.

"Sorry about that." His husky voice causes liquid lava to stream between my legs.

"It happens," I murmur back with a one-shouldered shrug. My own voice sounds unnaturally low. I move to stand between his legs so I can reach his chest. He must have read my mind because he spreads his legs wider, and I step into the space. I keep myself edged closer to his right leg so I don't accidentally touch his... python.

I avert my attention back to the evidence of his burns, sliding my hands around his non-injured side to relax him entirely, and Alex sucks in the air. I still my movements again and frown.

"Is that too painful?" I whisper.

He croaks a low chuckle and rasps, "No."

The opposite? I think but don't say.

"Okay. Tell me if it's too bad. I'll stop the second you

want me to." I don't *want* to stop though. And I don't think he wants me to, either. His face is calm and relaxed, his mouth slightly ajar. The tension in his shoulders is barely noticeable, and his jaw is slack.

He grunts an incomprehensible response that I take as a *yes*, and I continue massaging his chest, noticing that the scars are slightly more pronounced here than on his back. While shifting my hand, I accidentally brush my fingers over his nipple, and his jaw sets, but he doesn't say anything.

So I do it again. I feel a hot glare on me, but I ignore it and continue playing with fire. *Yikes, that didn't sound right.*

He doesn't close his eyes, keeping them locked on my face with almost unnerving concentration. My fingers continue down his chest, running over his nipple again and again, getting a slack-jawed exhale as a response every time my fingers graze over it—and yet another twitch in his jeans —and I decide to move to more neutral areas for the sake of my own sanity, and the hormonal unbalance currently unraveling in my lower areas.

I progress to his face and hesitate. Somehow, it feels even more intimate than running my hands over his chest. I step farther between his legs, and he spreads them a touch wider for me to fit. I graze my fingers up his neck to his face, gently cupping his jaw in my hands and stroking my oiled-up thumbs over his cheeks and back again.

This doesn't feel like just a massage. It's healing.

Which of us is receiving it, I have no idea, but it's healing nonetheless. For me, it is a force built from connecting with another human being who's managed to grant me a feeling of safety and calm. For him, I'd say it's remembering how to feel human touch again.

He opens his eyes, and their blazing green stares back

into mine, a mixture of pain and pleasure, fear and confidence, *no* and *yes* warring in his gaze. He says he doesn't like to be touched, but this is not a man who doesn't like to be touched. This is a man who has denied that part of himself. He doesn't *allow* himself the freedom of being touched. He has trouble accepting his scars, but for the love of God, I have no idea why. He has a story written all over him, branding him.

It's a story of survival. And it's beautiful.

When I'm finished with his scars, I move to his brows and forehead, trying to find the pressure points to help release some tension. He's still watching me unyieldingly, but his eyelids have become droopy. The two deep grooves carved between his brows finally disappear when his eyelids close, and the breaths leaving his lips are heavy with sound while I gently swirl my thumbs in tiny circles where the lines had been.

I lift my hands into his hair and rake his scalp with my nails. He moans loudly and unapologetically. I almost choke on my own tongue from how delicious the sound is. It's the sexiest thing I've ever heard. Suddenly, he wraps his large hands around my small wrists.

"Enough," he rumbles, sounding like he needs to clear his throat.

His face is still relaxed, but some tension has seeped back into his neck and shoulders. I sigh.

"Thank you for your help," he adds roughly.

Feeling suddenly irritated, I step back—not very carefully though, because I accidentally brush my leg against his. Right where the python is hiding. He hisses and lurches up from the stool.

"Is it better now?"

He gives me a weird look and answers slowly, "Yeah,

sure," then disappears into the bathroom. It took all of three milliseconds, and now he's gone. The shower turns on. Why would he take a shower and wash off all the oil I've just rubbed in?

I shake my head as I trudge across the floor to scrub my hands in the sink. *What was that, Freya?*

He comes out five minutes later... still covered in oil.

Hmm, I wonder to myself. *What was he doing in there?*

Then I see it. The python is gone. Oh. *Oh!* The python is gone! That sneaky bastard.

"Did you have fun?" I just can't help myself. Color visibly rises on his neck. Did I just manage to throw this mighty man off his grouchy game? He grunts something in return and goes for his shirt that's still lying on the table.

"Don't put it on yet. Let the oil set for a bit." And maybe let me ogle your oiled-up body some more.

He looks at me, then at his shirt, then at me again. I witness him in fascination. One might think I just asked him to jump into a snake pit. Then his shoulders drop, and he lets go of his shirt. It's like watching a lion on the Discovery Channel, I swear. His face is stoic, but little movements give him away—he can't find a place for himself in this confined space, being so on display. I try to ease his discomfort—even though I really want to rile him up over his recent activities in the bathroom because I certainly could use some of that myself—so I start talking.

"If you do this every day, the pain will lessen."

"Who says I want it to lessen?" His question-like statement throws me a little off-balance.

"Nobody wants to suffer from pain," I reply matter-of-factly.

"I do." He barely whispers, and I know it was not meant for my ears. Is it survivor's guilt? I see a lot of issues in him from a professional point of view, but I don't think pursuing that angle is the right approach here. So, I turn off my medical knowledge and just be... me.

"You think you do, but you really don't," I say carefully.

He lets out a sharp, sarcastic huff through his nose. "And you know me so well after ten minutes of meeting."

"Well, it's been a little longer than that." I dismiss him lightly, ignoring his answering scowl. "But yeah, I think I'm starting to get to know you." I curl a lock of hair around my finger.

"Don't dig too deep. You won't like what you find." Then, after a pause, he adds acidly, "Or do, on second thought. That way, you'll be out faster."

"How very welcoming," I deadpan. I know why he's speaking so caustically, why he wants to alienate me, but it doesn't hurt any less. I've been unwanted far too many times in my life. Meaning that I have plenty of issues of my own, and I really have neither the energy nor time to placate his. "You're right."

"About what?" Interest piques in his voice.

"I can't stay here." I dig into the cabinet over the sink, looking for a glass, fill it with water and chug it in two gulps. "I'll leave in the morning." Then I walk to the couch, lie down, pull *his* comforter over me, turn on my side, and close my eyes.

I don't hear Alex moving, but the desire to peek and see what he's doing is strong. But just to spite him, I resist. Eventually, he lets out a heavy sigh and lumbers to his room.

My craving for validation just keeps getting me into weird positions throughout my life, and I don't need a random guy on a random mountain in a random town in

Maine to add to the list of people who don't want me around.

Despite the thousands of thoughts running through my mind and my slightly hurt feelings, I fall asleep very fast, as if I'm in a hurry to meet the demons of my past, all waiting for my arrival to a Morpheus land every single time I get a wink of shuteye. One particular demon is standing front and center.

I open the door to our apartment, dreading meeting him there. I've been held up at work longer than I anticipated. There was a huge pile-up on the highway, and all the hospitals were overflowing with patients with all sorts of traumatic injuries. Everybody was pulling their second or even third shifts.

But no matter what I say at home, he won't believe me.

I've been thinking about stopping it for a while now. Stopping all of it. But I don't know if I have enough guts. That's the only thing I've ever known, and it's casual for me. I'm not even sure I can separate a good relationship from a toxic one. Toxic is my norm, and I don't know how to behave when the person next to me isn't my bully but my supporter. What do you do with that? How do I accept their help and be grateful for it?

I open the door as quietly as I can and hear his voice from the living room. He's on the phone. I silently set my shoes aside, noting with a mental spasm of panic at the foreboding of it that there's a spot of blood smeared on the left toe from the gory shift I'd just survived. I'm barely breathing, hoping to sneak into the bathroom and lock the door behind me. I might be able to convince him that I've been there for a while, and he just didn't notice I'd come home a while ago. Right. Like he wouldn't have noticed me gone for hours. I texted him that I'd be late, but he didn't respond, and that's even worse than if he'd have yelled at me. The heat is explosive, but the cold is deadly.

While I'm tip-toeing to the bathroom, I hear a few curt phrases here and there, and one particular string of fearsome words causes me to freeze.

"Yeah, I'm tired of her too. Should have gotten rid of her when I had the chance, but now, with this fucking money..." Then he's quiet, listening to whatever the person on the other end of the line has to say. "I know, baby. I know. That was dumb, but we did it anyway. Now I need the money back, and it's a little more complicated." He's quiet again. "Yeah, maybe you should call your contact. We need it done, stat." He's silent for a long time after, and then he says with a voice I know he reserves for the bedroom: "Yeah, baby. All of it."

Then he's listening to his baby speaking on the other side of the call and finally says, "Yeah, we know that already. It's on the flash drive." He hums softly as he hears the response as if considering it. "You think? It's the only place I store the info... no, baby, not even you." He laughs at something the other person says. "That's my insurance, you know that." He chuckles. "I need to move the assets into my account, and then I'll just slip a few pieces of information that she knows their names here and there, and she'll be as good as gone. They pay me to keep my mouth shut, what can I do if she's nosy, right?" He laughs again as if he's just told the funniest joke in the universe.

I stumble over something on the floor and knock over a cat statuette from the coffee table behind me. It shatters into tiny pieces—I always hated that ugly thing. His head snaps to me, and he barks into the phone, "I'm gonna call you back."

"Hi," I mumble.

His face changes, a mask of fury washing off every single

human detail that's left in his features. "I see you're home."
He pointedly looks at his Rolex. "Just in time."

"For what?"

"You know what," he says, folding the sleeves of his white button-down.

Fuck.

I move backward toward the bathroom, but he's faster. He's always faster. He pushes me into the wall, and I hit the back of my head. You don't see stars when you get hit, you see black spots everywhere and blurry objects in constant motion that can't be collected into one, no matter how hard you try to focus.

He smacks my body against the wall again. "How much did you hear?" he hisses into my ear after licking it, and I'm just about ready to vomit.

I should keep quiet. Now is precisely the time when you keep quiet and stay alive. You escape and do all other crazy things later, but today I decided to do crazy before, so I whisper in his ear, "Everything."

"The fuck did you just say?" He pulls back to look at my face.

"I said I heard everything you just said." I smile through the headache already blooming.

His face becomes feral. Holding onto my neck, he hammers my head harder against the wall. I try to fight. I always fight, but this time is different. This time he is different. This time I'm fighting for my life.

So, I fight like a hellcat. He's stronger, but I'm determined. I've finally had enough.

Struggling to get free of his hold on me, I reach out to the ceramic lamp on the accent table by the wall. My favorite lamp—weighs a ton and cost a fortune. It takes me two more blows to my cheek for me to reach it, but when I finally do, I crash it with all my might into the side of his head. He collapses instantly. Unlike in the movies, when the villain keeps looking at you and blinks a few times before falling backward, no. He just collapses to the floor. I should feel bad and check his pulse because he's a human being. But I don't see him as one. I hope he never gets up. I hope his "baby" finds him dead on the floor days from now when he's rotting right where he hurt me for the last time.

I snatch up my purse, pull my shoes back on, and get the hell out of that cursed condo of hell, still wearing my scrubs. But right before I do, I glance at Erik—he's still unconscious, so I run to his office, pull the picture from the wall above his desk and rip out the backing of it. Here it is—the flash drive I found a long time ago when I was cleaning the room. That must be what he was talking about on the phone. Yeah, asshole, I'm taking this with me.

I rush to the elevator and press the button again and again and again. I might have only seconds before he wakes up. Right before the doors slide open, I hear footsteps behind me, accompanied by a roar. I fly into the elevator without waiting for the doors to fully open and smash the button for them to close. C'mon. C'mon!

"Freya!" Erik's yelling. "Where are you, honey?"

Fuck! Finally—finally! —the door starts closing, and he dashes out of the apartment. Please, God. Please, just close these doors! He sees me and rushes toward me, and right before he's about to reach me, the doors shut right in front of his face.

I slide down the back wall of the elevator, sucking in deep, shuddering breaths. My head is pounding, the back of my head is itchy, and I reach out to scratch it only to see that I'm bleeding. Head wounds bleed like nobody's business, and I need to stop it ASAP.

I run outside the building and smack right into a person, and when I glance up to see their face, my heart leaps because they happen to be a police officer. Thank God!

"Ma'am, what happened?" he asks, looking behind me and reaching for his gun.

"Help me," I whisper and collapse into his arms.

Chapter Seven

J USTIN, **The Fairy Godmother**

I smile, congratulating my brilliant self on the way home from Alex's cabin. I couldn't have planned it better. A hot chick dumped onto his doorstep. If it's not destiny, then I'm the Pope.

Alex's been stuck in this loop of self-hatred for years now, and nothing seems to get to him anymore. He doesn't talk to people, he doesn't date—as far as I know—and I know everything because my brother is Jake, the gossip queen of Little Hope. He should make a club with Donna; they're two peas in a pod. I also know that Alex doesn't fuck—again, courtesy of the local gossip mill. Hell, I'm not even sure if *it* still works for him. He has very excessive damage that I still haven't seen the extent of yet, and it's not like we've chitchatted about that.

And yet here we are. The moment a damsel in distress

shows up, Alex peeks out from under his shell, looking to save somebody. Isn't it adorable?

She's not the best candidate, per se. Not even close. Yes, she's beautiful enough to draw anybody's attention. But even though I can smell trouble following her from miles away, it might be precisely what Alex needs. Some trouble to stir up his perfectly boring life.

I've been trying to knock on those reinforced walls he's built since the explosion, but nothing's worked. Nothing. When he came back after staying so many months in the hospital and who knows how many reconstructive surgeries later, another accident happened. I'm not even sure which one caused more damage, but that was the time when I lost my best friend. He pushed me as far away as he could, and there was only so much I could take. So far, the guilt for leaving him there has forced me to close my eyes to all the shit he's been saying and doing, but even I have a limit. And I'd just about given up right before Freya showed up. The perfect opportunity wrapped in a small, pretty package.

All I needed to do was to force them together and leave the rest to some explosive chemistry happening between them. Thank fuck we have shitty roads here during the winter, and the weather sucks right now.

Talking about chemistry. There is good chemistry, and there is bad chemistry, and I've been experiencing a lot of the latter lately. Every time I see *her*, it's like... like I want to grab her and shake, shake, shake. Every time *she* looks at me with those huge, seemingly innocent eyes... I get zips in the pit of my stomach. Very low. *Very* low in my stomach. Like right now, as I remember the moment when I came to pick Freya up from the diner, and *she* was there, of course. *Fuck*, I think as I shake my head, trying to clear it of all the thoughts. All of them.

I park my truck and go to the garage. Mack and Joe are working on a salvaged car that Mrs. Jenkins totaled. The old lady doesn't have a scratch on her, but the car is junk. I towed it here to see if it can be fixed, and of course, it can. Insurances always write off those cars when they're perfectly fixable. I say my hellos and get to the office to work on bills. That's my least favorite part. I need to hire somebody for that so I can focus on what I really love to do—getting under the hood and getting dirty.

The day's gone in the blink of an eye, as usual. Besides us, there is only Alex, who knows shit about cars, but he doesn't work with the general public, so we're always busy.

The guys leave for home, and I go to lock the doors. As I check everything before closing it, my mind drifts to Freya. I didn't fuck it up, did I? I know what the rumors say about Alex, but I don't believe them. Yes, he has anger issues. Yes, sometimes they're bad, but I believe with the right stimulant, he could make a miracle happen and choke his angry nature before it explodes as usual, burning everyone around, no pun intended. Or shall I say a suppressant? I have a gut feeling she could be that suppressant.

Still, she clearly has some issues... Maybe my idea of matchmaking wasn't so great after all. *Hmm.*

Nah, it was a good one. I shake my head and go upstairs.

I'm on my non-sleep cycle, so I pop my AirPods in, turn the PlayStation on, and get back to my game. The idea of random fucking doesn't excite me as much as it used to, so gaming it is.

Around four in the morning, I make a fresh pot of coffee and head downstairs to start work early, but I immediately know something's wrong. The back door is open, when I know I locked it. My instincts are on high alert as I quietly move about the garage. As I check everything, I figure out that nothing's been stolen and nothing's broken, so it leaves only one thing that's new in here and might be what they were after—Freya's car.

I go to check her old Chevy—still beats me why she has it—and see that it was given a thorough search. The trunk has been popped open and not even shut again, same with the driver's seat. The contents of her suitcase are spread all over the floor of the trunk, and some are on the ground below it. Such rookie work.

I briefly assess the insides of the car—someone was clearly looking for something, but I don't think they found it.

Yeah, she's trouble, all right. For a moment there, I wonder again if I did the right thing, but the part I feel sorry about is Alex this time. What sort of troubles is she bringing with her? Will it be too much for him and our little town to handle?

At this point, even if it's too much, she's become a *person*, not just a tool in unshelving Alex. I can't let her roam on her own with her problems *out there* when we can protect her *here*. And knowing Alex... Nah, he won't let her go either. All I need to do is to hint here and there that she's *in* trouble and she *is* trouble, and his protective nature toward everything and everyone will take care of the rest.

Whistling a happy song to myself, I grab the rim from the floor, carry it to the storage shed, and hide it under a tarpaulin, where it will wait for its finest hour to happen in a week. Just as I promised.

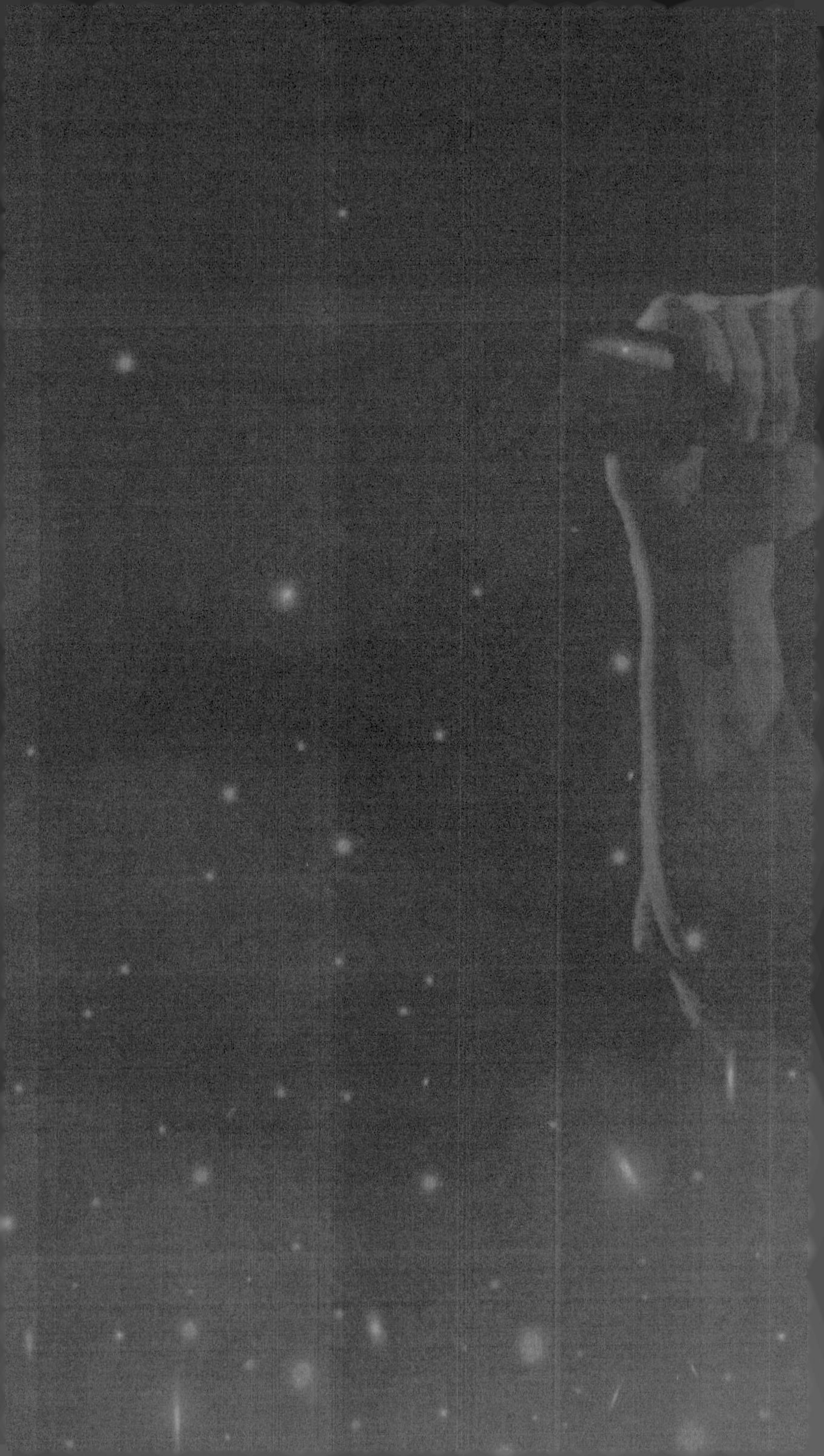

Chapter Eight

A^{LEX}

I lie awake for hours, wondering how the hell a chick I stumbled upon on the road back home on the mountain during a storm managed to get so far under my skin in such a short amount of time. And how the fuck did she manage to get me so riled up with just a simple massage.

Nah, that massage was anything but simple.

Not even getting anywhere near my dick, that I almost came in my pants? Hasn't happened to me since I was twelve. I groan loudly and wipe my face with my hands. Fuck. She's stirring something that's not supposed to be touched, and I'm not talking about my cock.

She can't stay here, not with me jacked up as badly as I am right now. I know myself, and I know I could go from zero to psycho in the blink of an eye from here. And when I do, people get hurt.

I get a text from Justin just after six in the morning and bolt out of bed in response to it, making my way to the windows surrounding my cabin and casting my gaze warily.

Justin:

> Garage got broken into. Nothing stolen. Nothing damaged. Your girl's Chevy got a nice thorough search, though. Her suitcase's been ransacked. Whoever wants her knows she's here.

That fucking matchmaker. Seasoned hardass who only cares about the town, my ass. I know him better than that. I've known him since we were in diapers, and I can tell that the asshole cares about Freya. That's why he wants to rile me up by reviving my long-dormant protective instincts, so I stick around her. Plus, my suspicion—and Justin's—about Freya's situation being odd just got confirmed. She *is* running from something, and now we know it's from some*one*.

I scan the scenery with a trained eye but see nothing that indicates anyone knows Freya is here. It's just habitual at this point, not like I'm planning to enlist as her bodyguard.

I pad silently over to where Freya is sleeping on the couch in the living room, completely buried under a huge, goose-down comforter that I picked out at West Elm for cold nights. The only part of her body exposed to air is her nose, sticking out from under the covers. She's snoring gently, and I find it oddly adorable.

I look around and notice her phone sitting on the edge of the dining table, and I contemplate picking it up, curious as to why she'd left it out here. She's always been so careful about keeping it on her, as far as I could see.

It lights up as soon as I touch the screen, and I frown. No wonder people know where she is. They've been able to track her. Yeah, it's a cheap burner phone, but I bet she paid for it with a card.

Fuck. Such a foolish fugitive.

She's led them right to my front door without realizing it. An old, buried-deep spark of excitement stirs in my chest. My heart begins pumping, and adrenaline kicks in. Anticipation of a battle. Any battle. I might yell from the rooftops that I'm fed up with wars and conflict, but once you touch that adrenaline level, you're done. You become a junkie, and once a new fix is on the horizon, you're all for it. No matter the cost.

And I understand that I am, indeed, a psycho who missed the exhilarating highs of war. But I'm neither the first who has nor the last who will.

There are text messages on the screen from an unknown number, but the sender of them is obviously who Freya's running from.

[Unknown]:

You can't run far, bitch. I'll get what's owed to me.

You're not as smart as you think you are. You're worthless. That money is mine, and I'll make you pay back every single fucking cent.

You'll get what's coming to you. Stop making me chase you. It's only making me angry.

I know you took it. And now, it's not only me who you should fear.

It's personal now. You WILL regret it.

I frown and check through her contacts to see if there is anything saved. There's Justin's number and The Dancing Pony's. There's a number saved as *DON'T ANSWER*. I copy it down and confirm there's nothing on the rest of the phone before taking out the SIM card and snapping it in half. I switch the phone off and set it down on the kitchen counter. It's too late now for the precaution since whoever is chasing her is now here in Little Hope. But at least he won't be able to track her exact location. Anything to make the life of a motherfucker who can talk to a woman like that more complicated.

I glance at the mass of material where Freya's sleeping. What money is he talking about? Is she a thief? The guy is an asshole, and he deserves what's coming to him when I get my hands on him, but I don't know anything about her. Nothing. She's a wildcard to me, and right now, I have no idea how wild she could turn out to be.

I'm sitting at the table and keeping an eye on the windows when Freya gets up, smiling warily through sleepy eyes.

"Morning," she says, punctuating her greeting with a yawn.

"I need all your phones," I demand sharply. Her gaze drops to where she'd placed one on the edge of the table. "I got rid of that one," I inform her brusquely when she finds nothing there. "I need the rest."

She gulps and steps backward. "What?"

I grit my teeth. "Whoever the fuck is looking for you is here in Little Hope," I respond, "and they're using your phone signal to find you. So, *phones*. All of them. Now."

She goes from deathly pale to bright red in a moment.

"Did you go through my stuff?"

"I don't need to go through it to know you fucked up."

Her nostrils flare. "Right. And *you*," she defends in a mocking voice, "*never* do. You're so mighty on your high horse that you're just always right."

"You brought that shit to our doorsteps," I snarl. "*My* doorstep. And now you're raging about *me* being an asshole?"

Her face changes in an instant, guilt washing all over it. She looks... *devastated.* Her eyes are wide and afraid, and I can tell she's biting the inside of her cheeks to stop tears from forming.

"I need to know what happened so I know what to expect." My voice is stern because I forgot for a moment that I'm not a drill sergeant commanding a rookie soldier. Pinching my lips together for a moment, I strain to change my approach, softening my tone as best I can. "Can you answer my questions, so I'm... prepared?"

She shakes her head silently, and a tear springs free from the corner of her eye.

I sigh heavily. "Freya, I can help."

"I didn't ask for your help." Her voice is detached.

"I know you didn't, but you clearly need it."

She gulps and takes a shaky breath, finding her way to the sofa. "Fuck," she exhales. "There's no chance my car is ready, so I can't get out of here."

"No." My tone is short again, but she brought it on herself. Yes, I wanted a battle, but no, I didn't want to get tangled in someone else's drama. Fuck knows I have enough of it on my own. "Who sent you those messages?" I spread my shoulders wider, appearing more threatening. The only thing missing is a light shining into her face. I know I'm acting like an asshole, but I need to know what the fuck is happening here.

Her face pinches with pain, and I almost feel guilty. Shoving that feeling down, I get up and sit on the armchair, eyeing her closely. "What money are they talking about, Freya?"

She closes her eyes, and I think she's going to deflect the question again, but she doesn't.

"I'm sorry, Alex." Her voice is as weary as it is plaintive. "I didn't think my problems would follow me here, and I most certainly didn't want to bring them to your doorstep. I thought I was careful." There's no sarcasm in her voice; she sounds and looks absolutely miserable.

"I need to leave, Alex," she adds. "Like, right now."

"Why, Freya? Who are you running from?"

She stares desolately out of the window and sighs. I can't help somebody who doesn't want my help, I remind myself. I'll just keep offering while she'll just keep refusing, and the cycle will eventually drain not only the two of us but all those around us.

I sigh along with her because this hits awfully close to home.

I'll drop her off at Justin's. Once upon a time, I trusted him with my life. I can trust him with hers, too. He'll watch over her while she's in town. Little Hope is small, and a stranger surely won't get far without being pointed out at every turn. And if that happens, I'll know. Then I'll come. Otherwise, she probably just made the smartest decision of her life by deciding to stay away from me.

In the end, she is just yet another person in my life I will let down. No sense in dragging it along; I might as well just do it now.

I nod slowly, resignation filling me as I gaze at her tense frame. "Have it your way."

FREYA

I don't say anything as Alex nods, then hefts himself up and into the bathroom. Fifteen minutes after I hear the first spray of the shower nozzle, he's striding out to get his coffee. Ten more minutes, and we're ready to go. He takes my bag before I have a chance to, so I trail after him to the truck.

"You're gonna stay at the Dancing Pony?" he questions gruffly.

I shrug and settle in to stare out the window. He starts the engine and takes off a bit faster than necessary.

Once we reach Justin's shop, I climb out with a quiet thank you, take my stuff, and walk to the main door, praying it's open. It is. Alex is still sitting in his car waiting for something—maybe an orchestra performing a symphony about my disappearing from his life. And being *the good girl* I am, I can't disappoint him, so I yank open the door and duck inside. The engine outside roars to life, the jerk finally taking off.

Inside, the shop is empty and quiet, so I cautiously call out for Justin. Nothing. I call louder.

"What the fuck?" He comes down the stairs located at the back of the garage. He's wearing jeans that aren't even buttoned up. Oh goody. I'm anticipating a nice tingling sensation down south or some sweet heat rising up my body, at least, but neither comes. Son of a bitch—that grumpy jerk broke me. "Oh, it's you," Justin realizes with a sigh.

"Don't look so excited," I chuckle. Somehow his dry

remark doesn't bother me in the slightest. Quite the opposite, actually—it puts me at ease.

"A little early for a social visit, don't you think?" he queries, quirking a brow at me.

"It's past eight," I deadpan. "Aren't you supposed to be open?"

"Yeah, well." He wipes his face and yawns. "It's been a rough night."

"Insomnia?"

"Yeah, and I still can't crash. Dammit." He yawns again, this time adding a full-body stretch.

"I'm sorry, Justin. I really am. I know it sucks."

He must believe my sympathy because he waves my apology off and asks instead, "What's up with you? Did you have a good night?" He has the audacity to smirk. "Alex didn't say you were coming."

"You mean after you dropped me off on the doorstep of your supposed *best friend* with attitude problems?" I arch an eyebrow.

His brows shoot up suddenly. "Did he hurt you? Shit, he did, didn't he?" He winces. "Should have thought about that before. Shit, I'm sorry."

"He didn't hurt me. Why does everybody think he's some violent monster?" I drop my hands.

He gives me a side-eye. "Because he kinda is."

"And that's why you sent me into a lion's den?" I want to smack him too, but harder. "If you really thought he was that bad, why the hell did you do that?"

"I didn't think he could hurt you," he defends. "Still don't, honestly. But people talk." He shrugs his massive, bare shoulders. And again, nothing stirs. "And besides that, you clearly have some problems. Whatever you're running from, Alex is your best bet for protecting you from it... no matter what 'it' is, really." He waves his hand dismissively. "The skills he has... man, they don't just *go away*."

"Aren't you his best friend? And you served with him, too, right?"

"Yeah, we did, and about the friendship... It's a long story." He lightly touches my shoulder. "Look, I really didn't think he'd hurt you. He's not that kind of man."

I raise my brows. "But people talk?"

"They do." His shoulders sag.

"He is an asshole, but he didn't do anything." I finally give in. "And I honestly doubt he would. I felt safe there. But..."

"But?" He nudges me to keep talking.

"But the situation we found ourselves in... well, it wasn't great." I wince a little.

"Did you fuck, and he didn't deliver?" He grins crookedly, hooking his fingers into the belt loops on his jeans.

My jaw drops. "What? No!"

"So he *did* deliver," Justin crows. "That's my boy!" Pride shines on his face, and it's disgusting.

"No! I meant we didn't sleep together!" I almost yell.

He laughs, probably at my beet-red face, then sobers up with some effort. "He's worried about you, you know."

"Yeah, sure." I shoot him a sarcastic look. "He's so worried that he dumped me on you."

"Hey! I'm tough too!" He sounds almost offended, then his eyes focus on something behind me—something that I don't think is present. "We enlisted together, you know. Picked different branches though. We were *this* tight before." He shows me a little space between the pads of his thumb and index finger. "And after, he was just a different person. Completely changed."

"War does that to people," I acknowledge solemnly.

"It's not only that. It's like all his old issues came to the surface at once. His anger was pretty bad before, but after... I've never seen anything personally, but—" *Again, people talk.* That's what he wants to say.

"And you never tried to talk to him?"

"All the fucking time. All the time, man." The poor fella looks defeated. "I talk to him, but it's... one-sided, I'd say. He's just... not here anymore. Sure, he answers, but I'm like this mosquito always buzzing in his ear. It's not a friendship anymore." Then he seems to realize that he's shared a little too much, and on his cheeks form twin splotches of light pink. Clearly pushing away his melancholic confession, he flashes me the same devilish smile he did right before he dropped me off on Alex's doorstep and took off. "He does talk to you though."

Realization slowly dawns on me. "That's why you decided to play matchmaker?"

He nods before amending, "Not matchmaker. But he responded to you in a way he hasn't with anyone in a long while. Maybe you're a genuinely nice person." He shrugs his wide and still-naked shoulders. I expected him to have a tattoo, now that I think about it, since he exudes a "bad boy" vibe, but what's visible on his body is squeaky clean. "A nice person who brought not-so-nice problems to our sleepy little town," he adds with a raised brow.

"Well, this 'nice person' needs to get her 'not-so-nice' problems the hell out of this place 'cause there is *no* hope for me left here," I retort. "So how about fixing my *nice* car sooner and sending me on my merry way?"

"Ha." He smiles teasingly. "Little Hope is growing on you."

"It *so* is not," I deadpan.

"Is too." He keeps his flirty smile plastered on his too-handsome face.

I exhale a long, exasperated breath. "Can you fix my car faster or not?"

"No can do, ma'am." He spreads his hands wide, accenting his nicely shaped pecs. And again, not a flicker of attraction. Grr.

"Could you tow me to the next city? Maybe they can help," I hopefully suggest.

He shakes his head. "The next city doesn't work with cars like yours."

"Why the hell not? It's in the middle of Maine, for fuck's sake!" I vent in frustration. "Does everybody here have the newest models of BMWs and Teslas?"

He smirks roguishly, and I so do not like it. That mysterious smile is hiding something, I just know it. "We do have old cars, but not like yours. You have special tires." He blinks rapidly as if he were a debutante at a ball coyly fluttering her lashes; the only thing he's missing is a decorative handheld fan.

I nearly throw my hands up into the air. "How special can they be that I have to wait a whole week?"

"It's the middle of nowhere. Give us a break," he replies, throwing my own words back at me, then bites his lips in a shoddy attempt to hide his laughter at my expense.

"Where am I supposed to live while I'm waiting?" It's my turn to spread my arms.

"Alex's?" he recommends hopefully.

"Do you think I'd be here begging to get the hell outta here if I could stay with him?" I hiss, but it doesn't seem to bother him. He just keeps on smiling. "He just accused me of bringing a shitstorm to all of your doorsteps. Not without your help, might I add—since you're the one who left me at his house in the middle of the woods with no car." I level him with a stare but then say on a sigh, "And he's right. Can't argue that." He tries to interject into my self-loathing as I start to descend into self-pity yet again, but I'm too far gone already. "Just leave it, Justin. Just... Can't you do *anything* to speed up the process? I'll pay you as much as you want. Just name your price."

"It's not about the money." He shakes his head. "I just can't get the wheels any earlier."

"But if you *do* get the wheels earlier, I can take my problems and get them the hell out of your wonderful Little Hope," I counter. "How about that?"

"Still a no-can-do, ma'am." His smile is lopsided and flirty again, and I want to smack him across his perfect face. Again. Since I met Alex, perfectly symmetrical faces just don't do it for me anymore. I want ragged and asymmetrical. Interesting. Unique.

Giving up, I officially resign from this conversation because nothing's working on him.

"Okay, how about you stay with me?" he offers unexpectedly. "Before you decide, you should remember that A: I'm a marine and can kick ass if needed." He rocks forward and back on his heels once, a proud look brightening his features.

"*Ex*-marine, you mean?"

"Once a marine, always a marine, ma'am." He corrects me defensively and a little too loud. I fight a smirk. "And B: you really don't have a choice."

There goes my smirk. I think his words are over. It's not like I have many choices; he's right. "Are you sure I won't bother you? Much," I add, wincing.

"Nah. You might even be helpful. If I pass out somewhere, just throw a blanket on me, so I don't freeze this fine ass to death." He shakes his booty playfully, and his pants, already hanging dangerously low, slide down a little more.

"Deal." I smile, averting my eyes from the taut V formed by his lower ab muscles. Ladies and gentlemen, he's got one too. But I look at it with matter-of-fact eyes, not admiring. He has it, I see it, moving on. All my admiration is wasted on a big jerk with a mouthwatering smell who wants nothing to do with me but to throttle me over my not-so-smart actions—and I'm quoting here. And I already do a good job on my own without his intervention on that part, thank you very much.

"Let me get your bag, and I can show you upstairs." Then he quiets for a moment. "Actually, I'll need you to see something."

"Okay," I say slowly, not liking his tone.

"Let's go." He nods for me to follow him.

He leads the way while I trot after him, and his pants are so low that I can see the top of his butt crack. Oh, dear Lord. Would it be polite to tell him to zip it up? "Are you checking out my ass?" He peers at me over his shoulder with a cheeky grin.

I've been caught. "Yeah, and I'm wondering how many flowers I can fit in between your cheeks."

He laughs and buttons his pants up. Finally.

"Don't freak out," he warns me as he leads me further into the garage, and I already know where this is going.

He brings me to my Impala. The doors are open, and my clothes are splattered everywhere. Fuck!

"I didn't touch anything," Justin says, carefully watching my reaction. I let out a defeated sigh, and he asks, "Do you think they found anything?"

He's not stupid; he knows whoever was here was

looking for something, so a little sharing won't do me any harm. "No."

"Okay. Let's call the cops." He's about to pull a phone from his back pocket when I yelp, "No!"

He watches me for a moment, deciding my fate, then nods, "All right. Let me help you then."

"Thank you," I say under my breath and get to work.

We manage to get all my clothes into the suitcase in under two minutes, with me shoving them inside and Justin politely trying to fold them to look more or less presentable. I feel guilty for the hassle I'm causing everywhere I go, and for the thousandth time, I wonder if that flash drive is worth it. When I opened it, it was a bunch of coded crap that I didn't understand, but if Erik wanted it so badly, it must be important. And I don't want him to have it, I just don't. I want him to be in trouble with his associates and their money.

"You okay?" Justin asks once I manage to zip the suitcase.

"Yeah," I answer.

"Cool," he replies and grabs my suitcase. We walk to the back of the garage to the stairs where he came from. It looks outdated and needs a good cleaning. If he doesn't want to take my money, maybe I can help tidy up his space. The apartment upstairs is small; there is no dining room, instead, it's an eat-in kitchen with a small round table and four chairs. The living room has an enormous TV hanging on the wall with a bunch of cords. I spot two different playing consoles and a bunch of other big-boy stuff. The leather couch lined up against the wall looks well-loved and cozy. It's a sectional and could easily fit four or five people. Justin points toward one door.

"Bathroom." The other door. "My bedroom. I sleep

naked," he cautions, "so don't come in unannounced if you don't want to be traumatized."

"Thanks for the warning." I cringe like the idea of snuggling with a gorgeous man would be painful.

He's just not the right *man,* my oh-so-helpful subconscious suggests.

"Thought so." He winks at me and carries my stuff to the last door. "Your room. It's not much, but in my defense, I didn't expect guests." The room is small. It fits a queen-sized bed with dark blue covers, two matching pillows, two white wooden nightstands, and a small chest. That's it, and there is no more space for walking. But it's more than I had in the last few months.

"It's great, Justin. Thank you. Let me pay you. I got enough money for that, trust me."

"Nah." He waves his hand. "It's fine. Towels are in the bathroom." His speech slows down, and his eyes become droopy.

"You're crashing?" I see the signs.

"Yep." He pops the *p* and glances over before he leaves. "You are safe here." He yawns. "I'm out." He barely makes it to his room—good thing it's just two steps away—and falls with a *fwump* to his bed. Almost all parts of his body made it to the bed, except his lower legs. He'll become a grasshopper if he sleeps like that through his crash.

I hadn't imagined that Justin had such a severe case of insomnia. When he mentioned crashing, I thought he'd just get tired and go to sleep once his body gave up. Now I know better, he'll be out for ages.

I walk to the bed and try to move his legs. The man is heavy, especially half-dead like he is right now. I walk around, take his boots off, and pull him by the shoulders toward the headboard. His bed is king-size, so I have to climb on top with him. The dude is tall, shorter than Alex by a couple of inches, but I can't find evidence of that difference now. He feels ten feet tall and six hundred pounds heavy.

Grunting and cursing, I manage to pull him up so his whole body is *on* the bed and there are no more hanging limbs anywhere. I turn his head to the side so he can breathe and pull the covers over him. I've done my civic duty, and now I'm free to explore his kitchen and satiate my rumbling stomach. I don't know how it's hungry in the current circumstances after having breakfast just an hour ago—heavy lifting must be a speedy calorie-burning activity.

The fridge is stocked with frozen meals, beer, and apples. An insane number of different sorts of apples. I don't find anything else appealing, so I grab an apple and go outside to explore the surroundings of my new temporary lodgings.

Downstairs, I'm greeted by three pairs of round eyes staring at me. Then somebody whistles, and someone else laughs. I roll my eyes. Some boys are still boys, no matter their age.

"Oh please, chill, would ya?" I say as I stride past them. Their laughter sounds like a conspiracy theory in the making, and I shake my head. "I'm heading to the diner. Anybody needs anything?"

A guy in his late forties with a voluminous mustache asks, "Worked up an appetite?" Then throws a wink in my direction.

I sigh. I want to tell him that, yes, I worked up an appetite by charitably dragging his boss's comatose ass to where he wouldn't roll over and break his nose falling flat on the floor, but I don't know if they know about his insomnia. Not my place.

"Sure did." I smile. Always go with the flow; it's easier.

"When will he be down?" the same guy asks. I try to think of an answer that won't point out Justin's problem, but he beats me to it. "He crashed, didn't he?" I don't know what to say, so I nod. He nods back at me. "All right, I'll look over the shop. Will you be staying here?"

"I need to go out, but I'm staying here for the night, yes."

He nods again. "All right. I'll show you how to lock up." He goes back under the hood of the Honda he was working on when I came here. Two of the others have already gone back to their business, their laughter having died out after the mustache guy asked about Justin. "I like Marina," the man in question continues. Then he lifts his head up from under the hood to look at me wide-eyed. His cheeks are scorching red, and it's adorable. "I mean, I like her pancakes." He turns even redder, if it's possible. "I mean, I like her food." Then he dives right back in, hiding his embarrassment.

Interesting. Now I want to know who this Marina is. Anything to take my mind off of my own drama.

The walk to the diner from Justin's place is short, and when I get there, the place is half-packed. I take my regular seat. Yes, it's my seat now, and I already have my usual order. So I sit and wait for Kayla to come and chat.

When she finally arrives, I immediately notice the stony expression clouding her previously cheerful face.

"What can I get you?" she asks in a neutral voice, almost mechanically. O-o-kay. I thought we hit it off yesterday.

My brow scrunches. "Hey, are you all right?"

Her expression doesn't change. "Sure, fine. So, what can I get you?"

"Kayla." I persist irritably, making sure I force her gaze to meet mine. "What the fuck happened?"

My cursing manages to crack her facade because she drops the hand clutching her notepad and stares at me. I stare right back. After a few seconds of mutual borderline glaring, she lowers her eyes and speaks, watching me from under her thick lashes.

"I heard you're living with Justin now."

Oh, goody.

"I've literally stayed with him for an hour," I complain. "And everybody already knows?"

"Small town." She shrugs her narrow shoulders. "So, are you?" She watches me like a hawk.

"And what if I am?" I ask just to push her because I see where this is going.

"Then nothing. Simply curious." She shrugs again, but it's an unnatural movement. She looks anywhere but my eyes. I take pity on her because Kayla isn't a bad person, she's just caught up in jealousy. Anybody could be in her shoes.

"My car is broken, and he's fixing it," I explain, softening my tone. "You already know that. I don't have anywhere to stay, so he offered me his second bedroom for a couple of days."

Her eyes light up a little, then they dull again. "I'm sorry I can't offer you to stay with me."

"Don't worry about that." I wave her off. I don't know her story, but I don't think it's an easy one. That's why I'll stay as far away as possible from her with my volatile problems. She doesn't need those tossed into her orbit too.

"It's just a matter of time before you'll be..." she continues after a moment, trailing off.

"I will be what?" I say a little harsher than I intended.

Her cheeks redden, and she finally meets my eyes. "I'm sorry, I'm being a bitch. It's just..."

I give her an understanding smile. "You like him, I know."

"No!" she yelps, but after meeting my eyes, she sighs. "Yeah." Her gaze lowers to the table.

"So why aren't you with him?"

"Are you joking?" She laughs. "Cause that's hilarious. You saw our interaction, right? He'd never pay me a second glance unless it were to sucker-punch me."

I look at her and honestly wonder why she thinks that. "Why?"

"Because I'm me, and he's Justin." She waves her elegant hand with long, artistic fingers like that's supposed to explain everything. It doesn't.

My brow furrows. "What's that supposed to mean?"

"He's, like, this gorgeous guy that everybody is tripping over to get with. He's slept with all the wandering vaginas, and they are fucking twenties out of ten." She rolls her eyes and lets out a little huff.

"Wandering vaginas?" I laugh so hard I snort, and Kayla starts laughing along with me. Probably at my piggy-like sound.

"Yeah, I call them that."

"And who are they?"

"You really wanna know?" Her eyes sparkle as she plays with her braids. The tips are colored red and match her painted lips. It's a cute look on her.

"Do tell!" I'm excited about some drama that doesn't involve me.

"Let me get you your food and coffee, and I'll be right back!" She flies away without asking what I want. I hope it's a Kurt, but I'll take anything she brings me.

Ten minutes later, she brings me my food and drink. And it is a Lonely Kurt! It gives me a bloom of warmth in my chest that she already knows my order like I'm a real regular—and she's already my friend. Then she plops onto the seat opposite from me, puts her elbows on the table, and smiles mischievously.

"Get ready for local gossip!" Her eyes sparkle, and I'm getting this nice, cozy feeling inside, like when you meet a long-lost friend, and you just click right back together like you never separated. "So, we all went to the same school together."

"You and Justin too?" I'm surprised because she looks younger than him.

"Nah. He was years older, but he was my first crush. Like, ever." She scrunches her nose. "Until one of the vaginas sank her claws into him."

"So they were together at school?"

"Yes. No. Stop interrupting!" she exclaims and throws a sugar packet at me.

I manage to catch it with a laugh. "All right, all right, but you're confusing me."

"We all went to the same school, but different years. It's like one school here and two in the next town. But we all mingled. Well, *they* mingled," she adds after a pause. "Any-way, there are Regina Georges in every single school. Popu-lar, beautiful, rich, you know the type." I nod. "So, they all stick together, and when the old squad leaves, the new one comes in. Every generation has them. And every one of them slept with him."

It's my turn to scrunch my nose in distaste. Not because

he fucked mean girls, who cares, but the idea of all those friends sharing one dick makes me cringe. "O-o-kay."

"Yeah, he's a man-whore. As glorious as they come." She sighs wistfully.

"And I'm guessing you wanna be one of them?" No shame here; he is a fine-looking man.

"I wish. I bet one ride with him would be enough to remember when I'm old and wrinkled." Her eyes glaze over like she's getting tangled in her imagination.

"So why not?" I ask.

"He hates me," she says quietly.

I feel like I'm missing a big part of whatever has happened between them, and I'm having difficulty reconciling the Justin he is to me with the Justin he is to Kayla. "He doesn't seem like the type to hate somebody, especially a hot woman, but since I saw how he talked to you... Man, it made even me uncomfortable."

She grimaces. "Imagine how it makes *me* feel."

"I'm sorry." I pat her hand over the table sympathetically.

She filches a strip of bacon from my plate and stuffs it into her mouth before I can snatch it back. What's wrong with people here constantly stealing my food? Are they unable to buy their own bacon?

"He, like, legitimately hates me," she continues as if she isn't a dirty thief.

Getting back on track, my mouth screws up as I reflect. "It's honestly hard to believe. He seems so easy-going and happy-go-lucky."

She shakes her head. "Yeah, not with me."

"Why?" I'm genuinely curious. Kayla is hot and smart; she looks like exactly the type Justin would go for—that any man would go for. He might be a flirt, but he isn't stupid in the slightest. I can tell that man has a big brain in that dangerously handsome head of his and the matching heart, even if he's behaving like a clown. Those usually have the sharpest minds.

"No idea." I give her a dubious look, and she throws up her arms in defense. "Honest to God, I have no idea. We were fine years back—well, not fine because he didn't know I existed—but at least he wasn't mean. Then when he came back..." She cuts herself off because she doesn't know how much I know, and here I see a beautiful person who's still trying to be loyal to the guy who hates her.

"From prison?" I help her.

"You know?" She seems surprised.

"Small town and all." I smile almost apologetically, embarrassed that it sounds like I've been gossiping.

"Ri-i-ight." She's hesitant now like she's said too much, and just remembered that I'm staying at his place—for tonight, at least. And she still doesn't know the length of my almost-nonexistent relationship with him, if you could even call it that. "Well, when he came back, he'd changed."

"Prison tends to do that to people," I suggest gently, and she shakes her head.

"No, he's changed with *me*. Like I'm his number-one enemy. He treats me like shit, and so does his brother." She grabs another piece of bacon, and I don't stop her this time, considering she needs it more than I do. In fact, I'm about ready to share my sacred Lonely Kurt with her.

I still can't imagine a flirt like Justin treating any woman like shit, especially a beautiful and quirky one like Kayla.

"Stick around, and you'll see more of that side of him in proximity to me. A sight to behold," she scoffs sardonically.

"I'm leaving soon," I say quietly.

"Bummer." Her face falls. "I was hoping to make friends with a normal human being for once in my life."

"Surely there are people our age here," I hazard doubtfully.

"There are, but they all grew up here." She says that like it should explain everything.

"And what's wrong with that?"

Her smile is sad this time. "I'm not the most popular girl here."

"Why don't you move?" That's what I did. Thinking realistically, though, I snort internally at myself. *And how is that working out for you, Freya?*

She stands and leaves. "It was nice meeting you, Freya."

I might have said something insensitive, but I have no idea what. Five minutes later, she returns with my wrapped-up food and quietly takes my card. When she comes back, I carefully grab her hand. "Sit with me for a bit." She doesn't budge, so I add plaintively, "Please." She looks me over and decides to grant my request. "I'm sorry if I offended you somehow, I truly didn't mean to."

"You didn't offend me. It's just… it's my own issues, and I preferred to escape from them just like I always do when I have to acknowledge they exist."

"Hey, I don't judge. In the end, that's why I'm here." I spread my arms with a self-deprecating half smile.

Her brow crinkles. "Are you hiding here?"

"Something like that." We're both quiet, each in our own worlds when I spot a familiar enormous body strolling down the street. I instantly perk up and follow his steps with my eyes. He must have sensed my peeping because his head snaps over in my direction, and our gazes meet. I swallow a huge lump in my throat.

Kayla kicks me under the table, and my sight snaps from

him to give her an indignant look. "Don't stare at him!" she hisses. "He came back from war with injuries. It's not his fault he's like that."

Oh, sweet Kayla. She's trying to protect him, thinking I'm ogling his scars. In fact, it's the last thing I see when I look at him. So I tell her the story of how I ended up sleeping at Alex's place and how I ended up at Justin's only a matter of hours later—minus a few intimate details of my special moments with Alex. Her eyes widen with every sentence I speak.

"You slept in Alex's house? Like *slept* slept?" She's so excited she's like a kid in a candy store. "I heard about your interactions with him, but I didn't know you'd actually *been* in his house!"

"I'd do more if he were up to it, but we kind of had a falling out." My lips curve downward in an admittedly almost childish pout.

"Holy crap!" she exclaims in a high-pitched voice.

Just then, a tall lady with big boobs and stylish red hair calls out from behind the counter. "Wanna come back to work some more, honey?"

"Be back in a minute, Marina!" Kayla yells back with a wave of her hand. So that's Marina, Mustache Guy's crush. "I'm so happy!" she gushes.

"About what?" I refocus from observing Marina of Mustache Guy fame back to Kayla.

"You have no idea how long he hadn't had normal interactions with a human being," she explains with bright eyes, "let alone a woman. Not until you."

"You seem awfully invested in his well-being." I squint my eyes at her in the same manner she did when she was vivisecting me about Justin.

She laughs at that. "Touché." We both look back at

where Alex had been, but I can't see him. "He probably went to get his delivery." She must see a question in my eyes because she explains. "He orders parts for the cars he restores online, but most of them get delivered to Mac's store over there"—she points to one of the buildings outside—"because nobody can find his address in the woods. Alex picks them up once a week or so. It's weird, though." She taps a finger on her chin. "Because he just picked up a delivery yesterday morning."

As she says that, Alex strolls out of the store empty-handed. His eyes are trained on me, bolder than I would've expected of him. When he walks by the diner, he averts his gaze to the road and walks back to his truck.

"I think I just got pregnant from the way he looked at you." Kayla laughs.

"What?" I ask, confused.

She looks at me like I'm missing brain cells. "He *looked* at you," she repeats. Then she sighs, and her gaze begins to look far away. "Oh man, you should have seen him when he was younger," she reminisces. "All-American pretty boy. He could get anybody, literally anybody." She wrinkles her nose. "And he used to get them. Right alongside Justin. Anyway, he's not the same anymore. And people who praised him now treat him like an outcast." Her sad gaze and the visible pinch of frustration in it follow Alex.

"So I've heard."

"Don't believe everything you hear," she reminds me almost darkly.

"Kayla!" Marina yells.

"That's my cue to leave. Give me your phone." I pass it to her. She punches something in and gives it back. "I sent a text to myself. If you decide to stay here longer, give me a call. I could use a friend."

"Kayla!" Marina's getting aggravated.

"I'm coming, jeez!" she hollers back. "Again, nice meeting you. And I mean that this time." She chuckles and leaves.

Glad I stopped to pick up a new phone—with cash this time—on my way here earlier. I grab it so I can program Kayla's number into it, grab my stuff, and exit through the double doors at the front of the diner. Then I suddenly stop because Alex's truck is still parked on the street. And he's inside. I need to walk past him to get to Justin's place.

I begin marching by, feeling on edge and trying not to look at him, then failing because he abruptly opens the door and jumps out of the truck.

"Hey," he says in his gruff, guttural voice.

"Hi." I just saw him a few hours ago, and we didn't part ways as buddies, but seeing him now makes something in my chest that feels suspiciously like my heart singing.

He seems to be searching for words because it takes him a minute to gather his wits. "Are you settled in your new place?" he finally asks.

"Yes." It's all the information I offer. Then a pregnant pause follows, but I don't budge.

He loses the battle and gives in first. *Ha. I win.* "Where are you staying?"

"At Justin's."

"The fuck?" Oh, do I enjoy this reaction. He doesn't seem happy, which means the tension and undeniable attraction I've felt all this time hasn't been one-sided. "Are you staying *in* his place?"

"Yes." I shrug. "I don't have anywhere else to go, and you dumped me at his feet. Why are you getting all snarly right now? I'm crashing in the guy's extra room. No big deal."

"The fuck you are," he snaps, his jaw taut. "Get in the car." He walks to the passenger side and opens the door. I'm standing in the same spot he left me, put off-balance by his unanticipated fury. "Get in the fucking car, Freya," he repeats in a low growl.

"Why?" His behavior is starting to get to me. All this hot-and-cold behavior where he lets me in his house then kicks me out of it, then lets me in, then kicks me back out again is messing with my head.

"So we can go there, get your stuff, and go," he grunts because he doesn't know how to speak like a normal, rational human.

"Go where?"

"To my place."

"Are you fucking kidding me?" I don't even care if anybody hears me, and I'm positive by tonight everybody will know I lashed out at a war hero—as overall unappreciated as he is by them—and escaping my abusive ex will instantly be the least of my problems. "You just threw me out this morning, and now you want me to come back?"

"Yes" is the only reply he gives me.

"That wasn't a question! It was a rhetorical statement, so I could point out how freaking absurd this is!" I'm certain by now I have steam billowing out of my ears. "I'm not going anywhere with you," I declare, crossing my arms over my chest.

"Get. In. The. Car," he growls, his words barely audible. And it's probably a terrible idea to poke a person who admits himself to be violent, but I can't seem to help myself. So, I walk to where he stands and right up close to him, right in his space.

With only inches between us, I hiss in his face, "No."

His nostrils flare, and his breaths come out short, shallow, and ragged. He grabs the open door so hard his knuckles turn white. His lips are one tight line. He looks scary, very scary, but somehow, I'm not scared of him. Not at all. Jeez, my survival instincts must be shit. God knows they are.

"Get in the car, Freya." He can scarcely contain himself, and I believe now that he has anger issues. Serious ones. Otherwise, there is no explanation for why he went from zero to a hundred in half a minute when I mentioned where I was staying.

"You're not yourself right now," I tell him honestly. "And I'm not going to be in the same car with you when you're like this." I take a tentative step back, and he takes a matching step forward like we're waltzing in the street together.

"This is exactly what I'm like." He spreads his hands sarcastically. "Just how you wanted, the real me. I warned you to stay away, but you didn't listen, did you? And now you don't leave me a choice but to get involved."

His eyes are focused on my face, and I might be a little scared now. Just a tiny bit. I've been in this same place before, where I let a man make me afraid, and I vowed to myself never to go back there. And yet, here I am.

I take another step back. "I've changed my mind. I'll be out of this town when my car is ready, and you won't have to hear from or about me ever again." I take one more step, and he must see something in my face or physicality that he hadn't before because his whole demeanor changes. He drops his intimidatingly demonstrative hands and steps back to the truck.

"I'm sorry. I'm sorry, Freya," he whispers and strides toward the driver's side. He's speeding away from this crime scene of a conversation in the next moment. I swallow another lump in my throat, along with the bitter memories that are resurfacing in the wake of this interaction. I take several deep, long breaths, and when I'm feeling closer to the normal me, I finally notice that we have an audience. At least a dozen people stopped whatever they were doing to watch our interaction instead.

Yep, my ex is the least of my problems right now, considering the faces full of judgment all around.

I pull my scarf tighter and restart my interrupted journey back to Justin's place.

Chapter Nine

F**REYA**

When I open the door to Justin's apartment, I let out a yell because there's a person in there, and I didn't expect anybody, given that Justin was likely to be out of commission for many more hours to come.

"Apparently, I was put on babysitting duty," Jake says instead of a greeting from the worn chair he's sitting on, speaking through a mouthful of chips even as he reaches for another in the open bag on the counter.

I glare at him. "That's the best you can come up with when I'm yelling bloody murder?"

He just shrugs and sends another chip into his mouth, following up with a loud crunch.

"And who put you on this duty?"

"Justin called earlier, said you were coming. He knew he was about to crash, so he called me to watch over you while he's out." He sighs deeply. "I knew you were trouble the moment I saw you in that parking lot."

Didn't know I was coming, my ass. Justin the Jerk! So Alex *did* tell him I was on my way, and he was just playing dumb.

"Yeah, I get that a lot. Get ready." I throw him the jacket that's newly hanging over the back of the couch, so I assume it is his.

"Where?" He doesn't sound thrilled.

I take perverse pleasure as I chirp, "We're going shopping."

I smile when I hear a pained groan.

It takes Jake an hour—an hour!—to get ready. What a damn diva! And that's considering he was already dressed! He needed to "take a leak," then he needed coffee, then his coffee wasn't hot enough, then it wasn't cool enough, and after a full hour had passed by, I gave up and left him there.

"Where are you going?" he yells after me. I don't grant him a verbal response, just a middle finger as I turn and walk down the sidewalk.

I've seen a small grocery store half a mile down the street, so I head in that direction. Jake rushes to the car and fumbles with the keys. Why would he need a car when we can just walk for five minutes and be there?

I slip in and walk quickly to the back of it, away from the giant window out to the street. There's an old lady trying to reach a bottle of milk that's too high up, so I walk up with a friendly smile and get it down for her. I might be —literally—on the run from a police officer, but I need to get my good karma points back up.

"You look familiar," the old lady says, squinting through her glasses. "Do I know you?"

"No, I'm not from around here. I'm only passing through."

She doesn't seem to believe me. "Did you date my son?"

I chuckle. "No, ma'am, I'm pretty positive I haven't. I'm only passing—"

"He's about your height. Has brown hair—"

A different voice comes from behind her. "*Gray* hair, actually, Nonna."

I turn to see a man about my age with sparkling blue eyes and a traditionally handsome face. Where Alex is rugged and looks like he could fight a bear with his hands, this guy seems like he'd win any office debate, wearing a suit while clicking a pen.

He extends his hand and flashes me a glittering smile. "Jonah. Her grandson. The son she's talking about is my father, and he hasn't had brown hair for two decades now."

I blush at the attention of a handsome man. Feels like Little Hope might give me hope to become a normal woman capable of enjoying male attention again, after all. "Freya. I don't usually have a thing for men older than me, so..." I turn to his grandmother. "Your son's virtue is safe."

Jonah laughs. Before either of us can say anything—or Nonna, for that matter—Jake comes flying down the aisle, red-faced and steaming.

"*You,*" he snaps. "Don't run away."

I purse my lips piteously and turn back to Jonah. "I promise I'm not a fugitive."

"You *are*, actually," Jake snaps, and I can't help but notice that Jonah's attention is no longer on me but on the cop. Hmm.

There's a flush creeping up Jake's neck that has nothing to do with me, I'm sure of it.

Jake glowers at Jonah before grabbing me by the arm and tugging me away. "It was nice to meet you, Jonah," I say over my shoulder while he chuckles and gives me a small wave. "He's cute, don't you think, Jake?" I ask slyly once we're out of earshot.

"No, of course, I don't *think*." He scrunches his nose like he just smelled something foul.

I shrug. "I mean, *you* said it."

He growls and forces me to a stop in the cookie aisle. I grab a box off the shelf behind his head and open them.

"You're not a very good babysitter," I inform him, crunching down on my first of many.

He gives me a look that could singe my eyebrow hairs off. "We're trying to keep you *safe*."

I frown. "No, you're trying to keep me *here*, and I want to know *why*." I turn and keep walking.

"Are you going to pay for those?" Jake barks after me. When I don't answer, he groans loudly and digs a handful of bills out of his pocket to shove at the cashier before chasing after me. He snatches them out of my hand and takes one. "What do you mean we're keeping you here? You're the one sticking around."

"*Yeah*, and you know *why*?"

Jake gives me a bored look and steers me in the direction of the car. "Your car broke down."

"Precisely. *My tire blew out.* This means I simply needed a new tire to replace it, and then I would have been on my way. But *your brother* claimed that replacement is going to take at least a week. He conveniently abandoned me at Alex's house, took away my car, and is now getting the police force involved." I tick each offense off on my fingers, then fold my arms and squinting at him. "Why am I still here? Are you really so bored in this little town that you need to make up problems for yourselves? Do you and all your cop buddies take turns breaking random laws so you can have fun arresting each other?"

Jake is looking more and more bewildered. "I don't know what you're talking about."

"Oh, c'mon. Why are you babysitting me, Jake? I'm a big girl. I vote. I pay taxes. I can even cross the street on my own, believe it or not."

He ignores my sarcasm completely, replying simply, "Justin asked me to."

"And do you do everything Justin says without question?" I round my eyes and stare at him unblinkingly, hoping he'll get the feeling I'm going for—mocking him for obeying his big bro.

"If he asks, yes," he answers, looking right into my eyes, and instantly, I feel like crap. This man right here loves his family so unconditionally that he even agrees to babysit a random weirdo who got into this town by accident and doesn't bring along anything but trouble. I gulp down a lump in my throat.

"Okay," I murmur, all antagonism draining from me. "I think you're a good brother, Jake. And thank you for keeping me company."

"That's it? You're not going to interrogate me anymore?"

"Nope. Just wanted to see you squirm a little after you made me wait for an hour."

"You little..." He doesn't finish, but I know what he was going to say.

The end of the day turns out to be a decent time. We have a nice dinner, where I grab a drink since I'm preparing myself to spend more time with Officer McGossip. I'm not ready to listen to Jake running his big, all-knowing mouth anymore, and I just want to step into oblivion where unicorns shit butterflies, and my problems don't exist. Taking my facial cues in the form of scowling to heart—thank God—Jake doesn't mention Alex the whole time, and I'm forever grateful for that.

By the time we arrive back at Justin's place, I see a very familiar truck sitting in the parking lot with no driver in sight. That can't be good.

Chapter Ten

A **LEX**

"You're both fucking idiots, that's what you are," I hiss as Jake and Freya stand in front of me with confused looks on their faces. They'd come here looking too happy and too relaxed—her for somebody who's supposed to be hiding and him for somebody who's supposed to be watching over her. And both of them are too comfortable together for my liking.

Justin is leaning against the mantel, his arms crossed and an amused smile playing on his lips, but I ignore whatever it is that has him so damn tickled. When I barged in, he had clearly just woken up after one of his insomniac episodes.

"*You,*" I snarl at Freya. "Your car got broken into and the person searching for you is clearly here, and yet you're traipsing around town for everybody to see instead of waiting safely here." I turn to Justin as Freya begins looking considerably small and frail. "And *you*. You couldn't do the *one* fucking thing I asked of you. You said you could help, and then you dumped her on your brother, who fucks up everything the second he touches it."

Even Justin stands up straight at that. "Hey, watch it," he snarls. Jake looks crestfallen, and the sight of it makes Freya snap back to her angry stance.

"Jake was with me the whole time." Freya crosses her arms across her chest, and my attention dips to her breasts for a moment. She isn't wearing a bra—I see her nipples poking through the thin material of her green sweater. And that asshole—an *officer of the law*—was with her the whole day, looking at... *it*. "He was watching over me."

"I can see that," I can't help but snarl.

Justin snorts and instantly earns a glare from me.

"What's your problem, Alex?" Freya steps into my space, invading it with the scent of my own body wash on her skin.

"You!" I say too loud and too angry.

"Nobody wants me out of here more than I do!" Freya hisses, poking my chest with her finger.

"Oh, really? So then why the fuck are you still here, disrupting everybody's lives?" The moment I say it out loud, regret fills me—and the moment I see Freya's eyes flash with hurt, I feel a stab of guilt in my gut like a physical assault.

Justin, an ever-present mediator, steps forward and holds his hands up between the two idiots and me. "Okay, let's just cool our—"

Moving without thought, I violently kick my foot into the table beside the couch, relishing not just in the release of inner tension but the slight physical pain it causes me. The table goes skittering across the floor while the lamp that had sat atop it hits the hardwood floor with a sickening crash, the ceramic base shattering on the floor.

"Out," I order, voice deadly quiet. "Get out. All of you."

I look around the room, scanning for more I can send careening into the wall, and freeze once my eyes land on Freya. She looks horrified and tiny. She's holding onto the back of a wooden stool with white knuckles. Her eyes are round, and two red blotches have appeared on her cheeks. I take a small step toward her, and she scatters backward, dragging the stool along.

Justin scowls thunderously at me, striding forward to clamp a firm hand on my shoulder and steer me out. "You're in my house, actually, so how about *you* get the fuck outta here."

Justin's voice is so hard it's almost calm, and I can see that his own beast is very close to the surface. He might seem like a sunny guy, but his demons are dark. Maybe even darker than my own. Once he walks me to the door—and I let him—he reaches out to Freya and gently touches her shoulder, causing me to see red.

"You're staying with me, Freya. I assumed too much when I sent you to Alex." I've never weathered this genuine disappointment from Justin before, and the hostility on his face toward me causes a trickle of plain discomfort to roll down my spine.

I catch a glimpse of fear lingering still in Freya's expression and swallow the painfully hard lump in my throat. It's the same look that kicks me in the teeth every time I see it. I turn on my heel and slam the door shut, letting the whole building shudder on its very foundation. I'm surprised the door didn't splinter. I didn't want to smack it so hard, I never do, but emotions get the best of me. They *always* do.

I asked Justin to find her a place to stay and maybe, just

maybe, put that useless baby, Jake, on her tail, so she's constantly under the watchful eye of one of us while she's here. But he had to go ahead and insert himself deeper into everybody's business, and now it's all a mess.

I drive back to my house in a fog of fury and something bordering on regret, trying to forget that fiasco back there. Somehow, I feel like I've not only lost Freya but finally lost Justin too.

The room still smells like Freya. I yank open the window to get the fresh air in and suck in huge gulps. It's always there, hovering on the outskirts of my brain. That feeling of walking into a trap. That *trust* that was so easily snapped and thrown away like it was nothing.

The storm was picking up on my way here, and I welcomed the natural outlet for my anger that was about to arrive. Now, I lean my hands on the windowpane, and when I hear the first crack of thunder, I let the flashback hit me hard and lose myself in the weeping, angry, fearful mess that I know I can't let anyone see.

The next morning starts with a bang. Quite literally. Somebody's banging on my door. I look around and inspect my surroundings. After my blackouts, I tend to be lost in time and space and flow within my emotions. Yesterday was no different.

When the weather is angry, I wallow in it. I let the demons of my past roam free because when they're trapped in their cages for too long, the inevitable outbursts will be more brutal, and I might accidentally hurt someone. This way, I only hurt myself.

Lying tiredly across my bed in the dim morning light, I

try to make a fist, and the battered skin on my right knuckles stretches and starts re-bleeding, undoing the small amount of healing sleep had offered. I move my wrist around—*fuck*, that hurts. Must have hit the wall or something. I look around, searching for damage, and there it is. A hole in the wall next to the door. Thank fuck I didn't hit the door; that shit's reinforced better than these paper-thin walls and could've done some nasty damage. Wouldn't want a trip to the ER. I've seen enough hospitals to last me a lifetime.

My head's pounding, like somebody keeps punching it with a heavy fist in an even beat. I should know the feeling by rote after my brutal childhood of proving to everyone around me that they don't get to call me a bastard. Soon, I realize it's the entrance door and not little gremlins in my head.

I groan and roll off the bed. This fucker—whoever he is —clearly doesn't know how to read the room and keeps making a hole in the wood of my perfectly handcrafted door. I'm about to rip my knuckles farther open when I meet my morning guest.

"Who the fuck—" I stop when I open the door and see Jake standing on my porch. "What do you want?" I growl.

"You're an asshole." He takes off his glasses and pushes them into his breast pocket. He rarely takes them off, preferring to hide his immature ass behind them. Interesting. Did he come to fight?

"What's new?" I scratch my scruffy jaw. A shave is many hours overdue.

He steps closer and—color me impressed—actually walks inside my house. Toe to toe with me, he takes his glasses from their pocket and moves them to the back pocket of his uniform slacks. Huh. Definitely looking for a fight. The fucker loves his Ray-Bans.

I lazily watch his movements without stepping back an inch. The little pest is in my territory, and the only thing keeping him from losing all his teeth right now is my respect for Justin. He has enough on his plate dealing with his siblings and doesn't need to add *this*.

"You've treated Freya like shit. Just like you treat everybody else. You don't deserve her," he says in disgust, and I clench my jaw. I can do that. I can stop myself from breaking all of his bones.

"I don't *want* her," I counter through clenched teeth.

He scoffs goadingly. "Yeah, that's why you ran at first sight of me and her together."

"The fuck are you talking about?" I'm confused here. When I heard that Jake and Freya were having mimosa brunches and painting each other's nails in public, I wanted to smack them both stupid. The chick's obviously on the run, and whoever's after her obviously knows where she is. I don't know her story, but her car got broken into, and her constant edginess speaks to some shady shit going on. She should be staying hidden until... until what? Until she leaves Little Hope and is alone with her troubles again? With nobody to look out for her?

"You're jealous," he declares with a megawatt smile.

"What?" The idea of me being jealous is ridiculous. I've never been jealous of a girl in my life. Yesterday, I was annoyed as fuck that I had to deal with them both. That was all it was. I've been jealous of my siblings and their family, yes. But not a chick. Never a chick.

"That's right. You want Freya to yourself, but you don't deserve her." He looks smug.

"You're right, I don't."

"You don't—wait, what?" He's blinking so fast that I wonder if he will fly away. *Please, God, let him fly away.*

"You are right, I was wrong. Are we done here?" I ask tiredly. I haven't even had a cup of coffee or a Tylenol yet.

"I'm not joking."

"Neither am I, and that's why she's staying with Justin." I hold his gaze, showing the heaviness of my words. The real meaning behind them. She's better off as far from me as possible.

When she took that shirt off, I nearly died. All my blood rushed south, and I almost got brain damage. Throughout my whole life, I've never seen a woman sexier than her. Sure, I've slept with a lot of women—not as many as Justin, thank fuck—but Freya... She stirred something in me. All right, I know exactly what she stirred, but she also touched something deeper with her vulnerability and how she shied away from herself after she gave me a run for my money like that and just about gave me a stroke, too. That's how I feel about my body. Though I have no idea why. She is breathtaking.

Her legs are long and muscular. Her stomach is flat. Her tits... Man, her tits are the perfect handfuls. I feel the blood rushing south again, and it's about to get awkward with Jake standing in my space.

"Good." *Speaking of whom.* "Good that she's staying with him. Me and him, we'll take care of her."

I nod because there's nothing else I can add. I know they will. I trust Justin. I don't trust Jake, but Justin does, and I have to trust Justin's judgment.

"Stay away from her," he says bravely.

I sigh. "You should really know when to stop."

He finally begins to sense the danger he's in and takes two steps back, nearly tripping backward over the threshold. I roll my eyes.

He looks back and starts walking toward his car.

Halfway down the stairs, he turns toward me and says: "You don't deserve Justin, either. For the love of God, I have no idea why he's still trying with you. He's better off without you. Just like Freya is." He pushes his chin forward, preparing to fight.

But instead, I just say, "I know." Then I close the door, leaving him outside with his mouth hanging slightly agape.

I don't know why Justin's still trying, either. Everyone else gave up on me long ago, but he's still around. He's still here.

Well, he's not anymore, I guess. I know how protective he is of his siblings, and I did a low blow saying all that shit about Jake. Intentionally or in self-sabotage, I still don't know. When the anger takes over, I'm not myself. Or maybe it's when I am the real *me* without this pretend bullshit.

When I was a teenager, and my father sent me to a therapist to try to fix my anger issues, I got even madder that they tried to change me. Taking the part from me that was still angry with my mom dying and my dad taking me in was done at the wrong time, so I resented the therapy, and I still do. By trying to fix the problem, my father created another one—now I avoid connecting with anyone because I'm afraid they'll try to fix me. So, I established my default setting as being an asshole to everyone around me.

I take a shower, drink some coffee, and patch up the wall. Then I go to the garage and try to work on the engine of an old Dodge that's due in a week, and it still has a shit ton of work to do since I've been distracted lately and haven't gotten much done.

As I'm fixing the scratches on the original bumper of the 1965 Dodge Coronet—which is a miracle on its own—my mind keeps drifting off to Freya and the look of pain on her face instead of admiring the old horse. The way her beautiful honey eyes glazed over with regret and hurt for a moment and then revived with a spark of fury. At me. I can take fury, but can't take her looking so vulnerable, so upset.

Yeah, I could relate to that. Besides Justin and my team—there goes another *ache* in my chest—I've never really connected with anyone else. Until Freya. That's why I sent her away. Jake's right; they're all better off as far away from me as possible.

As I get distracted with my self-beratement, I over-tighten the screw and the bumper cracks. *Fuck!* This boy survived fifty years of abuse, and now he's destined to die under my brute hands. That's it. I drop the screwdriver and stand up. I can't put this car through my bullshit, so I decide to distract myself with something. Take-out from Marina's sounds like a good idea.

Never mind that Freya might be there since she and Kayla are growing pretty close. I'll go there just to grab some food and leave.

I go inside the house to change, then, halfway through, I think twice and want to slap myself. The hell am I doing? Changing clothes to go into town? Since when have I become such a pussy? With a growl, I yank the clean shirt off and pull the old, grease-stained one back on. Better. I'm not there to impress anybody.

As I drive to the diner, I regret not changing the damn shirt.

I park in front of the entrance and take a peek inside before going in. I know Freya's habit of sitting in the same place she's occupied before and choosing the same mug she's already used, so I look for the same spot by the window she sat in the last time I saw her here.

She's there. Sitting in the same exact spot, eating the same exact food. I think they call it Lonely Kurt. Well, she's not eating but playing with the food, more like it. She's clearly in a foul mood, the corners of her lips dipping down. I watch her carefully, waiting for a sign for me on how to proceed.

And I get it very fast. My stepmother's walking on the sidewalk toward the diner, and that's my cue to leave.

I look once more at Freya, and she has a smile on her face because Kayla's sitting at her table now and clearly chatting non-stop. Good. That's the sign I needed—that she's okay and happy without my presence, so I can let her be.

I start my truck and drive off.

At home, I open a bottle of old Scotch bought back in the times when I still respected myself. The amber liquid burns my throat and washes the guilt down. The more I drink, the less guilt I feel. So I drink more.

Eventually, I ditch the glass and begin drinking straight from the bottle. By the time I can see the bottom of it, my brain is mush, and I stumble to bed, hoping that my constant nightmares will leave me alone tonight.

Little did I know that I'd face another sort of nightmare. A different kind where a certain pretty refugee is trying to escape from the demons chasing her, but she never can. In my nightmare, whoever is chasing her finds her every time, and I can only stand there frozen, immobile, unable to do anything to help.

I wake up covered in sweat. My breathing is labored, similar to how it always is after my episodes.

Her scared face will be forever branded on the insides of my eyelids. My heart stops beating the moment a hand reaches out to her, pulling her back from me. I shudder at the thought of something like that happening to her anywhere but in my nightmares.

Fuck, I couldn't see that one coming—her getting so deep under my skin, and after only a few days.

Is it because I haven't had sex in forever, and the close proximity of an attractive woman prevents my brain from thinking straight? She *is* hot, no question about that, and it'd be so much easier to think of her as just a fuck. But there's something else about her that makes my chest ache.

Fuck. Did I do the right thing by letting her leave my sight?

FREYA

I end up staying with Justin again, and Jake is crashing on the couch. I don't know why, but I think he wants to stick together because his cop pride was wounded and maybe because he genuinely pitied me too.

Jake's not as bad as I thought he was. Yes, he was talking shit about Alex before and gossiping non-stop, but this little town is immersed in gossip, and it seems like it's just a not-so-charming part of its culture.

And then there's Alex, with his anger Jake had warned me about, destroying a lamp and nearly scaring me to death. It had sent me into a flashback of my old life, leaving me happy that he had sent me on my way. I don't know how I would have reacted if I had been one-on-one with him during something like that. For the first time, I had feared him at that moment. *Feared.*

A knock startles me, and I jump again. Jake leans against the doorframe of my bedroom and smiles awkwardly. "Sorry, didn't mean to scare you." He's wearing pajama pants and no shirt. "You're stuck here with us for now," he says ruefully before adding with a sheepish smile, "With *me.*"

I shrug. "No big deal."

He sighs and enters the room, plopping down on the edge of the bed. "I know I'm not as good at... *guarding you* as Alex would be, but..." He purses his lips, then gives me a sincere half smile. "I'll do my best, I promise."

I wave him off. "I'm sorry about what he said. And I don't need a guardian."

He grins. "Well, maybe they want me to guard Little Hope from you."

"Yeah, that sounds about right." I offer him a smile in return and try to change the subject.

"So, what do you know about Jonah?"

"You're not his type. He prefers rugged and manly. Literally."

I give a little snort-laugh. "That's not what I was asking about, but thanks for letting me know."

He grunts. "Right. Well, what *do* you want to know?"

I could swear I recognize a hidden interest behind his words in the way he keeps averting his eyes and staring at anything but me.

"I don't know." I shrug. "Anything. I'm bored."

"Right." He's still avoiding direct eye contact. "He owns the local realty business, but he's not in Little Hope often. He runs it from a distance."

"Ah. And he likes you, apparently."

Jake rolls his eyes. "Yeah. Won't get the hint I don't play for his team." He sighs melodramatically, then grins. "Anyway. I'll let you get some sleep. If there's anything you need, just yell out. I'm on the couch, and I'm a light sleeper." Then he adds, "Not like my brother, who could sleep through a war, once he can sleep at all."

"Thank you, Jake, and thank you for staying here with me."

"Didn't have a choice," he calls out over his shoulder, a hint of a smile in his words, before shutting the door and leaving me in the silent room all by myself.

I try not to think of Alex and the sound of his foot crashing into the furniture as I curl up and eventually fall into a restless sleep.

I wake up with a foggy mind and an itching feeling in my soul. The fight with Alex left a bad taste in my mouth, and no amount of Colgate will rinse it away. I lay in my new temporary bed and think about how I am truly alone in this world. I'm infinitely grateful for Justin and Jake and their support, but they belong to Little Hope, and I don't.

My cheap flip phone pings, and I'm surprised and scared at the same time. I don't have people to ask about my well-being besides my shitbag of an ex. I take a deep breath before reaching for it, expecting to see a new cluster of threats, but instead get a pleasant surprise from Kayla.

"Meet me outside. If you come out the front door, turn left and walk to the bookstore. I'm here."

And then another one. *"Don't eat anything."*

Surprised and intrigued, I text her back, but my fingers keep pressing the wrong buttons. I get aggravated and hit *call.*

"Got tired of figuring out how to deal with your old dinosaur?" she starts, then adds without waiting for my answer, "You ready?"

"No," I groan, "I just woke up."

"Too bad. I gotta be in Springfield in the afternoon, but my morning's free. So put something on to cover your ass and come down."

"Fine," I groan again, even though I'm secretly happy she's here.

"Wait! Brush your teeth first!"

"Nope." I pop the *P*. "You're getting all of me." I laugh and hang up.

I quietly peek outside my room, trying not to wake Jake up. But he's already gone. Duty calls, I guess. I quickly brush my teeth and splash water on my face. She didn't give me time for a shower, so she's getting me au natural.

I trot downstairs and then through smirks of greased-up dudes to leave the garage, following Kayla's instruction. She's waiting for me on the bench by the bookstore with two cups of coffee and a take-out bag from Marina's. She's wearing her badass black leather pants, light red jacket, and white beanie that accentuates her ash-blonde hair. She looks both cute *and* hot.

I plop next to her on the bench and gratefully take a cup. "Oh, goody." I moan at the first sip—coffee does make life better, no matter what people say. "Why are you hiding here?" I ask when I finally manage to croak after caffeine hits its mark.

"Uh," she draws outs pointedly, clicking her tongue and jerking her head in the direction I came in, "do you really need to ask?"

I raise both brows in a challenge. "I guess I didn't think you'd be lurking in the shadows like a vampire when Justin's around."

"He's always around," she replies flippantly, shrugging. "Doesn't mean I won't try to avoid him whenever possible."

I'm getting a vibe of her mood heading increasingly downward, so I change the topic. "Thanks for the coffee, that was what I needed this *fine* morning." Then I point at the bag. "Whatcha got there?"

"Oh, I forgot." She passes it to me. "I got you a BLT. Figured bacon won't hurt after what you endured yesterday."

I nearly choke on my coffee. "What did I endure?"

"Survived a night in the viper's nest?" she clarifies with a clear question mark at the end and makes her eyes round, assuming I want to add something more. But I don't. Not now, at least, when the morning isn't looking so dull anymore.

"Yeah, Jake isn't so bad."

"Sure, he isn't," Kayla drawls sarcastically. "I've got at least a dozen unpaid tickets from him. My wallet doesn't think so highly of him anymore." Then she adds after a pause, "Not that it ever did. Never mind, let's go for a walk. I wanna show you Little Hope from a native's point of view."

As I follow Kayla's one-person, impromptu tour of Little Hope, chewing my amazing BLT and listening to her stories about the locals, I immerse entirely into a life of a small town. I've always lived in Baltimore, so I've never had this connection with the people around me. We usually just went about our own business without interacting much. But here, people *see* people. They ask how you're doing and if you're feeling okay. Everybody *knows* Kayla, but not everybody *likes* her, that much I can tell. They throw suspicious looks at her as if waiting for a bomb to explode. If I were to name those people, I'd call them uptight dickbags with sticks up their asses, but I'm happy to admit that they're a minority of the population of Little Hope.

I glance at Kayla, but she's so absorbed in a story about Mrs. Jenkins and her famous plants that she doesn't notice any hostility that might be thrown her way. When the next person throws a disgusted glare at Kayla, I scowl my face and scratch my nose with my middle finger. A middle-aged, pearl-clutching lady in an expensive cashmere coat nearly chokes on her tongue before spinning around, flipping her hair, and going about her business. *Good. Stay out of my friend's business.*

Once I think of Kayla as my friend, a warm feeling spreads inside my chest. I think it might be what we both are missing. Then I do something I never do because every time I see it in movies or on the streets, I nearly vomit—I hook my arm with hers and interlace our fingers. She stops talking and looks at our hands. For a second. Two. Ten. Until I begin feeling like an idiot and am about to pull my hand away—then a wide smile spreads across her face, and she squeezes my hand and keeps talking about Mrs. Jenkins and her crazy adoration toward her houseplants as if it's the most natural thing in the world for us to do.

The next couple of days passes quickly. Justin has been in and out of the apartment, mostly working down at his shop. Jake went back to his place once Justin became a normal human again after his insomnia incident.

I did some basic cleaning around the place because I needed something to do and to repay him somehow. Although I do have money and no problem using it, I get a feeling Justin isn't going to accept it. Kayla's story keeps nagging at me, but I've decided to wait for the right moment to ask.

As for Alex, I haven't seen him since the incident. I texted Kayla back and forth, and she said she saw the whole interaction near his truck from the diner's window—along with other patrons, and, of course, it was a topic of the day.

Two days, to be exact. Good thing she didn't see what happened at Justin's place, and I think it should stay just between the people present during that very enlightening conversation. Enlightening because I finally got what Alex thinks of me—a nuisance who's disrupting everyone's lives. But why am I here? Yes, I am waiting for my car to get done, but if I really wanted—*really* wanted—I could find a ride out of here. But I didn't, and I still don't. Even after Alex's hurtful words, I'm still here, in the spare bedroom of Justin's condo. I have been looking for a place I could call home for a long time, and Little Hope isn't my home. So, why does it feel like I don't want to go just yet?

Today I decided to resume my morning runs, so I woke up at six a.m., slid into my leggings, pulled on an old sweatshirt warm enough for chilly mornings, popped in my earbuds, and took off toward the woods. After a short warm-up, I begin sprinting at my regular speed, and after a mile or so, my leg muscles are burning with familiarly agonizing pleasure. I've missed that feeling, so I soak it all up, enjoying every tingle of muscle strain.

I'm just finishing up when I pass Justin's shop. It's one of the last buildings on a dead-end street, and it's just two hundred feet off the edge of the forest. I walked there yesterday, and there were a lot of clear trails acceptable for a run.

Until suddenly, there's a blinding pain in the back of my head, and I stumble forward with a scream, throwing my hands to stop smacking my face on the ground.

Before I can look to see what hit me, a blow comes at my side, hard and strong, leaving me winded. I roll onto my back and slam my feet as hard as possible into my attacker, trying to get a good look at him. This is all too familiar. Too... expected. Another blow to my ribcage and I grunt, struggling for air. He shoves my face into the ground as I cry in pain. I knew I said I would take my knowledge of the money to the grave, but I wasn't *ready* to yet.

As I sob loudly, the weight of him leaning hard on my spine, my arm pinned behind my back, he is suddenly wrenched off me. I hear a few heavy, distinct thuds of flesh hitting flesh, and when I manage to rise onto all fours and crawl a safe distance away, I turn to see Alex punching the ever-loving shit out of my assailant.

He isn't who I'd expected at all, though. I'd expected Erik because he liked to come from the back and leave bruises on places where others couldn't see them, but I've never met this guy before. It is a little hard to tell now that the man's face is a bloody mess, but I know for sure it's not my ex. Erik's way shorter than this guy and just a couple of inches taller than me, whereas this guy is tall and lean. Erik's built like a tank with wide shoulders and a thick neck. Erik maintains his perfectly conditioned brown mane with two-hundred-dollar haircuts, while this guy looks like he hasn't touched his hair in a year. Erik would never be caught in such a state of dishevelment. He had to look *good* to represent his brand of expensive, illicit activities.

"Alex, stop." My voice is raspy and barely above a whisper. Maybe even if he did hear me, he still wouldn't stop. "Alex," I say louder. He's too far gone in his rage. "Alex, *please*," I beg. My voice breaks as I say it, and he looks over at me, his arm raised once again.

He stands up slowly, my attacker well and truly unconscious beneath him, beaten to purpled unrecognition. Alex's eyes are fierce and dark, his fists still clenched. "I want to fucking *wreck*—"

"I know." I sink against the closest tree and close my eyes, nauseatingly aware of every inch of pain I'm in.

Alex looks down at the man before lifting him up by the collar and looking at his face. "Do you know him?" His voice is tight and restrained. I want him to come over toward me and hug me, but I'm too scared to ask him. Not when he looks like he wants to murder everything in sight of him capable of breathing.

He must have noticed my fear because he takes a few deep, steadying inhales and crouches next to me. Then he gently touches my pale face and inspects my arms. When he moves to my ribs, I yelp. His jaw sets and that muscle next to his eye twitches in a mad staccato.

He carefully pulls my shirt up, and his nostrils flare. The veins on his neck strain, his carotid visibly racing, and he makes a move to return to the guy who's groaning in pain on the ground. I grab Alex's sleeve. "Please, stay with me." After a long second and a tense swallow, he nods and pulls his phone from his jeans pocket. When somebody responds on the other side of the line, he instructs without preamble, "I'm on the old trail to the waterfall, two miles down from the sign. Come here. Now. Or you'll have a murder case in your county." Then he hangs up. So it must be either Jake or Ken, the sheriff guy I've heard about. *Good,* I tell myself. *Law enforcement should make me feel better.*

When the man making friends with the dirt off to our left grunts something incomprehensible, Alex is next to him in a second. He silences him again with one punch and trudges back to me without a word. Crouching next to my half-curled body, he inspects my stomach, finding and deciding to examine a few nice purple bruises already forming on my torso and abdomen—touching without too much pressure. He's so gentle that I can almost tell myself that he's never been violent, even though it was put on display for me personally no less than a minute ago. I should be scared of him because I just saw firsthand the beginning of what he could do to the human body, but I'm not. I feel safe, he is here, and nothing will hurt me now. It's that naïve sensation that got me in trouble in the first place, but I can't help how I'm feeling. No more than I can help how Alex is acting.

"Where is it hurting the most?" His voice is husky, even more now than usual.

"My stomach." And my ribs. "And only a little." It's a lot.

He doesn't believe me and keeps inspecting the freshly forming bruises. When he touches my ribs, I wince. Yeah, I might have some fractures in there. The kicks were vicious, and I didn't have a chance to protect myself. Though right now, it's hard to tell because everything aches.

He doesn't look at my face and keeps his eyes trained on my body.

"Alex," I call him quietly because I'm only a foot from him while he's so far from me. He doesn't stop, so I repeat his name louder. "Alex!" Nothing. "For fuck's sake, Alex, *look* at me!"

"I can't," he grits out.

"Am I that repulsive to you?" Such strong déjà vu. My ex-husband couldn't look me in the face after he smacked me around. This finally gets Alex's attention because his scorching eyes find mine.

"If I see even a *scratch* on your face..." He cuts himself off, takes a deep breath, and concludes, "I'll end up killing this motherfucker."

Be still, my heart. The man just admitted his desire to kill another human being for me, and I'm literally ready to jump in his arms. Even the sharp pains seem to fade away. Just as I'm about to say something I'll surely regret later, the rev of a car engine cuts through the sound of our heavy breathing—mine in pain and frustration, and his under the strain of talking himself out of a killing spree.

Then, Alex's face changes suddenly. *And... here it comes.* "What the fuck were you doing here by yourself?" he shouts.

"I was jogging," I whisper weakly. Now, the idea of jogging in the forest when my violent ex is trying to hunt me down doesn't sound very smart at all.

"Jogging? You were fucking *jogging? Alone? Here?* Are you out of your mind?"

I'm back to a curled ball of fear.

A police cruiser comes into view, moving toward us and saving me from Alex chewing me a new one. A guy around the same age as Alex jumps out of the driver's seat and runs to us. He's handsome in a classic, overly perfect, almost boring way, and he looks an awful lot like Alex, just a bit more civilized version. He kneels next to me and asks in a calm, sure voice, "Ma'am, I'm Sheriff Benson. Are you all right?"

"Of course she's not fucking all right. Look at her. She got fucking attacked," Alex sneers, and I sigh.

"I don't have any broken bones, just some bad bruising. He"—I point toward the still-prone body—"might need an ambulance though."

"He's not getting shit," Alex snarls again.

"Okay, let's all calm down," the cop says, then turns to me. "Can you tell me what happened?"

I expect Alex to interrupt, but he also stares at me, waiting for an answer. *Right.* "I was jogging."

"Yeah, smart move," Alex pipes up, still angry.

"Alex." The cop cuts him off in the kind of authoritative voice that compels soldiers to obey, and it seems to work on Alex, who snaps his jaw shut with a scowl. "Go on, ma'am."

"My name is Freya." He nods. "So, I was running and got pushed from behind. Got kicked a few times." Alex lets a breath out so fast he sounds almost like a huffing bull about to charge. "Then Alex knocked him out. You know the rest."

"What is 'the rest,' exactly?" Sheriff Benson asks warily.

I look from the cop to Alex to the body lying on the ground and back to Alex. "Alex stopped him from attacking me."

The cop looks at the defeated-looking body. "Looks like he did a little more than stopped him."

"I managed to kick him a few times, too," I add quickly because I don't want Alex to get into trouble. I don't know the nature of his relationship with the cop, but he already looks suspicious of Alex having overdone the protective task a tiny bit. A faint smile crosses Alex's lips.

The cop looks at me again with a raised brow. "I'm sure you did."

"Oh, I really did. I'm small, but I still know how to kick some ass," I rush to add, but maybe overdo it a little bit because the cop stifles a chuckle before going to check on the attacker.

"He's got a pulse," he reports.

"Unfortunately," Alex murmurs under his breath, and the cop shoots him a scolding glare.

"I'll take him to the station," the sheriff concludes before addressing me specifically. "You'll need to come over there to give a statement after the hospital."

"I don't need a hospital." I already know the severity of my injuries, and I don't require a hospital stay or even an x-ray. I've had this type of bruising before. It hurts like a bitch but isn't life-threatening and heals on its own. And if I have a fracture, it'll be good to let it rest for a week or so.

"You do," Alex argues.

"Trust me, I know when I do. And that's not now. I'm fine." My words must have been the wrong ones because Alex growls. *Really* growls as if he's a wild beast, and instead of sounding weird coming from a human throat, it sounds arousing to me. *Bad, bad Freya.* "Can I just give you a statement here?"

"You can't, unfortunately." The cop shakes his head apologetically while cuffing my now mildly grunting attacker. He gives him a few slaps, and the body comes alive.

"Kenneth." Alex's voice is a bit louder than necessary.

The cop sighs. "Okay, tomorrow morning, be there. But for that, you'll come to dinner on Sunday. Mom's missing you." Shocked, I snap my head toward Alex just in time to see him clench his jaw and send a glare at the sheriff—his... *brother?*—that could start a forest fire.

"She's *not* my mother."

"She might as well be 'cause she helped raise your ungrateful ass. So don't be a dick and come to dinner. Ms. Freya can have her rest today," he summarizes, gesturing at me before turning back to Alex, "and you come to dinner Sunday. That's the deal."

I can feel Alex's rage boiling inside him, his jaw grinding back and forth. I open my mouth to agree to go to the station right now when Alex blurts out a harsh "fine."

And it makes me warm all over. He clearly didn't want to go to this dinner with his family, and there's probably a good reason why, but he agreed to it anyway. For me. Tears burn the backs of my eyes, and I blink rapidly to prevent them from falling and embarrassing the ever-loving shit out of me.

The cop's face lights up like he just won the lottery. "Great! It's settled. Now let me give you a lift wherever you need."

"Can you drive me to Justin's place?" When I ask that, his brows shoot up into the stratosphere, almost disappearing for good.

"You're staying with Justin?" He asks to confirm it, like the idea of me being there is absurd. He eyes his brother before focusing back on me.

"Yeah. Can you give me a ride?" I lick my dry lips and taste blood. The flavor isn't one that brings happy memories to mind, and I fight a flinch.

"Sure. We will drop off this specimen on the way." He grabs said specimen and forces him into the back of the cruiser with a firm hand on his head. The attacker is barely moving, let alone talking, but that doesn't seem to bother Sheriff Benson; his approach to dealing with the man wasn't completely opposite of Alex's, evidenced by the less-than-gentle way he shoves him in and slams the door behind him.

Alex comes to me, and I lift my hand in hopes that he will help me to my feet—because, as of now, the task feels insurmountable on my own. Instead, he snakes one arm around my back, the other under my knees, and lifts me up.

"What are you doing?" I exhale in surprise.

"Taking you with me." His voice is full of determination.

"Where?" I ask, my tone hopefully not sounding *too* hopeful. He just kicked me out, and I already want back in. Aren't I a glutton for punishment? My own Marquis de Sade, no less.

"Home."

"What about Justin?" I try to make my voice as neutral as possible and not to show that secretly, I so wish to be whisked away from my problems in his strong arms.

"Forget about him."

"What are you doing, bro?" comes from the direction of the cruiser.

"She'll be staying with me. I'll drive her to the station tomorrow," he declares to Sheriff Benson—I can't bring myself to even think of him as Kenneth yet, not that he's invited me to—over his shoulder.

I glance briefly at the cop, and a small smile of satisfaction is spread over his lips. Whole dang town of matchmakers. Donna first, then Justin, and now Benson.

"Okay, then. See you tomorrow and Sunday. It feels like Christmas came early!" He salutes me with a wide smile on his face and hops into the cruiser.

"Put me down, Alex," I request, meaning for my voice to sound firm but instead sounding soft and plaintive.

"No."

"You can't carry me all the way to your house," I try again.

"Says who?"

"Nature, for one," I reply. "I weigh... a lot of pounds, if you must know." I cut myself off before I spill all the beans. Some things must remain secret.

"I don't need to know." His pace is brisk and steady. And I'm a hundred fifty-five pounds of bones and other stuff jangling around in this fabulous body of mine.

"Alex, please put me down. I really don't feel comfortable like this."

He stops immediately. "Why? Are you in pain? Am I hurting you?" His eyes roam over my face.

"No. I just feel bad that you have to carry me like I'm some... victim." There, I said it.

He finds my gaze and holds it. "There is nothing I want more right now than to hold you like that."

"Why?" I whisper.

"Because it's the best bet to ensure I don't double back to trick my brother and kill the asshole who hurt you." He sounds so serious that, somehow, I don't doubt him for a second.

"Okay," I reply quietly, tightening my hold around his neck.

"Besides that, I've carried heavier people for longer distances." Right, his training for the navy must have been brutal. "And the house isn't that far from here. About a mile or so."

"How is that possible?"

"You'd gone pretty deep into the woods, Frey. Plus, if you take the road to my house, it snakes all over the place, but from town, a straight walk through the forest is way shorter." Yeah, for a mountain man, maybe. For normal people, we need to Uber there. I relax in his arms, still trying to hold off at least some of my weight.

Chapter Eleven

A**LEX**

It's slow progress, but I manage to half carry, half drag Freya back to my house. It's only slow because she insists that she can walk herself but winces the whole time she does it. I carried her from the place of the accident, but then she began spitting some nonsense about being heavy and insisted on walking by herself.

"Can you just let me carry you?" I snap, my nerves getting the better of me.

"I am *fine*."

"You are *not*."

She glares at me, and we continue on this slow, limping torture. It's a surprising relief to have her back in my sights again. I'd spent the previous two nights lying sleepless, letting the panic wash over me. I let her out of my sight, and she got hurt. I knew I'd let her down eventually, like I do with others, but *this* level of "down" could've rivaled the loss of my unit.

She limps again, and my patience finally snaps. I gather her into my arms, and despite her protests, I keep carrying her. She finally quiets, and we walk in silence, thank fuck. It's better this way, or I'll say something I'll regret later. In fact, I should say something because it's the right thing to do after the traumatic experience she's just had, but all more or less coherent thoughts have escaped my mind, leaving only bright-red rage stirring inside. Freya sniffles quietly, and all the anger dissolves.

"We'll get him," I promise her woodenly, trying to focus on getting her back to my house and not turning around and finding the dickhead that ordered this. "The one who's looking for you."

She gives me a weak smile but doesn't say anything.

The house comes into view, and Freya relaxes. "I'm sorry," I whisper when we're on the steps.

She tilts her head up and studies me. "For what?"

She's really going to make me spell it out for her? "Everything," I clarify simply. "Can you push the door?" She gets the handle, and I walk inside and gently deposit her on the couch. I get an ice pack for her ribs—she swears they aren't fractured, but they're definitely at least bruised. She yelps as I place it on her skin and glares at me, but she doesn't tell me to remove it.

"We'll have to get your things back from Justin's."

There's a softening in her expression, and I'm surprised at the jealousy that rises in my chest. Freya isn't mine, but she sure as hell shouldn't be Justin's. He's got a shit-ton of women falling at his feet, and he would never understand a woman like Freya, ready to fight at the first sign of becoming caged again. A woman who's only just tasted freedom, I can tell. A woman too pure for the likes of him. Or of me.

"I know," she says softly. "I want to speak to him anyway."

"Yeah, about how he let you out of his sight, and you got attacked?" I sound a little hypocritical for a guy who let her out of *his* sight.

"It's not his fault, Alex," she growls again, and that jealousy rears its ugly head.

I pretend I'm not interested in her answer but still ask. "Did you sleep with him?"

"With *Justin?* Are you insane? Why would I?" She denies it so instantly that her posture stiffens, and she immediately begins to pant—she must have jostled her ribs. I tighten my grip on her, trying to ground myself from the ever-rising tide of anger inside.

"Because you spent a couple of nights in the same place?" I can't smoothen my voice, and it comes out as a rough accusation.

"You and I spent a couple of nights in the same space, too, and managed not to ravage each other." She stares at me with round eyes until I feel the heat rising up my right cheek; it would be on both had I not lost the ability on the left. "*No*, I didn't sleep with him because *neither* of us wanted to," she finally states. The relief in my gut is palpable. "More than that, we didn't even think about that! I mean, he's gorgeous and treats me with a modicum of respect, but no. I didn't. There are no feelings there whatsoever."

"Good." That's all I offer because I don't have an explanation for why I needed to know.

One of Freya's brows jerks up practically to her hairline. "Are you *jealous*, Alex?"

"Right," I drawl, as if it's a joke to even think of me being jealous over her, and the light in her eyes dims a little.

Her expression is impassive, but disappointment is too evident in her gaze. "Yeah, it was too much of me to assume. I'm sorry."

After her admission, I have to physically restrain myself, turning a dark glare to the view through the window. I want her eyes to shine again, especially after the day she had. But I can't, it's just not who I am—to admit defeat is *physically* painful for me, and accepting my growing feelings for her means defeat. For some people, feelings are their way of living; for me, it's my way of dying. Once upon a time, I let myself believe that I had a family, but then it was ripped away from me by guns and explosions. I won't let myself feel again. Never.

And even if I do ever feel again, I'll squash the sensation as I would a bug because if my brothers didn't get a chance to live, why should I? And being an asshole to everybody around me ensures I won't get the chance.

FREYA

I stay on the couch after my embarrassing moment with the jealousy thing while Alex locks himself up in the bathroom. When he emerges with a clouded expression on his face, I already know the evening isn't going to be getting any better.

"Do you know him?" Alex asks while pouring us both a whiskey in the kitchen.

Here is the moment I make a choice.

"No." I decide on a half truth. And I'm not even lying—

I *don't* know the guy. It's just that the way he executed the whole thing feels... familiar.

"The way he came at you... It seemed personal. Like he was doing it to *you*." He regards me with his full attention now. "Why are you here, Freya?"

I don't think he is asking about me chilling in his house. I hesitate and chew the corner of my lip.

"I need to know," he continues after a silent moment. "If I don't know the threat, I can't protect you." He sounds tired, and it's not even midday.

"I don't need protection," I dispute stubbornly.

"You do." He doesn't look at me anymore.

I can't share much with him, so I choose an avoidance tactic, hoping it will pass by. "Can you drive me to Justin's?"

He throws his arm out and knocks over the lamp that's been standing on the small side table, sending it to the floor. He's been taking his shit out on lamps a lot lately, though luckily, this one doesn't shatter. Unfortunately, my long-conditioned instincts kick in, and I react without giving my body permission, curling into a protective ball. His head snaps to me, and he jumps from the couch. He strides over to the wall and plasters himself flat against it. "See, right there. *That's* why I didn't want you to stay here." He presses the heels of his hands into his eye sockets and pushes hard.

Once I've gathered my wits, I stand up and walk to him. I'm not sure what I'll do when I reach him, but my heart demands I be near this broken man. *Maybe we can be broken together*, it sings quietly. He still hasn't removed his hands from his eyes. I reach out to him and wrap my arms around his torso, my head coming to rest on his chest like before. His heart beats loudly. I should feel like a fool, but I don't. Even when he doesn't hug me back. When I've gotten my share of this one-sided, healing hug in full, I pull away from him, but just then is when he returns my embrace and holds me even tighter.

I understand that I'm walking a very fine line here. The line where the victim is not simply a forthright victim anymore, but a Stockholm subject who comforts their abuser. Trust me, I know. I've been there. But this feels different. This *is* different. He isn't trying to place blame on me; it seems like his self-loathing mode is fully engaged. And no matter how hard I try to see all the warning signs—God knows they are there—I don't see an abuser. I see a broken man who can't put himself back together. Or maybe he doesn't want to. Isn't it the most delicious challenge for any woman?

"You need to tell me what you're running from," he asks in the throaty voice I've come to love. I try to pull back, but he holds me tighter.

"My ex-husband." My whisper is barely audible.

His body tenses. "You're married?"

"Did you miss the 'ex' bit there?" I pull away again, and he lets me go this time. "I'm not anymore."

"Did he hurt you?" His voice drops even lower.

"Yes. But it's been a long time." I'd work on the definition of *a long time*. "Now, I'm free."

"And that asshole in the woods is *not* him?"

"No." I play with the idea of sharing my thoughts with Alex. It couldn't get any worse than it is. "But I think he was hired by him," I admit.

"Why?"

"I might have or might not have walked out from the marriage with a lot of money." I look anywhere but at him—that wonderful picture on the wall beside the fireplace seems ideal. It's a huge oil drawing of a lonely house on a mountain hill next to a small river, surrounded by a blooming green forest. The picture has a dark, depressing vibe, but the house has two windows lit, and that alone gives hope to a whole picture of sadness. Huh, sounds familiar. "And some information that might or might not be related to some sort of illegal activities."

"Define *a lot*." Alex brings me back to the present from a lonely house in the picture.

"A few million. *Many* few." I give him a small smile. Alex's eyes widen.

"Okay. Wait up." He holds his hand up. "So, you got a divorce settlement?"

"Not exactly." Oh, this is not going to go well. I can smell the ashes in the air already. He folds his arms across his chest, waiting for an explanation. I take a deep breath and tell my story. Well, at least the short version of it. "He opened up an offshore company, and I was the CEO there. Without even knowing it," I mutter under my breath. That was a pleasant revelation after the divorce was settled. "When I got a divorce and a restraining order, I also got millions stashed in my bank account that I didn't even know existed. And here I am, stuck in Little Hope with no tire. Should have bought a regular Civic, dang it." I spread my arms as if to say, *That's all you're going to get, buddy*. But Alex has other ideas. Of course.

"Hold on. You missed something there." He holds his index finger up.

"I did?" I take a misstep back and almost fall on my butt, but Alex grabs my hand and pulls me up. My body twists, I nearly fall, and my poor abused torso screams in agony. The adrenaline is wearing off. He must have noticed the pain on my face because he curses and urges me back to the couch. He grabs my abandoned ice and presses it back to my stomach. This time, he holds it himself.

"I'm waiting."

"He needs his money back. And I'm not giving it back. I took it as a payment for all the shit he put me through. And other people too." I lift my chin defiantly, expecting a wave of judgment. Even to myself, I sound like a money-hungry bitch. "Besides that, I'm not giving it to him just *because*. He doesn't deserve it, it's not... clean money. I will put it to the right cause when I figure out... well, the right cause."

"And that info you mentioned?"

"I have no idea what's on there, but I have a flash drive that he's been hiding. It seemed important to him."

"And you still have it?" His forehead wrinkles.

I nod grimly.

"With you?" His brows shoot up.

"No." I accentuate the word with a shake of my head. "It's stashed in a safe deposit box."

"Good." He rubs his chin. "He doesn't have access to that, right?"

"Yeah."

"Good," he repeats. "How long were you married?"

"Six years." I look anywhere but at him. I know what I'll find if I'll look. The question why the hell I stayed with him for so long? And I don't have the emotional capacity to explain why or how. I know why. People who've been in the same boat know why. He will never comprehend the motives behind our actions. Every person has a turning point when you get tired of being slapped around, figuratively and physically. The main mystery is why we let the road to that exact point drag on so unnecessarily long.

"How old are you?"

"Twenty-seven."

"How come nobody at your work noticed that you... you had problems at home?" Isn't that the million-dollar question? We're going down a very unpleasant road, and Alex's opinion of me is about to be lowered to the floor.

"People can be very...unassuming when they want to."

"Yes, they can," he murmurs. "Why didn't you do anything?" He lets go of the ice pack, and I can sense the aversion in the air.

"You don't get to judge me, Alex. You don't know my life," I snarl defensively.

"I don't judge. I just can't understand." He scratches the back of his head. "I really can't. Why did you stay with him for so long?"

"None of your business," I hiss. I might be overreacting, but I've seen enough to know a judging person when I see one, and Alex is being one judgmental asshole. It's nearly impossible to explain to somebody who hasn't suffered the same exactly why you do what you do. It's not only about abusive relationships. It's about everything. Like, for example, I cannot fully understand what he went through, regardless of how hard I try. And only when I find myself in the same shoes or vice versa, then and only then can we talk the same language.

"Wanna share with me how you got your scars?" I wave at his chest, waiting for him to say something, but he doesn't, of course. "Yeah, didn't think so." The hurt inside my chest is stirring on its own, even if he hasn't accused me of being a weak person, but allegations in the air are palpable. The following silence is suffocating, and my labored breathing is the only sound.

"We were on a mission," he says quietly, and I snap my head toward him, straining my ears to hear. "Four of us. We were a family, and we all had some fucked family situation at home, so we stuck together and weren't planning on ending our careers early. We blindly followed the orders, as usual, because that's what we were taught to do. But that time..." His breathing speeds up. "That time... intel wasn't right. And *they* knew it." There is so much hate in that word. "God, they knew it and sent us in anyway." I touch his hand, but he moves it from me. I try not to take it personally because he's reliving his own hell, even if I want so badly to comfort him. "Archie and I came back. Four in and only two out." He stops and closes his eyes. His jaw is set. The desire to touch his skin and feel that he is alive and here is palpable, but I refrain. "Archie got it worse than me, though. He... he's not the same anymore."

He doesn't say anything else, so I nudge him softly. "That's where you got hurt on this mission?"

"Yeah. Was in the hospital for six months and did a few surgeries. Then came back here." He shrugs a shoulder.

"They released you? The army, I mean." I remember Jake saying about Alex's unfortunate discharge from the Navy.

His chuckle is dark. "The navy. They *dishonorably* discharged us both." He spits the words out.

"Why?" I didn't mean to exclaim so loud, but my voice is higher than I anticipated.

"We weren't quiet when we gave our statements. Not quiet at all." He shakes his head as if in disbelief and chuckles again, but there's no humor in it. "And they made us quiet."

"I'm sorry that you went through that. I truly am." I touch his thigh with my finger and quickly retrieve it. "But I still don't understand why you're hiding here on the mountain from people."

He raises a brow at me. Yeah, that sounded a little hypocritical. I sag into the cushions.

"Do you keep in touch with Archie?" He doesn't say

anything, so I take a glimpse at him and see that he's shaking his head. "Why?"

"We'd just remind each other of what happened."

"Does he feel the same?"

He scowls at me, but I'm getting immune to his bad mood. "I said I haven't talked to him."

"You didn't exactly say that." He glowers at me in his typical manner. "What? You didn't. You just said you don't keep in touch now. Maybe you talked a year ago. Or three."

"No, we haven't. Since we both got released." He presses the ice back to me, but I push it back.

"No, that's enough. Or I'm going to become an ice cube."

"You cold?"

"A little." As if on command, I shiver.

"Here. Take that." He passes a fluffy throw blanket to me, and I wrap myself in it. For such a hermit, he sure has a lot of cozy stuff. I would like to see Alex strolling through Home Goods looking for stuff for his cabin—that'd be something to record and watch on a bad day instead of cute cat videos.

We sit in silence until a car screeches outside to a stop, followed by a heavy pounding on the door. I shudder instinctively. I know the same guy won't come anywhere near me while Alex's here, but the memory is still too fresh, even though it's temporarily tempered by Alex's presence.

"Alex, open up!" It's Justin's voice. Alex walks to the door and opens it halfway. He doesn't ask anything, just watches Justin. It's interesting, considering they are, or were, best friends. It looks like Justin is trying to stick around—well, he *tried* before Alex went ahead and messed everything up by being an asshole to him, me, and Jake.

Justin pushes him out of the way and enters agitatedly.

When he notices me on the couch, he is next to me in three long strides. "Damn it, Freya. I almost fucking died when Ken told me about the attack. Are you okay?" He holds my chin with two fingers, trying to inspect my face. "Where are you hurt?"

"My stomach," I admit.

"Is it bad?" Genuine concern laced with worry drips from his voice. And a little bit of guilt.

"No, I'm fine." He gives me a suspicious look. "No, really. I'm fine."

"The fuck you are." Alex comes to stand next to Justin. "Where were you and Jake when she was attacked?" Oh, no, he did *not* just ask that, but before I can say anything, Justin pushes Alex back and yells back in his face.

"Where the fuck have *you* been? Hiding in your cabin like always?"

Alex's jaw starts moving side-to-side, and I'm looking for an escape pod from this about-to-blow spaceship. They are both excessively big guys, and if they go at it right here, I'm fucked. My heart starts racing as a well-developed habit of fleeing when the tension builds up in the room begins to spike in my chest. Alex's looking ready to explode, but his shoulders drop in defeat, to my utter surprise. It's like watching an inflated balloon being poked with a needle. Oh, no, no, no.

"Look, guys, I'm a big girl, and nobody is responsible for me. But I am incredibly grateful to both of you for all your help." I try to stand up between them, and they let me, separating enough to luckily ease the mounting tension in the room. The more distance between them now, the better. I offer them both a reassuring smile when the door bursts open without a knock. Kayla flies through.

"Oh my God, I was so scared!" She runs to me and

envelops me in the tightest hug. If I didn't have broken ribs, I sure as hell have them now.

I hiss in pain on impact. "A little less force, maybe?"

"Oh my God, I'm sorry. I'm so, so sorry!" She lets me go, then hugs me a bit more gently. And to my surprise, tears start pooling in my eyes. I guess all the stress finally got to me, and my mind decided to let it go when a friendly face showed me some kindness. I'm not used to either—friends or kindness. People giving a shit about me. So I hug her back and hide my face in the crook of her neck. She smells good, like fresh strawberries. She gently rubs my back up and down.

"What the fuck are *you* doing here?" Justin pulls me out of this wonderful, purging bliss.

"What?" I ask, confused, but he isn't looking at me. No. His stare is fixed on Kayla, and easy-going Justin's gone. He's replaced with some sort of an alien asshole version. He's glaring at her like she just committed a crime right here and laughed about it. That's the second time I've had the pleasure of witnessing this old feud and the first when it's so severe. Well, not exactly a feud—more like a one-sided dislike.

"I'm visiting my friend," Kayla answers calmly.

"Like you have those," Justin laughs, and it's bone chilling. I take my words back—not dislike, but hatred.

"You wouldn't know." Kayla shoots back, and even though I don't fully understand the meaning, Justin's face changes. It's become even darker. And before something bad happens and the rest of us will need to clean the blood off the walls, I pipe up, looking cheerfully at everybody. "Tea, anyone?"

Alex's head snaps to me. "My house is not a fucking tea party."

"It is now." I walk to the kitchen and pull Kayla with me. I look back to see what Alex and Justin are doing—they're staring at each other in silence, but the hostility is gone. That's all I can hope for.

"Thank you for coming. Really. Thank you. I didn't even think that somebody would want to visit me." I look at Kayla's face, and she looks sad and hurt. "I don't know what happened back there, and I'm really confused. Has something happened between you two?"

"No." She shakes her head vigorously. "I told you, that's how he is with me."

"That you did." I mull it over. I saw him being not very nice to her, but *this* goes way beyond.

"Yeah." She smiles sadly, and I see that despite how Justin treats her, she still has a massive crush on him. That's just how the majority of women—myself included—operate. We just can't simply walk past a good ol' asshole, figuratively speaking. "And about the visit, I think you underestimated our little town. I've heard Donna is making a special batch of donuts for you. And Marina sent you your favorite Lonely Kurt, but I ran here so fast that I forgot it on the counter." She gives me a sheepish smile.

"Really?" My eyes must be wide like saucers. "How does she know, though?" Kayla just laughs, and I wave my hand at her. "Right, forget I asked. But it's just... so unexpected. Why would somebody go to so much trouble for me?"

Kayla looks at me like I just spurt hairs out of my nostrils. "Because you're one of us Little Hopers now."

"There is so much wrong with that phrase."

Kayla only laughs again and then stops. "You have no idea how scared I was, Freya. No idea." I look at her carefully and see that she's telling the truth, not just saying it for the sake of making me feel better. "I don't like seeing people getting hurt. It's just not right."

"Really?" I pointedly look at her tattoos—those didn't come with pleasure. Unless I don't know something about her.

She looks down and responds, "Those were my choice. It hurt like hell, but you didn't choose yours." She shakes her head. "Who would do such a thing?"

"Yeah." I cringe, thinking about the unavoidable conversation. "I think I know who."

I call Alex and Justin and ask them to come to join us. When Justin walks into the kitchen, the hostility level shoots through the roof again, and I roll my eyes. He's just like a teenage boy. I'd like to know one day what went wrong between them.

Justin takes a seat on the window, Alex plants his butt against the counter, and I stay at the table with Kayla.

And I tell them my story.

Chapter Twelve

F **REYA**

My mom died when I was ten. Because I didn't have any known relatives, I got thrown into the system. I was lucky enough to be only in three foster homes, and my foster parents weren't that bad. But they weren't that good either. They were just collecting paychecks for the kids they fostered. I'd never been abused by either of them, was almost never hungry, and had wearable clothes—well, relatively wearable. But I'd never been hugged by them, either.

So I met him when I aged out of the system and didn't have anywhere to go. He was ten years older, attentive, and so lovable, everything a girl with daddy issues dreams of. And I did—and probably still do—have daddy issues. My father left us when I was three, and I don't even remember what he looked like. I didn't have anywhere to go, didn't have good friends—any, really—no money to last longer than a month, and no family. And here he was, a knight in shining armor, ready to save the day. We got married two months after we met when I turned nineteen. He paid for my nursing school tuition and supported me every step of the way. I thought I had hit the jackpot.

Everything changed when I went to work. I was at the top of my class and was able to score a starting position in one of the busiest hospitals in the city. The cases were many, and the hospital was always understaffed, so I picked up more and more shifts, day or night, willing to get as much experience as possible.

One day, I came home after the night shift to find him awake. He was standing looking out the window of our expensive condo—which was not exactly ours, but his, mind you.

That was the first time he hit me because he thought I was cheating on him. Then he properly apologized and groveled for a week, showering me with love and lavish gifts. And the naïve fool I was, I forgave him. Because he said that he would never do that again, and that was just one weak moment of insanity when he got caught up in jealousy. I believed him. And I'd been believing for four years after that. Then, it was so difficult to break that cycle that I couldn't even find the end of it anymore. He threatened me so I'd leave my job and focus on our family. He wanted a child. But I refused to quit what I'd worked so hard to do— and I would've died before bringing a child into a home ruled by a monster like him.

Especially once I got a sniff of his illegal business. Our child would never be safe; he or she could always be used as leverage against Erik, and I didn't even know what he did. But his regular nightly trips out of town when he came back with a load of cash in a bag made me question his line of work.

Then a few things happened that aren't easy to say, and I'd had enough. I grabbed my shit and left. Turned out I didn't have much of my own stuff. He used an LLC for all our purchases, including the cars and condo, and the CEO of this LLC was not him but a thirty-year-old brunette who had been fucking my ex for years.

I filed for a divorce. He tried to contact me a few times, but I wanted to deal with him only through lawyers. Then the threats started. And I filed a restraining order. He tried to get to me a couple of times, but he was hauled to jail due to a violation of the order. That seemed to teach him a lesson, but not for long because he had friends everywhere, and somebody helped him out of jail, of course. But after that, he stopped for some time. Then his CEO—I cringe, holding back the vomit that might come up—tried to do the same. Another restraining order. Sign here, please.

At the proceedings, I didn't fight for anything. The only thing I wanted was my freedom. And I got it.

But only for a few weeks. He started stalking me, and I could never get any proof of it, so I couldn't report a violation. I knew that he might have figured I had the flash drive at that point and wanted it back. And to punish me, of course—he definitely wanted to punish me.

So I left the city, knowing there would be no help from the cops, given how he seemed to own half of them, evidenced by how easily he could get out of assault charges. The cop who found me *that* day testified against him but then withdrew his statement without a valid reason. Well, I knew the reason, he knew, and the judge knew, but nobody could do anything. So, I went to Pittsburgh. Fled there, really.

I was scared to get a nursing job because that would be the first place he would look, so I found a waitressing gig at a hole-in-the-wall bar, where I was happy and free. My happiness didn't last long, though, because he found me. Stupid me, I still was using my old phone number. Right before I was about to cancel my plan, I got a weird phone call from a rival of his asking for a meeting. I knew the guy and respected him, and on the phone, he seemed like he wanted to share some good news with me. I didn't know if it was a trick, so I set up a meeting in a public place.

Turned out my ex scammed this guy, and as a gesture of goodwill toward me, he told me about the offshore company that happened to be under my name. And as the sole beneficiary, I am a multi-millionaire now.

He offered to buy everything from me for a price remarkably close to the market. I figured that by selling to him, I wouldn't lose anything, especially when five minutes ago, I didn't even know what I had. So I sold it to him, put the money into a trusted firm that deals with it now, and memorized all the information about numbers and safe combinations. I'm the only one who has access to it. What I don't say is that I also stashed the names of big people involved in money laundering in the same safe.

And now, I have more money in my account than I can spend and more information than I know how to handle. And I'm looking for a good cause to put it into and a good place for me to settle along the way. Whichever comes first.

Chapter Thirteen

F**REYA**

"So, what's the first thing you did when you got all that money?" Justin asks excitedly when I finish telling my story. By now, everyone has seated themselves at the table, with Kayla tapping her fingers on the surface of it, Alex leaning back on his seat with his arms crossed, and Justin resting his elbow on the back of his chair, all studying me.

I feel my cheek redden. "I got a car."

"That piece of shit?" His eyes bug out.

"It is not!" Alex and I exclaim simultaneously, and Kayla chuckles, which causes Justin to scowl at her, which causes me to scowl at him, which causes him to scowl back at me, which causes Alex to scowl at him. So much scowling, and just because Justin is an overgrown ass.

"Chill, Justin," Alex says in that calm, steady voice he probably used in the navy. I'm expecting Justin to blow up, but instead, he surprises me by clenching his jaw, and then we all watch him trying to relax. It's adorable, really.

I take a quick look at Kayla—she's shifting her butt from side to side on the seat and glancing at the door. If that's not the first sign of a person looking for an escape route, I don't know what is.

So, I change tactics.

"This car, if you must know, is the *Supernatural* car."

Kayla chuckles again and tilts her head in Alex's direction. "Well, aren't you a perfect match?"

Now it's Alex's turn to be embarrassed. His undamaged cheek pinkens, and he must have nudged Kayla's foot under the table because she laughs louder. Justin tenses more and moves his eyes from Kayla to Alex and back. And just now, I notice that Alex isn't wearing his goddamn default cap. He's comfortable and doesn't need to hide. Justin, I get it. Me—I've seen it. Kayla, on the other hand? *Huh, interesting.* Something ugly stirs inside my chest, and I try to press it down before it lifts its awful head. Damn jealousy. Because of a guy who I just met. To a girl who sincerely worries about me and genuinely wants to be my friend.

I shake my head and notice Justin's stare at Kayla. That is *so* not hate. Then I look at Alex—I must have been looking at Justin for too long because Alex's expression is clouded, and his nostrils are flared. Then his gaze slowly moves to Justin. Not jealous, my ass.

I hear a stifled sound to my right: Kayla is covering her mouth with her hand, trying to suppress laughter. Her eyes twinkle, and I know she notices all the awkwardness at the table. "What about that tea?" she asks nobody in particular.

"Yeah, Alex. What about that tea?" I ask him.

"What about it? You know where everything is," he tells me with a wave of a hand, and it warms my heart. He just gave me free rein to roam around his kitchen in front of his... let's call them *friends*. Because I just totally shared my life story with them, so they'd better be both of our friends, or I'd have to draw penises in Sharpie on their foreheads while they sleep.

I put the kettle on and prepare enough mugs. Everything here is the love child of West Elm and Pottery Barn, and even the dishes all match each other. For easily the tenth time, I wonder who designed this place. While I'm busying myself with getting the tea set up, awkward silence again hovers over the table.

I place the tea set—a very lovely one, white with gold trims—on the table and pour green matcha for everyone. When I asked, nobody cared, and that's why everybody will be drinking what I want now. The silence is suffocating.

Justin and Kayla are looking everywhere but at each other. I feel awkward because I don't know what happened between them, but I still pick Kayla's side. Girl power, yay. Only Alex seems fine. He leans back and watches my face. I wink at him, and one corner of his mouth hikes up.

"All right." Kayla breaks the silence finally. "What do we do now?"

"What do you mean? It's none of your business what we're going to do," Justin pipes up.

"Justin, shut up. It's none of yours either." I cut him off. "You need to stop this shit. I appreciate everything you've done for me, I do, but you need to leave if you can't keep your anger in check."

"I second that." Alex slightly turns toward Justin and adds in a quiet voice, "You need to let it go. It's been a long time." Justin's face begins turning red, his jaw ticks, and his eyes are focused solely on Kayla. He looks about ready to blow up—I probably shouldn't have said anything when I don't know the whole story, and just a simple mention of her name causes such a violent reaction. I glance at Kayla and freeze; she looks like she doesn't know the story either because she looks utterly confused. Shocked... and hurt. I get a bad taste in my mouth about her simple crush on him not being so simple. Oh, my poor Kayla.

A wave of protectiveness rises up in my already-tight chest. I turn to Justin and open my mouth to rip him a new one when Alex stops me with a quiet "Freya" and a shake of his head. I take a deep breath and count to five, and only after then do I talk. "Justin, Kayla is my friend. To be honest, probably my only friend." He looks hurt at my statement. "What? Don't give me that face. I meant a girlfriend. I've never had those. And I'm not about to lose her because you scared her away. Can you be civil for one day? For me, please. I got hurt today." I make my lower lip quiver to prove my point, and he sighs in defeat. Alex's chuckle eases up the atmosphere.

"You little minx." Justin laughs, takes a sip of his tea, then spits it back out. "What the hell is that?"

I scowl at him. "It's called green tea, jerk. Don't waste a good product."

"That tastes like piss on grass." He looks about ready to vomit.

"And you know how that tastes... how, exactly?" I widen my eyes at him, and he laughs again.

"Busted. Do you have coffee?" he asks me.

"Alex does." I point at him.

"Yep. It's in the same spot," Alex answers while throwing brief glances at Kayla.

Justin gets up and goes straight to the cabinet with the coffee supplies. He looks like he knows where everything is, and it makes me a little happier that Alex's friend looks to be back in his life. Even for only a little while. To think of it, I'd probably take the beating again if it meant that Alex wouldn't be alone anymore.

I've only known him for a couple of days, for God's sake. Where is all this coming from?

But then I look back at Kayla, who's retracted into her own shell and not smiling anymore, and I want to punch Justin in his handsome face. I take Kayla's hand and pinch her skin lightly.

"What was that for?" she hisses. At least I got some reaction from her, and some fire returned to her eyes.

"To wake you up, sleeping beauty." I stick my tongue out at her, and she cracks a smile.

"Amateur," she says, which causes me to stick my tongue out even farther. "Yes, c'mon, show me your glands."

Justin returns to the table, and just like that, all happiness evaporates. He is the definition of a party pooper if I ever met one. "Is he coming after you?" he asks as he settles back into his seat, his tone serious.

I sigh. "Most likely, but he's coming after the money."

"I think it's safe to say that you are not to go anywhere alone."

"I was fine before, Justin. I'll be fine after." What I leave out is that I'll be fine in another place. When he finds me, I move. I'm picking invisible dust particles from my lap when I feel heated stares at me. I look up and see three sets of eyes burning holes in my face.

"You're planning on leaving, aren't you?" Kayla's quiet voice is filled with sadness.

There is no point in lying; I've known these wonderful people—*Justin, you're destroying the statistics here for a moment*—for only a couple of days. I've left my whole life behind me in a heartbeat, and yet here, I don't feel the same lightness. "Yes."

"The fuck you are," Alex thunders, and I jump on my stool, startled. His anger issues aren't my best bet on survival at the moment, especially when he is the perfect trigger for my dormant flight instincts. The coffee machine beeps, drawing my attention from the murderous face before me.

"Yeah, I don't think you're leaving, Freya," Justin adds and stands to get his coffee. "To stay here is your best bet."

"And what will I do here? For God's sake, I can't even find a motel to stay in. And besides, I can't keep bringing my problems to your doorstep. They're only going to get worse." I throw my arms in the air too suddenly, and it stirs my bruises. Alex must notice my wince because his eyes become slits. "Haven't you heard when I said he's shady? Like, a *lot* shady."

"Doesn't matter." Justin shrugs. "We'll always be around. Let him come."

I roll my eyes. "I appreciate it, Justin, I really do, but it's my problem that neither of you needs to be involved in. Trust me, he's nasty; you don't want to cross Erik." At the mention of his name, Alex's jaw audibly clenches, and I'll be impressed if he has any teeth left after.

"You'll stay with me," he commands.

I give him a bored look. "Yeah, and how did that work out for us before?"

"You're staying with me. End of discussion." He leans back and crosses his arms over his chest.

I don't even know whether I should punch him in the face for his Neanderthalian alpha tendencies or smack a kiss on his lips. I focus on them as I keep thinking that the latter is winning by a long shot. The corner of his lips tips up when he catches my stare on his mouth. I scratch my cheek with my middle finger, and he laughs.

"Jesus Christ," Justin interjects. "I didn't know you had it in you anymore."

"What?" I ask.

"The Grinch over there laughing." Justin waves at Alex. "I thought he forgot how to do that."

"Fuck off." Alex flips him off, and Justin laughs.

"I think you should stay, Freya," Kayla says. "I honestly can't imagine anybody better who can protect you." She gestures at Alex and then points the finger at her own chest. "And little ol' me here has a shotgun. I can sleep on the couch and guard your asses."

I try to imagine Kayla with a shotgun, and it's not that difficult, honestly. The girl's got some serious badass vibes. Just when Justin is not around, that's all.

"I feel safer already." I smile at her.

"You should be. My trigger finger never wavers."

"Little Hope is just as good as any other place." Justin shrugs his shoulders, surprisingly not commenting on Kayla's words. "If you were planning on finding something, why not settle here?"

I stop breathing, dumbfounded. Why, indeed? I peek at Alex—his posture is relaxed, forehead lines smooth, a corner of his lip lifted. "I have enough space, you know," he says.

"Do you, now?" I quirk a brow, referring to our first encounter and my escape-slash-eviction from his house.

"I'm the lesser of two evils at the moment."

I sigh. It's not right the way he sees himself.

"All right, it's decided then. You stay here. I'll bring your suitcase." Justin leans on the back of his stool.

"Trying to get rid of me so fast?" I reach over to pinch his arm.

"Yeah, you snore louder than your old piece of shit on four wheels." I pinch him harder. "Ouch, fine, fine! She's all right for an old lady." I shake my head—what a dang joker. He stands up, washes his cup, and comes back to the table. "I need to go, got a few cars getting dropped off today for a big job."

"Racing again?" Alex asks.

"Nah, just fixing them cars for a good buck."

"You aren't back into it, are you?" A genuine concern rounds the edges of his voice, and I'm mentally doing a happy dance, celebrating Alex's coming out of his shell.

"Nah, man. I was young and stupid once, but I'm not anymore."

"Doubt that." Alex chuckles, and Justin punches his arm. Alex swats it away and laughs harder. Is that a clue as to why Justin went to jail in the first place? Alex's smile dies when he says, "I hope you're really done, Justin."

Justin sobers up and nods. "Okay, gotta go. I'll drop your stuff in the evening." He kisses the top of my head and leaves. I'm speechless. Nobody's ever done that before. It was so... tender and brotherly. I feel my eye swell and start blinking rapidly. It doesn't help, so I jump up to action and clean the table. I don't think I succeeded in hiding my true emotions because Kayla clears her throat and draws Alex's attention from me.

"I don't know why you always wear that stupid hat. You look like a superhero," she says, and I almost drop a teacup on the floor. Carefully peeking at Alex, I wait for a giant volcano to erupt, but instead, he just pats her head. "You were always too mouthy for your own good, Kayla."

I watch oh-so-carefully the way they interact because I want to choke the slithery snake of jealousy stirring in my chest. I hate that evil bitch, I hate her, but I can't do anything about that. With every second of their comfortable being with each other, I choke on it more. My movements are stiff, and Kayla must notice it because she tells a story that is supposed to be for my benefit, I just know that. "Alex was always the only one who saw me as more than trailer trash"—Alex tries to protest at her choice of words, but she silences him with a wave of her hand—"so he stuck up for me all the time when we were in school. Sort of like a big brother would." She accentuates the words, pointing out the real relationship between them, and I feel better. I mouth "thank you" to her, knowing she'll understand.

When Kayla leaves, I turn around and stay by the door in awkward silence. Alex is still sitting at the table, checking his phone. "Apparently, we're having dinner on Sunday, and everybody's coming." A heavy sigh. "I hate those dinners. I'd rather pull my wisdom teeth without anesthesia. Again." He shakes his head.

"Okay. Sorry about that. I hope you won't suffer too much." I'd kill for a family dinner where people are dying to see me at the table.

He finally lifts his head from his phone and looks at me. "Oh, no, no, no. You don't get it—*we* are having a family dinner. You're coming."

"What? Why?" I try not to show how excited I get at the prospect of a family dinner. Any family dinner. How pathetic am I?

"Apparently, my brother's been running his mouth, and now everybody wants to meet the woman worthy of me agreeing to this damned torture. But you were coming anyway, even if he didn't say a word. I'm not gonna suffer there alone." He snorts at the last sentence.

"Okay."

"Okay?" He looks confused.

"Yeah. What else do you want me to say?"

"I don't know, it seems like you're almost happy to go."

"That's because I am," I say when he raises eyebrows in a silent question. "What? I haven't had many of those. Foster child, remember?" He swallows hard and rubs his face with his hand.

"Shit, Freya, I'm sorry. I didn't mean to sound ungrateful."

"But you are."

"I am what?"

"Ungrateful. You have a brother and a family who want to be in your life, and you keep pushing them out of it."

"That's 'cause you don't know the whole story. And not just one brother."

I walk back to the table and sit next to him. "What's the whole story?"

"It's too long and messy to go into detail."

"Do you have anywhere to be? Because I don't." I spread my arms as if to show that I'm all his. All of it, soul and *body* and all that, if he only advanced a little bit.

He sighs. Seems like all he does today is sigh. "Not tonight, Freya. Really, not tonight."

"Okay." I sense that this story would be too much to add to today, and I'm not pushing more because I don't think either of us can handle it now.

Alex walks quietly to his room, and I follow him. He takes clean sheets from the dresser and is about to strip the old ones, when I grab his hand. "Stop, I like the smell." His eyes are full of confusion, and I don't blame him—I just blurted out some random shit. My cheeks are heating up in a fiery blush, and I try to crawl out of the hole I fell into. "I like the smell of your cologne."

"I don't wear any," he says after clearing his throat, still looking confused.

"Oh, right." *Earth, just please swallow me whole, would you?* "Anyway, I'll sleep like that if you don't mind."

"Okay." He hesitates. I would too if I had a loose cannon on the run from their ex like me around. "I'll be here if you need me." And he leaves.

I dig through my suitcase that Justin brought from his condo and find the most unsexy pajamas I can find: a dark-red T-shirt a size too big and oversized matching pants. It's shapeless and should serve its purpose—to make me feel as unsexy as I can. Because the sexier I feel, the braver I get, and the braver I get, the more openly I salivate over Alex. That's a big no-no considering our issues and an extra problem I can do without.

After my shower, long and luxurious on my sore and tender muscles, I go to the kitchen and feel Alex's eyes on me as he surveys my choice of sleep attire. "The shower is all yours," I say without looking at him.

"Thanks," he mutters and disappears into the bathroom.

I sit on the sofa and try to focus on the TV that Alex had on, but my mind keeps wandering about what Alex is doing in the shower. The water was turned off almost ten minutes ago. I strain my hearing to know what's going on behind those doors. I wonder if he... is getting some time alone. Heck. I should have thought of that. Here's a man that is so used to being at home alone whenever he wants it, never having to censor himself for anyone around.

I get up and walk closer to the bathroom door before stepping back with a grimace when the floorboards creak underfoot.

There are a few curses and groans in the bathroom, and my mouth drops open in surprise. I cover it with my hand to stop the giggle before there is the sound of a bottle lid clattering to the floor and a frustrated sigh sounds through the door.

"Alex?" I walk and lightly rap on the door. He doesn't respond. "Alex?" I ask louder.

The door swings open, and blazing eyes are met with mine. "What?" he barks. He wears only plaid pants, the scarred side of his body glistening with something that looks like oil.

"Are you okay?"

"Fine."

"Do you need some help?"

Yeah, because this turned out so well the last time. I'm sure he's going to refuse, but instead, he surprises me with a faint "Please."

I walk inside, and with Alex here, the space feels cramped. Good thing I picked these pajamas because the shower steam and Alex's presence make me hot and very bothered. "Sit. I'll teach you how to do it yourself." He sits on the toilet as I pour a small amount of oil into the palm of his hand and massage it in, taking care to remember that it's not a body part usually massaged. His stare is transfixed on my smaller hands in his large one.

"Okay, now here, let me show you." I bring his hand up to his shoulder, keeping mine on top of his. "Small, slow circles. See? It should soften under your touch."

Then I take a step back and wait for him to repeat what I just showed him.

He looks at his hand on the burn before looking up at me, clearing his throat, and asking, "Can you do it?"

I hesitate. I want to say yes. I do. I want to be the one touching his warm skin, releasing painful knots with my fingers. But I also know that I'll have to leave, and he will be in pain again. He needs to learn.

"Yeah," I whisper anyway—the anticipation of the feel of his skin under my hands has won.

I pour more oil into my own hands while his rest on his lap. I'm slowly warming up the oil, and the wet movements of my hands are the only sounds around us.

Alex seems mesmerized by my hands. Only one small step separates us, and I take it. I begin rubbing his chest. His skin is taut and angry. He must have exhausted himself somehow because it feels even tighter than it was a few days ago. Probably from carrying my weight around. I feel guilty, so I pour more oil and put a little more pressure with a dead-set determination to ease his pain.

He doesn't say anything else, and I move my fingers to his neck, tilting his face up to mine, his green eyes searching mine as he opens them and looks at me. His pulse flutters under my hand, and I unintentionally caress it with my thumb. He swallows, and I move my palm to the front of his neck. He swallows again, slower this time, and I feel the movement. I keep caressing his pulse as it starts to beat faster while my palm rests on his Adam's apple. I press with a little more force and move my gaze to his eyes.

His next swallow is hard and raw. I move my thumb to his chin. And then to his lower lip. I press on it, and he opens his mouth. I move my thumb across his lip when his tongue darts out and licks my finger. Now it's my turn to swallow hard. He bites my finger with his teeth and sucks it in. My knees buckle, and the wetness nearly pours between my legs. I swear, it's the most erotic thing I've ever experienced in my life.

If I take another tiny step closer, I'll be standing between his legs. My eyes dart down, and here it is—the python. Then I look up. Alex's arm snakes behind my thighs and pulls me closer. With my finger still in his mouth, he licks and sucks on it. I put my other hand on his shoulder for support and to feel more... of him.

His pupils are dilated, and I almost can't see the green anymore. His hand is joined by another, and now they both crawl up to uncharted territory. When they grab my butt, he jerks me on top of him. My legs are spread over his thighs, his hold on my bottom strong.

I gently pull my thumb out and wipe his saliva over my lips. It feels dirty and hot. He follows my movement with his widened eyes and, without a word, crushes his lips on mine. The air sizzles around us as his tongue darts into my mouth and finds mine, eliciting a low moan in the back of my throat.

He tastes like mint and feels like a warm, cozy evening. His body under me feels solid and steadfast. His hands on my ass promise total control that I find horribly arousing, and when he squeezes me harder, I gasp. He uses it to deepen the kiss, stroking my tongue in an aggressive dance.

I rock my pelvis over his lap and feel his hard length beneath me, feeling his breath leave his lungs as I shift indelicately to get the right spot for the both of us.

I'm so far gone that I could come just from rocking a few more times, but I want to hold this off. My pajama pants are wet. I wouldn't be surprised if even his plaid is soaked, too.

His hand on my back pushes me harder into him, and it's almost painful, but I lace my fingers through his hair and angle him in a way that gives me better access to his mouth.

Alex stands up, me still on his lap as if I weigh nothing, and he pushes me against the wall behind me, growling into my mouth as his kisses grow sloppy. I wouldn't be able to move even if I wanted to, and to my surprise, I realize that I *don't* want to. The security I'm feeling in my soul and the safety in his arms enhance my body's desire.

He bites at my lower lip, and I whimper at the heat that floods my poor pajama pants, probably utterly destroyed by now.

He suddenly stops at the sound and lowers me to the floor, bracing his hands against the wall on either side of me. He has a massive hard-on tenting his pants, his lips are swollen, his chest is red from friction, and his eyes are wild. He looks so delicious that I unconsciously lick my lips. He groans as if in pain.

"What happened?" My voice sounds foreign to my own ears.

"You're in no position for this." His is raspy and so wonderfully low that it releases butterflies into my belly.

"I'd say I was in a perfect position." I'm still panting.

He shakes his head. "You were assaulted today. The last thing you need is to be mauled by me."

"Again, I'd say that's just the thing that I need."

"No, you don't," he says on an exhale, closing his eyes. "I haven't had sex in fucking forever."

"Again, I don't see a problem here."

"There is a good reason why I don't have sex." His nostrils flare while his gaze is trained on the wall behind me.

I wait. And then wait some more.

"I'm violent everywhere, Freya," Alex murmurs. "I've always been rough. No, more than rough. After I came back... it's worse. I can't have sex, Freya, and especially not with you. I can't do that to you. Knowing your history... I can't risk it." He shakes his head again. I knew it. I fucking knew it! Oversharing is evil in its purest form.

"Do you remember you told me you hurt somebody

before?" He nods at my question. "Was it during sex?" He nods again. Holy shit. I press the heels of my palms into my eye sockets. Just great. I escape one wife-beater just to get myself drawn to another? "Okay. How did it happen?"

"Freya..."

"How, Alex? I need to know if I plan to stay here with you." And I mean, just to sleep in separate beds.

His admission sounds tortured. "I was... rough with her."

"How rough are we talking about?" I swallow nervously.

He scratches his chin. Then scratches his ear. Then his forehead. "I'm not a small guy. And I have a lot of power. And sometimes... sometimes, I can't control it very well."

"It doesn't really explain anything. Did you hit her?"

"No! Yes!" He seems offended by my suggestion. "I don't know, Freya. I don't know what happened, but she didn't like it."

"You don't know, or you don't want to talk about it?" When I don't receive a response, I shrug my shoulders. I've had two men in my life, two. I don't trust easily, and here I am, ready to trust a large, physically intimidating man when he doesn't even trust himself. For a second there, I wanted him to take charge of everything, and I never do that. Never. Even with my ex being an abusive asshole, I submitted physically but never mentally. At least, not completely. There were moments when I was so close to giving up, but years in foster care made me grow prickles. That was another reason why my ex got crazy—he wanted a full submission during his outbursts, but I didn't give in. I want to though; I want to give up control completely, and Alex looks like a guy who would be able to take charge and, as a bonus, knows what to do between the sheets, but his story... I'm not sure I want to go there. Or need to.

"Have you heard a word I said? You don't wanna talk about that?"

"Yep." I pop the *P*. All this rubbing in the bathroom just went to waste. "I'm tired. Good night, Alex." And I go to the bedroom. No more action would be happening today, and to be frank, I'm not sure it would be a good idea either way. He might be right about this one. What is wrong with me, anyway? I can't be so horny that I want to jump in the bed with the guy who says that he hurt the last chick he slept with, can I? I need a good shrink, dang it.

Besides that, he wasn't wrong. I was assaulted today, and as the adrenaline from our bathroom encounter begins wearing off, the bruises remind me about themselves once more.

The sheets smell like Alex, but I'm so frustrated with him and more with myself that I don't even want to smell him anywhere near me right now. I toss and turn for what seems like forever before drifting off to sleep.

And *he* is there. Again.

"Hello, wife," he says, walking into the motel room I'm currently staying in just as I step out of the shower. I screech like a banshee, and he moves toward me in two big strides. Covering my mouth with his hand, he crushes me into the wall. "Did you really think you could escape me, hmm? Did you?" He brings his nose behind my ear and sniffs. "You changed your body wash." He hums to himself. "I do not approve."

I mumble into his hand that I don't give a shit what he thinks, but he just laughs, not removing his palm from my mouth. "What did you say? I couldn't hear."

A knock comes on the door. "Everything okay? We heard yelling." A gruff male voice comes through.

"We're fine, my wife just saw a mouse," Erik calls back good-naturedly.

There's silence for a brief moment, and then, "Ma'am, are you all right?"

Erik whispers to me, "You're gonna go, open the door, and say that you saw a mouse, or I'll shoot your nice neighbor right in his face. Are we clear on that?" I nod slowly. "Good." He removes the hand from my mouth and gestures for me to go.

I swallow and pad to the door. Opening it, I meet a pair of worried eyes. He's a trucker in his forties, very tired, with bags under his eyes. "Are you all right, ma'am?" He watches me carefully, and he looks like a good man. He is a good man —not many would come to check on their neighbor in a cheap motel—and I don't want anything to happen to him, so I nod. "Yes, thank you. I'm good."

My throat is dry, and I swallow. He glances behind me and then back to me, and I try to smile. "All right, then. Have a good night."

"Thank you, you as well," I reply meekly and close the door, resting my forehead on it. I know what's about to follow.

My towel flies away when Erik pulls me backward by my hair and throws me on the floor.

"You lost weight. I approve," he sneers, lecherously watching me. "Where is it?"

"What?"

"Don't play dumb with me. I know you're not very bright, but not now, Freya, not now. Where is the drive?"

"Fuck you, Erik." I look at him, smiling despite the fear.

"You little bitch!" He advances on me and delivers a kick to my stomach so brutal it causes me to curl into a ball.

He's about to deliver another when the entrance door bursts open unexpectedly, and three cops rush in with guns blazing, literally and figuratively. "Hands up!"

"Fuck," Erik mutters and steps back.

The youngest of the cops grabs a blanket from the bed and covers me with it. "Call an ambulance," he says over his shoulder, and I follow his gaze to his colleague, who mutters our address into his radio. And then I move my eyes to a trucker who's lurking behind their backs with the same worried eyes. Once I catch his eyes, I mouth a thank you to him.

ALEX

The whimpers and sobs start at about one in the morning. I'm lying awake on the sofa, as expected, trying to figure out what the fuck I'm doing. I'd been seconds away from ravishing her where she stood. I wanted to slide into her, grab those delicious hips, and pump into her until those gorgeous eyes roll back in her head. God, the way she wiped *me* over her lips. I almost came right there, imagining what else she could be wiping like that.

I slide my hands into the front of my pants to try and fend off the desire steamrolling through me. I'm so wound up that I need to close my eyes to get my thoughts under control.

Although... I open my eyes and peek at the closed bedroom door. Would it be *terrible* for a quick release of pressure while Freya is asleep? It's better than the alternative, and I don't want to be so riled up around Freya's presence for the next couple of days, and blue balls tend to do just that.

I pull my pants around my thighs and grip tight on my erection. I'd seen Freya's glances at it, and the idea of giving it to her had seemed so appealing. It still does.

Before I can lose myself in my thoughts, the commotion from the bedroom starts. I still and sit up, one hand on my dick, my ears pricked and listening for trouble.

I'm on my feet, my pants yanked back at my waist when there's a scream from the bedroom. There was no way that anyone had gotten through that window, and even more unlikely, they'd managed to sneak past me, but I grab hold of the nearest weapon I have, a table lamp, pulling the cord from the wall, and push my way into the bedroom.

She's alone. And asleep. And thrashing on my bed from side to side. I can see her form clearly through the window light; the moon is bright today, and no clouds. Freya's forehead is covered in sweat, and her pillow looks to be drenched. I sigh and put the lamp on the nightstand—carefully this time, before sitting on the edge of the bed gently. I'll just have to get rid of all the lamps in my house if they're going to have such a short lifespan around me.

"Freya," I whisper urgently, carefully resting my hand on her arm in fear of making it worse. Her bruises are visible in the moonlight, where her sleep shirt has ridden up, large, dark islands all over her pretty skin. "Freya, you're having a nightmare." But she's too out of it, so I shake her a little. "Freya, it's me." She doesn't respond and begins thrashing even more violently. I can't watch this anymore and crawl onto the bed toward her. "Freya, wake up." Nothing. So I do the only thing I can think of right now and pull her into my arms, giving her my strength to live through her nightmare and come out victorious.

FREYA

"Freya, wake up." A familiar man's voice is calling my name. *"Freya."*

I jerk awake. My body is pressed against a hard, warm, breathing surface. My skin is sleek with sweat. I grab the arm that's hugging me and hold on to it for dear life. "Alex?"

"Yeah, it's me. You had a nightmare." He's sitting on the bed with me. My side is pressed to his front. Both his arms envelop me in a mighty hug while he strokes my wet skin with his thumbs.

When my brain is fully awake, and I comprehend that it's Alex who is next to me, I relax and sink into his embrace. "Sorry." I must have been loud if he heard me from the living room and came in here.

"Don't apologize for your nightmares. Ever. It's not your fault." He takes two deep, calming breaths. "When I put my hands on your fucking ex…" He inhales deeply and exhales through his mouth. "You're okay."

"When?" I repeat. "Not if?"

He chuckles and ignores the question. "Do you want me to stay with you until you fall back asleep?"

"Can you just stay here? Maybe it's a paradox, but I feel safer when you're around."

I feel his chest expand under my cheek, and I smile to myself. Somebody likes to be a hero.

"Yeah." It's all he says and slides down from the headboard to the pillows. I move with him and nestle closer, my face pressed to his chest. He stiffens for a moment, then puts his arm under my head and tugs me into him. I'm sweaty and gross, but I don't care at the moment. Right now, all I think is that I'm safe and nobody will hurt me while Alex's arms are wrapped around me.

I take in a good, long inhale; the smell of his just-woken skin, male sweat, and just... *him* is intoxicating. And calming. He chases the shadows of my nightmare away. And the shadow of my ex is not even close to being visible behind his wide shoulders. "Sleep, Freya," he rasps and kisses my forehead. It should feel weird after our hot bathroom encounter, but it feels right instead.

I'm in so deep.

Chapter Fourteen

F REYA

I wake from the deepest sleep I've had in a long time to an almost overwhelming warmth surrounding me. My head lies on a hard bicep, and a heavy arm rests on my thigh.

My backside is pressed against Alex's front—even barely awake, I know it's Alex, the man I've known for a few short days but seem to recognize instantly. The python is present as well, and by the feel of it, it wouldn't mind snaking its way in. Not that *I* would mind that, either. So I push my butt against him, and Alex groans. The arm on my thigh digs into my flesh and holds me still.

"Don't move, woman." His voice is groggy with sleep, and I practically melt. I wiggle my ass against him. "I said, *don't move.*" In contradiction to his words, he rocks his pelvis into me and groans louder. "Evil, evil woman." He pushes himself off me and flips onto his stomach. His face is buried into the pillow as he grunts. "So evil."

I feel like a reborn Aphrodite, making a man like Alex suffer from desire. That's what he's suffering from, right? I close my eyes and try to remember this is not the right time for us to be together in *any* way. Not when I'm still looking over my shoulder for my ex or when he's still a walking pipe bomb with a short fuse. We both have to face our issues on our own, and only then can we move on with our lives. I know that. He knows that.

But I look at the man lying next to me and wish that we could be waking up like this every morning. Like a normal couple. I know that we will never be a couple, or a normal one at that, and this is pure fantasy, but there's something lovely about having that dream of being happy and content with that one person who is always looking out for you. *That's* what I want. I want a protector, but not a guard. I want a safety net, but not a superhero. I want someone I can call home who won't try to control every aspect of my life. I want a *friend*.

I look at Alex again and smile. He's still wearing only the plaid pajama pants from last night, and I'm happy that he's comfortable around me and isn't trying to hide his scars.

He rolls onto his back and pulls the comforter over his lap. It doesn't hide much but gives some comfort with the heavy covers, weighing his python down. Comfort for both of us, I suppose. It's sort of distracting. An involuntary giggle escapes me, and I widen my eyes. I'm not usually the giggling type. Alex's eyes twinkle.

"Are you laughing at my misery?"

"You turned me down, remember?" I remind him teasingly. "You wouldn't be in so much misery if you let me help you."

He narrows his eyes at me and flops his arm over his face. "Yes, well, you're making me regret everything," he mutters, and I think we're both surprised that it came out of his mouth. He clears his throat and rolls onto his side, propping himself up on his elbow. "We need to go give your statement. You should have told me about him the first day so we could have protected you better." He looks into my eyes seriously. "I won't let him hurt you again, Freya. I promise you that."

"I know," I whisper, and somehow, I *know*.

"Ken is an asshole, but this is his job, and he's a good guy. He won't make you uncomfortable."

"That's not what I'm worried about."

"Then what is?"

"It's just..." I cut myself off, thinking over carefully what to say next.

"Just what?" He leans closer, and the covers slip lower, baring his ripped stomach. My gaze dips, and I get distracted. "Freya," he says carefully, a smile in his voice.

"Right." I clear my throat, looking back up. "I just don't want to go through all that." I sigh. "Again."

His face hardens. "How many times have you done this already?"

"Once." I barely recognize my own voice. "Or twice."

"How many times did he hit you?" His voice drops to the point of growling.

"It doesn't matter now."

His jaw works, and he grabs my hand, tugging me toward him. It's supposed to be a hug, but I end up toppling and landing on top of him. I straddle his thighs, my arms around his neck and his face in the crook of mine.

"Fuck," he says, muffled. "That was a terrible idea."

To prove him right, I rock my hips, trying to get some

sort of friction on the spot between my thighs, already prepped and ready for him. Turns out, to be prepped for Alex, I just need to be in close proximity to him.

I scrape his neck lightly with my teeth, and he mutters something roughly under his breath, tightening his hold on me. I let out a breath that tickles Alex's ear, and he lets out that delicious growl of his, and, just like that, I'm high. He slowly lifts my top off, his gaze searching me greedily, and I want nothing more than to feel his lips on me.

"Fuck it." He moves quickly, so he's on top of me in a flash, his eyes hungry and his breath ragged. His eyes drop down to my lips, and he licks his. "Tell me if you want to stop."

I can't talk with all the anticipatory fire burning in my stomach, so I just nod.

He draws up onto his knees and tugs my pants down over my hips, scraping his calloused fingertips over the sensitive skin of my belly. His eyes are focused on mine, watching my reaction. He slides his hand into my panties, and his middle finger immediately finds its target, making me arch off the bed with a moan of approval. Alex brings his face closer, and I'm expecting the kiss. I'm *hoping* for a kiss, but he doesn't grant my wish. He keeps moving his finger in little circles, staying just out of reach with his mouth. His head drops to take my nipple in his mouth, and I cry out at the intensity of his talented lips.

Alex presses his forehead to mine and keeps his eyes open. I can't do the same with mine anymore, so I close them and let out an embarrassing moan, all while digging my fingernails into his shoulders. Under my hand, I feel his scars, tight and raw. He tries to pull away, but I hold on tight. He might be thinking they repulse me, but it's the opposite. Somehow, it makes it *more*—his trust in me and ability to bare his body when he seems to hide himself from the rest of the world. It makes me feel oddly special, and my feelings intensify with the feel of his fingers touching me in all the right places.

His thick finger moves and slips inside of me. "You're so wet. And so hot," he rasps, and I lick my lips again because his face is right here. So close. Just a movement away. But he doesn't kiss me. Instead, he moves his middle finger in and out and presses his thumb to the small nub of nerves. The feeling of the end is so close, just within reach, and I press my pelvis into his touch, trying to speed it up a little because I can't take it anymore. "So greedy," he whispers, and I for sure can't fucking wait, so I grab his face into my hands and pull him closer. Or pull myself closer.

It feels like he is just waiting for my permission because he moves his other hand to the back of my neck and devours my mouth. His pelvic rock over me, and just now, I remember how selfish I'm being. I drop my hand from his shoulder and follow my index finger down between his pecs. They are magnificent. Then his abs, where I can trail every bunching muscle of his six-pack with my finger. Then I pull away the waistband of his pants and slide my hand inside.

When my hand makes contact with his heated python, he exhales loudly, and his stomach muscles contract. His fingers slow inside me as I run my finger along the length. It's a powerful feeling to know that I have Alex entirely at my mercy. I'd never had this sense of control before, especially not with Erik.

It feels like Alex is giving it over to me, *letting* me be in charge.

I wrap my hand around the python, and yes, I was right. It *is* a python. So thick that my fingers don't meet. I'd be so upset if something small would be attached to the frame he possesses. To be honest, I'd love everything he has, but this right here is a lovely bonus.

I rub my thumb over the crown, and it's slick with precum. He groans again into my mouth and rocks himself into my grip, reminding me that I'm the one in charge of his pleasure. I smile into the kiss and begin pumping his length. Up and down. Up and down. Slower and faster. Slower and faster.

Our kiss becomes frantic and sloppy as we both speed up. He can sense I'm close as I drop my head back away from his mouth and groan loudly as the climax hits me, my fingers accidentally squeeze his python harder than I intended, and he comes all over my hand. Thick ropes coat my fingers and his stomach. We both pant heavily, like a fish out of water, and our eyes meet, both of us suffocating in breathless laughter. Our sweaty foreheads are resting against each other.

"That was not supposed to happen," he says through more panting.

"Yeah, bad idea," I agree eagerly.

"Very bad." He nods and pushes himself from me. I move back while trying not to drop his come from my fingers. When I'm safely off the bed, he follows me. I'm about to go wash myself when I notice him lifting his fingers to his face and sucking them into his mouth. I think I stop breathing for a moment. There is pure bliss on his face when he closes his eyes. Never in all the years, I was married did my ex-husband enjoy going down on me. He always found excuses. Always. I probably got it on our anniversary or my birthday. So, I wasn't really enjoying it, not really. How could I when I knew that it was like torture for him? But now, I can't stop imagining Alex's face between my legs, and that picture is forever imprinted in my mind.

I feel my face heating up even more than it already was, and I do something I've never done. I mean, I've done blowjobs before but never *wanted* to taste the aftermath of one. And I certainly want to know how Alex's pleasure tastes. I suck my index finger inside my mouth and remove it with a pop. His eyes go saucer-wide. He stumbles while standing in one spot, and I find it hilarious.

This new feeling of power is something I could get used to. It's new and raw, and I don't know what to do with it yet, but I feel like I'm moving on the right path.

I give him a saucy smile and go to the bathroom, swaying my hips as much as I can. When I'm closing the door behind me, he's still standing with big, round eyes.

Chapter Fifteen

FREYA

I'm sitting in the County Sheriff's office, receiving a patient, yet curious, stare from the said sheriff, who, yes, just happens to be Kenneth Benson, Alex's big brother. On the way here, Alex told me a shortened version of the overly complicated story—his words, not mine—of his extended family.

Kenneth is the eldest brother at thirty-four; he did a couple of tours as well but got out before it irrevocably impacted his life. Came back here and became a deputy until, fast forward a few years, he won an election two years ago, and now he's the sheriff. And we will be having dinner in Kenneth's "real" mother's house, where she lives with her husband, their shared father.

Turns out, Alex's father had strayed from his wife with Alex's mom, and Alex was raised by a single mother.

On the question of if his father had been in the picture while Alex was growing up, I got a few unintelligible and by no means friendly grunts, so I dropped the subject. His mom died when he was twelve, so he had no other option but to move into his father's house. And with a wild guess, I can assume that's when all the *fun* started. To lose a mom at that age—at any age, really, but especially at the time when the whole world feels against you for the first time...

Alex also has other siblings, too—well, half siblings: a sister and a brother, neither with whom he is close. Just as he isn't with anybody else either, it seems. But I'm starting to gather a picture as to why. From the way Alex talks about Stella, his father's wife, I sense she is the big bad wolf in this story—the archetypical evil stepmother lifted straight from *Cinderella*—and with that realization, I begin dreading this Sunday dinner.

When I first saw Kenneth, I didn't pay much attention to his appearance, but now I see the resemblance between him and Alex. They are both of a mighty build, both have dark hair and moss-green eyes. I'm guessing those must be his father's traits if they both inherited them. He has a few extra fine lines creasing his face in small places where Alex doesn't, like the corners of his eyes and around his mouth, and a deep groove sits prominently between his brows. I'd take another guess his job might be doing a number on him already.

Kenneth offers me a cup of coffee, and I take it just to keep my hands busy, absently rubbing my thumb over the lip of the mug, which is chipped but clean.

"Okay, Freya," Kenneth commands. "First of all, I'm so very sorry for what happened to you, and we're all sorry something this heinous happened in our town. We do expect the assailant will be locked up." Then he adds, after a pause, "After you give your statement, of course."

"Did he say anything?" I question, forcing even, relaxed breathing.

"He did," he replies, slowly and with suspicion, mulling words over.

"I see." I smile placidly at him. "Are you letting him go if he's cooperating?"

Kenneth leans over his desk closer to me. "Don't mistake this, Freya. For what he's done to you, he is not walking out of here under any circumstances. And whatever fairytale he's produced, well..." He shakes his head. "We don't believe in fairytales here."

That manages to make me feel a little better—as if the whole world isn't against me. I've been down that road, since what happens to so many abuse survivors has also happened to me: when the cops believe the abuser's story over yours because they make you look melodramatic, manipulative, and overreactive.

I take a sip of mind-bogglingly disgusting coffee and wince. Kenneth laughs. "Yeah, sorry about that. We ran out of the good stuff, and I'm sort of on Donna's shit list right now. So"—he waves his hand at my mug—"that's the only thing we have."

"It's not that bad," I try.

"Oh, it is." He chuckles.

"Yeah, it is." I smile back, small but genuine.

"If you're done flirting, maybe we can go back to that statement of yours." Alex cuts in with a bite in his voice that could slice through glass, which I notice makes Kenneth smile wider.

"Sure thing, baby brother." This only makes Alex grind his molars harder, and the sparkle in Kenneth's eye only intensifies. "So, Freya, what can you tell me about the attack?"

I let out a long exhale before explaining it. "I was jogging, he came from the back and hit me in the head."

"Have you been checked out by a medical professional?" His voice is all business.

"No."

He frowns. "You might have a concussion."

"I don't," I respond instantly, shrugging it off. "And if I do, it's mild. Nothing they can do for it anyway, just monitor it."

"You seem pretty familiar with that kind of process." His voice is unassuming, but he squints at me as he says it—I get the feeling he's trying to gauge my reaction to certain thoughts—and for a moment there, I see Alex. The way Alex squints his eyes when he's suspicious or being sarcastic. It warms my heart, and suddenly, the situation becomes just a little more bearable.

"I am a nurse." I chew the inside of my cheek. "Well, I used to be one."

"And that's the only reason?"

"For what?"

"It'll be easier for us to figure this out if you'll be honest with us, Freya." Now, he is a person of authority.

"My ex-husband was an abusive son of a bitch, so yeah, I'm familiar with bodily harm," I deadpan and don't miss the way Kenneth's face hardens at my words.

"The guy in the cell is not him, I assume?" he asks, tapping a pen on his notebook.

I grimace, thinking of Erik. Of how my body would shake if *he* were in that cell, too, so close to me. "You'd be right. But the way he acted, he was—"

"Was what, Freya?" He leans closer over the table again.

He keeps calling me by my name, and I think it's a psychological trick to force my brain to want to respond every time he does it.

"Was familiar. I think my ex sent him here. Can you give me a piece of paper?" He passes me his notepad with a clean sheet, and I scribble on it. "That's his website, it should have some basic info and his image."

Kenneth nods pensively, taking the notepad back. "Now would be a good time to tell me the whole story. If you want Alex to step outside—"

"The fuck I will." Alex strides from his corner to the table where we sit.

"If you want Alex to step outside, he will." Kenneth's voice is firm, and his unapologetic gaze is trained on his brother.

"No, he can stay," I allow with a resigned sigh. "He already knows everything."

"Okay then."

I take a deep breath and tell him a short version. "I got divorced when my ex became extra abusive. I have a restraining order against him and his girlfriend."

"Do you have them on you?"

"Yes." I dig into my bag and produce two papers that I carry with me wherever I go, rolled up tight to save space and try to keep the contents from any possible prying eyes. "Here." I pass them to the sheriff, and he quickly scans them. He grinds his jaw again, just like Alex, and I can't keep a smile from my face, even if the moment doesn't call for one.

"Okay. If you don't mind, I'll need a copy of those, and I'll send an official request to Baltimore for more information so I can better protect you." He looks up from the papers. *"Officially."* He holds my gaze steady. "Off the record, Freya: he will never touch you while you are here. I promise you that."

I nod, feeling the sting of tears threatening in my eyes. "I filed for a divorce about two years ago, but it was finalized only last year."

"Why?"

I'm sure he knows why. According to all the books about the psychology of sociopaths and abusers, they can't let go and can't accept rejection, and obsessive behavior is normal for them. "He didn't want to let me go." I shrug. "And he didn't want to let go of the money that I have."

"What money?"

"Without my knowledge, he created an offshore shell company under my name, and now I'm a millionaire. Yay," I say without enthusiasm. "I think that's the main reason why he didn't want to sign the papers. He knew about the money." Then I tell him the same story I already told the guys and Kayla—about my ex's frenemy, who approached me and bought the company from my hands, about my ex and his hoe, how I got restraining orders. And pretty much everything else. No more enigma in this girl left but a little extra about the flash drive. I wait for Alex to pipe in and remind me about that, but to my surprise, he keeps quiet. I know Kenneth is Alex's brother, and I trust Alex. But I have a love-and-hate relationship with the law, seeing as it wasn't able to protect me. Some cops were nice and helped me out big time when I was down and bloody—quite literally—but others tried to cover up Erik's crimes, so yeah, I'm on the fence here.

Kenneth looks to be pondering all this new information

about me being a millionaire. "So, you think he hired that guy to... what? Rough you up a little?"

"I dunno." I shrug again because I really don't. "Maybe he wants to get me back to the city so he can get the money. I'm sure he knows that I've sold it, so he can just come after the cash. But another thing is, he needs to know where it is."

"And where is it?"

I raise my brows at him. "Not on me, if that's what you're asking."

"Okay." He nods. "That's good."

"What did that asshole say?" Alex asks his brother from behind me.

"I can't repeat it, Alex. You know that."

"C'mon, Ken."

Kenneth sighs heavily. "In a big city, that would cost me my job."

"We're not in a big city," Alex reminds him needlessly.

"Thank fuck for that." He scrubs his jaw before revealing, "The guy there, Bobby Linsky, was hired by your ex-husband. His job was to get you to Springfield, where your ex patiently awaits your arrival."

"What?" I yelp, jumping from the chair. "You know where Erik is?"

"Calm down, Freya." A big hand lands on my shoulder and pulls me into a big, warm chest. "I won't let him touch you ever again."

"He's right. Normally, I'd put a cop outside your door, but you don't have a door. Or a house." He chuckles.

"Asswipe," Alex growls, but Kenneth's amusement is unwavering.

"You're a little insensitive for a cop," I comment dryly.

"Occupational side effects," he rationalizes with a wave. "In reality, though, Alex is better than any cop I have. In fact, I've asked him many times to come work for me." I look at Kenneth, but his eyes are trained on Alex and, strikingly, filled with silent pain. He's worried about his brother, and even though he can't influence Alex's decisions much, he wants to be in his life. I can see that. But Alex is too blind to. "You're going to stay with Alex; he has the best door around here." He laughs under his breath, then sobers and adds seriously, "It's the best course of action now. Do you think you'll be comfortable with this plan?" His solemn focus is solely on me now, and his tone is laced with concern.

"Yeah, I'll be fine with it. Can I stay with you?" I ask, looking at Alex.

"Stupid question." He looks down at me, then back at the sheriff. "Are we done here?"

"Yeah, we are," he says and starts stacking papers on his desk. "I'll call you when I have more news."

Alex grabs my hand and leads me to the door.

"Alex," Kenneth calls out. "Try not to kill him when he shows up. We need him to be prosecuted properly, so he can get life for all the shit he's done. It's a lot of charges we can pull here. You hear me? He's going to keep paying and paying and paying for that." His voice is stern. Alex stops for a second but doesn't say anything, probably considering his words. Then he gives a curt nod, and we continue walking, Alex leading the way.

"Alex," Kenneth calls again. "Can you come back here for a second?"

"Can you wait for me?" a slightly exasperated-looking Alex asks, turning to me.

"Yeah, sure."

As he disappears back through the door to Kenneth's office, I spot Jake sitting at what looks to be his desk, head down, studiously filling out paperwork. I didn't see him when we came in and had hoped to. I sigh with resignation and walk over to him.

"Hey," I whisper, cognizant of the other officers and staff who might decide to snoop on us.

He looks up in surprise before looking back down at his work, the surprise disappearing into aloofness. "Hi."

I purse my lips. "How are you, Jake?"

"Fine," he says shortly, then, after a long pause during which his entire aim is to make me feel uncomfortable and unwanted, he finally lifts his head from his papers again. "Heard what happened to you. Sorry about that."

"Thanks. Not your fault, though." I shrug because he doesn't sound sincere.

"I know."

"Okay." That's weird. I clearly meant it as a figure of speech.

He throws a bored look my way. "Is there anything I can help you with?"

I stand there awkwardly, feeling like I just lost a friend. Another one. And I don't even know why. The last time we saw each other, we were fine, I thought. I shake my head, giving up, and make my way to where Alex is standing and watching me. When I turn to look back at Jake, he's fully reabsorbed in his paperwork and refusing to register my presence.

My shoulders are drooped as I walk out into the blinding sun, Alex following me. His calm presence makes the moment more bearable, but the sting of Jake's unwarranted rejection doesn't feel like it'll heal over completely in the near future.

"Are you sure it's a good idea for me to stay with you?" I ask when we reach his truck.

"Why?" he asks immediately, stopping abruptly to turn to me. "You wanna stay somewhere else?"

"No, I don't." I lick my lips, and Alex's gaze dips down. "But we have a weird tendency to say mean shit to each other."

"You mean *I* have that tendency?" The corner of his lips lifts, and I find it annoyingly charming.

"Yes. I mean, no," I stumble. "I'm no angel either. What I'm saying is it all happened too fast. My car problems, our weird, unplanned sleepovers, among... *other things*, and now I'm going to be living with you." I press the tips of my index fingers to my temples and try to massage away the once-in-a-millennium headache that's bearing down upon poor lil' me. "It's too much for one week. I should just get out of this town and take my problems with me."

"And where will you go?" he challenges.

"I don't know." Because I don't. I have been thinking the same thing—where would I go if I left Little Hope. Nowhere. I have nowhere to go. And the funny thing is, I don't even *want* to go. This little town has grown on me, and, well, these people have grown on me. Alex, and Kayla, and even Justin (when he's not around Kayla, of course). And I thought Jake, too...

"Back on the road, then?" he responds, and there's something angry in his voice. "You like that nomad life so much, huh?"

"I don't. Not at all." I shake my head, which causes my headache to intensify, feeling like a metal clanging is taking place just behind my eyes. "But I'm not worth all this trouble."

"How do you know that?" He squints at me.

"I'm not, trust me on that. It's not self-pity or anything.

It's just that the number of problems that seem to follow me is completely disproportional to any good I bring." I shrug.

Alex's reply is clipped and confident, throwing me. "I'll be a judge of that. We need groceries."

"What?"

"Groceries. You know, the things you buy at the store and eat?" He speaks slowly, like I'm an idiot. If he tries miming eating to me, I'll kick him.

"I know what groceries are, smartass. I'm asking if you heard a word I said."

"I heard." He opens the passenger door and gestures for me to get inside. "Now, we need groceries."

Shaking my head, I let it go.

The grocery place we go to is a big, Walmart-like convenience store about twenty-five minutes out of town. Alex grabs a cart, and we follow down long rows of food. I wasn't joking when I told him I didn't know how to cook much. Just a few simple dishes and lasagna. Growing up, I didn't have many resources to discover the Gordon Ramsay within myself, and when I got married, Erik and I used to eat out almost all the time. Now, though, I'm willing to try and learn. It's not as if there are hundreds of take-out spots in Little Hope, and as I've mentioned before, the primitive part of me wants to feed my man, and I think of Alex as mine from time to time. We will be living together; it sounds very domestic to me. Sounds very *mine*.

"I want ice cream," I declare suddenly.

"Do you now?" His eyes twinkle as he stops to look at me.

"Yep. Be right back." Then I do the unthinkable, I rise on my tippy toes and kiss his cheek. Then I'm off to find the freezers in search of ice cream. Also, on the run from what I just did.

I'm browsing through containers of frozen goodness when someone suddenly knocks into me from behind, hard. A flash of my attack strikes a jolt of panic in me, making me jump and accidentally smack my head against the glass.

"Jeez, what the hell is wrong with you?" A feminine voice brings me back to reality, and I understand that it's not my attacker anymore. I spin in place to see a tall, beautiful brunette, probably in her late twenties, looking me up and down with unmistakable disgust on her face. "Wow, even more trailer trash. Alex just can't help himself." She snorts. "Though only the likes of you will look at him now, I guess."

"Ah, you must be one of those wandering vaginas," I say, pasting on a smile.

"What the fuck did you just say?" she sneers.

"A wandering vagina," I repeat. "You know, making rounds through the town?"

Her jaw slackens in shock. "Did you just call me a whore?" She raises her index finger and pops her hip out, and I swear she's only missing only big ear hoops and pink lipstick to be a character from a nineties teen flick. The image is comical.

"Did I?" I blink at her innocently.

She scoffs dismissively. "I saw you around town with that tattooed trash, Kayla," she tells me as if I should be embarrassed. "I guess you found your circle around here. Don't get comfortable, though, because she isn't staying here much longer. And neither are you."

"Adison, are you running your big mouth again?" Alex's deep bass booms from behind her. I didn't even notice him coming.

Her demeanor changes completely at the sound of his voice, and she turns around to greet him with a sickeningly sweet smile on her face.

"You used to love my big mouth," she says as she steps into his space. She runs a finger down his chest, then lifts her eyes up and winces. Her finger drops, and Alex's jaw tenses.

Okay, this is awkward. She might be his ex, but from the reaction on his face when she drew attention to his scars, he probably isn't over her. Is he? I feel a lead ball forming in my stomach, hot and uncomfortable.

"Don't come close to Freya and don't talk to her." His voice is menacing.

Her lip curls in a sneer. "Or what?"

"I don't know, Adison. I guess you'd have to find out." He steps around her and takes my elbow. "Did you find your ice cream?"

"Yes," I say and grab the first pint I can reach. "Let's go." I'm holding too tightly onto the cold box as we make our way to the registers, causing it to start to melt its little ice shards into puddles in my hands. "You don't have to protect me," I inform him once we're well out of earshot. "I've dealt with mean girls my whole life." I force my voice to sound reassuring—a complete one-eighty from how I'm actually feeling.

"You don't have to anymore." His voice is even and unaffected.

I don't respond to that, just swallow down this odd, itchy feeling stuck in my throat before asking, "Was she your girlfriend?"

"No."

"She seems to think otherwise." I cock a brow, hoping with all my little heart for him to refuse my stupid suggestion.

And here comes the blow. "I slept with her a long time ago, and that's all it ever was."

So, I was right—he isn't over her. Oh, boy. It's just my luck to start falling for a man who's already fallen for another woman.

Something must be showing on my face because Alex asks, "Do you have a problem with that?"

I play dumb. "With what?"

"With me sleeping with her."

"Are you sleeping with her currently? Because I'll feel weird staying in your house after what we've done if you have a girlfriend." The words taste like acid, but I'm careful to say them flippantly.

"I said I don't have a girlfriend," he grunts. "And I haven't slept with her in years."

"Okay," I say quietly, then the lightbulb goes off. "Wait. Was she the one you—was that her? From what happened the last time you...?"

His jaw sets, and I've got my answer. *Motherfucker.* I knew something was off with her the moment I saw her. It's like this weird woman's intuition to spot your love interest's ex, who still seems to be very present in his current life. Grr, so aggravating.

And now, my sole purpose in life is to figure out what the hell happened that last time between them. The story with my attack and my ex fades away into the background, which I take as a win for now.

"So, that was her, huh?" I chew on the inside of my lip. "What did she say to you?"

His nostrils flare. "Why don't you ask what I did to her instead?"

"Why would I do that?"

He leans closer. "Because I told you I hurt her during sex. I *did.* And yet here you are, thinking she's the one to blame."

I see red. Now, right now, I understand the meaning of this phrase. I want to cause violence. On him, on her, on the poor rows of canned goods stocked up in neat piles to the left of me. Instead, I rise up on my tiptoes until I'm as level with his face as I can be. "Because, Alex, no matter what they say, and no matter what *you* say, I simply cannot see you as a person who could harm somebody. You might be all big and growly, throwing lamps and stomping around like you do"—I wave my hand at his height, build, and general demeanor—"but in reality, you are soft and fluffy. You'd rather break your own hands than use them to hurt a woman."

Probably wasn't the smartest idea to call him fluffy, so I grab my card out of my pocket and zoom down the rows of food. "Let's go, I'm paying." I leave him speechless and almost run to the cashier. Hopefully, we had time to grab everything we needed, otherwise, I'll have to raid Alex's pantry again.

We drive home in silence, and after Alex unloads the bags and sets them on the counter, he leaves with a quiet, "I'll be back soon."

Sometime later, a knock on the front door cracks the silence, and I stiffen immediately from where I'm reading on the couch. This cat-and-mouse game is finally getting to me. I wish Erik would just come here already and be done with it. The anticipation slowly eats away at my soul as if with a teaspoon.

The knock comes again, followed by Kayla's voice. "It's me, Frey, open up."

I let out a sigh of relief and tread to the door in my sock-feet. Kayla looks like she just ran here on foot. Short wisps of wayward hair, the ones always escaping from her ever-present braids, stick to her temples, there's a wet spot on the front of her green shirt, and the top of her lip is glistening with sweat.

"Jeez, did you run here?" I ask, opening the door wider for her to come in. She flies past me straight toward the kitchen.

After chugging down a huge glass of water, she looks at me with round eyes. "Adison stopped by."

Could I not be done with that woman for the day? "Alex's ex?" I respond tiredly, as if I don't already know.

"That's her. Though I wouldn't say they were ever really dating." Her brow furrows. "Never mind that. She stopped by with her new boyfriend."

"I'm... happy for her?" I half ask, half answer.

"He asked an awful lot of questions about you." She looks at me pointedly. Dread begins to settle in my stomach.

"About me?"

"Well, not exactly about *you*, but about any recent newcomers. And he was pretty specific."

"And you think it's Erik?" I just know it's him. The cold sweat breaking out on my body is pretty sure of it, too.

"I don't know. Do you have a picture of him?"

I smack my forehead. Of course, I should have shown everybody his picture long ago. I did mention his work website (the legitimate one he uses for cover-ups), which has his picture to Kenneth, so he has an idea of who he's hunting. I'm sure he shared with Alex, but I should be the one doing that. Dummy.

I pull the phone out of my pocket and then remember that I have a cheap pre-paid crap one that can browse nada. "Give me your phone." She passes hers to me, and I find a few pictures of my ex from the same company website I mentioned to Kenneth and show it to her. Kayla's face falls.

"It's him. I didn't say anything. Obviously." She makes a face as if assuming her saying a word about me sounds ridiculous. "But I'm sure he knows everything there is to know. Adison likes to run her mouth. Especially after your recent encounter."

"And you already know about that, of course," I sigh. Not that I mind, but I'd like to have been the one who told her about that on my own terms.

"Small town." She shrugs with a smile.

"Right." This small-town thing is getting annoying.

Kayla walks to the kitchen and pours herself a glass of water, still panting. "Yeah, I think he's collecting as much info as he can to catch you when you're alone."

My eyes roam to the window. Why am I still here? Erik found me, it's time to move on to another place. But then what's next? New place, new faces, same problem. Unless I face him. But what would I do then? He's already begun his campaign where he charms everybody to take his side, starting with my foes, and eventually, everybody will think that I'm crazy, my friends included, and no one will believe my allegations about him being an abusive asshole.

"Man, it's like watching that movie *Split*."

Only then did I remember that I'm in Alex's cabin, and Kayla's watching me. "Huh?"

"I swear, I just witnessed a conversation happening over there." She circles her finger next to her head and mouths, "cuckoo," making me laugh.

"That bad?" I wince.

"Yeah, man, you had me scared for a second." Her eyes are round and unblinking now. "Care to share with the class what the fight was about?"

I laugh and put the kettle on to make some tea. "I was just thinking about what I should do."

"And what is that?"

"I don't know, Kay. I honestly don't know."

"Well, you have Alex here. And Kenneth. You do understand he isn't that kind of cop who can be bought, right?" She's watching me while pouring herself another glass of water. How much liquid can she fit in her stomach?

"I don't know." Even to myself, I know I sound concerned.

"I get that you don't have a good trust record with law enforcement, but you shouldn't fear it here. Small towns are different from big cities, Freya. We're a tight bunch, we don't do bad shit to each other."

"Yeah, I've heard a few people calling you... names." I pointedly look at her, and she just waves it off.

"Please, there are rotten apples everywhere," she dismisses. "The majority are nice folks. Honestly. And Kenneth is very fair and loyal. Plus, he's Alex's brother. He will do everything possible to protect you, I'm sure."

I give her a grateful look for easing my doubts.

Chapter Sixteen

ALEX

This is going to be hell, I think as Freya and I sit in the car out front of Dad and Stella's house. And sit. And... sit.

"You know, we do have to actually *go inside* eventually," Freya finally whispers teasingly. "It's just a dinner; you'll be fine."

Little does she know that it's anything *but* "just a dinner." I throw her a glare and try to find the willpower to open the door and get out. I haven't been here since my discharge. The disappointment on my father's face when he heard the news of how my career had ended would be forever drilled into my brain. No matter that he was an asshole—*is* an asshole—it would be a lie to say that I wasn't looking for approval. I was always a bastard, and I wanted to prove myself to be better, to be more than just the product of an affair to him. But I never was.

And now I'm destined to suffer through this disaster just so Freya could have one evening to herself. Was it worth it?

I look at Freya while she flings open her door with a bounce in her movements. She took forever to get ready, changing her outfit hundred times, fixing her hair and makeup, and now she seems so happy to be here that suddenly I decide that, yes, it *is* worth it. I take a deep breath.

"Two in, two out," she instructs me. "Let's go, soldier." She flicks her hair over her shoulder, and I growl as she strides toward the door.

"*Marine*," I grunt, falling for her bait. "Wait, *Freya*. Stop." I get out and chase after her. She grins in satisfaction and rings the doorbell before I can stop her.

The door opens, and my stepmother's face appears, grinning with knowing eagerness. She knows I'm breaking my neck by coming here, and she *knows* I'm bringing someone into this hell with me. She's probably heard all about Freya amongst the gossip circles in town, and I want nothing more than to turn around and leave before she gets the wrong impression of us becoming one big, happy family. I'm here, sacrificing my principles and my peace, only so Freya could come back home after the day she'd had and not go to the station to give a statement when she was so shaken up. *Who the fuck are you, Crowley?*

Both Stella and Freya are waiting for me to do the introductions, but I narrow my gaze at both of their expectant expressions and step past Stella. "You both know of each other. Don't expect me to help."

I walk farther into the house where my younger half sister, Leila, my half brother, Aiden, and Ken, are sitting around the lounge, looking like they're trying not to make a big deal of my presence in the room. It's the first time all four siblings have been in the same place in a very long time. I don't find a common language with any of them, even though Ken has been trying for a while. He's a bigger man than I'll ever be.

My dad walks into the room and smiles at us all. "Ah. You *did* show up. I thought Ken was lying to us." His presence's the same as it was when I was twelve. He's big, and not only physically. He is a large man, but it's his *presence* that makes me feel like a little boy all over again.

"I'd hoped you were bringing someone," Ken says, and I catch the glint in his eye as he says it, eyeing Freya at the door chatting with Stella about God only knows what. That fucker, like he hadn't orchestrated this scheme.

"He is," Freya speaks up from the doorway, and the whole family turns to look at her. Sure enough, Stella's hand is on her shoulder, and they already look like the best of friends. "Hi, I'm Freya." Leave it to Stella to hijack the latest person to become someone to me.

Ken looks past me and grins. "Nice to see you again, Freya. I've been meaning to follow up about—"

"No police work tonight, Kenny," Stella says firmly. For a pint-sized woman, she always knew how to put us in our places. "I'm sure whatever it is can wait for one evening, and then Freya can hear about it while you're on duty." She claps her hands. "Right, everyone, into the dining room for dinner."

I shoot Freya a look, but she smiles placidly at me and follows Leila into the dining room while my sister sneaks curious peeks at her.

This can't go well.

. . .

FREYA

By Alex's description, I'd assumed Stella to be an evil bitch of a stepmother straight from the Cinderella story, but instead, she's the nicest, most maternal woman I've ever met. The four boys are mostly quiet during the meal. Alex and his dad, Keith, are completely silent, while Ken interjects occasionally, and Aiden spends the whole meal glaring at everyone and angrily scraping his fork down his plate whenever he feels it necessary. Halfway through the meal, his dad abruptly snatches the fork from his hand and stabs it into the table, making us all jump. Me higher than most.

My eyes dart around the room nervously, looking for an escape. My heart's beating so fast it's about to spout wings and fly away from my chest. My breathing becomes heavy, and I'm about to lose it...

Until a large, warm hand lands on my thigh, grounding me to the present, to the family dinner with no threats around. Alex gently pats my thigh and then squeezes it gently. I let out a loud breath through my mouth and try to relax my hand, gripping my fork so tight my knuckles have turned white. I glance at him while he keeps his hand on me and give him a grateful smile. The corner of his lips perks up, and he lets go of me, returning to his own plate.

I carefully peer around the table. Stella quickly averts her eyes, and there's an awkward silence. I also return to my plate and start slowly nibbling on food while throwing careful looks around.

I can see the resemblance between Alex, Ken, and Aiden—they're all large men, clearly taking after their father. Even though Aiden is a teenager and still has some growing up to do, I can predict he will be huge, maybe even as big as Alex. Ken is a big guy too, but he can't beat Alex there.

As for Leila, she takes after her mother—petite and ginger. I've yet to hear her speak. Looking to be in her early twenties, she's an unapologetically observant person, sliding curious looks at me from across the table and even smiling conspiratorially like we're sharing a joke. I don't know what the hell we're joking about, but I smile back.

Stella continues with her story, her tone darkening as she glares over at her husband and youngest son.

"So, Alex, how are things?" Stella tries, but Alex sends her a glance and continues pushing his dinner around his plate.

I twist my lips around each other before answering for him. "Things are going really well. Alex has discovered a love of needlework and embroidery. And his *poetry*. Something else entirely. I burst into tears when he performed a dramatic reading for me. So heartfelt. So passionate." I even go so far as to pat him on the shoulder.

Alex slowly looks over at me while Ken leans back in his chair and smirks.

"Anyway," I continue. "How are you all doing? I'm not sure what specific things you do—"

"Since Alex never mentioned us?" Ken offers helpfully.

"Yeah, that." I smile awkwardly. "So, how are you guys?"

"Well, Leila is volunteering at the senior center," Stella says.

"Mom," Leila warns her.

"What? I'm proud of you, baby. Why can't I tell it to the world?"

Alex tenses next to me, and I place my hand on his knee on instinct, just like he did with mine.

"Anyway! She goes over there once a week and…"

I pay close attention to what she's saying, but I'm aware of the silent man sitting next to me. I'm slowly beginning to understand the dynamics here. Stella is trying her best, and she's one of the purest women out there. She took in the child of her husband and another woman and treated him like her own. Even from the thirty minutes, I've been here, I can see that she cares about Alex and wants him to be a part of the family.

The only problem here is *Alex,* who doesn't want to be in one. Who assumed that he's unwanted by everybody. And his father. I think he's the even bigger problem. Stella, while not having blood relation to Alex, tries fifty times harder than his own father, who seems untouched by the whole situation of his child being present at the dinner table after such a long time.

When Stella is done praising her daughter, which I find adorable, Keith clears his throat and tries to ask Alex a question, finally finding his paternal instincts buried under a truckload of unaddressed emotional issues somewhere deep inside.

"Friend of mine over the hill has an old Royce that needs fixing up. Wanna take a look at it, Xander?"

Alex drags his glare over to his father before looking back at his plate.

I look at *Xander* and raise my eyebrows at him. When it's obvious he's still not going to speak, I do.

"Actually, he's really into *boats* at the moment. Sailboats. He's making them from scratch. With zero tools, can you believe that? Takes up a lot of his living room."

Keith sniggers. "I believe the embroidery junk more than that. Since he was a kid, Alex wouldn't know the difference between port and starboard."

For a moment, I wonder if I've misheard him, but when I glance confusedly over at Alex, he's clenching his jaw even tighter and staring with laser-like focus at decidedly *not* his father.

Turning my head back to Keith, I frown. "You think?" I ask frostily, and he raises his eyebrows at the bite in my tone. "You don't think the man who was *in the navy* for seven years knows the difference between port and starboard? He would've been turning around in circles for half the damn time." I squeeze the fork I'm clutching so hard my knuckles turn white.

The whole table falls silent, and Keith pales, his gaze dropping to stare at his plate. I look at Alex in disbelief, understanding more and more why he dreaded coming here, and find him trying to hide a smirk. So *that* gets a response.

Keith clears his throat. "I... yes, well, I forgot about that."

"How could you?" Aiden mutters. "It's written all over his face." I'm about to rip him a new one when I realize that he's not aiming a distasteful look at Alex, he's glaring at his father. God, he's just a boy—a boy who doesn't have the right words to express himself but is speaking up anyway, chastising his father for forgetting his older brother's story. I glance at Alex instinctively and see him staring at Aiden with a weird look on his face. Alex's head is slightly turned to the side, and his eyes are glued to Aiden's face as if he's noticing his brother for the first time, too, for what he is—a future protector. Just like Alex is.

There's another awkward silence before Stella laughs nervously. "Freya, how long are you planning on staying in Little Hope? I'm having a big birthday party for my fifty-fifth next month, and I'd love for you to be there! You can bring Alex with you." She chuckles. "I know I should be asking the other way around, but..." she trails off, and I know why.

"Of course!" I reply warmly. "I'd love to come!" Then I hesitate, thinking twice before adding a little awkwardly, "If I'm still here."

I feel Alex's stare on me.

ALEX

"You're the *most* frustrating woman I've ever met," I snap at Freya as soon as her door has shut, and we're alone again in the car. It's the first time we have been the whole evening.

"Why, because I actually have your back? Because I don't just roll over and let people walk all over you or me? Trust me, been there, done that. Got it tattooed on my forehead. Not doing it again."

I scowl and steer the truck in the direction of home. She's right. Mostly. I *haven't* had a woman who fought for me. I've had brothers who would die for me, and I'm not talking about the ones I share genetic material with. The people I served with were my family, and that's one of the reasons I enlisted. Even though I lived with my father's family, they were never mine. And I desperately wanted one.

As for the women, everyone I've been with has easily wilted under pressure. I'm not a light person to be around. Adison stuck around longer than most, but even she did so because she wanted to be popular at school when we fucked casually whenever the urge struck. But I saw every time she shrank away when anger took hold of me how she became bored when I didn't engage in chatter about shoes, clothes, and other shit she wanted to talk about. And how she was scared of me when I came back. She wasn't my girlfriend, and I treated her like shit, taking her for a ride only when I wanted to. No surprise there that her desire for me was superficial as well. When she saw my scars, she winced. The only time we tried to have sex—it didn't go further than a few kisses—after I came back, she got blackout drunk, probably because she couldn't bear looking at me, I could assume. She was talking nonsense about my injuries and my teammates who died, and I lost it. I ravaged the room we were in, and she ran away sobbing. I had just come back from the hospital and had pretty bad PTSD-related blackouts. That night I had an episode of one. She told me and everybody else afterward that I was a monster who hit her, and I believed her because I didn't have a reason not to. I still don't. I do have anger issues, and when I came back, it was fifty times worse.

Freya acts differently. It's like my scars don't bother her in the slightest, and a couple of times, I've caught her looking at me like a starving man would at a piece of freshly roasted prime rib. I know I look at her like that all the time, but I can't do that to her. I haven't had sex with anybody but my hand in forever. What if something triggers an episode, and I black out again and hurt her?

"I think it's cute that your dad calls you Xander and not Alex," she remarks, bringing me back to reality, and I realize that I've been staring ahead for some time already.

"Xander is what he wanted my name to be in the first place," I say shortly. "Mom wanted Alex. Dad wanted Xander. They compromised. Not that dad should have had a fucking opinion on the matter."

"To be fair, you haven't seen him properly in years."

"To be *fair*," I grit out, "I went to fucking *war,* and he *forgot*."

Freya winces. "Yeah, that was very awkward to bear witness to." She waves the topic away. "But I love Stella. And Leila. Your brothers look like you. A lot, actually."

"Half brothers," I mutter. "And we all look like our father. It's why he couldn't even look at me." I feel Freya's gaze on me, but I don't look over to acknowledge it. Why would I? To see her pity or judgment? I'll do fine without either.

After that, a heavy silence descends upon us. The kind when you want to jump out of a moving vehicle. A few minutes pass until I start figuring out that I'm lashing out at the wrong person, but I'm too proud to admit it.

I wait until we pull into my drive and turn the car off before sighing. "Thank you," I say through an exhale.

Freya turns back in surprise, one leg already poised halfway through the open door. "For what?"

"Coming with me."

She pauses and then gently places her hand on my arm, the fire burning under my sleeve. "You're welcome. I'm glad I could be of assistance to you." She taps her finger on her chin. "I think I forgot to say thank you for convincing Ken to postpone my suffering. So I sort of owed you for that."

"That you did. And I'll still be collecting."

She turns to me with a devious smirk on her face. "I sure hope you will," she replies with mischief in her voice, then jumps out of the truck and strides into the house. I stare at her ass as her hips sway with the movement and try to ignore the swelling in the front of my pants.

Our little interaction in her bedroom the other day is going to be the last of the encounters of *that* sort between us. I can't risk her getting hurt. Not now—not ever. I sit in the car and wait for my thoughts to remind my body of my decision before dragging myself into the house just to spend a sleepless night on the sofa, wanting nothing more than to climb into bed next to Freya and ask her to stay there.

But I don't do that. I can't do that. And when she leaves eventually—because I know she will—I won't wash the sheets she slept in, keeping the scent of a woman around me instead. *This* woman.

Chapter Seventeen

Alex

"I'm *actually* worried about Jake," Justin says as he sits on my front porch in the morning, eating some of the cookies Freya and I bought during our first—and last—*family* grocery trip. He frowns at the box before screwing his nose up, yet eating another one anyway.

I glare at him as I bring the axe down to split another firewood log. The weather's getting warmer, but right now, I'd rather be out here chopping wood than in there watching Freya dance around my space as if she was the one to drive to West Elm for three hours through fucking traffic and pick furniture herself. She integrated herself into my life in the blink of an eye, and I'm helpless to change it.

"I don't care," I mutter. "He wouldn't care if the situation were reversed."

Justin can't disagree. "I think he might have liked Freya," he comments after a pause, his voice unassuming.

My spine straightens, and I look over to glare at him through narrowed eyes. "Why the fuck are you here, Justin?" I snap. "I didn't invite or ask for you to be here."

"I thought you might like the company."

I scoff harshly before reassuring him with more than a bite of sarcasm, "I don't. Trust me. I've got plenty of company at the moment." I scowl at the house.

Justin raises one brow and smirks. "I heard about your dinner."

I groan loudly. "What? That I went? That's hardly noteworthy."

"*Freya* went," he clarifies. "And Jake was upset."

"I don't fucking see how any of that is Jake's business," I growl and once again stand to my full height, bringing the axe to my side. "Why are you here, Justin?"

Justin tosses another cookie into his mouth whole. "I'm actually worried about Jake."

"So you've said." I bring the axe down through another log and hear the satisfactory crack as it splits. "But I still don't care. And if you weren't still under the very *wrong* impression that we are friends, you probably would've figured that out by now." My scars are stinging with the force of my arm, and I make a mental note to ask Freya to massage it later. I *can* do it by myself, but why would I want to when Freya's fingers on me feel so unbelievably good? It's like it forms direct contact with my cock every time she touches me, and, fuck, that will get me into trouble. The thought—and consequent frustration—means I crack the next log with much more force than necessary.

"Woah, *friend*," Justin says, flinching his arms up to his face as a wood chip flies toward him.

I scowl at him. Now that all of the wood is cut, I have nothing else to distract my thoughts with. "Not a friend, Justin, not a friend. We haven't been those for a while."

He stops smiling, his gaze dulling in a way that's almost startling. "I think you might be right," he responds quietly, then spits on the ground and leaves me standing with a sudden ball of lead in my stomach.

FREYA

"This one is cute," Kayla says, holding out a dress. We're trying to each find something to wear to Stella's party, but apparently, there are only two styles of dresses for people my age in Little Hope—tramp or nun.

I didn't know I'd still be here for the party five days later, but here I am. Why? Still beats me.

The garment Kayla is holding out is cut out in very unflattering places and has a bright-orange leopard print. I pretend to gag. "Hard pass."

She puts it back and sighs. "You're too fussy." I snort and keep searching. "Have you heard from he who shall not be named?" she asks casually, but I feel her sharp gaze on my face.

"Not a word. Have you seen him again?" I know she hasn't, otherwise, she'd let me know right away. She's my town watchdog who has constant access to the gossip in the diner, which manages to cover everything ever happening in Little Hope.

She shakes her head. "No. Nor did I see Adison, to think of it."

"The quiet scares me," I admit.

"You shouldn't be scared anymore."

"Why?"

"Because Alex will protect you." She puts so much faith in her words that I grin. "How are things going with Alex, anyway?"

I glance over at her, but she is conveniently looking through a rack of dresses, ignoring my narrowed gaze. "Fine. As well as unexpectedly having a roommate can be."

Kayla hums at the back of her throat. "There's only one bedroom in that cabin, isn't there?"

I yank out a random dress. "Ooh, this is nice."

Kayla smirks, knowing it's meant as a distraction. She's right, it's a terrible dress. Again.

"I'm beginning to think I won't find anything," I sigh, shoving the eyesore back from whence it came.

"I'm beginning to think you're avoiding all questions about what your current relationship status is." She clicks her tongue.

I flash her an eye roll. "I don't have a current relationship status, if *that* answers your questions."

"Okay, yeah. *Sure.*" She grins and turns around. "I'm just *thinking*... one bedroom, a sexy man who oozes pheromones..." I whip my head toward her, and she laughs, continuing, "pheromones that don't do anything for me, of course, but your face was priceless. Anyway, you, a sexy beast, and his pheromones are all alone in a cabin in the woods... Seems like everything is pointing toward some hot action between the sheets."

"You read too much into our situation." I shake her off, trying to ignore my rapidly reddening cheeks and hoping she does too.

"Do I?" She taps her pouty lips with her fingers, colored bright pink today to match her hair ends.

Frowning, I ponder that as Kayla wanders away to try her luck in a different section of the store. Why *haven't* Alex and I slept together yet? She's right; it's one bedroom, one sexy man, and complete solitude from the rest of the world. Minus some sniffing around from Justin from time to time. That *should* be the perfect recipe for bliss. Instead, Alex has continued to sleep on the sofa, doesn't look me in the eye, and spends a suspicious amount of time chopping wood. At this rate, we won't have any forest left in a month.

Yes, once upon a time—more like a few days ago—I thought we weren't at the right point in our lives to jump into each other's arms, but so much has changed since then.

Hmm.

That one morning before I gave my statement is all we've had so far, and it's frustrating.

"Well, going back to Adison, I haven't seen her, but I heard she's back in town," Kayla says, making her way back to me with several options slung over her forearm. With her unique looks, Kayla can get away with so much more than I can. I grimace as I feel a sudden wave of jealousy run through me. God, what is wrong with me? I just don't know how to be friends with a female. With anybody, really.

"With Erik?" I check, dreading what she might say.

"I haven't heard anything about her having a sidekick anymore. You know I'd tell you," she assures me. "He couldn't collect anything from us, and she, well... she isn't very bright, so there isn't much information she could give him."

I roll my eyes because Kayla is being Kayla, and I love her for that. I pull out a sexy black number that leaves little to the imagination. It's more revealing than I wanted, yes, but I'm getting too desperate to put it back.

"She's been talking to Jake." Kayla raises her eyebrows in warning, and I feel my shoulders drop.

"Jake? Really?" My spirits plummet. She's going through every man in my life. Well, Jake wasn't really my man, but he sort of was. Soon, there will be no man uncharted. She's like Erik in a skirt, taking everybody from me.

Jake is still an enigma to me. He is mean, then he is nice, then a minute later, he is a total asshole, and now he's cozying up with Alex's ex. Weird.

I straighten my shoulders and go back to searching.

ALEX

I notice Justin standing next to his truck and glaring at his phone as I walk down Main Street. I want to pass him by, but I don't—something in his face makes me slow down. I'm about to ask who pissed in his Cheerios when I freeze in surprise at the image of Adison, smiling and laughing with Jake across the street, her hand on his arm. "What the—"

Justin lifts his gaze from his phone and scowls at the picture in front of us. "Yeah," he says with disgust.

"Fuck. *Adison?*"

His nose wrinkles as if he just smelled something foul. "I know. It's worrying on so many levels. She's found her target, apparently."

Jake is twenty-two, a baby compared to her experience and how she can claw out mortal men's jugulars. I don't like the kid, but I wouldn't wish that snake of a woman on my worst enemy. Shaking my head, I postpone turning into the grocery store to ask, "Is that why Jake's been treating Freya like shit? I saw their run-in at the station."

Justin just shrugs and keeps throwing daggers at the happy couple.

"Did you sleep with her?" Justin comments out of nowhere, his eyes still trained on Jake and the viper.

I spin and grab the front of his shirt, pushing him against his brand-new truck. "How about *it's none of your fucking business?*"

He pushes me back and smiles reassuringly at a wide-eyed elderly woman coming out of the door nearest to us before looking back at me. "I'm not worried about *you*," he hisses, his eyes narrowing. "I'm scared for the woman who's living in your house. So is Jake. Why do you think he's shackin' up with her?" I give him an uninterested look, but he doesn't care and keeps going. "Yeah, to see how much fucked up shit he can find out about you from her, seeing she was the last one and all that."

"I don't give a shit about him playing a little detective. A little bit too late to worry about Freya, don't you think?" I hiss back and see guilt written all over his face. "Yeah, didn't think I wouldn't recognize your meddling, didn't you? You were so eager to throw her under me before. What changed, Justin? Huh?"

He steps closer to my face, his eyes turn into tiny slits, and I see the Justin not many people can see. The Justin he lets out very rarely. The one who followed hard, unimaginable orders, and when most of us were vomiting after the mission for hours, he just stood and smoked a cig, blank and emotionless. One might think he's a sociopath, but I know he feels—a lot—but shoves those emotions inside and suffocates on them when he's alone.

"I didn't know her story before, but *that's changed*," he says calmly, and I know it's false.

I shift my jaw, trying to control my own anger that's rising up right alongside bile. What if he's right to be worried? I know he's right.

"Do you think I hurt *her* that night?" I whisper as all fight leaves me, and I genuinely need to hear his answer because I still don't know what happened that night. Once upon a time, he was my best friend. My family. His opinion still matters, no matter what I say. The only difference from back then is that I don't deserve friends or family anymore.

He is quiet for a moment, searching my face, then he says in a firm tone, "No, I don't think so." Then he adds quietly, "I never did."

FREYA

I rest my head against the headrest of Kayla's car and pout. "Thanks for the ride."

"There's a town an hour's drive away that might have some more options," she offers apologetically.

I chuckle wearily and heave myself out of the car before holding up the Lonely Kurt I'd picked up from the diner. It was going to be a treat for Alex, but I'm hungry enough to eat it all by myself now. "Thanks for this. I'll talk to you soon." I hesitate. "Should I say 'babe'? I feel like chicks say 'babe' all the time. Do we need to?"

"Oh, hell no. Bye, bitch!" And she drives off, flipping me off as she goes.

I wave good-bye with a laugh and sigh as her car disappears before spinning slowly on my heel and ambling my way up the rest of the drive. I can't see Alex's truck anywhere, and it makes me groan.

First no luck in finding a dress—although I bought a little black number that's not suitable for wearing to my roommate's mother's birthday—ugh, *roommate*—and now Alex isn't even home to take my mind off things.

I hear a rustling in the leaves near me, and I slowly turn my head, suddenly expecting to see another one of Erik's attackers. Instead, my eyes widen as I come face to face with a huge, furry, angry bear.

"Oh, shit," I breathe. The bear starts making a beeline for me, and I turn with the intent to run toward the cabin. "Oh God! I thought everyone was joking!"

Fuck. Can bears climb? I can't get my keys out of my pocket. I can't even say what *type* of bear it is, which makes all of Alex's half-hearted attempts at instruction utterly worthless. Was this the type of bear that you should play dead for? Or one where you should *not* play dead? Either way, I won't be just *playing* it soon.

All of Erik's hard work and I die by a bear. Pity.

Just as the bear comes too close for comfort, my heart beating erratically in my chest at the large wild animal in front of me, I hear a noise to my left, which grabs the bear's attention.

"Hey! Hey, bud! Over here, you big lump." Again, Alex is saving me, and I'm so relieved I could weep. "Frey... stand *up*," he orders me firmly. "Big stance. Look big. Look *human.*"

I whimper and force myself to slide up the porch railing and stand dead straight.

"You look like a fucking tree, Freya. *Human.*" There's a different voice in front of me, and I take a swift glance away from the bear to see Justin standing in the drive, a shotgun hanging loosely in his hand. The bear is now confused, with Alex off to his side, Justin behind him, and me standing in front of him.

He apparently decides I'm not worth the effort and ambles off into the forest to my right. I sink to the floor and put my head in my hands, trying to ease the headache rapidly spiking in my skull due to the blast of adrenaline I've just had course through my body.

Alex stomps his way through the undergrowth, and I can already tell I'm about to get a lecture. "Fuck, Freya. What happened to what I—"

"I don't know! I couldn't remember any of it!"

He opens his mouth to scold me again, but Justin clamps his hand down on Alex's shoulder. "Get her inside. She doesn't need this from you right now."

I throw a grateful look at Justin, but he's already walking back to his truck.

Alex watches him for a second before turning back to me and gesturing into the house. "A minute later, and you would have..." He doesn't finish his sentence, and I'm glad about it.

"I know," I whisper, my legs unable to keep me up anymore. "Everything went out of my head when I saw it there."

I stumble in and fall to the bed, curling up in a ball, shivering despite the warm temperature in the house.

Alex stands in the doorway, and I hear his exhale from here. His footsteps sound heavily toward me, and then the bed dips with his weight. He easily pulls me back, and I'm suddenly resting in his solid embrace, looking up at the ceiling and feeling safer with every passing second.

My heart's still pounding as if I just ran the Boston marathon and almost about died on the finish line—a metaphor that's close enough.

Alex's hand moves to the curve of my lower back and starts making calming little circles there. My mouth goes dry, and I lick my lips, trying to return some moisture to them.

My hands slowly move to fully embrace his wide torso, until he startles when I accidentally scrape my fingernails over his sides, exposed by his shirt riding up with his movement, so I do it again and force a chuckle out of him.

The adrenaline slowly dissipates into sexual energy, and I unfurl from my ball and look up at him, finding his gaze already on mine. His tongue peeks out to touch his top lip, and his eyes drop down to my mouth.

Without waiting for him to take charge, I twist in his grip, lift up, and fervently crash my lips on his. I open them almost as soon as he starts kissing me back. His strong hand grips my hip and pulls me flush against him, letting my knees slide on either side of his legs to allow the both of us to rock against each other.

He shifts his lips to my neck hungrily, roughly making his way down the slope and fueling the almost painful desire to have him close that is swirling in my clenching stomach.

I feel nothing but his solid frame under my body, the weight of his heavy arms surrounding me, and his wet lips on my skin. My mind is sufficiently scrambled enough that I can barely remember my own name as I'm panting through his kisses.

Just as I'm settling into the rhythm of his hips pushing into mine and his fingers trailing down my skin toward the spot where I'm burning for him, he pushes me away from him, his eyes wide and feverish.

"Fuck, no, Frey... I don't want to..." He scrambles away from me, leans back on the headboard, and lets out a loud exhale.

"You won't," I whisper. "You won't hurt me. I *know* you won't."

"You can't know that. *I* don't know that."

I sit up to face him and slowly run my fingers down the scars on his cheek, tracing down onto his neck. "You've so far been the one to *save* me, Alex Crowley."

I follow the gulp as it goes down his throat, lick my lips, and move to him, then I move on my knees toward him before bunching the shirt at his front in my fist, tugging it over his head. He lets me take it off, and I slowly crawl on top of him, knowing he's allowing me to. The scared look still lingers in his eyes as I completely straddle his lap, grinning with a new idea.

"How about..." I whisper, leaning over to get the tie to my robe that's hanging on the edge of the bed, "we make you feel more comfortable?"

He studies the tie in my hands before looking up at me in wonder, lips parted and holding out his hands, pinned together at the wrists.

ALEX

God, how can this woman go from the scared victim of a near-bear attack to one of the most sensual beings I've ever met? The tie around my wrists is loose enough for me to escape if I wanted to—I don't—but just having the pressure around them is enough to keep the fear in my stomach from spreading and my mind from racing to the places I can never find my way back out of. She motions for me to lift up my tied hands, and I do just that, a little curious about her plan. She grabs my fists and brings them to the headboard, securing them to the slatted headboard of my rustic, wooden bed. Grinning widely, she admires her handywork.

With my hands tied, Freya's in control of the way everything will go, and it's pure torture; I want to snap these pitiful restraints and wrap myself around her, so I feel *all* of her, but I can't. I need to stay still and give up full control to her. So she's not scared of me.

So *I'm* not scared of me.

She shoots me a playful smile and goes for the belt on my pants.

"Wait!" I say as I pull on the ties. "Freya, wait!"

"What?" She freezes, scared by my abrupt tone, and I mentally kick myself for being an idiot—she doesn't react well to loud noises, I know that and just keep fucking it up each time I open my damn mouth.

"I don't have condoms." If my hands weren't tied, I'd smack my forehead.

"Oh." Her plump, red lips form a perfect O.

"Yeah," I groan in pain. Real, physical pain, as all my blood is pulsing below my belt.

She plants her ass on my thighs, not making it any more comfortable for me. "I haven't been with anyone since my divorce and got tested when I figured out he was cheating on me. I'm clean, and I'm on the pill."

My mouth goes dry. "I…" I swallow a lump in my throat, "I've never done it without a condom, plus I got tested when

I was in the hospital." Yeah, and it's been a really long time since.

"And since then?" she asks, licking her lips.

I shake my head.

"What?" she prods, nudging me to answer.

"I haven't been with anyone since then," I say, half-embarrassed.

"Oh." She bites her bottom lip. "What about Adison? I thought you were together after you came back."

"Never got... that far." I wish we never got even to being in the same space again. I so fucking wish.

Her eyes widen and then turn into tiny slits as a mischievous smile spreads across her face. "Good. All that" —she points her finger at my torso—"is mine now."

Freya hooks her fingers in the waistband of my blue jeans and swiftly removes them, leaving me dry-mouthed and lying naked. The anticipation of feeling her bare is enough for me to be done awfully fast, so I try to recreate a grocery list of what my pantry could benefit from, just so my excitement will... turn down a little.

And it works until she places her finger under my navel and starts moving it downward. Just like that, the fucker is back in full force. Her mouth works in a silent murmur of approval, and I grin.

"C'mon, you're going to leave me like this?"

She smirks. "Maybe." She flips her hair over her shoulder before slowly pulling her clothes off, leaving on only a sexy pair of lacy black panties and a matching lace bra. I can see her tight nipples peeking out, begging for my attention. God, she's gorgeous. "Maybe I like you all tied up," she teases in a suggestive voice. Then she climbs back onto my lap and positions herself, keeping her sultry gaze on my face the entire time. From timid creature to seductress in the blink of an eye. I'm a lucky fucking bastard.

Her heated pussy is right above my cock, and I push my hips toward her, urging her to take me in. She just laughs, the little minx, and leans over, giving me a quick kiss—*on the mouth*, but I'll take anything at this point—without going deep. I groan in frustration, and suddenly the idea of being tied up doesn't seem so fun anymore.

Freya moves her mouth to my ear and bites the lobe, sending a shudder through my body. She clearly likes the reaction of my body to her teasing because she alternates between bites and kisses and soft puffs of her hot breath. My dick is painfully hard, and I press my hips once more, hoping she'll give in.

But the little devil doesn't. Instead, she peppers my chest with her soft, featherlike kisses, and I'm about to come just like that, without her even directly touching my cock.

"Fr... Freya." I manage to say only on the second attempt.

"Yes?" There is a smile in her voice.

"Freya, please. You gotta do something about that, or I'm ripping these shitty binds to shreds," I rasp, holding onto the bed's headboard with my last slivers of willpower.

"Oh." She lifts her face from my chest, and her mouth forms a cute little O. "You think we should?" she asks and looks down at my poor, straining dick.

"Yes, Frey, we should." My throat's dry. It's been a long time since I've had a woman doing unthinkable things to me, but none of them, even from before the accident, were Freya. She makes everything *more*.

She smiles mischievously as she slowly strips off her bra and panties. It's pure torture, and I want to close my eyes to preserve the sanity I have left, while at the same time, I'm afraid to lose even a second of this show that I might never get to see again. Once she's done with her lingerie, she *finally* moves to my tormented dick.

I groan in the back of my throat when she takes my tortured, twitching fucker in her hand and guides it in, slowly sinking down, her eyes fluttering closed as I fill her completely. "Oh, fuck," I murmur. "You feel so fucking good." I was scared that she wouldn't be ready, that it would be painful for her, and this... *urge* to make it pleasurable for her... turns out, I have nothing to worry about since she's so slick it's easy for me to slip in. She got like that just from kissing me. From *kissing me*. How the fuck did I get so lucky?

She's too busy focusing on the sensation to respond, adjusting to my size, and as she starts to move when I'm fully settled in, I try my best to hold onto those miserable ties that are about to give in to my straining arms. Her eyes roll back in her head, and that's my last straw. I snap my restraints and grab her tight hips, helping her retain her balance and get lost for a long, blissful moment. Forgetting who I am and how badly this could all end up. Only her body in my arms matters.

Her eyes widen, and she places her palms on my chest to leverage herself. Then she starts moving up and down. If she continues, this will end fast, so I dig my fingers into her thighs and slow down her movements. She whimpers and attempts to move again.

"You gotta slow down, baby." My voice is coarse from the overwhelming pleasure. "Or this is going to be over too fast."

Her chuckle is sensual and carefree. "We can go for round two after."

"We will." I give her ass a light slap, and her eyes twinkle. "But I want this one to last."

She bites her lips just as she squeezes her inner muscles. My balls draw, and my head falls back.

"Shit," I hiss. "Stop."

Of course, she squeezes it again, and I nearly come. Done with her games, I grab her waist and throw her on her back.

We both freeze. I think I've scared her—not knowing the whole extent of what shit her ex had done, I should have been more careful. Shit, I knew I'd fuck it up somehow.

But she surprises me—as usual—and grabs my butt cheeks with her hands. "Show me what you've got," she says in her sexy voice and bites her lower lip. It just about undoes me.

I guide myself inside her soaked pussy and start moving. It's like riding a bicycle—you remember how to the moment you're in the seat again. I'm a large man—everywhere—so I spread her legs wider to fit between them better. She foresees my every move and meets me with one of her own. It's a perfect rhythm right away. It's unsettling.

It's amazing.

I don't remember any of my partners being so intuitive before, but Freya is. She anticipates my every move, the tiny switch in my rhythm and position. My mood.

My hips move faster. She bites her lips harder. I lean toward her and wrap my arms around her torso. I want to feel her whole body shaking when she comes. She digs her fingers into my back, avoiding the ultra-sensitive spots on the burns. I don't know how she knows where she can't touch. She's so gentle, yet her nails are deep.

I press my lips to hers, and her tongue instantly peeks

out to meet mine. I increase the movements—everywhere, and she moans into my mouth and arches her back.

I continue holding her with one arm still wrapped around her, and I move the other one down between us. When I find her swollen, sensitive clit, I start rubbing it. She rockets in seconds, squeezing my cock with her tight, spasming pussy. And then I let myself follow her into this oblivion I've missed so much. The one that only she could lead me to.

Chapter Eighteen

F REYA

I sprawl out in bed as Alex appears in the doorway, buck-naked and grinning. I guess empty balls can do that to a person. His impressive-even-in-chill-mode python's swinging from side to side, and that image will be imprinted on my retinas for as long as I live.

"Someone's pleased with himself," I say as he climbs over the bed and crawls back beside me.

"Oh, I am," he informs me. "Say that wasn't the best sex of your life, I dare you."

I beam and draw his face to look at me so I can kiss him slowly. "I'm really not that great," I whisper against his lips.

"Oh, I wasn't talking about you." He grins and gets a smack on his chest. "Okay, okay," he says with a yawn, stretching out his sore shoulder. "I might be a little rusty, but it's not like you were on a constant roll either," he quips with a mischievous smile that gets a hot glare from me.

"I didn't hear you complaining," I shoot back.

"Well..." he singsongs and gets another smack on his ass this time. "What? You said so yourself."

I roll my eyes and climb off the bed to pick up the bottle of lotion I'd bought in town earlier, specifically to help with his burns, from the bathroom. He closes his eyes as I settle into what's now a semi-regular position for me and slowly start massaging it into his skin. "Do I have to get attacked by a bear every time I want to have sex now?" I ask, mock-pouting.

"Oh, no, I'm *happy* not to go through that again." I widen my eyes, and he laughs, adding, "The bear part, I mean."

"Good save," I snort, poking him in the chest. "You were about to end up sleeping outside with those very bears tonight."

With him still naked, I get to watch his python roaring back to life as he relaxes in the lulling quiet after our banter recedes, and while I keep one hand working away at his scars, I trail the other down to his impressive length and circle my hand around it, feeling it harden completely under my touch. That right there, that's art. Nature created this masterpiece so I could enjoy it. He moans softly, and I grin at the effect I have on him. It's a powerful feeling I can't get enough of.

I press a kiss to his chest before looking up at his closed eyes and softly kissing him a little bit lower beneath his ribs. His mouth pops open a little, but his eyes remain closed. I dip my tongue into his navel, and his breath catches in his throat, his erection pointing straight up to the ceiling.

I plant a kiss on the head of his angry-looking cock, and he gasps. When I look at him, he's staring at me, eyes wide and hazy with desire. I smirk at him and turn back to the straining flesh in front of me, dipping my head and laying a good, long lick on its head. I haven't voluntarily given a blowjob for as long as I can remember—the whole thing always turned out to be torture or a part of an abusive episode with Erik—but Alex isn't demanding it. I'm offering. Of my own free will. So I place a hand around the base of him, the other low on his stomach, and I allow myself to feel *powerful*—so much so that I can bring an equally *powerful* man such as Alex to his knees.

"Oh God," he hisses, muscles on his stomach contracting under my palm as he restrains himself from lifting his hips and pushing farther into my throat. "Please, *Freya*."

My name, along with the *begging* from his lips when he's as relaxed as he's now, sends shivers of pleasure down my spine. I didn't know *giving* could be so rewarding.

I shift so I'm lying between his legs, and he moves a hand to rest under his head, tilting his head down to look at me better. His other hand is firmly placed on the bar of the headboard, preventing him from reaching out to me and pushing me deeper into him. The veins on his neck and forearms are straining against the skin, looking ready to burst with the pressure. My mouth waters at the sight. God, he's gorgeous. I stop getting distracted by his face and get back to business.

A few hours later, we still haven't left the bed. For a guy who's been starved for sex for however many years, he sure tries to compensate for the lost time in one day. One more time and I won't be able to walk straight tomorrow.

But Alex has other ideas. As does my stomach, which reminds us both of its hungry state with a loud rumbling. "Let's feed you, or you'll pass out from exhaustion," he says, but along with concern for my starving organism, I also see male pride—and probably more of that than the other, honestly.

"Should we be worried about the lack of curtains?" I murmur as he picks me up with very little effort from the bed, carries me out to the kitchen, and places my bare ass on the countertop, all while kissing my neck and collarbone. I wear only Alex's shirt and the remaining sensation of his kisses on my body. The sensation of cold granite under my naked skin and his hot frame pressing into mine is intoxicating.

He's sucking on my skin like a starved animal, and I'm his feast. I'll definitely have hickeys tomorrow, but strangely enough, I want the whole world to see that I belong to Alex.

I *belong* to Alex? I shake my head, trying to get rid of a terrifying thought I promised myself I'd never have again. I don't want to belong to anybody anymore. Do I?

He must have sensed my withdrawal because he pulls me off the counter and spins me around, letting me look out the expansive evergreen forest out the window. His finger slips inside me, making me gasp and forget about *any* thought I might have. "If someone's watching," he hums in my ear, "why don't we give them one hell of a show?"

"All the way over here, they can't see much," I pant, every nerve in my body singing for his attention.

He chuckles, low and deep in his throat, and the sound is so sexy and so relaxed that it makes me even wetter than I already am, so I urge his face to look at me before biting at his lower lip. It's so much plumper than the top one that it causes me a constant desire to nip on it. "Are you seriously suggesting we go *closer* to the window and let whoever might be coming watch as I give you yet another orgasm?" he manages to ask between bites.

I pull away and look over at the window. "Yes. But only if that orgasm is given with your tongue."

His mouth drops open before a sexy smirk crosses his face as he accepts my challenge. "Perfect."

"You say that now, but when you have to get down to business..." I murmur under my breath.

"What?" He begins laughing. "I honestly don't know what you're talking about, but it sounds very suspicious, I just don't know why." He laughs louder.

"Sure you don't." And just like that, at my words, the sexy mood evaporates instantly. Ruined, just like it always is when I run my mouth.

Alex grabs my chin and lifts it up, so I face him. "What are you talking about, Freya?"

"You know. *That* morning?" I offer, hoping to freshen his memory.

"Yeah, what about *that* morning?" he says, mimicking my tone. Either he's playing dumb, or he is dumb.

"You know, you were moving around but never did it." He keeps looking at me with no comprehension on his face. "Oh, c'mon! When I was next to your python, I didn't play hide and seek!" I exclaim when I'm done with this game.

He gives me a dubious look before he bursts out in laughter. He's laughing until his eyes start tearing up while I'm standing here and getting aggravated. Once he's done laughing, he looks up at me and begins laughing again. "C'mon! It's not funny!" I protest.

"You—" he stutters, unable to talk through his laughter,

so I wait again. "You called my dick a *python*." He chokes on the last word.

Oh boy. And I begin laughing along with him. Yeah, that piece of information was supposed to go with me to my grave, and I just vomited it all over.

"A python," he repeats with a self-satisfied grin.

"If the shoe fits." I shrug.

"Oh, man. Freya, you are something." He looks up at me, and his whole demeanor changes. There are smiley crinkles around his eyes, his mouth forms a sexy, wicked smile, and his shoulders don't hunch anymore. He needed that laugh. And I feel like a champion because I was the one who gave it to him.

"But really, you're talking about me not going down on you that morning, is that right?" I nod, embarrassed. Though I don't know why I am—it's a very legitimate question at this point. He grabs my chin, firmer this time, and forces me to look into his eyes. "I didn't do it because there was no fucking way that I wouldn't want more after I had tasted you. I can't control myself even when your scent reaches my nose. I don't know what I'd do if I tasted you. Do you know how good you smell, Freya?" I shake my head like a mouse hypnotized by a snake. Not a python this time though. He brings his face to my neck and inhales deeply. "You smell fucking delicious." I shudder at his words. "Are we clear on that?" I nod. Turns out, I've lost my ability to speak.

"Where were we before all that nonsense?" Alex picks me up again and carries me closer to a window. He makes me stand facing the window, my palms pressed against it. He encourages me to spread my legs wider before falling onto his knees behind me.

"I have *this* in my view and plan on being quite busy,"

he murmurs, smacking my ass, sending a pleasurable jolt of barely-there pain. "So you'll have to keep a lookout for anyone that might be a witness. Do you think you can do that?" he asks from my feet, and I nod. "Good girl. Now"— he licks his lips—"I can do what I've wanted to do since I saw your angry ass on the side of the road."

He touches my knee with his finger, then begins moving it up my thigh, closer to the place where I want it the most. He wets his lips, and I'm mesmerized by his movements, just like he was when the roles were reversed.

When he's close to the center of my ache, he stops, and I'm ready to smack him. "Alex." My voice is hoarse and pleading, and he's smiling.

"Payback tastes so sweet," he murmurs, grabbing both my thighs with his hands and spreading them wide. Then he dips his head, and his tongue, warm and wet and touches my aching clit. Right at the core. *Thank you, Alex.* I wouldn't survive more teasing. It's not like I'm big on foreplay nowadays. Yesterday, when I climbed the mountain named Alex, I got so excited just paying attention to his body alone that I completely forgot about my own. It would be a huge mistake if I weren't so attuned to his pleasure and got nice and prepped on just seeing him fighting for breath and thrashing in those restraints. I was never a dominating person in the bedroom, but, as it turns out, Alex can bring a new me to the surface, and I'm happy to meet her.

I moan loudly as Alex brings me here and now and moves his tongue between my folds, drawing out sensations I've never experienced before. The heightened thrill of potentially being seen and the expertise that Alex is showing brings me closer than anything ever has. Turns out, it's like riding a bicycle—once you learn it, you can't unknow it, even after years of non-practice, as he claims, and I believe him. Even left on my own with a vibrator hadn't felt as good as this does, and I'm a slave to every dip and flick of Alex's tongue.

"Fuck, Alex. Yes. *There*. Oh, God."

I explode over his tongue, and he holds my quivering thighs with his large hands, keeping me steady as the earth ricochets around me.

"Stay there," he orders. "Just like that." And he moves away.

I plant my hands back on the glass and smirk. I *wish* Erik saw that. That would be quite some payback.

Everything looks peaceful and calm, a high contrast to the explosions that are still going off in my heart and body. I feel sensual for the first time in my life, and when I hear movement behind me, I turn around. Alex is standing still and watching me.

"What?" I ask, confused.

"Just admiring the view." He groans as his gaze sweeps up and down my figure. "God, woman. You're so gorgeous."

The compliment settles in my heart, firing up my awoken sensuality. He places one hand on my hip, the other around the python as he slowly guides himself in me, filling the void that's been there since the moment he first growled at me. He is so large, and he thinks I need a moment to accommodate to his size when I just want him to start moving.

"I need to move, Frey, or I'm going to die," he whispers into my hair.

I hum in agreement and stand up more, pushing off the glass. With our height difference, I need to go on tippytoes while he needs to seriously bend his knees for us to "align" in this position. With shuffling behind me and then a muted curse, I know that Alex has had enough. "Brace yourself, Frey" is the only warning I have before he brings his hands to my hips and lifts me from the floor. With one hand lightly pressing on my chest and forcing me to lean on him and the other firmly holding me across my pelvis, he begins moving.

This is a new position for me, something I could never have done with Erik because... well, I hated Erik from behind, or everywhere for that matter. The sensation of being so tiny—when I am not—and him being so big makes me feel like a fragile woman in the hands of a strong and capable man. I guess it just takes the right sort of man to make a woman feel this way, and not her size or appearance.

Once Alex picks up the pace, I forget any comparison with other men or possible voyeurs out there.

ALEX

I watch Freya as she frowns at some recipe she found on my phone. She's wearing granny panties and my wrinkled shirt and still looks like a sex goddess. I've spent the whole time she's been cooking trying not to salivate over her. I feel like a valve has been opened, releasing my hormones, and now I don't know how to patch it up again and stop myself from craving every ounce of her attention all to myself. The concentrated look on the face of this woman trying to figure out how to decode a not-very-complicated recipe has chipped away at my carefully constructed walls, and I don't know how I should feel about it.

"Do you remember your mother?" I ask, lost in thought.

She turns to me in surprise. "What?"

I shrug. "We lost our mothers at a similar age. Wondered if you remembered her at all."

"Um... not really." She distractedly stirs something in a pot that smells a little bit burnt already, but I'll eat whatever she gives me and not bat an eye. "A few specific memories, but I have a certain level of selective memory suppression. I don't know what I've forgotten, but I know it's there. It's like my brain erases something I don't like. Or need." She waves her hand. "Mom was a mess most of the time. At least her death meant I didn't have to attempt to return to her care every time she came home from rehab."

"She was an addict?"

"An alcoholic."

"I'm sorry," I whisper. I regret bringing up the topic, but it's doing its job of stopping me from wanting to pick her up over my shoulder and take her back to bed. Even to my own ears, it sounds selfish. "Who did you stay with when you weren't with her?"

"Foster care. Social workers were our frequent visitors. I'd pack up everything I owned into a bag and disappear to a nice house with perfect children and perfect parents, and then I'd go back to my optimistic mother for a few short months. Rinse and repeat."

My gaze drifts to the bedroom, where I see her suitcase. *Everything I owned into a bag.*

"I thought I had it tough," I murmur.

"You did. You can't compare our traumas. We both have different scars, but they're still there." She shrugs, not looking at me, instead turning to place whatever she'd been making into the oven.

I think about what she said. "Can you choose what memory to suppress?"

"No." She hums for a second before walking to stand next to me, leaning on the benchtop. "You know how you have PTSD from your trauma?"

"Mmm..."

"So, your PTSD makes your brain *remember* everything that happened to you and relive it repeatedly. It finds stimuli from your everyday life and finds its way into that memory. My brain does the opposite in response to trauma. It *forgets* it. All of it. It finds stimuli to *help* forget it. I can't find it even if I want it. It's filed in a box somewhere in my brain, with padlocks and alarm systems on it. It'll never be opened again unless something forces it."

"Huh." I study her for a moment. "So, the bear attack from earlier. That could potentially be filed away, and you'd never know it existed."

Her brow furrows. "The what?"

My mouth drops open, but she grins before I can really believe her. "Just kidding."

I reach out and grab her, lifting her up over my shoulder. She squeals and laughs breathlessly, and I deposit her on the couch, climbing on top of her, and trapping her in my arms. "That was mean."

"I know," she murmurs, leaning up to kiss me. I keep moving out of her way, my lips always just out of reach until she pouts. I grin as she gets frustrated, and she wraps her hands around my neck, pulling me down until I lose my balance. We both chuckle as her lips find mine.

"You win," I whisper, deepening the kiss and letting her take the lead. For a person with such a dominating nature, I sure give up control quite often when it's about her.

"That's what I thought."

We're so distracted on the sofa that Freya's carefully scheduled timer goes ignored. I can't say I regret it since it smelled burnt from the beginning; plus, I've discovered I'm no longer interested in food. I've found something *way* better.

Chapter Nineteen

F **REYA**

"Hey, what do you think?" I ask Alex, twisting my hips to show off my dress. "Does this make me look like a ten-dollar hoe on the corner? Or does it make me look like a respectable lady that you can take to your stepmother's birthday party, where your entire family and the whole community of this wonderful, hopeful town will be?" There is only one right answer, and I hope Alex won't let me down.

He looks over from the bed and whistles. "Ooh... wow, Freya."

"It's the first one, isn't it?" I say with a sigh.

"Er..." He looks at his watch before walking over to me and scooping me up in his arms. "*Yes*. But I don't think that's the problem."

"I want to be *liked* tonight. I don't want to look like a—"

"—an outsider?"

"Exactly."

"That has little to do with your outfit, Frey. It's you who just appeared in Little Hope and dragged a town weirdo to a family dinner that he hasn't been to in years. They're gonna look no matter what you're gonna wear."

"You are not a weirdo," I hiss a little too forcefully—I hate when Alex puts himself down like that.

"I am." He taps my chin.

"Yeah, you are." I chuckle and get a smack on my butt for that.

I wiggle in his embrace so he'll let me go. "Wait. I have another dress option. Put me down, and I'll show you."

He complies with a heavy sigh, and I disappear into the bathroom.

"How much did you buy on your little shopping expedition?" he calls out.

"Why? Are you stressed about my finances?"

He snorts. "I'm stressed about how much room we have in this place."

It's not the first time he's made reference to this *relationship* between us being more permanent and the *"we"* thing. Erik is still out there, Alex is still mentally recovering from his Navy years, and I am still on the run and no less damaged than he is, just from different things.

Nothing good can come of this, and it's something that I force myself to remember. Alex has clearly given up on that task—and to think I blamed him for backing out from my advances before.

He needs therapy, *not* a live-in girlfriend in a small, secluded cabin in the woods. And I need to get the hell out of here, dragging my problems along for the ride. I don't like Adison, but I wouldn't wish Erik even on her because she doesn't know him as I do, and if she gets sucked into that nightmare, it will take years to get away. And by the time she's ready, it might be too late. I feel like Erik is my problem that I'm handing over to her, knowing the bad outcome.

I shake my head, trying to get rid of pessimistic thoughts just for today because I sure don't want to show up with a sore look on my face to a party for Alex's stepmom.

"Ta-da!" I say, leaning dramatically on the doorway. It's a short, flowy mint-green dress that accentuates my chest, waist, and legs all in the same go but doesn't yell from the rooftops that I work in the red-light district. "What about this one?"

I know the answer by the grin on his face.

"What is it on a hoe scale?" I check.

He chuckles. "It's perfectly in the middle of bringing you home to meet the family and maybe a hundred bucks an hour, not ten."

I burst into laughter and turn back to look in the mirror. "I can work with that."

"I know I can too," he mumbles under his breath.

"We're not leaving this house if you don't get ready." I lean closer to the mirror to put my mascara on. "*Or...* I will go to Stella's party all on my own and dance with Justin all night long." I raise my eyebrows as I peer around the corner.

He throws me a dirty look and grunts as he gets off the bed. *Right*, like I'd let somebody else touch me after Erik did such a number on me. Since him, I can look but not touch. No amount of naked, bulging muscles caused my insides to melt and my fingers to tingle in the desire to touch.

Until Alex.

Oh, how did I want to touch his imperfectly perfect face. I'm still surprised that I feel so free and safe around

Alex. I feel safe with Justin too now, completely, but my mind sees him as a friend. A good, loyal friend that I gained in such a short term. No butterflies in my belly at the sight of him. Plus, I love Kayla. There is no way I'd hurt her by even looking at Justin as anything more than a friend.

I get distracted watching as he fills the space of the room, his large shoulders coming into view as he peels his shirt off and discards it behind him. *God.* I step back toward the mirror and ignore the wetness growing in between my legs, and if it were a pair of pants, this new dress would be about to bite the dust. How does he turn me on so easily? I'm like a teenager again.

"Is there anything I should know about the people that will be at this party tonight? I know I've already met your family."

"Nope," he says shortly, and when I look around the corner at him again, he's wearing a white button-down that hides his scars, and his hair is brushed over the damaged part of his forehead. He's wearing black slacks and shiny shoes, and the whole outfit makes my breath hitch in my throat. I thought he looked hot in lumberjack clothes, but this outfit takes the cake.

He looks over at me, and we both allow each other to size the other up for a moment before he smiles.

"How about we do this one hundred-per-hour thing first?" He tries his luck with a lopsided smile on his boyish face.

I almost give in. Almost. "No. We'll go with the 'meet your family' part first."

He chuckles and nods his head toward the door. "Let's go, then."

. . .

Of course, everyone from Little Hope is at the party that Stella hosts in their big house, and if Alex had had his way, he wouldn't have been. The place is decorated with balloons saying *Happy 85th.* I don't see that joke going over well with Stella. And another saying 21 *again, a few times over.* Long tables by the walls are covered in food and all sorts of drinks. There are two separate tables designated for the flowers, and there is already no space left on them. I clutch a bouquet of white roses and a little bag to my chest. We stopped by the florist on the way here, and Alex gruffly suggested that white roses might be good, and when we were picking dresses with Kayla, I also got Stella a beautiful bracelet, hoping it would be an appropriate gift.

As we move through the crowd, I hate to say it, but Alex was right: every single person's staring, and not at me. At him. I look nervously at Alex while he mutters under his breath and tries to make a beeline for the bar. I grip his arm tightly, forcing him to stay by my side.

"You won't get lucky if you don't make it through this with a smile on your face," I mutter low in his ear while he glares at me. "*Smile*, Alex. It's a party. And they have to see you have the capacity to smile."

"They don't see me as you do, Freya. They still remember shit about me, and the way they see me will never change for this town."

"Your army story?"

"Navy," he corrects automatically with a scowl that I've come to love, "and no, not that one."

"Which one, then?" I narrow my eyes at him.

"Another story," he murmurs under his breath.

I'm about to drill him about this mysterious story just as Stella arrives to greet us. She gives me a warm smile and pulls me into a tight embrace just after I squash the flowers into Alex's hands. I melt into the hug. It feels so... *motherly*. Alex is missing out, the dummy.

"I'm so glad you both could make it!" Stella gushes with a grin. She reaches out to touch Alex on the arm, but he stiffens, and she retracts her hand. I notice the hint of pain behind her eyes, and I look up at Alex with a frown, but he refuses to look at me. I could back him up here if she was evil, but she's not. She actually cares about him, and it pains her to have him reject her attempts of connecting with him over and over again. I nudge Alex's shoulder, and he clears his throat, passing the flowers to Stella.

"For you," he grunts.

She takes the bouquet with a warm smile and sniffs it. "Thank you, they're so beautiful! I can't believe you remembered my favorite flowers!" Her eyes are misty. So are mine.

I push the delicate little bag into her hands, sniffing discreetly. "That's for you, too. From us."

"Oh, dear, you didn't have to." She clutches the flowers and the bag to her chest.

"I know. Just wanted to," I answer with a light smile. Because that's how I feel—light.

"Well, thank you! Now, you two, mingle and have fun! Excuse me," Stella says with a genuine smile. "Ken and the girls just got here."

I wait until she's busily greeting them before turning to Alex. He shrugs and tries to walk to the table where the food's placed.

"That was sweet," I comment, biting my lower lip and hinting that he might be rewarded for good behavior later, but he just goes and ruins it.

"I don't give a shit about this party." He glowers around us.

"Uh-uh. Not this time." I stand in his way and fold my

arms. "*She's* not the one that you should be having issues with," I hiss. "And especially not at her birthday!"

"We're only here because *you* wanted to come. I wouldn't have been invited if you hadn't been here. So, me being here by myself and not *mingling* doesn't change shit." He's sulking like a teenager just hitting puberty and not knowing how to control his hormonal emotions.

"You know why? Because they don't want it to turn into World War fucking Three every time you *do* get invited. You make it so everything's all about you."

He glares at me, grabs my arm, and roughly pulls me to the side of the room. The action should be a trigger for me, and I expect my heart to palpitate in familiar fear... But nothing comes. It makes me wonder if my body knows it's Alex, someone safe.

"Oh yeah?" he says, oblivious to the way he's grabbing me. "Why didn't my *dad* acknowledge me for the first twelve years of my fucking life, huh? Why was my mother left scrambling to find the money to raise *me, his* child?"

"It's not Stella's fault," I argue, "or yours. You were both thrown into a shitty situation, but she's actually trying to be a better person and make it work for both of you." I think a little and add, "Actually, she's trying to make it work for *you.*"

"Then she's an idiot for trying. And for not leaving that sorry excuse of a spouse."

I fold my arms over my chest and look over to where Alex's dad and Stella are having a similar conversation to the one we're having, judging by the hissed exclamations emanating from their corner. Alex looks similar to his father, and it's a comparison I know he'd resent me commenting on. "That woman raised the son that her husband fathered while still married to her. Think about it.

Think about what that must have felt like. *She* paid for *his* indiscretion. Your mother did too. Your problems aren't with your mother, your stepmother, or any other member of that goddamn family—they're with your *father*."

"Are they? I didn't know," he growls. "Thank you, Dr. Phil. Thanks for your input."

He stalks away from me before I can say another word, so I'm left to stand awkwardly until I notice Kayla being a wallflower by herself on the other side of the room. She's wearing a long, sleeveless black dress with a long slit cut up to her thigh that hugs her shapely figure, accentuating her tattoo and making her look like a seasoned seductress. If I'm not mistaken in my calculations, Justin will go home with blue balls. Serves him right.

I stomp over to her and scowl as a greeting.

"That good already, is it?" she says with a chuckle. "I feel you."

"I'm happy to see you here," I tell her sincerely.

"To be completely honest, I don't know *why* I'm here," she murmurs.

"What?" I turn to her and watch as she chugs a full glass of champagne. "Okay. Spill."

"Nothing to spill," she responds as she grabs another glass from the table nearby. "Never been a part of this crowd. Never will be. I think I got invited out of pity. And I came here because I wanted to be a part of *that*." She waves her hand around the room. "How pitiful is that, huh?"

I grab that waving hand and bring it to my chest. "You came here so I don't feel stupid and out of place, so thank you for that."

A beautiful smile spreads across her face, and I can't understand how men in Little Hope can be so blind when such a gorgeous woman's hiding right under their noses.

I keep people-watching for a few minutes until I notice a heated glare directed at Kayla. A very heated one. In fact, a bead of sweat slides down my temple just by looking at *that*. Justin's standing by the door, and judging by the lack of glass in his hand, he's just come in. His hands are fisted by his side. He squeezes them harder and then moves them inside his pockets. His jaw's clenched, and his whole posture is rigid. He looks like he's on the verge of murder. But his eyes tell me that he would be murdering with orgasms, most likely.

I carefully glance at Kayla and see she's oblivious. She doesn't see or feel that. How? How on earth can't she feel him eye-fucking her? I look at Justin, and when he notices my attention, he switches back to his joker self and smiles at me. Nah-ah. I saw it. I saw it. *Hates her guts*, my ass.

I'm finishing my second glass of champagne when Marina catwalks toward us. She's wearing a skin-tight red dress, stealing the show from half the ladies in the room, and they're throwing her dirty looks. She stops next to us, looking us up and down, obviously.

"You both cleaned up nicely, girls."

"Thank you, ma'am," I answer, and Kayla snorts.

"I see you're dead-set on giving Paul a stroke," she laughs, nodding toward Mustache Guy, who's been eyeballing Marina the whole time she was doing a podium walk through the room. Marina blushes sweetly and glances at him without saying a word.

"I have no idea what you're talking about," she shoots back, fidgeting with the strap of her purse. I exchange *looks* with Kayla, thinking it's all adorable. "Okay, I need another drink."

As soon as she walks off, we burst out laughing. "Poor guy. He's had a crush on her for as long as I can remember,"

Kayla explains, grabbing a tiny tartlet from the nearby table.

"I think they would look cute." Sizing them both up, I finally announce my verdict. Cute would be an understatement. Marina is a six-foot-tall lady, and the Mustache Guy —fine, *Paul*—is at least one head shorter.

"Oh, they will. Eventually. He will wear her down, I have faith in Paul," she answers, shoving another tartlet down. "Incoming," she warns, hiding behind her half-full glass.

"I knew you're exactly what he needs!" Donna comes out of nowhere and swallows me in a bear hug.

"Thanks?" My voice is muffled by her generous chest.

"So happy to see you both together, honey. So happy!" She keeps squishing me with love.

"Donna, I need your help here, if you can." I hear Stella call out from the kitchen, remembering Donna mentioning that they were good friends.

"Gotta go help the birthday girl. See you, ladies!" And she flies away, nearly knocking down the tray with drinks that have been so conveniently put next to us. I look at Kayla, and she just shrugs with another tartlet in her mouth.

After a few drinks, I've reached the level of tipsy that has me rearing to face Alex again, and I look around the party to find him. I stop in surprise when I see his tall figure across the room, talking to Adison. I narrow my eyes and watch the exchange, getting more and more irate the longer I watch them. Alex lifts his hand and touches her gently on the arm, smiling at her. Smiling *wide*. He smiled that widely at me only a number of times because usually, he's scowling, unhappy with literally everything. He must sense my glaring because he lifts his head up and meets my angry eyes across the room. He looks confused and... happy?

I give him one more glare and turn away, disappearing into the crowd. Here is yet more proof of exes being everpresent. If she truly was in the past, she wouldn't be ruining our first outing together with my... boyfriend? Friend with benefits? I still don't know who we are to each other.

ALEX

I scowl as Freya turns and disappears into the mass of people in the room. I don't like how she was staring at me, so I leave Adison to follow Freya. I've said everything that needed to be said anyway. Freya sure is fast for such a small woman, so I have to speed up if I plan on catching up with her before she reaches the Canadian border.

"Everything okay?" A familiar voice calls out to me, and I turn to see Leila leaning against the wall, her sharp eyes noticing everything all at once. For such a young person, she is extremely observant; if she were in the army, she'd be a strategist or a sniper. She's got a wine glass in her hand and an amused smile curving her painted lips.

"Yes. Fine," I bark.

She's in step with me as I start to follow Freya across the room. "I'm glad Freya's here. She's perfect for you." That's one of the very rare occasions Leila has talked to me of her own free will. I throw her a questioning look, but she just shrugs. "You're acting like a human being." Then she chuckles and adds, "Sort of."

"What's that supposed to mean?" I stop and look at her. I could never have imagined that my younger—much younger—and supposedly less wise sister would make me feel so uncomfortable just with one comment. And then I notice that I just called her my sister in my mind. Not *half*, but *sister*. Well, I guess she might be right after all.

Before I can question her on her statement any further, she veers off to the side and returns to her position by the wall, turning her eye onto someone else. My eyes linger on her for a few more seconds longer, and I wonder how the hell my sister grew up so fast and I haven't even noticed it. Maybe I should take her out for breakfast and... I don't know, talk?

I sigh and follow Freya, knowing Leila is right. The old me would have never even thought of chasing after Freya or anyone that I was seeing. I wasn't even seeing anyone before. Well, I've never used that word anyway and never wanted to be exclusive. Though, the thought of Freya with somebody else sends a cold sweat down my back.

"Hey, wait up." Ken's voice stops me.

"What?" I growl. Why do my siblings keep getting in my way today?

"I gotta ask you something." He catches up with me and nods for me to follow him to the side, where nobody can hear us. "Do you know what's happening with Jake?"

"How the fuck would I know that?"

"He's been acting out since your girlfriend showed up here. I was hoping you knew something." Kenneth looks serious, and since he knows I don't have warm feelings toward the brat, asking me about Jake must really be his last resort, so I soften my attitude a little. Grudgingly, I internally reflect that Freya would approve.

"I don't know, Ken," I sigh. "I know he's been a dick to her recently, but that's pretty much it. I don't know what's happening with him, but he's been on my ass even more lately."

He watches me carefully for a moment, then nods.

"Okay, call me if you hear anything. The idiot got suspended, I don't want him to throw his life away over a fling."

"Fling? They didn't have a *fling* if that's what you're implying." I'm getting mad at the thought of Freya and Jake together. And to think of it, I pretty much put them together in tight quarters when I was being a dick to her myself. I didn't see him as anything other than an annoyance. To be honest, I didn't think of Freya as anything else either back then.

"I'm talking about you."

"Yeah, how is that?" I take a step toward him while he holds his ground. He knows me too well to let my anger dictate his behavior. Plus, he's older, and I always wanted his attention. I've finally gotten it. Now what?

"If it's a fling, and she moves on to another town, you'll forget about her as she will about you. No harm done. But he's all riled up on protecting her from big, bad Alex. He's young and doesn't separate a fling from a permanent fixture." He must see the dumb look on my face because he sighs and continues, "Look, if you just fuck her and then send her on her merry way, it's one thing. You won't have time to show her all your shades of fucked up, but he doesn't know that. So he'll lose his job over your fling. He wants to protect her, do you get it?"

"From what?" I swallow.

"You know from what." He levels me with his stare.

I know, and he knows that I know. "I'll call you if I hear anything," I mutter with resignation, and he nods. Now, I need to go and find that sexy little fling... who looked pretty upset just minutes ago.

I look around and don't see her. I assess the room again

and finally notice Kayla pointing at the door and mouthing "idiot." Don't I know that.

I almost run outside just in time to see Freya slipping her high heels off, preparing to start walking.

"*Freya*," I growl. It's freaking freezing, what the hell is she doing? I have no fucking clue where she thinks she's going, but I run over to her and grab her hand, spinning her to face me. Her hand comes up as I do, and she slaps me hard on the non-scarred side of my face. Anger bursts to life inside me, and I grip her tight on both her upper arms, lifting her clear off the ground. Her eyes widen in fear, breaking through my anger.

"Put me down," she says through gritted teeth.

I gently place her on the ground and put several steps between us, turning away. "You shouldn't be outside, at night, alone, Freya. *You know this.* And put your fucking shoes back on." My voice is vindictive, I know it. Also, I know I should be soothing her and not scaring a woman who was abused by her husband, but I can't help myself. Not when my own issues are flaring up.

"Yes, well, right now, I feel like I'd rather take whatever punishment that's coming to me from Erik than stay here and watch you all over your ex in there." Her voice quavers, and I don't like the burning hole it's searing in my chest.

"Put your shoes on." My request comes off more as a command, and she shows she doesn't like it by sticking her jaw forward. I sigh and add more gently, "Please."

She glares at me for a second, but then common sense wins out, and she slips her shoes back on. Her ankle boots are torturously sexy, but the heels are so high my feet ache just looking at them.

I look over at her in alarm, but she's not looking at me; her arms are folded, and her hip is popped as she glares at the ground. I sigh and take a step toward her. Her defiant eyes lift to me, and I stop in my tracks. I swallow my anger and close my eyes to calm down. "You've asked me before what story the town remembers. Well, here is your story." I sigh and prepare myself for the inevitable when she learns the truth. "When I came back, and we tried to have sex"—Freya winces, but she had to hear that—"I had one of my flashbacks and hit her. And that's what everybody remembers when they see me. Not a war hero, but an asshole who hits women," I say flatly. "I was apologizing to her, something I can only do because you're in my life now." I shake my head. "But you will always follow your assumptions before asking me. Just like everybody else."

"I believe what I can see, Alex. And what I saw was a reconnecting of two old lovers." She points dramatically toward where the sounds of the party are filtering through the open doors. "You just spent the whole *hour* we've been here ignoring everyone, ignoring *me*, but you're more than happy to flirt with her. Oh yeah, and I forgot to add—right after we fought about you refusing to mingle with anyone." The grown-up Freya, who can reason with everything I came to know, is gone, and a brand-new teenage Freya is out. She just needs to stomp her foot, and the picture would be perfect.

"As I said... I was *apologizing*." I accentuate the last word, trying like hell to sound calm even though I'm anything but.

And why the hell is she focusing on that part? Hasn't she heard what I just said? Or is flirting a bigger crime than abuse in her eyes?

"Well, where is *my* apology for leaving me in there alone?" Her lips are pursed, and a deep crease appears between her eyebrows.

I groan loudly and throw my hands up. "You shouldn't fucking need one. You just assumed I was flirting with her right after I crawled out of *your* bed." I pace a few steps away before jabbing my finger in her direction. "How did you make this all about you, huh? Will it happen every time I speak to another woman?" I can't stop anymore.

My frustrations reach a boiling point. At Freya for stirring something in me that was supposed to be long dead to life. At Justin for always trying to stick around, even when I don't want him to. At Adison for running her mouth all those years ago, even though I deserved it. With this town, who thinks of me as a monster. With my family, who sees me as a fuck-up and an outcast.

She stares at me, not blinking, her expression blank.

"What happened with you, Frey? You're different somehow. You were this carefree, intelligent woman, and now you're—" I cut myself off before I say something even worse.

"I'm what?" she says through gritted teeth.

"Nothing." My sigh is defeated. "Let's go home."

"I'm what, Alex?" she repeats stubbornly.

"Let's go home, Freya."

"I'm *what*, Alex?" Her voice raises to almost yelling, and that does it.

"Clingy. You're fucking clingy." The moment I say it out loud, I regret it because the corners of her lips dip down even more, and I want to punch myself in the face. She stands there watching my face.

"Why are you so quiet all of a sudden? You had so much to say to me moments ago!" I breathe heavily before pointing toward where my truck's parked.

"What if it's the real me?" She finally confuses the hell out of me with her question.

"What?" I stumble back because this admission seems... a breakthrough of sorts.

"What if this *is* the real me? Clingy, needy, and crazy, huh? What if, for the first time in my life, I let myself just be me, just so I can feel a freedom of being weak, of needing and wanting something I'm not supposed to have, because I'm free to do so, huh?" She advances on me, and I take a step back, not because I'm scared, but because I know I did the wrong thing at the wrong time. "What if this is the first time I've wanted you to tell me that I'm special and deserving, but you just went and threw it all away. Threw my feelings away. Huh? The first person I wanted to show my real self to, and you just... disregarded me. Fuck you, Alex Crowley. Fuck you." And with those last words, she storms to my truck. I take a relieved breath, thanking the universe for her not having a choice but to go with me.

I want to tell her that I see her, that I want to understand her and to take all the shit I just spouted back, that I want her to give me another chance and be silly with me, throwing tantrums left and right if she wants.

I want to tell her that I'm scared of change. I'm scared to live a life when *they* can't anymore. That I'm scared to leave that dark, dark place I've been stuck in for so long of my own free will. That she was the one who pulled me out of it. That I'm scared and ashamed that I like my new life in the light. I hate her for that. And I love her for that.

But I don't tell her any of that.

Chapter Twenty

A^{LEX}

Freya doesn't say a word during the entire drive back to my place, but she stays in the car when I switch the engine off. She stares out the window. I don't know how to express all the things I'm feeling; they suffocate me after being suppressed for so long. I don't know how to, so instead of something sensible and nice, I say:

"Are you going to go inside or camp in the car for the night?"

She continues to ignore me, and I shake my head in frustration.

"Fine. Stay here." I can't trust myself around anyone right now, especially her; I'm feeling a familiar tingling in the back of my head, warning about a new outburst coming. Eager to escape. I slam the door behind me and storm inside, keeping an eye on the truck, anxious at her being by herself in the dark night. I switch on the porch light and can just barely make out her face in the shadows.

She's so *frustrating*. A complication that my life doesn't need. No, my life hadn't been great before she'd showed up, but I made peace with the way I'd never be happy again. It had been okay. I *chose* to be the way I am. People left me alone, and I left them alone. And now I'm drowning in these feelings, and I hate that.

Eventually, a few minutes—or hours—later, I watch as she gets out of the truck and walks slowly toward the house, and I'm alarmed at the sudden ache in my chest at the determined look in her eyes. She's about to leave again, and the idea's surprisingly terrifying.

She sighs and stands in front of me, shutting the door behind her. "You're right, for once. Everyone's better off if I leave." She folds her arms and tilts her jaw. "As soon as I'm gone, my problems will be as well. I'm more trouble than I'm good for, which is what I said to you right from the very beginning." She shakes her head, and I can tell... I can just *tell* she's not being petty, she actually believes it, and *I* was the one who put those thoughts in her head.

"Freya..." The ache in my chest intensifies.

"No, Alex." She turns and strides to the bedroom, pulls her suitcase out from under the bed, and places it heavily on top. "You're the one who's constantly telling me to trust you, and then you never give me any explanation for your actions." Her voice is getting louder. "I don't know where I stand. I really don't." She's throwing clothes into her suitcase angrily, the colors of the fabrics blurring with her speed. "We're never on the same page. We're barely reading the same *book*. I thought I could let myself be... different around you, but I was wrong, and I apologize for assuming too much."

I scowl. "And you're going to solve all your problems by running away again? Just like you always do?"

Freya stands up straight, then steps in front of me and holds her hand out, eyes narrowed. "The keys to my Chevy, please. I know you have them. I saw Justin pass them to you."

I stare at her outstretched hand, then cross my arms on my chest. "No."

"Why?" she challenges, her voice bordering on pitchy with agitation. "Because you can't live without me?" She rolls her eyes sarcastically. "*Give* me my keys."

"Were you not listening to anything I just said?" I implore.

"*Keys. Now.*"

"You don't understand anything, do you?" I shout. "You, leaving this—*me*—will make everything go back to being *bad* again." I close my eyes and inhale deeply before letting it out. Freya's determined look fades to uncertainty, and her arm drops.

I step closer to her and tilt her face up to look at me, my hands gentle on her skin. Freya's right, and it pains me to accept that. I never told her where we stood, sure as fuck never mentioned exclusivity, and she doesn't seem like the type who likes to share. Seeing me with Adison might have looked like something more than it was. "I thought that apologizing to Adison, accepting what I've done, would let me move forward. With you. *Any* of you." I cover my face with my hands. "Man, I'm just fucking everything up. She doesn't want me, and I don't want her. It was like doing a fucking twelve-step program for an alcoholic." I take a deep breath and back away from her. "You know, until this moment, I wanted to believe that I didn't hit her that night, but I *don't* remember. I don't fucking remember! And all their stares reminded me of that. Reminded me of who I am and that I have to be around you, a person with a fucking abusive ex-hole. What if I slip up again and hurt you? How would I live with myself after that?" Only now do I dare to look at her.

"Alex," Freya says slowly, and I hear resentment in her tone. She's given up on me.

"I want you here, I do," I say in defeat.

"That's not what you said."

"I know, but I didn't mean that. I promise. I'm just scared about what will happen when I hurt you." How can I explain it so that she understands?

"Alex," Freya whispers, her eyes trained on my face. "You are not the monster you see yourself as. You won't hurt me or anybody else."

I slowly shake my head. "I am."

"I don't think you are. I *know* you're not." She carefully walks toward me and stops one foot from me.

"But what if I am?" I whisper as I lean closer.

She gently grabs my face and pulls it to hers until our foreheads rest together.

"I'll never believe that," she whispers back.

I sigh, long and low. "Why are you on my side, Freya? Why do you believe in me so blindly?"

There's a long pause. "I wish I could answer that," she says quietly.

I tilt my head and press my lips to hers, bored of talking about how much I want her to stay and itching to prove it. She tastes like alcohol and has a flavor that is uniquely Freya. It's deadly and intoxicating all in the same breath, especially when she dips her tongue into my mouth and her fingers tangle into the hair in the back of my head.

I pull her closer and lift her up in my arms, her legs

hitching to wrap around my waist. Carrying her over to the bed, I push her suitcase off and growl at the back of my throat as she tightens her grip on me until it's almost painful. "Stay," I breathe in her ear as I slide my hand under her dress and reach the edge of her panties. "Don't leave." My fingers find her wet center, and she whimpers with need, dropping her head back on the bed and squeezing her eyes shut. "Promise me you'll stay."

"Alex," she gasps as I gently pulse my fingers in and out of her.

"Promise."

She gasps again when my movements pick up speed.

"Alex," she breathes out, and I nearly come undone.

I drag her lips back to mine in a fierce kiss and let my fingers work their magic to bring her to a fiery orgasm, hoping with it I imprint on her the feel of me, the taste of me, and the *knowledge* of me.

I don't notice until much later that she never did make that promise.

Chapter Twenty-One

F**REYA**

Kayla screws her nose up when we sit in a booth at the diner the following morning. "I can't believe I'm at work on my day off," she complains in a low voice.

"You love Marina too much to let her work alone when her back's hurting so bad."

Kayla's face changes instantly—she looks like she's about to puke—and then she covers her ears with her hands. "La-la-la, I don't want to hear anything else!" Considering the fact Kayla thinks of Marina as the mother she never had but always needed and the fact that we saw Mustache Guy sucking on her neck yesterday at the party, she probably doesn't want to think about the nature of the activities that threw out Marina's back.

I grin and order something a little lighter than a Lonely Kurt this time. There are only so many Lonely Kurts I can eat and retain my shape. No amount of running can save my waist from Marina's delicious cooking.

"Have you heard that Jake got suspended?" Kayla asks after she stops fake-gagging.

"Really? No! What happened?"

"I don't know the details, but I've heard he failed the shooting range or something a couple of days ago," she elaborates between sips. "I think Kenneth even took his badge and gun."

"For failing the range?" I'm confused.

"I guess." She adds more coffee. "I also heard that he got into fights with a few people while on duty, so Kenneth didn't have a choice." Then she looks at me and adds with a cheeky smile, "I guess." Right—she doesn't feel bad for Jake because he's been an asshole toward her for a long time, and in her eyes, he deserves that. In mine too, a little. He clearly uses his badge to bully her.

"How do you know that?"

"Small town," she explains with a shrug.

"Ri-i-i-i-ght," I singsong. By now, this phrase should explain everything.

"Anyway, are you going to come with me to the outdoor movie night tonight at The Dancing Pony? Or is Alex going with you?"

I snort. "Alex? At a screening of *The Hobbit*? No. It'll be just me. I can't wait. Though it will be freezing." I shudder at the thought of watching an outdoor movie at close-to-freezing temperatures.

"Nah, it'll be fine," she assures me. "Just put something warm on. You have a costume?" She sounds excited.

I grin. "All ready to go! Stores here sure sell a lot of themed stuff."

"Yeah, it's one of our few activities besides drinking.

Small towns." She shrugs her shoulders. "The Dancing Pony has a *lo-o-o-ot* of different themed nights." She bats her eyelashes at me, and I choke on my bacon, remembering my initial thoughts about The Dancing Pony.

"Right." *These small towns...* "Anyway, I'll meet you there tonight. I'll get Alex to drop me off if he's not too pissed off with me."

Kayla sees Marina walking from the kitchen with two heavy plates and jumps up to help, but Marina waves her off. "Chill, will ya?"

"Thank you, ma'am." Kayla grins and grabs a fork from the table. Once Marina's gone, she turns to me. "I feel like something might've happened again. What was it?"

I let out a huff and roll my eyes. "The same as always. Tells me one thing and then tells me another right after it."

She shakes her head in sympathy and disgust. "*Men.*"

"Mmm... tell me about it." I look over at her and raise my eyebrows. "How's Justin?"

Her expression shutters. "Ignoring me. Like always. Jake is too now." She picks at her fries almost dejectedly, then sighs. "At least he stopped giving me speeding tickets. So that's a plus." She mock-cheers me with a forkful of potatoes and tries to smile, but I see through it.

"Jake's ignoring me," I offer in sympathy. "Probably for the best. Since he's with Adison now." I shrug, pretending that it doesn't bother me in the slightest.

Kayla rolls her eyes. "Yeah, you won the lottery here. Jake isn't such a good guy, Freya. And he likes to run his mouth a lot, just like Adison. Who knows what they could tell Erik? Now we at least know that Erik doesn't have very direct contact with her. Did you tell Alex about Erik and Adison being together?"

"No," I mutter.

"Why? I think Alex should know."

"You might be right, but I don't think Adison could offer any vitally important insights to Erik, given that she doesn't actually know anything. Besides that, every time Adison's name is mentioned, Alex and I fight. Like, every single time. I don't want to destroy my last days in Little Hope by mentioning the Wicked Witch's name."

Her eyes go round as she sees something over my shoulder, and she subtly nods her head toward the door.

"Speak of the devil," she mutters.

I glance over to see Adison. She meets my gaze instantly and plants a fake smile on her lips. I give Kayla a meaningful look as Adison begins picking her way over to us. "'Devil' wasn't exactly the word I would've used..." I murmur back. My word would've rhymed nicely with a *witch*.

Adison comes to a halt in front of our table, flicking her hair over her shoulder. "Look what the cat dragged in," she drawls. "It appears trailer trash likes to stick."

Kayla looks down at her food, and I take a shaky breath, trying to remain calm and think about Alex's words to me. He felt terrible for what he supposedly did, and I'm supposed to feel bad as well for what he might have done or not done. Unfortunately, for that to happen, Adison needs to shut her goddamned mouth, and since she doesn't look like she's prepared to do that, I'm not prepared to see her as a victim—because she sure as hell doesn't look like one.

"It looks like Alex's taste has gone downhill since he left me, hasn't it?"

"Oh, honey, no," I croon. "He could have only gone *up. Look* at you. Any day now, and that thick layer of foundation won't be able to cover up the Dorian Gray painting you're hiding underneath."

Kayla nearly chokes on her food and Adison's jaw tenses.

"The fuck do you mean? I don't have a—a Dorian Gray on my face." She scratches the corner of her lips, and I smile.

"But you *so* do."

Kayla is visibly struggling not to laugh out loud.

"Your eyes give away your dark, dark soul. Just like Dorian's." I smile sweetly. "Dorian kept his portrait in his attic though." I paste on an exaggerated expression of mock contemplation, then wave a hand in the general direction of her skull. "You *do* have a lot of empty space available there, so maybe you should think about giving that a try."

Adison's jaw begins moving from side to side, and I'm a little scared she's about to spurt fur and transform into a she-wolf. I'm starting to think perhaps it's time I stop poking the bear—or she-wolf, as it were—but Kayla finally looks like she's getting more self-assured in Adison's toxic presence; she's sitting up straighter and can manage to look Adison in the heavily-mascaraed eye.

"So *he* was right," Adison spits, before looking at me, and lead slowly settles in my gut. I know who she's talking about. She's clearly standing with a smile on her face, waiting for me to question her about who she assumes is a mysterious he. But I won't give her the satisfaction. Or him.

"Oh, yes," I say dryly. "I bet he was."

"He's all over me now. Just like Alex will be again soon. *I* know what he likes." She waves her hand in the general area of her chest.

"People with hearts?" I say bluntly, trying not to dwell on the idea of Erik intervening in my life once again. "Who stays loyal despite appearances?"

I can see Adison knows precisely what I mean instantly

because an unbecoming flush stains her cheeks; she looks furiously between Kayla and me, then turns on her heels and storms out.

I feel a little guilty about the way I spoke to her, but I also know the utter bullshit that she's said about Kayla in front of me, and I'm not about to sit here and take it without comment. Why do people keep calling her that? Living in a trailer doesn't make you trash; talking shit about people does. Kayla is one of the purest people I've ever met. The sooner Adison, Jake, Justin, and the rest of Little Hope figure that out, the better.

Chapter Twenty-Two

FREYA

Alex is already glaring at me when I arrive home. He's leaning on the counter with arms crossed over his chest, waiting for my inevitable arrival. I don't have time for this. I'm already running late to get to The Dancing Pony before they start the movie. From what I've heard from Kayla and Donna, a lot of the town goes to these things, and everyone goes all out. It means I have no time for an argument with Alex, which has already been penciled in on the schedule, so I walk to the bedroom, knowing he'll follow. He's after my blood now, he'll come for me anywhere.

"Did you have a nice conversation with Adison?" he drawls darkly, leaning on the bedroom doorframe.

I tilt my head from where I'm sitting on the floor, digging into my suitcase as if considering. "Not particularly."

He doesn't look to appreciate my humor. "I thought I told you to leave her alone."

I shrug and keep looking for the hobbit costume I picked out a few days ago. All my life is still in one suitcase, nothing has changed, even though I got a little too comfortable. "*Told me to leave her alone.* Right. Like I'm a paradigm of pure evil over here. You have an Adison-shaped blind spot because you feel guilty and don't see her faults."

He tracks my movements. "What the fuck is that supposed to mean?"

I throw him a frustrated look. "It *means* she walked into the diner, started calling Kayla names, and made a scene. I could have easily left her alone, but *she* didn't leave *me* alone, and I'm going to stand up for myself and Kayla because nobody else in this shitty town does."

Alex takes a calming breath, but the anger doesn't leave his eyes. "You're saying she just walked up to you at the diner and started being a bitch for no reason."

"Yep," I respond, popping the P, "that's exactly what happened."

Apparently, he doesn't believe me. "You insulted her physical appearance, Freya. She had to protect herself. I didn't know you had such a mean streak in you." Alex shakes his head disappointedly.

I begin laughing at that. "Really? That's the version you're going with? So, what exactly did I say to her?"

"You know what you said."

I cock my head at him, pausing in ravaging my suitcase —this moment deserves my full attention. "I do, but you obviously know better than I do, so please enlighten me." I'm about to be *so* done with this situation.

"You told her that she looks old and ugly," he claims. "I

didn't know you say that shit to other women. I didn't expect that from you."

I freeze. Turns out Alex doesn't know me at all. "You really believe that?"

He presses his hand to his forehead. "I don't know, Freya. I don't. I've seen you from a different side these days, so I really don't know what to believe."

Ouch. That one hurts. Especially after my heart-wrenching admission about showing him my true self. I've never been a Band-Aid who sticks to the guy and doesn't let him pee alone, but even if I were, so what? It wouldn't make me any less of a person. Besides that, once in a while, everybody deserves to be a little clingy and a little dependent, and today is my turn.

"She's vain. She can't even look you in the fucking *eyes*, Alex. And you're protecting her right now? Really?"

"This isn't me protecting her," he argues stubbornly, even though we both know it is.

"Oh, really? So what's *this*, then?" I point at the space between us.

"It's me being disappointed in you."

"Fuck you, Alex. I didn't tell her she looked old. I told her she looked like Dorian Gray with all her vanity, cruel jabs, and all that evilness. If she only reads the instruction labels on shampoo bottles, that's her problem, not mine," I almost yell, but I don't care anymore.

Alex looks confused. "Dorian Gray?"

"Yes, Dorian Gray. You know, the guy who sinned like it's nobody's business and tried hiding it in the painting so he could act ugly without looking ugly? Sound familiar?" He doesn't say anything, and although I see that my words are getting to him and he would understand my side should

I push a little more, I'm done explaining, and I don't want to hear a word he wants to say.

I get my phone out, stride away, and dial Kayla.

"Change of plans. Can you pick me up?"

ALEX

When I got the call from a hysterical Adison, I was so mad that I had to go outside to chop wood to release steam. The amount of firewood I've sliced and diced since Freya came into my life is alarming, and the pile is still steadily climbing.

I didn't imagine Freya to be so malicious, but it turned out I was wrong. And I had told her Adison's story! Why would she exacerbate that? I had traumatized Adison, and I don't even know if she's ever had a normal relationship after that night. God knows I haven't. And I'm forever in debt for ruining her life.

But after that fight with Freya, I'm not so sure anymore. Freya looked sincerely hurt, and my instincts have always said she's a good, honest person. What happened? Clouded judgment on my side? God, I might have made a huge mistake. Again. Why would I want to protect Adison and not Freya? Was she right, and I just feel guilty? Freya had been abused for years, for fuck's sake, and I just disregarded her feelings and took Adison's side even before hearing Freya out.

I growl in frustration and smack a new lamp on the side table. The lamp goes flying to the wall. Fuck that, I gotta fix the mess I've made. Again. And I'm not talking about the damn lamp—I just have to stop buying those fuckers; they don't survive long around me.

Kayla's already smirking when I walk up to her at the outdoor *The Hobbit* screening. Everyone's dressed up and excitedly sitting on piles of blankets or low chairs, facing the projector screen on the side of the building. Emma's waving at me excitedly from the chair in the first row—it's my first time ever showing up at one of her events.

"Cute ears," Kayla taunts.

I move my attention to her and narrow my eyes, ignoring that. "Where's Freya?"

"Restroom." Kayla cocks her head and clicks her tongue disapprovingly. "You've really gone all the way and fucked up pretty bad this time." She huffs a humorless laugh. "What's up with guys protecting their exes from their current girlfriends right to their faces?" She looks at me as if expecting an answer. I can't give her one because I wasn't *trying* to protect Adison, I was scolding Freya—which is probably even worse. Kayla looks me up and down. "This might do the trick. This costume makes you look almost like a cute little hobbit. Almost." She winks at me, and I feel lighter. If she approves, I might stand a chance.

I sigh. "Almost is not enough this time."

"Yet you're wearing elf ears and have a ratty blanket around your shoulders like a cape. That might look like you're saying you're very sorry for something." She folds her arms and squints her heavily painted eyes. "So what were you doing with Adison?" She's asking like she hasn't just sent me through a washing machine cycle on high heat. Sounds like cheap fishing.

"Not you too," I growl. It's bad enough I've got Justin and Ken trying to weasel their way into my relationship with Freya, let alone *Kayla*. "I think you'd do well to keep your nose out of my business." And just like that, all the brownie points I'd gained are most likely revoked. Damn it, I need her on my side.

"Mmm... I'd love to. But your business keeps rearing up in my face, Alex. And we *both* know I don't mean Freya." She glares at me, and I close my mouth again for a moment just so I can grind my teeth together in frustration.

"Adison is not my responsibility, and she has never been." I'm growing aggravated and regretting ever letting my dick near Adison.

"You do realize that she's sleeping with Freya's ex, right?"

My eyes widen. "The fuck?"

"Oh please, don't pretend you don't know. The whole town knows."

I take a step closer to her while she holds her ground and tilts her head back so she can meet my eyes. "What are you talking about, Kayla?"

The array of different emotions that runs over her face is almost comically varied—surprise, comprehension, fear, and then clear, *oh fuck*—before defeat eclipses the rest. "She slept with Erik while he was snooping around," she admits. "I didn't know it was him, but I had my suspicions. And now, she's sleeping with Jake. I can't say for sure, but she may be using him to fish for info he might've gotten from Justin or you or Ken. That's my suspicion, at least."

Motherfucker.

Right here, under my nose. I'm an idiot, and I messed up with Freya. She saw right through Adison while I was blinded by my guilt, which she was right about too. Another problem rises to the forefront of my mind—what did she tell *Erik?* Saying his name even mentally threatens bile to rise up in my throat. There isn't much that she could share as far as I know, but she's been in my cabin plenty of times enough to have learned strategic entry points, and she knows my schedule well enough to share when I'm around or not.

"Oh, I see a fun scenario running through that big, stupid brain where you end up alone in that cabin of yours with thirty cats because you couldn't stop being a jerk."

I scowl at her, but she's not done.

"Oh, and here's a hot tip for you—*don't* flirt with your demonic ex at a party right in front of your girlfriend." She smacks her forehead with a little too much force that she begins rubbing it right away.

"I did *not* flirt with her," I growl. "I was trying to apologize to her!"

Kayla frowns in bemusement. "For what?"

"You know what."

"No, I don't." She only looks more perplexed.

"For... the *incident*," I say, embarrassed.

I see the moment when she realizes what I'm talking about. She lifts her hand and puts it on my forearm, which is taut with tension.

"I never believed her, Alex. Not for a moment. And there are quite a few of us who never did."

And she turns back to the screen. Just like that. A woman who's been referred to as "trailer trash" more times than not by a few big mouths says that she believes in me. When even *I* don't believe in me. She has trust in me, while I don't have trust in her. When I was still a part of society, I used to be around those loudmouths a lot and heard some shit being poured over Kayla's head, and I said nothing. Even though I don't think she deserves to be called that—or anyone does, for that matter—I still kept out of the drama.

But that's about to change because there are people who need me. Even if it's only sometimes.

I realize that Kayla is a good person, and she will be a great friend to Freya. And that story with Justin... it will have to be forgotten somehow. The talk with Justin is long overdue.

I'm about to thank her when Freya arrives with narrowed eyes. "What are you doing here?"

I eyeball Kayla one more time and take Freya by the arm. "Let's talk."

"I'd really rather not. I want to watch a movie and have a good time. We can have an argument... oh sorry, I mean chat... when I get home."

"Please," I implore, and her attitude wavers a little, but then she's back to freezing me out.

"We already had plans," she informs me as she shakes her arm out of my grip and walks back to sit next to Kayla. I take a deep breath to calm myself before walking to sit next to her.

"Okay," I say simply. "Let's watch a movie." She studies me warily, then turns her attention to the screen as the movie starts playing.

FREYA

I'm a little confused by Alex's presence at the movie night, but he leans back on his hands and watches the dragon hovering over his gold with surprising focus. I'm still mad at him for confronting me about Adison and taking her side, but I'm also a little touched by his gesture of coming here. I know how much he hates socializing and coming down from his solitude on the mountain, but he is here, watching a long-ass movie with almost the whole town. For me. And he looks adorable in those ears. I guess this is as close to a date as I'm going to get with this guy on such short notice. Why not enjoy it a little while I can?

I hear shuffling and notice Kayla looking for an escape route. When she meets my eyes, she stands up. "Need to pee," she announces loudly and winks at me. I smile gratefully and lean into Alex's embrace, getting comfortable. He nuzzles his nose into my hair, and I snuggle deeper under his arm.

Alex sits up properly and grins. "Good. Now we're alone."

"We are not. We have people all ar—"

He tangles his fingers into the back of my hair and covers my lips with his. I gasp in surprise, and he uses it to dive in. I let my hands roam over his chest and dig nails into his muscles. I hear his growl, and I'm about to respond in a similar manner when I suddenly remember we're not alone. I push him gently off and hear a few chuckles around us.

"What was that for?" I whisper when he finally pulls away.

The grin that's spreading over his face, changing the very shape of it, makes my breath catch for a second. He runs his arm around my shoulders, pulling me in tight. "A few reasons. *One*, I've wanted to do that for ages. You've been sitting here next to me for almost an hour now, and you've given me a boner for almost the same amount of time."

I roll my eyes, but he continues.

"*Two*, you're mad at me, and I don't want you to be. That's not how I want to spend my evening. *Three*, I was an idiot."

"This is a long list." I chew my lower lip.

"*Four*, I'm bored." He kisses my hair. "And this movie is fucking long, and I want to whisk you away from here and have you all to myself." I tilt my head up to look at him, and he plants a gentle kiss on my lips. "But I guess I can tolerate being here as long as you can forgive me."

"I think I can manage," I whisper. "But *The Hobbit* goes for nearly three hours. How much of a guilty idiot do you feel like?"

His mouth drops open. "*Three* hours? What the fuck?"

I smirk and glance over the people to see Kayla sitting with Marina. She notices and gives me a wave and a wink, so I know I'm free.

I turn back to Alex and purse my lips. "I've seen this movie five times." I shrug. "Do you have anything else in mind?"

He throws an excited grin my way before helping me to stand. "Come on. There's something I want to show you."

Alex drives the truck off the main road, going deeper into the dark, quiet forest. "Are we going to get eaten by bears?" I probe. "Because I've already experienced that enough for one lifetime."

He grins. "The only bear who's going to be eating you is me. You'll just have to see when we get there."

There's a clearing that Alex stops in before grabbing a backpack by my feet and hopping out of the car. "Come on." He pulls a huge puffer jacket from the back seat and hands it over to me. "Put it on, it's going to be very cold this high up."

"It was already freezing down there, not sure I can

handle any colder," I complain as I get out into the chilly air and suddenly notice how clear the sky is above us. The stars glitter brightly; you can never see them so clearly in the city if you ever can. "Wow."

"This way. Stay by me."

I put the jacket on and hurry to catch up to him. After a couple of yards into the forest, a large tree appears in my vision. Alex hands me the flashlight he's been carrying and positions my hand to show the beam on a wooden ladder nailed to the tree. The beam above me can't see the top of it.

"Trust me," Alex whispers low in my ear, and I take a deep breath, put the flashlight in my mouth, and start climbing.

There's a state-of-the-art treehouse at the top. It's sturdy, large, and obviously professionally built.

I wait for Alex to catch up, and he grins, switching on a dim bulb. "What do you think?"

"This is... *incredible*. Is it yours?"

He shakes his head. "Not really. My grandfather made it for my dad and his brothers." He grabs the picnic blanket I had used at the movie and spreads it on the wood before pulling out a bottle of wine and two glasses from the backpack. I narrow my eyes at him. "You were planning this?"

"No, but I was sure hoping."

I grin and accept the glass from him.

I sigh happily and look at the dark scenery lit up by the moonlight. "This is magical. I bet you spent a lot of time here as a kid?"

He shakes his head slowly and takes the glass out of my hand before tugging me back, so we're lying down. Above us is open, the beautiful sparkling stars glittering peacefully at us. "I didn't know it existed until I was twelve." The time his mom died, he moved to his father's house. "I only found out when Ken and his friends came here to smoke weed, and I followed them to spy on them."

"Ken? Smoke weed?" I'm shook.

"Yeah, believe it or not, he was a naughty kid growing up."

"I don't!"

He chuckles. "You'd be wrong."

"Did you come here with them then? After you discovered the place, I mean."

"No," he admits with sizable regret.

I'm so sad for him and so enraged on his behalf. He should never feel like an outcast with his own family, but he did. He still does. No wonder he dreads family gatherings.

I let the silence surround us before gasping when I see a shooting star above us. "Aw!" I squeeze my eyes shut. "Starlight, star bright, first star I see tonight. I wish I may, I wish I might have this wish I wish tonight."

"What did you wish for?" I can detect a smile in his tone.

I open my eyes and grin over at him. "Can't tell, or it won't come true."

Alex smiles and props himself up on his elbow, nudging my face with his nose to get me to look at him again. He feathers a kiss against my lips before coming back for more.

"You're right." I sigh contentedly. "This is better than *The Hobbit*."

"Told you."

"Although I think it's adorable that you're still wearing your elf ears." I carefully pinch one of those.

Alex pulls back in surprise before reaching up and tugging the ears off, flinging them off the side of the treehouse. "What elf ears?"

I burst into laughter and pull him down on top of me.

Chapter Twenty-Three

F REYA

"Freya! Darling!"

I turn in surprise as the next morning, I'm walking down Main Street and spot Stella hurrying out of the grocery store, her arms loaded with bags of groceries. I rush forward and take one of the bags just as it's about to tip forward.

"Oh! Thank you!" she says, nodding her head as I take another one so she's not overloaded. "That'll teach me for trying to carry it all at once without a cart. My car is just over there."

I grin and start following her. "I swear it's a universal human compulsion. We're just trying to do as much as we can in one go."

Stella chuckles. "Yes, I think you're right. Sorry I didn't

get to see you much at the party, dear. There were a lot of people."

"We left early too, so no worries."

Her eyes go soft. "I... wanted to say how grateful I am that you got him to come in the first place. He's so..."

"Frustrating?" I say dryly.

She laughs. "A lot of us are, but... he's so tied up in a mess that should never have been put on his shoulders. His parents, *me* and I put too much responsibility on him. Involved him in the adult drama that was not suitable for a twelve-year-old. Especially not a twelve-year-old grieving the loss of his mother."

I smile awkwardly. "I know it's none of my business, Stella. I only know what Alex has told me, and it's not a lot."

"I know. The fact that he's told you *anything* says more than you know." She smiles and pats me on the cheek. "He's been through a hard lot, Freya. A lot of change, a lot of pain. Remember that."

"I will. I would also love to have a talk with his father," I state in a stern voice, understanding that I'm utterly over-stepping.

"Yes, somebody has to," she agrees sadly, and I can see there are still many unresolved issues between her and Keith. "I'm happy that Alex has somebody like you in his corner."

"I'm in your corner, too," I tell her sincerely.

"Thank you, dear," she replies through a light sheen of mist in her eyes, then she blinks rapidly and adds, "Oh, darn it. Freya, love, are you able to send this letter for me? It has to be dropped off at the post office."

"Sure thing. I was heading in that direction anyway." I wasn't, but I take the envelope and scan the address on the front. It's for a competition out of an old-fashioned magazine.

"I'm hoping to win a car, so I can get rid of this old piece of junk." She grins cheekily and climbs into her car, which, admittedly, isn't exactly a newer model. Weird. Keith has a lot of money, from what I can tell. Why wouldn't she just buy a new car?

She rolls her window down and says, right before she leaves, "I never believed the stuff Adison was spewing. I know that boy, and what she said about him... It's not him." She gives me a grateful smile and drives off.

Huh. I chuckle and wave good-bye as she drives away, her car imitating the noise of a jet engine trying to take off. She does need a new car.

And Alex needs to be spanked for how he treats this wonderful woman who is more mother to him than he realizes.

I walk toward the post office and study the envelope. "Good luck, Mr. Car. Stella needs you."

I'm coming out of the post office when I nearly smack into Jake. Despite the cold, skinny jeans, and dark Ray-Bans, he's wearing a tight tee and is chewing gum like a cool kid. He looks like the bad-boy villain in a teen rom-com. By the way he freezes and jumps away from me, you'd think I had some disease. It's hard to remember that I might have called him a friend not long ago.

"I don't have the plague, Jake," I growl. "I don't know what your problem is. And if it's about what happened with your little girlfriend, she had that coming. I won't let her talk like that to my friend."

Jake stiffens. "This has nothing to do with Adison, Freya. Even though she's right—you shouldn't waste your time on trailer trash."

"You better watch yourself, Jake," I hiss in his face, "Or soon you'll have to cover your ugly, over-judgy nature that's peeking through, just like your new girlfriend already does."

"The fuck?" he rears back. "What are you talking about?"

"You know what." My humor isn't back yet to explain to him the beauty of Dorian's hidden ugliness.

While I'm fuming like a bull in an arena, he looks gobsmacked for a moment and then begins laughing like a maniac. "Jesus Christ, *Dorian.*" He wipes his face. "That's what she was talking about. Dorian *Gray,* oh my gosh." He is panting through his words. "I was wondering what the hell a Dorian is. I even Googled that shit. Oof." He laughs again.

"I'm glad somebody's happy," I say dryly.

"Oh, man." He pats his chest, and for a moment, the old Jake is back. "She sure does have a lot of it on her face. A lot of Dorian. Sounds so wrong." He chuckles again, hopefully not to some naughty memory, then sobers a little. "But honestly, Freya, you shouldn't hang out with Kayla."

I lift my finger to his face. "Here, right there, is the *last* time you talk shit about Kayla in my presence. Are we clear on that?" Hurt crosses his face for me choosing Kayla over him, but I'd do it again in a heartbeat—he has so many people in his corner, and Kayla doesn't even have a water boy. I'll be the one for her, even if no one else is willing.

Jake thinks my words through and finally nods slowly.

"Thank you." I tap his chest and gesture to his general appearance. "So, what's up with you leaking asshole-y vibes all over me?"

He ignores me, searching for something in my face. "You're still here, Freya."

I look around. "O-o-kay. Guess I'm leaving, then." I begin walking around him, but he grabs my hand.

"No, I mean, you're still *here*, in Little Hope. Your car is ready. Why, Freya?"

That's a loaded question I don't have an answer to. Why *am* I here?

"Exactly," he says. "You're here because of *him*. He's already sucked you in. He did the same with Adison. See how that worked out for her?"

"And how is that, Jake?" I ask with a sweet smile.

"You know how."

"I don't. And *you* don't. *Nobody* does."

"Stop protecting him, Freya. He doesn't deserve it." He's getting aggravated that I won't cede to him, his voice rising.

"That's not for you to decide." I yank my hand from his.

"He doesn't *let* anyone get close," Jake snaps. "He uses people. Stella Benson raised his ungrateful ass for years, and he can't even stay long enough at her birthday party to watch her blow out her fucking candles."

"You don't know the whole story, so don't judge."

"Freya, he's violent, selfish, and dangerous. I'm just saying. Alex brings everyone around him down."

He tries to walk away after, but I run to jump in front of him, halting him. "Jake, you can't blame Alex for everything like that."

He holds his hands up. "Don't hate me for this. I just don't want to see you hurt. Not again."

"Jake—"

"*No,*" he hisses, his anger finally reaching the surface. "Alex is the one who forced Justin to join the navy with him. *Everything* that has turned to shit in my life is because of *Alex Crowley*. If Jus hadn't joined the military, he would've been here. For my *family*. For our sister and me. And *that* decision landed him in *prison*, Freya. Him and your wonderful trailer trash friend who you're protecting so fiercely. My whole life would be different if Justin had just *been here*."

I blink at him in surprise. That's a lot of information, none of which I knew about. I didn't even know that Justin and Jake had a sister.

"Uh, wait... You have a sister?"

Jake scowls. "We do. You *clearly* don't know any of us as well as you thought you did."

This time, I let him walk away, my mind whirling. What did Justin going to prison have to do with Alex and Kayla? Did they keep some significant secret from me? And why haven't they mentioned their sister before? Justin doesn't have any family pictures in his place, and I didn't even bother to ask about his personal life. He offered me a roof over my head, and I don't know anything about him. Maybe I've been on my own—truly on my own, even while being married—for so long that I've become selfish.

I take a deep breath and head in the direction of Alex's cabin, hoping to find some answers to the many questions Jake just raised.

ALEX

I stand across the street, glad that neither Jake nor Freya saw me here as they had their argument.

I'd seen my name on their lips plenty, and I can only imagine what the dispute was about.

Of course Jake is trying to meddle again. Adison

reminded him of all sorts of things that should have been left buried. And now I see why Freya doesn't like Adison very much—she brings destruction in her wake wherever she goes, but I recognized it too late.

I can see by the determined gait of Freya's strides that she has questions, and I'll be damned if I'm answering any. She's caused enough trouble as it is without trying to dig back into ancient history. *Especially* history that isn't even mine to talk about.

She can spend her evening with Jake for all I care since they're such close buddies. I head to the nearest bar, The Cat and the Stallion, and order a large drink of whisky.

"Girl troubles?" I hear from across the bar and tense before turning to face my father.

"At least it's not daddy troubles." I take a gulp of drink before adding darkly, "This time."

Dad smirks and moves to sit next to me. "Your girl sure stirred our sleepy town up."

"Do you need anything?" I ask without looking at him.

I hear the eye roll in his voice. "It's been eighteen years, Alex. It's time to let it go."

"Eighteen years since *what?*" I tap my finger on my chin. "Oh, that's right! Eighteen years since my mother's death, and you were burdened with the result of your own mistake for the rest of your miserable life."

My *father* has enough decency to look a little ashamed. He chugs down his drink and waves to the bartender for another one. "I mean, you *could* have gone to live with your mom's Aunt Beth and Uncle Joe on their farm in Nebraska. Figured you might want to be near family. Near us."

"Well, you figured wrong. Now, fuck off and let me drink in peace," I growl, staring at my glass.

Dad stays seated for a minute before shaking his head

and moving away, taking his drink with him. Two seconds later, he comes back and says quietly, "I want to fix it. I just don't know how." And leaves.

Good fucking riddance.

Now I just need to drown my thoughts until I can bear to face the woman that is slowly wriggling her way into my soul little by little. She's stirring up not only this sleepy town but my dormant heart as well, and that shitty organ needs to stay fucking dead.

Chapter Twenty-Four

F**REYA**

I scowl at the dark living room, my hands on my hips. Where the hell is Alex? It's been hours, and he's not answering my calls. I have so many questions, so many. And with the time I've had to think, I have more and more, and they're only getting more complicated by the second.

I've been thinking for a long time about calling Kayla and asking her, but I need my answers. The first doubts crept up on me after the conversation with Jake. She picked up the phone on the second ring.

"Sup, biatch?" Her voice's too cheerful, and I almost feel bad for bringing it down in a minute. Almost.

"Kayla, what did you do to Justin?" Yeah, that didn't come out right. I should have found a more delicate way to address the issue. Diplomatic, I am not.

"What?" She sounds genuinely surprised, and my gut

twists with uncertainty. "Please don't tell me you're one of them now too."

"I know you and Alex did something to Justin and Jake's family, but I don't know what. Can you tell me what it was, please?" My tone changes to pleading.

"The fuck, Freya?" Now she sounds offended. "You really think I did something to them?"

"Did you?"

There is a pause and heavy breathing on the line. "No, Freya, I did not."

"Okay, I'm sorry for asking, but I had to."

"Is there anything else you need?" Her voice is curt and official.

"No," I whisper, and she hangs up. How could I so easily be led by Jake's words? It feels like I've just lost a friend. One true friend that you come across only once in a blue moon.

I sit on the bed and sigh, trying Alex's cell again. Where the hell is he? I need to talk to him, so I can ruin one more relationship in my life.

Hours pass, but the feeling of emptiness that the talk with Kayla left in my chest doesn't waver, and I need a distraction. Pronto. I'm about to go and search for him, bears be damned, when I hear the front door open.

"*Finally*," I say, getting up and making my way out to the main room. "There you are. I've been calling—"

I stop in pure horror as Erik stands in the middle of the space, a calm smile on his face. "Here I am," he says, spreading his arms, his smile widening. He looks just as I remember: big and imposing. He has a few gray streaks in his brown hair, a few more wrinkles, and a lot more Dorian trickery.

My heart starts beating as if it were caught in a trap and

trying to get out of it by thrashing against its walls. "What did you do to Alex?" I whisper.

"Nothing. I didn't have to do anything, surprisingly. He's out drinking himself to death at the only boring little bar this fucking town has to offer." He draws my attention to his hand as he slowly reaches down to lock the door. "Really, babe. Keeping this unlocked was *very* irresponsible of you. Or did you think that you were safe all the way out here, in this sleepy little town, with my money under your mattress?"

I think I was for the time being, but I had almost forgotten that Erik was still around. I haven't heard about him or about his shenanigans with Adison anymore, so I'd assumed the threat was no longer an issue. I realize now that that was what Erik was waiting for: for me to get complacent. To stop running and relax. The perfect prey for a predator like him.

"What do you want?" I demand coldly.

"You *know* what I want, Freya. Don't do this. Just give me the information I want and my money, and we can all go our separate ways."

"Sure, you'll do that," I retort sarcastically.

Erik shrugs and wanders into Alex's kitchen, finding the bottle of whiskey Alex keeps in the liquor cabinet. He opened exactly this drawer, meaning he knew precisely where it was. He's been *watching*. Maybe even that time I had extracurricular activities with Alex out here.

"Ooh," Erik says, opening the bottle and smelling it. "My replacement has some expensive tastes. Is *this* what my money is being spent on, hmm? Buying your little guard dog gifts for his troubles? You're paying him with sex, too, I imagine. Knowing you." An ugly smirk crosses his face.

I try to think about what to do while he's distracted, but

I can't stop focusing on the way I can hear my heartbeat, and my legs are shaking. *God, Freya, focus!* Erik will kill me if I let him get the upper hand. He's the calm before the storm; I've seen him like that so many times and can never forget the pain that followed.

He's locked the door, and it would take one hell of a distraction to get out, get to my car, and run for help.

"Have you heard about the awful traffic accident just down the road?" Erik murmurs as if he can read my mind. "Such a shame. Beautiful old Chevy, too."

I gasp as I lean my head slightly to the right and see the missing car from the drive.

"Made it really difficult to get to this house. It will be at least until everything is cleared up." He looks over at me and smiles blandly. "God bless our police force, right?"

I can't breathe for the pain that is enveloping my body. *He destroyed my car.* Alex isn't answering his phone. The cops—Ken, because I don't think Jake would come to help me anyway—won't be able to get here even if they knew about my situation. And by the time the road clears out, that would be... too late. I just know it. It's *today. The day* is today.

"Bad news for the other driver though. Her car was rundown enough for it to cause some serious damage. God, that car sounded like a plane was trying to land. You could hear it from a mile away." He chuckles.

I slowly turn my head to look at him. "What did you do, Erik? What did you do?" I whisper hoarsely. "What do you want from me? The money? *Take it,* it's yours, take it!"

The car with an airplane engine... *oh no, God, please no.*

"Oh no, sweetheart." He chuckles patronizingly. "*You* have alluded me for *months.* You've been jumping from place to place, *teasing* me with your escape every single time. You know, I was actually starting to get impressed!" He takes a swig of the whiskey before dropping the tumbler on the floor and picking up a shard of glass when it loudly shatters. "But then your precious little heart got in the way, didn't it, baby? That's always been your problem. You get too attached to people. *Real* people on the run know to keep that urge buried deep down inside."

As he wanders around the house, I step closer to the door, trying to figure out my game plan.

"Oh, honey, I wouldn't do that if I were you," he murmurs as I throw a quick glance at the lock on the door. I don't have my keys, so I'll have to sprint out of the house, through the forest, until I get to the road. When I reach the road, I'll be yelling and running and yelling and running until I can see Ken on that road near the accident and beg for his forgiveness for what happened to his mother because of me.

He puts both hands on his hips underneath his jacket, and I spot the gun tucked into his pants. My heart sinks. I'd be dead before I could get out of sight, who am I kidding?

"Besides," he says with a smirk. "I've heard you've had a problem with bears recently. I tell you what, *that* was a hard one to pull off. The *amount* of food I've had to bury nearby." He shrugs and turns to face me quickly, making me jolt with fear. "Ah well, it makes it easier for me when I leave here. It'll be just another statistic on bear attacks here in Maine."

"You won't get away with this," I hiss, trying to delay the inevitable. If my car is in an accident, it's only a matter of time before someone realizes that I'm not in it and come to the rescue after they help Stella. *God, please, I don't pray often, but let her be fine.*

I feel sick to my stomach.

"Why so quiet, *wife?*" Erik croons. "What are you realizing?"

"I just thought you'd forgotten that there's only one person alive who knows how to access the money. *Me.* You need me alive to get it."

He smiles and walks closer to me, pulling the gun out, pressing it to my throat, and pushing me up against the door. I can smell the whiskey still on his breath. "And you are going to tell me."

"No, I'm not," I whisper. "I will take it to the grave, *honey.* I'm not scared of dying. I've been running from it for so long that it's almost peaceful to know it's here." I smile, noticing the moment of hesitation passing in Erik's eyes. "So go on. Do your worst. Have my blood on your hands. You won't get away with it. If I've let myself get known in this area, *so have you.* Your face is as well-known as mine now. So, do it. Kill me. Murder your *wife,* like you've wanted to for so long." I reach up and wrap my fingers around his hand, holding the trigger. "I loved you," I confess. "I thought you could be my family. But you never were. Now I made another family here, and you hurt one of them."

I yank his fingers back, hearing a satisfying crack as Erik's index gives way to the sudden pressure against the joints. He yells and doubles over, the gun clattering to the floor. Rage fills his expression, but I manage to smack him in the nose with my elbow and my knee into his groin at the same time. Him being this close to me has its advantages.

In his distraction, I scramble for the gun on the floor and train it on him. I've never even held a gun before, and it's heavier than I thought it would be. It's cold and impersonal and very unstable. A gun doesn't remember who or why it kills, only the owner of it does.

Before I can decide what to do next, Erik slowly rises,

his eyes murderous, his nose bleeding. In one smooth movement, he pulls the gun out of my hands and knocks me to the floor with a blow to the side of my head. I can't think much beyond this point; the only comprehensible thought is that I am truly and wholly fucked. Erik points the barrel of the gun at me, his face that of a maniac, and I do see my life in front of my eyes like they always say. The worst regret I have right now is not telling Alex how I feel about him; now, he will never know.

Then a shot rings out from the silent forest surrounding the cabin, slicing cleanly through the glass window, and lands directly into Erik's chest cavity. It looks almost comical, the way he slowly lowers his eyes to the open wound in his chest before he sinks heavily to the floor with a solid thump. I stare at him wide-eyed before gingerly stepping toward him to make sure it is real. Is this a dream? I change course at the last second, realizing that I desperately *don't* want to see up close what's become of him on the floor, where he is very, very quiet. Instead, I look out through the now-punctured windowpane to the forest beyond.

By the trees, wearing a puff jacket, skinny jeans, and sunglasses, unnecessary in the night around him, stands Jake, his gun by his side.

For some reason, seeing him breaks something inside me, and I sink to the floor, retching violently.

I was prepared to die, and now this new life I've been given feels wrong. Not at the price of the blood of my abuser on somebody else's soul.

ALEX

. . .

Justin slowly sinks down on the stool next to me, and I let him because I'm close to being wasted. Jenny, the bartender and owner's daughter, has been glaring at me for the past half an hour, and I feel like my time to be escorted out is upon me. "You haven't been answering your phone." He grabs my drink and drinks it in one gulp. *What the fuck?*

"I needed *one* night off," I grunt. "Can you—"

"Stella is in the hospital after her car *mysteriously* collided with Freya's apparently empty Chevy." His voice is exempt from emotion. "Freya's ex found her, and now he's dead with a bullet where his heart was supposed to be. She tried to call you. You never showed up. She's refusing to let anyone into the house, but there's a clean bullet hole through your window. Current word is that Freya shot him with his own gun in self-defense. It's up to Ken, but he *might* forget to mention that mysterious little hole in your windowpane." He drops the keys to his apartment on the counter. "Go to my place and get your shit together before you show up looking like that. And Alex," he commands, looking pointedly at me, "walk there."

Then he stands up and leaves the bar as if he didn't say anything.

I gape after him, my brain going haywire with the overload of information. I try to stand up but wobble in place, and when I try to move, I stumble over nothing. I'm in no position to drive after spending several hours trying to drown my sorrows away; I can barely walk straight. I open my phone, and nauseating dread and panic slam into me at all the missed calls and texts from Freya, Ken, Justin, and Jake.

Fuck.

What do I do? How do I fix this? Freya is there alone. Well, she's surrounded by people, but she's *alone, without me.* She's scared and maybe even hurt, and I'm still fucking here, unable to even stand on my own feet. How do I unfuck this mess? I need to get to her. Now. I need to see her and make sure she's okay. *Dumbass.* She won't be *okay,* but I need to know she's not hurt physically. Fuck, I wanted to be the one to wring her ex's neck, and here I am, missing my fucking shot because I left her alone to get piss drunk.

Fuck Justin and his orders. I'm going to Freya.

I pull my keys out of my pocket, and they fall on the floor. *Fuck.* I struggle to pick them up, but when I eventually manage, they fall right back down again. Fuck, I won't make it far driving, I need an atle... alre... alternative plan.

I stagger out onto the street, and my gaze lands on Kayla's car. Good. She must be around somewhere. She's my alternative plan to get to my cabin. To Freya. The diner's closed, but I spot a thin, flickering light shining from the bottom of the kitchen door through the window. The flickering is what sets me off. I frown and try the lock. I open it with brute force when it refuses to budge and squint when no alarms go off. I know Marina. She'd have this place locked up tighter than a maximum-security prison in Russia. Her life's work is attached to this diner.

I'm getting soberer by the minute. I take my phone and call Justin.

"Yeah?" he answers hoarsely.

"Where are you?"

"Driving to your house."

"Are you far from the bar?"

"No, why?" He sounds suspicious.

"You need to come to the diner. Now." And I hang up. He knows me well enough to understand when I mean business.

I see Justin walking up to the diner thirty seconds later with a deep frown. "Alex. The hell's going on?"

"I think there's a fire, Jus, and I think Kayla's in here somewhere. I saw her car in the back."

His eyes widen in panic, showing an impressive amount of emotion for the woman he claims to detest. He takes off without saying a word. Fuck, I can't leave him like that here with Kayla, probably still inside. But Freya's waiting for me. Fuck, what do I do?

"*Kayla?*" Justin yells, opening door after door until one of them doesn't budge.

The heat level is rising, and the smoke finally reaches my nose. No, I can't leave him here, it's all too familiar. Freya is with cops now and protected; I'll fly to her on my fucking wings the moment Jus and Kayla are safe.

"Kayla!" Justin keeps yelling until we hear sobbing, clear as day, and without a second thought, he runs to the last locked room and knocks it down without breaking a sweat. *Hates her, my ass.*

I can hear the sirens through the crackling of the diner, and I try my hardest to stamp out the flames as they try to spread into the dining room. The spot where I know for a fact usually houses a fire extinguisher is empty.

A flame licks at my hand, and I stagger backward with the familiar sensation. My skin burns with the memory, the flashback hitting me hard. That mind-numbing torture that never seemed to go out, the screams of agony of everyone around me, the *silence* that followed it. And I am gone, I'm not in the diner anymore. I'm in my head.

I'm vaguely aware of Justin appearing with a tied and bound Kayla in his arms, his face weak with relief, and when the fire crew screams up to a halt in front of the diner,

I make it out to the fresh air, turn in the direction of home, and I run.

Chapter Twenty-Five

A^{LEX}

My property is swarming with police and medical professionals. Thank fuck Ken didn't allow any onlookers on the scene. The red and blue flashing lights are piercing against the night sky. Ken is pressed up against my living room window, his shoulders tense.

"Freya, we just want to make sure you're okay. Can you let us come in, please?"

Freya's strangled *no* comes through the noise, and I walk quickly toward him. Shouldering past him, I stride straight to the front door, digging my keys out of my pocket.

"Alex, *don't*," Ken warns from behind me. "She needs to give us permission."

"It's my fucking house," I hiss. "My *girlfriend* is in there with a fucking dead body! Don't tell me I can't go in!"

I put the key in the lock and hear Freya let out a high-pitched, devastating scream just as I swing open the door. She scrambles backward until she hits the wall of the bedroom, and I can see even from here the wild look in her eyes. She doesn't see me. She is still seeing him.

The blood from Erik's body is on her hands and in her hair—*fuck, I hope it's only his blood*—and beginning to seep across my floorboards and into the rug.

I jump backward in fright, slamming the door shut again, and yank the key out. My keyring drops to the ground in my haste, and Ken turns a frustrated look at me. "You don't think we would be able to get in? She is one woman, and there are plenty of us, but she's in shock, we don't want to traumatize her more by storming in. She's had enough of that for a lifetime." He takes a deep breath and turns back to the window. "Freya, we're not here to hurt you. We just need to make sure you're okay."

I look around at the many men that are hovering around, the red and blue lights, and the stern looks on everyone's faces. A few people glance at me before nervously looking away, probably remembering the last time they'd been called to this property. It was with Adison; she'd called the cops that night. *Another Alex Crowley call. Figures.*

"Turn the lights of the cars off," I instruct him softly. "Get rid of most of these men. You and I will get her out, and then we'll sort out the rest."

Ken slowly turns to look at me before reluctantly turning to his men and relaying the instructions. More than half of them leave, the lights switching off and the forest becoming dark and relatively quiet again.

"Frey?" I murmur gently, walking over to the window. I twist a finger over the bullet hole through the reinforced glass to follow its trajectory. Ken says quietly behind me,

"Jake's suspended, and his weapon is supposed to be locked in the station." I hear him swallow. "But it wasn't there this morning. Do you get me?" I nod, understanding what he's asking of me. Then I try again. "Freya, can you hear me?"

She has her knees up to her chest, her gaze trained on the body in front of her, but when I speak, I see her gaze flicker to the window.

"Can you hear me, Freya?" I try again, and she shifts her whole head in order to look at me. "I'm going to come in now, okay? I'm going to come inside, place a sheet over whatever is in front of you, and then we're going to work on getting you to a hospital just to make sure you're okay. All right?"

"No," she says, but it's weaker than her other protests have been.

I slowly reach for the door handle and manage to get it unlocked without triggering a response, but the second I start to open the door, Freya screams that bloodcurdling scream again and flies backward, tumbling through the open door of the bedroom and smacking her head on the bed frame. She groans and puts her hand on the back of her head before looking at it. Her eyes widen in fright as she sees Erik's blood on her hands, thinking it's from her own head, and she looks at me with panicked eyes.

It's the same look. That panicked, betrayed look. Freya, Adison... Their faces merge in my mind, and I can't move from the spot I'm standing in. I'm doing the same to the woman I love without even trying.

Love? *Yes,* I realize I'm in love with Freya. And I don't deserve her. And she sure as fuck deserves so much more than the damaged asshole I am.

"Let us do this," Ken says firmly, two of his men and a paramedic going around me. I wouldn't be able to move even if I wanted to. "I think it's best if you're not out here when we come out with Freya. You appear to be a larger trigger than any of us." He disappears into the house, but I barely register what he said.

I wasn't here, and Freya was hurt. I'd left Freya alone because I was claiming some bullshit, like I needed time alone when I knew her ex was around. I let people down, one by one—every single person around me goes down because of me, one way or another.

In the quiet, I hear the sound of someone vomiting in the forest near the house, and I turn woodenly in the direction of it.

It's Jake, his hands and knees in the dirt, violently dry retching. His stomach is empty, so it's clear he's been at it for a while. His hands are shaking, his elbows wobbling as they keep him upright, and I see the gun by his side in the dirt.

I make my footsteps loud, but he makes no move to hide what's happening.

There are many things I can say, but I don't voice any of them. I haul him back onto his ass and pull his face to look at me. "I remember my first kill too." It's all I say, and his eyes widen in surprise at first, then pain.

I still remember the gasp of air that turned out to be his last. His face when he knew life was leaving him. The thud of his collapse. No amount of training or simulation, or expectations can prepare you for it. And no one tells you that *that* face will plague you forever until eventually you succumb to the darkness and give up on fighting your own end.

Jake's eyes water, and I nod, pulling him into my arms. "I know," I breathe in his ear.

His body wracks with sobs, and I hold him tight, knowing that this night will be one that haunts Jake forever.

Just as it will haunt me, too, as the night when the only woman I'll ever love was hurt because of me.

FREYA

I wake up from a groggy sleep to find myself in a hospital bed. My head is pounding, and my whole body feels stiff and unsure of itself as if it just discovered gravity and is trying to work out how to use it.

I lie awake for a few minutes, trying to piece together everything that happened after that sound of a gun that had ricocheted around my brain, but everything is either fuzzy or completely absent. All I can remember is the dead body. As it flowed toward me, the blood seemed like a river of premeditated assault, Erik trying to crawl inside me even after death. I'm about to drift back off to sleep when a nurse peers around the corner and smiles too enthusiastically.

"Oh goody, you're awake!"

"What happened?" I croak.

She checks my vitals and smiles. "I'm not the best person to ask that, but Sheriff Benson will be here soon to check on you. In terms of your health, Ms. Cunningham—"

"Kennedy," I say quietly. The nurse looks at me blankly for a moment. "My last name. It's Kennedy. Cunningham is my ex-husband's last name." *My dead ex-husband.*

The image of his bug-eyed look and the trickling blood flashes in front of my eyes, and I shudder.

"Ms. *Kennedy,*" she corrects meaningfully, "you're only here under observation, given that you went through quite a difficult experience last night. You're healthy, and none of our tests came back with anything of concern. A psychiatrist is going to be along in a few hours, and she will go through a few things with you, and we can work out when you're getting out of here."

There's a tap on the door, and the nurse smiles.

"Ah. Here we go."

I think it's going to be Alex, but I'm disappointed when it's Ken with Justin trailing behind him.

The disappointment must be visible on my face as Ken chuckles softly. "I've asked Alex to wait until you're cleared by the psychiatrist, Freya. He's not pleased with me at all, but it's for the best." He sits on the chair by the bed awkwardly. "We wouldn't want any more setbacks."

He exchanges a look with Justin but doesn't elaborate. "Do you remember what happened, Freya?"

I dig into my memory, looking for the past twenty-four hours, but the last thing I remember is the phone call with Kayla and Erik and his gun, nothing after that. "No, not everything," I whisper with a light shake of my head.

Ken looks at Justin and then back at me. "You were attacked at Alex's house."

"I know that."

"What do you remember from that?" Ken asks.

I think for a moment. *Stella! Oh my God, Stella!*

"Is your mom all right?" I yelp. "You shouldn't be here with me. You need to be with your mom!"

"Mom has a broken arm, was on watch for a concussion, and has an excuse for a new car," Ken says with a chuckle. "She's at home already and is being doted on by Dad and Leila. She'll be milking this for all it's worth. Don't worry about her."

I smile weakly. "I hate that she was involved in this. I

hate that anyone else was involved." I gulp and play with the blanket in between my shaky fingers. "How's Jake?"

The image of him standing there with the gun at his side, sunglasses on, appears in my head again, and I gasp through the fear that plummets through my body.

Ken automatically reaches his hand out to try and soothe me, but Justin pushes it back, replacing him.

Ken shifts in his seat and gives Justin a grateful look, clearly looking uncomfortable. He clears his throat while Justin settles on the bed with me, gently rubbing my shoulder. "Jake is doing fine. We're keeping a close eye on him on the force. Don't you worry about him. And Kayla's okay too, a little shaken up—"

"Kayla?" I whisper. "What happened to Kayla?"

Justin exhales slowly. "Kayla apparently got a text from Marina to say that the alarms at the diner had gone off," he explains in a tense voice. "Kayla said she would check it out on her way past. She was tied up and locked in the pantry while the kitchen was set on fire."

I stare at him, my heart breaking more and more. "This is all my fault," I whisper. "I *knew* I shouldn't have stayed. I just put everyone in more danger."

"The actions of a psychopath are not your fault, Freya," Ken states firmly. "I don't ever want to see innocent people harmed in such a way, my own mother included, but you've helped us uncover a much larger criminal ring that is going to save many more lives. Erik wasn't alone in his dealings, and now we can send everything to the big boys in the big city to stop this business that they've been laundering through offshore accounts. We're a small-town precinct that doesn't normally get that sort of drama. So, you will be a novelty for a while—just be ready."

I lick my dry lips and say quietly, "I have more information."

Ken and Justin share a look.

"Okay," Ken says, "let's get you cleared by the doc so you can give us a statement."

I give another weak smile as there is another knock on the door, and a stylish woman in her late thirties wearing a smart business suit and blonde hair tied neatly back quietly steps in. Ken smiles at her. "Jenna. Nice to see you."

"Sheriff Benson." She extends her hand and gives him a warm smile. She turns toward Justin, and her smile drops for a fraction of a second before returning. "Mr. Attleborough. I wasn't aware you had a part in all of this."

Justin dips his head. "Just friendly business. I promise." He turns to me and smiles. "I'll see you later, Freya." He nods his head at Ken and leaves, giving Jenna a wide berth.

Ken stands up too. "Freya, this is Dr. Jenna Morton, the psychiatrist. I'll leave you in her very capable hands, and I'll check in with you in a little bit."

"Will you send Alex to see me?"

"I'll do my best."

I watch him leave pensively before reluctantly settling in to talk to the psychiatrist.

I spend two more days at the hospital and get cleared to leave as long as I get several more sessions at Dr. Jenna's office in town over the next few weeks. All my weak suggestions that I needed to leave town were thoroughly ignored. She says she wants to try to work through what happened to me before it turns into PTSD, and I can't help thinking that Alex should have had the same treatment.

The efforts to treat his PTSD when he came back should have been more aggressive. Knowing Alex, I can tell that the right words from the right people might have done the trick —and probably still could.

On the morning of my discharge from the hospital, I give Ken my statement. I warned him what sort of information and about whom I wanted to share, and he decided that it's above his paygrade and called reinforcements in. There are a few big, black suits present who happen to be FBI. I stick close to Ken, as he's the only familiar face I know in the room; he treats me as if I were his little sister, and I'm eternally grateful for that. I don't think I'd be able to survive this interrogation if it weren't for him. The suits are intimidating, but Ken stands his ground against them, backing me up. Every time I get spooked, he puts his heavy hand on my shoulder and squeezes with encouragement, and that's how I make it through the process.

As a result, I give them access to my trusted company, which has been instructed to share the info I stashed with them. Because I'm sharing it of my own free will, they'll only take the information and leave the money to me—I'm not under arrest, so there's no need to confiscate the money. Fair and square.

After the statement, I feel two thousand pounds lighter —I'm not sitting on a time bomb ready to explode at any moment, and I'm helping people. I'm happy with both.

Ken kisses my forehead and leaves with the suits, saying he needs to finish giving his own statement at the station.

Alex doesn't come to see me. At all. Not before I got discharged, not after. I call Justin out while I was in the hospital the first day since Ken avoided the question like the plague, and he claims he hasn't seen him or heard from him since they rescued Kayla from the fire together.

Ken already left for the station. And I can't call Kayla, not after the way I doubted her and not after being responsible for her attack. The groveling will take more than a simple phone call asking for a favor to get me from the hospital.

Alex is MIA. So, the only person left on my close friends list is Justin.

"Hey, Jus. Can you pick me up from the hospital?" I ask him when he answers on the second ring.

"Sure thing," he chirps without hesitation. "Be there in a few."

As I'm sitting there waiting, the nurse that was with me when I woke up steps out. "Sorry! Freya, right?"

"Right," I say slowly.

"Here. This was left for you."

I take the extended envelope and stare at it in bewilderment. "Thanks," I mumble. I turn it over and take the card out.

It's a gaudy "Get Well Soon" card with a pink teddy bear holding a balloon. The contents make me freeze.

Freya,
Your belongings are at The Dancing Pony. I didn't think you'd want to go to the house, and it's still technically a crime scene. I fought to get what I did, so it's not much. My truck is there for you to use. I won't need it.
-Alex

My heart leaps into my throat as I read the card through several more times. I try and read every word as if it has an alternate meaning, but nothing occurs to me.

Justin pulls up in front of me and chuckles at the card in my hand. "Who's that from? I bet it's Donna. Pink is her favorite color."

"Is Alex dead?" I whisper.

"What? No!" He looks bewildered.

I hand him the card and watch his eyes widen as he reads it.

"What the fuck?" he whispers.

"What the fuck, indeed."

He frowns and opens his truck for me to get in. "I guess The Dancing Pony then?"

I slowly inhale and exhale, feeling the life rush through my lungs. "I guess so."

Chapter Twenty-Six

FREYA

I spend four nights at The Dancing Pony, and all four nights end with me waking up covered in sweat, still imprisoned in the memory of Erik's blood slowly crawling to me and soft sunset shining through the deep-red liquid replaying in my mind on constant repeat. On the fifth day, Dr. Jenna Morton appears at the request of Emma. Her smile is professional yet understanding, I think.

"So, how is everything going?" she asks calmly once she plants herself in a vintage chair by the window, as if I don't look like hell on earth—or like I'm trying to survive it. "How are you feeling now that you've had a bit of time to let it all sink in?" She takes a seat on a chair next to the window, and her blonde hair shines like a halo.

"Fine," I whisper from the bed. I haven't taken a shower since I came here, and I'd rather hide under the covers than let her get a whiff of me. I don't see how that could do me any favors.

"Fine. Okay..." She makes a note on her clipboard. "And how are you sleeping?"

"Fantastic."

Jenna taps her pen against her paper a few times before giving me a sympathetic smile. "Freya, this has been a very traumatic experience for you. Talking through it will only do you good."

I stare at a spot on the wall behind her and don't respond.

"Why don't we start by saying whatever is on your mind right now? The first thing that pops into your head... say it."

"I'm... free," I whisper, letting the waves of painstakingly planned sentences wash away.

"Do you think that your being free is the wrong answer?"

"I don't know." I look down at my lap.

"There is no wrong answer here, Freya. It's not a test."

"But I feel... *good*... about another person being dead. How is that not wrong?" I can't look up. I just keep digging my nail into a flower embroidered on the comforter.

"You're not feeling good because he is dead, Freya— you're feeling good because he can't hurt you anymore." There is a flicker of emotion in her carefully controlled voice.

"Is there a difference?" It's the first time I have had the courage to meet her gaze. She looks at me openly, not hiding behind her professionalism or smart words. *She understands.*

"Yes, there is. The first thing that popped up in your head wasn't about him, it was about you. You finally got free from the hell he put you through. You didn't plan for it to happen, you just tried to survive. And you *did*. You survived."

"I thought I was a victim," I mutter under my breath.

"Do you want to be one?"

"No," I say after thinking her question through.

"Then you are not. You're a survivor, Freya, and I'm proud of you."

"Thank you," I say, feeling the burn of tears in the backs of my eyes.

"And a lot of people here are proud of you, too. Don't doubt that." Jenna leans forward and lowers her voice. "Can I ask you a question?" I look up at her. "Have you felt recently like Little Hope was your home? That this was somewhere that you felt safe and understood? Even for a bit?" I stare blankly at her, and she chuckles softly. "I'm asking as a friend, not a counselor."

I nod once and then nod more and more because, yes, Little Hope has started to feel like home.

"With time, the trauma will fade, Freya. It'll get washed away by good memories made with the people around you."

That only makes me feel worse. How can I possibly look at Stella or Kayla or Jake again?

It's not like Alex is here to help, "a pro" in dealing with PTSD. Or just *living* with it, to be precise. According to Justin, he's gone. His cabin's a crime scene, so he couldn't stay there anyway. No one knows where he is, and each morning when I wake up, I lose a little bit more hope that he's coming back for me. He wasn't interested enough in me to even see me after the attack. Maybe he hates me for the mess I created at his home and his life. Ken has tried to convince me that Alex was at the cabin that night, but I don't recall seeing him. A flash of his face, shrouded in red and blue lights, comes to mind, but I can barely figure out if it's a part of my imagination or memory. It's like I've taken what Ken told me and tried to morph it into an image that doesn't quite connect with my own memory of what happened that night.

"Freya?" Jenna says softly. "I think it's time to go see someone."

I shake my head firmly. She doesn't mean a shrink because she *is* a damn shrink, so she means someone else that was involved. She means Kayla, Jake, and Stella. "I can't."

"You *can*," she persists gently. "And you don't have a choice. This is a bed and breakfast, Freya, not a psychiatric hospital. Emma's been worried about you, and she called me."

I gulp, and Jenna must notice my guilt as she stands up and opens the door to my room, nodding at someone on the other side. She holds the door open wide, and Stella's concerned face looks through. Her arm is in a cast, but she's wearing long sleeves over it to hide it from view, clearly for my benefit. Ken, Alex's dad, and Justin are standing behind her too.

"Freya," Stella murmurs. "Oh, darling. It's so nice to see you." She rushes forward and cups my face in her hands. "When I heard about what happened..." She searches my features as if inspecting for cuts and bruises. "I did not expect you to look so... *uninjured*."

I manage a weak smile, and she pulls me into her arms, hugging me tightly. I can feel the cast against my shoulder, and a new wave of guilt suffocates me.

"Are you okay?" I whisper.

"I'm fine, sweetheart." She releases me and sits down on the bed, keeping her hands on mine. "We were doing some thinking, Freya. Would you like to come to stay with us instead of here? I think it will do you good to be around people."

Tears spring to my eyes, and I look at my fingers. "Do you know where Alex is?" I ask quietly.

I hear Stella's sigh and know the answer before she says anything. "I'm sorry, dear. No. None of us have heard a word."

"Where is he then if nobody knows?" I cry out suddenly. "Why isn't he here? How could he..." I burst into tears and can't finish my sentence.

Justin steps into the room. "I know where he is, Freya," he says softly.

Everyone turns to look at him in surprise, and I frown, mumbling, "But you told me you didn't," just as Ken murmurs, "asshole" under his breath.

"I didn't when you asked." Justin gulps. "It's not my place to say, but I can tell you he's safe and alive and—"

I scowl. "He told *you* and didn't tell me? I don't even deserve a phone call?"

Justin slowly shakes his head. "I think it's the opposite, Freya. I'm sorry, I really am. He's going to come back, but only when he's ready."

"And you can't tell me where he is or when he's coming back?"

"I wish I could." There's a deep wrinkle dug between his brows that hasn't been there before, and a new look of suffering has become a constant presence on his face.

I take a deep breath and close my eyes, trying to soothe the disappointment in my chest. It's not heartbreak anymore; it's the fury. Why does *he* deserve a little break? Why does *he* get to decide when to come back and do what he told me he would? He said he'd protect me. He said that I wasn't going to get hurt if I was with him. Well, all those promises have turned into shit. His leaving without a word hurt.

I look at Stella, whose face reflects my sorrow and conflict in a way that nearly overwhelms me. "If that offer was sincere, I accept," I whisper. "Just until I can buy a new car, and then I'll be on my way. I'll get you a new one too. Whichever flashy new car you want, it's yours. I don't want to hear a word about it."

"No need, dear. Alex got me a new car already." Her smile is bittersweet.

"What?"

"The day after you were released from the hospital, I had a brand-new BMW parked at my driveway with a note. I think he dropped all his savings on that car." A tear slides down her cheek.

"What did the note say?"

"'I'm sorry.'" Stella's eyes are misty, and she's talking through a lump in her throat. And I know, I just *know*, he didn't mean the accident.

This gesture—one of a person who is finally beginning his healing—warms my heart despite how badly it bruises that I've been cut out of it all.

I look over at Justin. "Was the diner badly damaged?"

"Uh, the kitchen and the pantry were. It hasn't been opened since. Marina's trying to figure out—"

"I'll pay for it to be fixed." I interrupt him. "Any upgrades Marina wants, tell her to throw them in. Any at all." I turn toward Ken. "If there are any upgrades the station needs, you've got them. And..." I smile sadly. "If Jake needs anything *in particular*, let me know. I can pay for therapy or something. Whatever he wants or needs, he has."

Ken sounds neurotic as he assures me, "Jake is fine, why would you be asking about Jake?" he says, throwing looks at

Dr. Morton. Something's happening that I don't understand. Then he adds quickly, covering up the awkwardness, "None of us need all that, Freya. We just want to make sure—"

"Not a word." I cut him off. "FBI said I can keep the money. It feels wrong to keep it for myself." *Blood money*, I think to myself with a shudder. "I want to help as many people as I can."

He nods slowly. "The money does look like it'll stay yours. You technically acquired it legally, and everything is in order. I'd be a little worried about someone taking Erik's place. The black suits didn't share many insights with me, but they looked really excited. In fact, a little too excited, if you know what I mean." Ken, in fact, does look worried. Since the flash drive isn't in my hands anymore, I don't see how I can be of interest. *They* will know the government has it now.

"Then I just need to spend it as soon as possible," I say bluntly. I don't want to be in the same situation again, the situation where my life flashes before my eyes and other people get hurt...

And then it hits me. The *whole* story. Behind my eyelids, a shot rings out, and there's a perfectly clean bullet hole through the glass window. I used to think the glass always breaks, and the hole appears only in movies. Jake stands there and takes his glasses off, the shock on his ashen face obvious even from a distance. His gun is still pointing at the window, at *me*, and I stare directly at the barrel. Jake lowers his arm and sinks against the tree, sliding out of sight. I slowly turn to look at the dead body at my feet.

Sometime later, there was a lot of yelling and calling my name. Somebody's trying to get inside the house. Suddenly, Alex is there, turning the key in the lock, Ken warning him not to. I see his face through the window, lit with blue and red lights. "Frey?" he says, his voice distant and wavy. "Freya? Can you hear me?"

The blood from Erik is crawling toward me, fingers of it scampering closer.

"I'm going to come in now, okay?" The blood hisses. "Can you hear me?"

It reaches my foot, and I scream.

"Let us do this," Ken orders, his voice the most solid thing around me. "You appear to be a larger trigger than any of us."

He's not talking to me. I look up and see Alex's face, lit by the floodlight on his front porch.

"I think it's best if you're not here." The words vibrate around my brain, and Alex's face is still in the moonlight. He tilts it up to the moon, stars falling to dance around his face. "You're a trigger. You're only hurting her more."

I gasp back to reality, finding myself back in my room at The Dancing Pony, struggling vainly to ground myself. My head is pounding from the repressed memories flooding back into my brain, my stomach roiling as if I were being rocked in a boat. Ken, Stella, and Dr. Jenna are standing around me at careful distances, looking as if they were desperate for me to wake up from the nightmare I was reliving. Justin stares at me from the doorway, eyes wide with fear, and for a second, my gaze locks with his.

"Freya?" Jenna murmurs. "Can you tell me what happened?"

I slowly sit up and let the tears roll down my cheeks. "I remember everything."

Now it all makes a little more sense. Alex left his home because of *me*. I forced him away with my episode. He probably thinks he did something to trigger it, and he doesn't want a repetition of it happening to me. I just wish he stayed long enough for me to explain that he wasn't the one to blame. That Erik was.

But he left. Without hearing me out. I wish I only knew where he went and how to bring him back.

Jake slowly sits opposite from me at Donna's donut shop. He's wearing his running clothes and an old, battered cap that reminds me of Alex's one on my nightstand at Stella and Keith's house. Jake's eyes are droopy, and there's a blue haze under them.

We sit in silence for a minute, Jake staring at the table, me looking everywhere but at him, until he softly speaks.

"I didn't want to ever use it."

I glance at him. "Your gun?"

He nods, swallowing. "I don't even usually carry it." He finally looks up and meets my gaze. "Justin's been in trouble before. Our dad, too. So, I decided, too much temptation in that power you hold in your hands. Didn't want anything to do with it."

I reach out and place my hand on his as he draws a shaky breath. "If you didn't, I'd be dead," I remind him. "I'd never even *held* a gun before. He took it from my hands in a blink."

He moves his hand until our fingers are laced together and gives me a weak smile.

"Your life is worth it."

I catch his eyes and hold them. "I sure hope you're right."

He doesn't say anything.

"You never said you saw me pulling the trigger," he ventures after a long moment, his voice aloof.

I give a solid nod. "That's because I didn't see you doing it. I saw you in the woods, jogging."

His serious expression breaks, and he chuckles. "Only here can we cover our asses like that. But anyway, thanks."

"No problem. You don't need it on your record."

"Ken surprisingly turned a blind eye to it," Jake remarks. "Didn't see that one coming." He stares emptily forward.

"I did."

He looks up at me. "Huh?"

"He appreciates you, Jake."

His cheeks turn an adorable shade of pink.

"Do you know where Alex went?" I whisper after a long pause.

Jake shrugs but with no malice this time. Something has shifted in him regarding Alex, and the mention of his name doesn't cause an angry outburst anymore. "A facility, I think. I overheard Justin talking to Alex about it on the phone. All I heard was Justin saying, 'just get some help and come home to make this right, 'cause that's all too fucked up.' So, anyway, I *assume* that was Alex."

Oh. Alex is getting help? A ray of hope shines through the dark clouds that have colored my days.

And that Justin, the Jerk who refuses to share with the class where Alex went.

That Justin, the Good Friend who keeps his promises to Alex.

I chew on my lip before asking a question that's come to my mind after I have time to process everything. "Jake"—he looks at me when he hears his name—"what you were doing in the woods that night?"

His jaw shuts tight, and his eyes turn dark. Even the angles of his face turn sharper.

"I feel like it's a very important question." I look for the right way to say what I'm thinking. "Like it's something important to understand *you*."

"There is nothing to understand there, Freya." The muscles on his jaw pop.

"But it's not true, isn't it?" I hold his angry stare.

His face instantly changes, and a wide smile stretches his face. "I just wanted to get a glimpse of a beautiful woman in the window." He winks and rises to his feet. "I gotta run, Freya."

With a quick brotherly kiss on the top of my head, he strides away before I collect my wits to ask him another question.

Chapter Twenty-Seven

F**REYA**

I've been dreading talking to Kayla. Considering she never replied to my text message and her phone went right to voicemail every time I called, I couldn't help but wonder if she'd blocked me. The idea that she did hurt.

But enough is enough. I need to put on my big girl pants and go see her. Since I still don't know where her trailer is parked, I head to the diner when I know she and Marina are fixing something up. Marina didn't want to take money at first, but I convinced her after a long and heated argument. She took the money but insisted she would do as much work on her own as possible. I hope she will not realize that I've been secretly paying off her debts.

The paint on the walls and ceiling is fresh; the furniture is brand new and stylish. Kayla is wiping the new counter, frowning at something. The tips of her hair are dyed red.

Uh-oh. That's a bad sign. I should probably come back another day. I'm about to spin around and escape when Marina yells from the kitchen, "One Lonely Kurt is coming right up for our biggest sponsor, Freya!"

Oops. Looking up, I see Kayla's eyes on me. She frowns for a suspended moment while I stand there practically holding my breath—then begins bawling like a child. Stunned, I'm next to her in a moment. We hold onto each other like we're each other's lifelines.

"I'm so sorry!" she stutters into my ear, her voice choked. "I'm sorry I didn't come to you, but I just couldn't."

"No, *I'm* sorry for saying all that stuff to you. I'm sorry, Kayla, I don't believe that shit I said, and I hope you never did," I cry into her neck.

"Screw that, I don't care about that nonsense."

I pull away from her. "I—wait—I'm so confused."

Her brows shoot up, her eyes round. "Why?"

"I'm confused about how you can forgive me for doubting you." I haven't even tried to forgive myself for it.

"Water under the bridge." She waves her hand at me.

I squint at her. "So why didn't you respond to my texts?" I accuse. "Did you block me on your phone?"

"What? No!" Kayla's face scrunches unhappily as she adds, "I lost my phone, man. Got no money to buy a new one yet."

Stupid me. I should have thought about that before I started feeling sorry for myself for being ignored. I'll take care of it, though I won't say anything to her because she won't accept it.

I have another question though. And Kayla, foreseeing my question, lifts her hand in a defensive gesture. "And before you go bananas on why I hadn't visited you at the hospital, well... I was a little *tied up* at the moment," she jokes. "But honestly, I just couldn't come. Justin or Jake was always around you, watching you twenty-four seven like a couple of infuriating, stupidly handsome hawks. I love you, I do, but I was waiting for you to get out of there."

I smile, feeling happy that my Kayla is back.

"Hey, Stella? Did you need anything from town?" I call out in the direction of the kitchen from the bottom of the staircase.

"No, we're fine here, sweetheart!"

I take a deep breath and walk out toward my new car. It's not a Chevy—Justin, Jake, Kayla, and almost everyone else in the town talked me out of it—but it's a car made for *staying*. It gets me from Benson's house to the diner and back again. Although today it's going to take me to Alex's cabin in the woods. According to Ken, new flooring has been installed, the rug removed, and the windowpane that bore the bullet hole replaced, but I've yet to return to the place since the night of Erik's death, which had been close to two months ago.

I drive the well-worn route I know by heart and park in front of the house, accepting the rush of fear and adrenaline that comes to me. It's something I've learned to do since the attempt on my life; I accept what happened here and allow it to flow through me before remembering that it is over and that I'm still safe.

I step out of the car and stand in front of the cabin. It's still as beautiful as when I first saw it, although it's looking a little overgrown now.

I breathe in and out rhythmically as I unlock the door and slowly step inside. The floor definitely looks to have been ripped up and replaced like Ken promised, meaning the sofa and the rest of the furniture in the room have been moved to the side, and everything is now rearranged. I can't have that. It looks like a storage unit. After putting the kettle on the stove to boil, I grab the arm of the sofa and haul it back into its rightful place. I place a new rug I bought on the floor, reinstate the books on the bookshelf, dust off the mantel and windowsill where the window was replaced, and set the chairs up around the dining table.

"Better," I whisper to myself. I look around, avoiding the direction of the window through which I'd seen Jake, and I turn around and start adjusting the bedroom again. I've told myself that Alex would be coming back sometime soon, but no one has told me that he *is* coming back. For all I know, he's decided to stay wherever he is forever.

I fix myself a mug of tea and sit at the dining table, trying to figure out how to deal with all this *silence*. It's the same everywhere I go. I can't seem to escape it.

Little Hope without him is almost unbearable. I love people around me and think of them as my family already, and they make me feel closer to Alex, like I can almost touch him when I'm touching Stella or Kayla, like I can almost hear his voice when I talk with Justin or Aiden. It's torture to be surrounded by people and things connecting me to him but still feel him just out of my reach.

My days have fallen into a routine. I wake up at the same time every morning, I help Stella out at the house with cleaning—she doesn't let me touch the cooking though—as I would with Alex. I discuss with Leila a new story she's been reading as I would with Alex. I bicker with Aiden over random stuff as I would with Alex, then I go into Little Hope and either sit at the diner and share scraps of gossip with Kayla or wander around town trying to find something of interest to do that will distract me from the ache of missing him—though nothing ever does.

And I've had absolutely no contact from Alex. Even Justin hasn't heard from him recently, and it's been two months. I've had to learn to stop asking.

I can see it on Stella's face whenever I bring up Alex's return that she's losing hope that he will. I'm trying to stay optimistic, but it's practically impossible when there hasn't been even a hint of the man that I've grown to love for over two months.

And Justin, the Silent Monk, the only person who knows Alex's location, steers clear of everybody because they all keep asking about it—so to avoid answering those questions, he just secludes himself in his garage.

I exhale loudly, place my mug in the sink, knowing I'll be back tomorrow anyway, take a long look around the cabin that represents so many mixed emotions to me one more time, and walk back to my car.

ALEX

I stand in front of my house and crack my neck one way and then the other after the long drive. It was the most freedom I've had in two months, yet the drive felt almost as constrictive as the rehab facility.

But I'm home now, and I know I have a lot to do to convince Freya that I'm home for good. I wouldn't be surprised if she's moved on while I've been away, even though that very idea makes jealousy rise up my throat and threaten to explode with fury at whoever the lucky dick-weasel is. I take a deep breath, remind myself what I'd been taught to manage my anger properly, and step toward the house. If she is with a new guy, I'll have to forget the therapy for a few short minutes while I beat the shit out of him.

There must be some way to win Freya back even after I murder the bastard. The anger is still there, ready to override my brain at the thought of Freya entertaining her new boyfriend in my house, especially when I walk in and see the bed made with fresh sheets, the living room slightly rearranged, and a new rug on the floor, but I try to keep a tight lid on the jealousy. No point in getting angry over nothing.

"Freya?" I whisper, too scared to say anything louder. Someone *has* been here. Recently too. There's still wet mud on the porch and a warm mug in the sink. "Frey?"

There's no response. I take a deep breath and tug my phone out of my jeans pocket. I find her name and hit dial.

"I'm sorry, the number you are calling is out of service," says a tinny voice on the other side of the call before it even rings once.

I pull it away from my ear and stare at the screen numbly. Did she change her number? Of course she did. She's no longer on the run from Erik. She can get a new number, get a new phone, and *keep it*.

I stare at the space around me. Will my return undo her progress? Will I make her *worse* even than before? I'm everything she's been trying to forget. I'm the trigger that sent her into a tailspin, and I don't deserve to be around her.

But I can't think like that. Not anymore.

I dial the number for The Dancing Pony. "Hello, Emma speaking," greets a human voice this time. "This is The Dancing Pony, the number one themed Bed-and-Breakfast in all of Maine!"

"Hey, Emma," I start awkwardly, "it's Alex Crowley."

She gasps. "Alex! Hello! So nice to hear your voice again. What can I help you with?"

I surprisingly gulp down a rush of emotions that threaten to embarrass me at hearing her excited welcome. Excited for *me*. "Um, thanks. I'm... uh, I'm looking for Freya Kennedy. Is she there?"

Emma hesitates. "Oh, I'm sorry, Alex, but she hasn't stayed here for ages. I could probably find her number in our system, but I've been banned from giving out her details to anyone who asks for it. Sorry!"

"Banned? Why? Has she been getting hate?"

She sounds dumbfounded as she responds, "Hate? No, of course not! No, journalists keep wanting to write her story. It has been great press for The Dancing Pony, but not great for Freya, who really doesn't want the attention—understandably."

After rushing out a good-bye, I end the call with Emma, my brow now furrowed in confusion. What would anyone want with Freya's story? Sure, she's been through a lot, but would that make a good journalistic story?

I hit call on Justin's number and put it to my ear.

He answers it with a yawn. "Long time not *seeing your name on my phone screen.*"

I wince. "I know. I... needed to focus."

"Uh-huh. Right," he responds flatly. "So... are you focused now?"

"Yes. And I'm back in Little Hope."

Justin pauses on the other end of the phone. "Is that so?" he asks slowly.

I lick my lips, mentally preparing for my next question and dreading what answers he might have for me. "Does Freya..." I clear my throat and start again. "Is she still here?"

"Yes," he says bluntly. "She's still here. Last I heard, she was going to see Jonah today. You'd probably catch her at his real estate offices."

"Jonah?" I parrot, my nose wrinkling in distaste. "Is that the guy with the fancy suits who breezed in here thinking he owns the place?"

"That's the one. He does own the place though. He owns the real estate business and a few stores in town. Freya will probably be there. If not, she'll be at your parents' house."

My brows shoot up. "My... *why?*"

I hear Justin yawn again. "That's where she's been living. She only stayed at The Dancing Pony for a couple of days. She checked out when Emma became concerned about Freya's nightmares."

My stomach drops. I'd left Freya alone after being nearly killed and expected her to be okay with it... and without me. "Oh." I clear my throat and close my eyes, gripping tightly to the phone in my hand to stop myself from throwing it across the room, enraged with myself. "I just spoke to Emma," I all but grit out. "What is this about journalists hounding Freya?"

There's suddenly a commotion on the other side of the line. "I have to go, Alex. I'd either go to your parents' house to wait for her or go to the real estate office. Bye." He hangs up before I can say anything else, and I stare at my phone in bewilderment.

I take a deep breath and wince as I think about either of those options.

FREYA

· · ·

"Thank you so much for this, Jonah," I say, squeezing him in a grateful hug.

His smile is warm and friendly. "I'll send you through all of these options over e-mail so that you can go through them yourself."

I wave goodbye to him and make it out to my car, mulling over everything in my head. Using the money to open up a facility close to Little Hope for people with PTSD symptoms was a no-brainer. Especially after Jake was sent to the coast for fresh air since Kenneth couldn't announce to the whole world that he shot somebody off-duty with a government-issued weapon when it was supposed to be locked up in the station for the duration of his suspension. I'm not sure how Jake got ahold of his gun that day or what Kenneth did to him for that because I don't presume that he just patted him on the back, even for saving my life—Sheriff Benson loves rules a little bit, too much to disregard the matter.

Jake wrote to us constantly—real letters, no less, he said it was part of a program—but there was still that missing part in my life where Jake was supposed to be, to my utter surprise, seeing how we started. But a shared trauma and someone saving your life tends to unite people. As for Justin, I felt weird hanging out with him much because he knew—still does—where Alex was, so I don't think it's comfortable for either of us.

The only problem with opening the center was *where*. Stella and I had thought we'd found it—a large building close enough to town for easy access but far enough away to be secluded for the people in need to have the privacy to recover in peace—but the sale had fallen through before we could sign because of the same developer who messed with Donna's coffee shop. Jonah has now given me three other options, each slightly different from the rest, so I have to try to get someone to come with me. Kayla might be available, but she doesn't really care what they look like since she's been stuck in her own drama, so her presence is not really helpful.

I'm so withdrawn into my mental calculations that I almost crash into a bear. A huge motherfuckin' bear. At midday. On the outskirts of town. His huge mass is standing in the middle of a road and baring his enormous teeth at me as if I'm at fault for not letting him pass and he's about to demand my car insurance information.

"It's two-way traffic, you furry asshole!" I yell as I roll the window down.

He's looking at me like I'm an idiot, while I'm glaring at him like he's a jerk. *That's right, boy, I got some guts too.* He lets out a loud roar and charges toward my car. I quickly close the window and let out an embarrassing shriek. He slows down and completely stops next to the passenger window and roars at me, covering the glass in disgusting saliva. I almost pee my pants while he lets out a sound that reminds me more of a groan than of a roar and abruptly trots off.

A typical day in Little Hope, I think as I shake my head.

I pull into Benson's driveway and hop out, my head churning over the decisions I need to make. "Hey, I'm home. You'll never believe what just happened!" I call. I'm a little distracted by the papers in my hand and by the recent encounter with the bear. "Had another little *date* with Jonah and with a bear!" I quip with a laugh. It's been a running joke in the household about how often I'd seen Jonah over the last few weeks, and now, we should probably add bears to that, too. "I'd love it if you came with me to look at these new properties, Stella. He says we can go see them anytime."

I amble into the kitchen and absently go through the motions to pour myself a glass of water using only one hand so I can still read off the descriptions of the options Jonah gave me. One of them stands out to me as more like what we need than the other two: an old stone mansion nestled deep in the mountain, surrounded by raw Maine nature. It would involve a *lot* of renovations, as the stonework would need to be almost entirely redone, but there is enough space for offices, sleeping quarters, a spacious central kitchen, and several communal areas. The place is perfect; Jonah was right.

"Freya." Stella calmly beckons for my attention, and I turn to look at her. I almost drop my water as I finally spot Alex standing along the back wall of the kitchen, his arms folded and his expression nervous.

"Alex," I whisper.

"Hey, Frey."

I can't look away from him, and he doesn't drop eye contact either. He looks... good. Well rested. He gained a few pounds, which makes him even more imposing and threatening to somebody who doesn't know him. To me, he looks cuddlier.

Stella clears her throat and ushers Keith, who just came in and stopped abruptly with mouth ajar just like I am, out of the kitchen. "Yell out if you need anything," she says softly. "We'll be upstairs."

I barely register her speaking, but I'm aware of her lack of presence as soon as she's gone. It's only Alex left, his broad shoulders taking up most of the room, as usual.

"You're back," I breathe.

His breath catches in his throat, and he manages a slight nod.

I smooth my hands down the tops of my pants, nervous all of a sudden, and I sink into the dining chair in the kitchen. I don't know where to start, and, by the look of him, neither does Alex.

"Um... how... how long are you back for?" I venture to ask quietly.

"Oh... I, uh, wasn't planning on leaving again." His eyes widen. "Unless you want me to."

I chuckle, the absurdity of the statement hitting me. "Of course not. Also, I'm at *your* parents' house. So maybe you want *me* to leave."

"No!" he exclaims a little too loudly, his good cheek turning pink. "I don't want you to."

I try to hide my smile, biting the inside of my lips.

He smiles and sits too, folding his hands on the table. He clears his throat and looks nervously around us. "I know I shouldn't have left as I did," he admits softly. "And I know that seeing me is probably the last thing you want right now—"

I interrupt his ridiculous assumption. "Seeing you is the only thing I've wanted for two months, Alex. Well, for a few weeks, to be honest," I correct, rolling my eyes at myself. "All the time before then, I wanted to throttle you."

"I'm surprised the weeks of wishing to see me didn't come *before* the weeks of wanting to kill me," he jokes with a self-deprecating half-smile.

I chuckle, shrugging. "Me too."

His eyes look into mine, and I'm amazed at the reserved hope in them. "But... what about Jonah?" he asks. "You just said you went on a date with him."

I should play along with that for a bit and make him

squirm, but I can't help myself. I laugh. "He's the real estate agent. I'm opening a rehab facility close by to help people with PTSD. Jonah's helping me with that."

"You spend so much time with him every day, and there's nothing going on?"

I suppress a smile. "You know that Jonah is gay, right?"

Alex sighs with audible relief as his shoulders relax, and I realize just how jealous he was at the thought that I'd found someone else in his absence. Should serve him right. The first days after the attack, when I needed him the most, he left me behind.

"There's no one in Little Hope for me other than you, dumbass. Not that I don't love my friends here and your family, but do you *really* think I'd stick around for so long just for shits and giggles?"

"You waited for me?" he whispers, eyes round.

I shrug. "Waiting *has* been pretty boring, I must admit."

A grin bursts out on his face, and I can't help but smile too. I abruptly reach over and hold my hand in front of his. He frowns at it, bemused, before taking it hesitantly.

"Hi, I'm Freya Kennedy," I say on a long, happy exhale.

He smiles as he realizes my objective. "Alex Crowley," he replies quickly. "It's nice to meet you."

"You too. New to town?"

"Mmm-hmm... I was trying to find somewhere I can stay, actually." He cocks a roguish brow at me.

"Oh, I've got a great place for you," I respond innocently. "It's remote, currently empty, and seems like the perfect place for someone of your temperament. All the lamps have been nailed in place."

"Sounds perfect." He chuckles, keeping his hand folded in mine, warm and everything I need. "I was also looking for something else." His face turns serious.

"What is it?" I perk up.

"Some*body*, to be clear," he amends. "I was looking for the woman I love. Do you think I still might have a chance with her?"

My gaze blurs with unshed tears. "I think you might."

He grins and gets to me in two long strides. He picks me up from the stool and envelopes me into a tight hug, burying his face in the crook of my neck. He's sniffing my skin, causing tingles all over.

"I missed your smell, Freya. I missed you so much." His voice is muffled. "And I love you. *So* much. I promise I'll never hurt you like that again. I'll fuck up for sure, but I swear it'll be minor. Please, give me another chance."

That's more than I ever had hoped to hear from Alex, but there is something I need to tell him too.

"Alex," I say, pulling away from him and taking two giant steps back. "I'm sorry too."

"For what?" His forehead crinkles.

"For making you leave." I hold his eyes, trying to convey that I understand why he left.

"What are you talking about?" He looks confused.

"I remember what happened when you came inside the house. I didn't mean to freak out, I swear. I didn't want to send you away from your own home." I pinch my forearms, trying to dissolve embarrassment into pain. The latter is familiar, I can handle that. "I was just... out of it. I don't know. You didn't do anything wrong. I wish you had been here so I could've told you that." My gaze drops to the floor, and I begin counting nonexistent scratches on Stella's pristine hardwood floor.

There is a stunned silence, and then Alex moves carefully toward me. One step from me, he touches my chin with his finger and gently forces me to look up. I resist, but he doesn't stop until he catches my eyes. "Freya." His voice is velvet, embracing me in his calmness and strength. "You didn't do anything wrong. Nothing. I left because it was long overdue for me to get help. I needed it for *me*. I just wished I had picked a better time. I'm a dumbass, you were right." His smile is half-mocking, then instantly sobers. "I left you at the worst time possible."

"No, you didn't. I forced you to—"

"Shh." He presses his finger to my lips, silencing me. "Never again say that it was your fault. It wasn't. It was his. And it was mine for leaving at the wrong time and the wrong way. I should have talked to you first, I should have." I try to speak, but he still keeps his finger on my lips and presses again, keeping me quiet. "Not your fault." I try to speak again. "Nah-ah, not your fault. Got it?" He's waiting until I nod, and then he drops his finger. "I love you, Freya, and I want you to take this stray dog back. If I still have a chance," he adds quietly.

"I love you too," I whisper when I'm finally allowed to talk.

Alex loves me. A man like Alex *loves* me.

Sure, we'll have to discuss a whole lot of things, but the feeling in my stomach that's dropping lower and lower at just the sight of him means that all else is about to be put on hold until the both of us can get some semblance of satisfaction.

And, boy, do I plan on dragging it out for as long as possible.

Chapter Twenty-Eight

F REYA

I peer into the oven to check that my lasagna isn't bubbling over, and when I stand, I feel large, strong arms wrap around my waist and pull me back.

"Smells delicious," Alex whispers, nuzzling his nose into the crook of my neck. "And the lasagna smells good too."

I giggle and surrender myself backward into his embrace, closing my eyes and letting him easily pick me up and move me toward the sofa. "The lasagna isn't even for you," I inform him teasingly.

He tilts my head with a gentle hand under my chin so that he can look at me. "Wait, why not? Who deserves a lasagna more than I do?"

I laugh at his playful indignance. "Your stepmother does. It's for the opening this afternoon. She asked people to bring a meal for the party, and we both know lasagna's the only thing I can cook."

He chuckles and dramatically drags me down so we're both lying on the couch. "Well, how about you make it up to me in other ways? I can't have a lasagna, but I *can* have—"

"A sense of self-control and the promise that you can have me later as well as a plate of lasagna at the event this afternoon?"

"Wrong answer," he replies matter-of-factly, twisting so that he's on top of me. "The correct answer is *you*. You're all I want or need."

I pout at him as his gaze sweeps over my body, and he sighs, a groan rattling the back of his throat.

"It's still that time of the month, isn't it?" he whispers.

I nod regretfully. After almost a year and a half of being too thin, too stressed, and too panicked, my monthly cycles have come back with a vengeance, and it's something Alex has had no choice but to come to terms with. He's been perfectly wonderful when I've been immobile due to the intense cramps I've been gifted by that bitch Mother Nature. "But we can cuddle if you like?"

I open my arms wide, and he studies me for a moment before grinning and settling himself back into my embrace, nuzzling his face into my hair again. "I love you," he whispers, and I get the same giddy feeling in the pit of my stomach as I did the first time I heard it.

"I love you too." I hold him tight and sigh happily.

"*Jake!*" I yell as the familiar figure climbs out of the cab and grins as he walks toward us. I run forward to meet him in the middle, and he catches me in a hug. "You're back!" He has on his ever-present Ray Bans and a boyish grin.

He laughs. "I am," he confirms, sounding so cheery my heart swells.

"Feeling good?"

"*Much* better."

I step back and look him up and down. "You look good," I comment approvingly. "'Fresh air' was kind to you."

He wiggles his eyebrows. "I'll tell you all about it later. First, though, you have a big project opening today, and that's what we need to focus on."

I grin and loop my arm in his. "Promise me, later—"

"Martinis and gossip." He cuts in with a confirming nod. "Don't worry, Frey. It's been *months* since I've been home, and I need to catch up on everything that has gone on in my absence."

Jake chose rehab, and I insisted on paying for it. Nobody but me, Justin, and Alex know about that, though. He was told it was a government program because I didn't want him to feel like he owed something to me when, in fact, it's the opposite. The official report still states that Erik was killed in self-defense by me from the gun I was supposedly holding until the bitter end. When I offered to tell him the truth under the table so he'd know, he told me he already knew "the truth," and it's been filed in the report. And I'm okay with that. Nobody will touch me, but Jake's badge could suffer. We need good cops who can protect us day and night, and Jake became just that—a damn good cop.

I beam at him, and we walk toward where everyone has gathered for the grand opening of the Little Hope Rehabilitation Facility.

. . .

ALEX

I stand to the side and watch as Freya talks excitedly with Kayla and Jake. I owe the man a whole lot after saving Freya, but I don't know how to go up to him and say that. He looks better than when I last saw him when his whole body shook in shock after killing a man. I'm so busy observing him that I don't notice Stella walk up to me and join in watching the three of them, too.

I gulp when I realize she's there, knowing that this is the first time it has just been me and her alone since my return all those months ago.

"Thank you for the gift, my boy. I love that car as if it were my fifth child," she tells me warmly, and I feel a sudden lump in my throat. *Fifth. I'm* her fourth.

"Thank you," I quietly reply, "for looking after her when I couldn't."

Stella sighs with a smile. "We would do anything for you, Alex. That will never change. You're my son. A vital member of this family."

I flash a smile back at her. "You're pronouncing '*pain in my ass*' wrong."

Stella laughs. "You were asked to shoulder more than you should have been. Adult responsibilities should have never fallen onto you to carry on your back or hold in your heart." She smiles at me. "I know it wasn't easy. Coming into our family the way you did. But I'm proud of you. Everything you've done has been to stand up for what is right."

I can't speak for the lump in my throat, and I stare intently at Freya as she laughs with Kayla.

"This place was created for *you*, Alex," Stella continues. "For *the you* who should have received this care years ago."

I look at her and manage a smile through the emotions that truth drags to the surface. "I know."

She places a hand on my arm and tells me, "I'm proud of you for doing therapy, son," before walking away. My eyes sting. Somebody's cutting some damn onions around here.

Taking a deep, calming breath, I look over at Justin, who's got an arm around his little brother, pleased to see him back. I clear my throat and tread over to the two brothers.

"Officer Jake," I say quietly, holding out my hand with a warm smile. "Welcome back."

Jake stares at my hand for a minute before breaking into a smile and shaking it firmly. "It's good to be back." He cocks his head before tugging me forcefully toward him. "I'm a good shot. Let's remember that." Then he lets me go and stands there, chewing the inside of his lips, contemplating saying something. "You know..." he finally starts, then huffs. "Oh, fuck, I'd never thought I'd say it, but yeah, I was wrong."

"What?" I say at the same time as Justin.

"Yeah." Jake looks sheepish now. "That thing, years back."

"What thing?" I ask, cocking my head.

"The Adison thing," he clarifies uncomfortably as I clench my jaw. Now isn't the time for this. "Yeah, well, she lied."

"What?" I exclaim at the same time as Justin says, smacking my shoulder, "Told you so."

"Yeah." Jake looks at the ground guiltily as he explains further. "She told me she couldn't sleep with you when you… well, looked different and acted different than before, so she made it up so people wouldn't call her vain."

"That bitch," Justin hisses. He never liked her, even though she was always around Ashley, his years-long fuck buddy.

His brother grimaces. "Yeah, I learned a lot while I spent those few days with her."

"Man, I still don't know why you did that." Justin shudders in disgust.

"Yeah," Jake drawls with a note of sarcasm in his voice, squinting his eyes at Justin, "so horrible of *me* to do while *you're* fucking just another viper from the same nest."

"Not anymore. Not for a while," he states firmly. *Hmm, interesting.*

Jake regards him with silence for a few moments, then turns to me. "Anyway, yeah," he tacks on while scratching the back of his head, a nervous tic. "I needed to get some info on you, so I got cozy. Not that she minded," he adds quickly, "but turns out, I got the complete opposite. So yeah, I believe you now, and I'm sorry for all that shit I've been spouting off." He offers me his hand, and I take it.

I didn't do it. I fuckin' didn't do it. Freya knew it before I did. And Justin did too. Stella truly loves me as her own. My siblings are trying. I have amazing people around me, and without Freya, I'd never know how truly blessed I am. I glance at her while she laughs at something Kayla said. She radiates newfound freedom and happiness. And she is mine.

Jake notices my stare because he squeezes my hand that he's still holding, then leans back, giving me a gentle pat on the shoulder, "I'm still a better shot, remember that," he quips and walks away, leaving both Justin and me smirking after him.

"Your brother shoots once and thinks he's better than all of us," I mutter.

"He's got a point. He has better aim than me."

"Wouldn't be hard."

He rolls his eyes. "To be fair, if he *didn't* have good aim, we wouldn't be standing here."

"No," I murmur. "The worrying thing is that he *didn't know*."

Justin places a hand on my shoulder. "You didn't either the first time, and hey, I'm still alive."

I nod, then aim a smirk at him. "God help us all."

He chuckles before turning to the front steps of the beautiful stone building that my girlfriend has spent so long getting renovated and ready for anyone who might need its services.

She arrives at my side, and I kiss her forehead as the official opening of the facility begins.

"I love you," I murmur in her ear.

She looks up at me and beams, squeezing her arm around my waist. She doesn't need to say it for me to know it's true that she loves me too. Somehow through all of this, through all of the shit that we've been through—separately and together—we've found each other, the pain and suffering *almost* made it worth it.

Kayla smiles over at us before her gaze drifts to Justin, and I know Freya catches it, too, from the way the arm she has wrapped around me tightens briefly.

If only everyone were so lucky…

Afterword

Dear Reader, welcome to Little Hope!

Thank you for reading my book! If you want more books and news and freebies from me, you can find me on Social Media by typing this link https://linktr.ee/Ariana CaneAuthor into your browser. Or you can check out my website arianacane.com. It has a special about a very special character everyone loves (hopefully, you will too, after Guilty Minds).

I'm happy to see you here!

~Ariana

Also by Ariana Cane

<u>The World of the Fallen Gates series</u>

Dystopian, paranormal, urban fantasy romance series

Tale of the Deceived, Book 1 of the duet

<u>Story of the Forsaken , Book 2 of the duet</u>

-vampires, werewolves, faes

-true enemies to lovers

-the life after the World has ended

-super slow-burn

-one bed

-true series

-scorching tension

-tons of secrets

<u>Little Hope Series</u>

Small town, slow burn, contemporary romance stand-alones.

Haunted Hearts, Little Hope Series, Book 1

Alex and Freya,

-one bed

-grumpy-sunshine

-strangers to enemies to lovers

-an ex-navy veteran with PTSD

-woman on the run

-woodchopping

-cabin in the woods

-damaged MMC

-all the bears of Maine

Guilty Minds, Little Hope Series, Book 2

Justin and Kayla

-true bully romance

-groveling

-tattoo artist-waitress/mechanic

-miscommunication for a good reason

-wildlife of Maine

Broken Souls, Little Hope Series, Book 3

Mark and Alicia

-fireman and author

-strangers to neighbors to lovers

-hurt/comfort

-trauma recovery

-man's best friend

-protective MMC

Fragile Lives, Little Hope Series, Book 4

Archie and Leila

-enemies to lovers

-one bed

-cabin in the woods

-age-gap

-brother's best friend

-the most beloved character

-wildlife of Maine

-trauma recovery/PTSD (MMC)

-lots of tattoos and piercings (MMC)

<u>Book 4, Kenneth's story, is coming soon...</u>

Acknowledgments

I have many names, and it's my first book, so please be patient with me.

First of all, this book is dedicated to my husband. Even though you don't read romance, this book happened because of you. Because of your support for any crazy ideas I might have. You are truly the best person out there, even if you annoy me fifty percent of the time. You're my rock and mountain I like to climb from time to time.

To my friend A.. I don't need to say anything—you know it all.

To my grandad, who's not with us anymore, but who taught me how to love books and let my imagination fly. I bet you didn't expect it to fly this way, though, oops.

To my assistant, Sarah, a true gem I found among the internet fields—thank you for your constant presence and the right words all the damn time. You're better than Google, and you know way more. And you can find anything I didn't even know I needed.

To my editor, Ivy, who found me crying in a bush when I was in a desperate search for a decent human being after a certain editing disaster, and who spent days and nights editing and loving my characters the way I do (not Jake, though, but he'll grow on you). Accept that bear as a thank you!

To Kayla, my amazing beta-reader with a 'don't take BS'

attitude. Please, keep it! And thank you for your supporting words when I was feeling down.

To Elizabeth Dear, who spent her time explaining the ropes when she could be writing Knox's story. Thank you!

To my ARC team and Bookstagrammers who took a chance on a baby-author (yours truly). Nobody will read a book if they don't know it exists. Thank you for reviewing and helping me spread the word.

To Bookstagrammers and authors who became my friends! Wow, I didn't expect so many people to be so nice.

And now, last but not least, my readers! You're the MOST. You're the ones who make all of THIS possible. Thank you for picking my book among thousands of amazing stories out there. I hope you will not be disappointed!

Thanks to all of you who gave *Haunted Hearts* a chance!

~ Love, Ariana

*All roads lead to
Maine.
But do they end
there?*

www.ingramcontent.com/pod-product-compliance
Lightning Source LLC
Chambersburg PA
CBHW051311190726
48290CB00001B/109